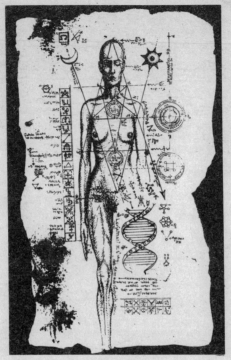

Hermetech

Storm Constantine

First published in 1991
by HEADLINE BOOK PUBLISHING PLC

First published in paperback in 1991
by HEADLINE BOOK PUBLISHING PLC

A HEADLINE FEATURE paperback

10 9 8 7 6 5 4 3 2 1

ISBN 0 7472 3609 7

Typeset in 10/11½ pt Times
by Colset Private Limited, Singapore

Printed and bound by
Collins Manufacturing, Glasgow

HEADLINE BOOK PUBLISHING PLC
Headline House,
79 Great Titchfield Street
London W1P 7FN

This work is dedicated to
Magan and Carl McCoy, and Scarlett,
for Sheer Faith.

With recognition to the following,

Caroline Oakley, my editor at Headline, for her patience and understanding; Vikki Lee France and Steve Jeffery for initiating the information service; Dearest Darren for his Deathly Dreams (From Within); Matt Collis for life-lessons; Priestess RIO for magickal BACKUP (and RESTORE); and a salutation to the Falconeers for everything.

Especial thanks to Magan and Carl for the artwork and superlative jacket design, and to Jay Summers for realtime enhancement and post-production.

'With light poise and counter-poise nature oscillates within her prescribed limits, yet thus arise all the varieties and conditions of the phenomena which are presented to us in space and time.'

Johann Wolfgang von Goethe

It was only a dream. She had grains and grass for protection, the grass sickly and pale, rolled into a small ball. The grain should have been gathered from a fertile field, she knew that, but there were no fields around there any more. She hoped pre-packed rice, bought from the co-op gypsies, would be as powerful. *Don't doubt. It's the intention that makes it work.* Both ingredients had been carefully arranged on the dry ground before her; a circle of grains surrounding the grass ball. Arani Shala Famber, fourteen years old and determined to heal her mind of fear, squatted in the long early morning shadows of Taler's Bump monument, making magicks to protect herself from evil.

She had had nightmares before, even those that persistently lingered in the mind for days, but never before had she woken up feeling so threatened, as if the substance of her dreams could follow her into the day and become real. A rational part of herself knew she was the one giving her terrors life, simply by believing in them. It would be more sensible to stand up and do something physical; run around the silent stones until her heart pumped the memory of the dream away, truly woke her up. More sensible, yes. The grass ball was beginning to uncurl; she pressed it together again. *Has everyone felt like this at some time? Has Mom?* She settled into a straight-backed, crossed-legged position and closed her eyes. It felt as if her body was going wild; she could sense the beating of her heart as if it had become small and hard, the rhythm erratic. Her spine ached, her stomach felt unsteady. Ari sucked in a deep breath through her nose and concentrated on relaxing. Even after several minutes, there was still a furrow between her eyes.

Over a decade before, Austin Grant, a rich young eccentric previously more famed for his excesses, had undergone a public and feverish conversion to Naturotech. The faith, if it could be termed that, was a mutation of the more informed brands of neo-paganism, and had arisen through people's belated concern for the fate of the planet, radical liberalism and a desire to utilise new technology to overcome the depredations of old technology. Large areas of the world had become virtually uninhabitable – certainly uneconomic – and the elements of chaos appeared to have taken over the climate completely. Eventually, politics and corporate interest just had to nose their way in, and a splinter movement, Tech-Green, had been formed. Recognising a life-saver when it was thrown to them, powerful people worldwide clamoured to embrace the new ideals and secure comfortable positions for themselves within the organisation. In an environment where the richest and most influential agencies had moved off-planet to the gradually expanding orbital communities, there were effectively no individual economic nations left on Gaiah.

Naturotech, still operating largely as a planet-side movement, secretly considered Tech-Green to be a brutish parody of their original ideals. However, because of T-G's encompassing control, Naturotech maintained an uneasy alliance with them; ostensibly their goals were the same. Attempts at assuaging the planet's wounds and diseases had been sporadically successful, but largely uncoordinated. Monstrous domed cities had been constructed in an almost indecent haste, to which earthbound people flocked in their thousands, believing this was the best way to deal with the problem. Nomad natros, who still stoically tried to survive on the land itself, often referred to the city dwellers as 'ostriches' (an extinct giant bird that allegedly believed it became invisible once its head was buried in sand). Sadly, the irony of the metaphor was lost on the majority.

In order to demonstrate his own loyalty to the New Goddess of Naturotech, Austin Grant had dubbed himself a geomancer and swiftly squandered considerable amounts of his family's fortune on constructing grandiose sacred sites, which he envisaged could be used as places of worship by all. Other natros had not discouraged him. They did not point out that one of the freedoms of their chosen system involved scorning fixed temples and that worship itself was generally considered to be outmoded, if not downright suspect. However, they believed everyone should have their own way of expressing themselves. Grant enthusiastically supervised the erection of dozens of henges around the country, in areas where it was still safe to cavort about outdoors. Some of these were based on existing ancient sites – or the memory of them – some were stamped with his own artistic mark. The latter generally consisted of imposing stone pyramids surrounded by rather bashful groups of menhirs that, even though lacking in antiquity themselves, seemed embarrassed being used out of context. Natros, because they had a sense of humour, had first begun to use the monuments for their festivals as a bit of a joke, but eventually for convenience's sake. Every site had its own facilities (accommodation, heating, running water, artificial attendants, occasional special effects in the stones themselves), which the natros had to admit were useful when large amounts of people wanted to gather together. Grant achieved his dream.

Taler's Bump was such a monument; not a very grand one, consisting merely of a single trilithon and seven monoliths, but people still came to use it. Ari Famber had lived all her life in the shadow of the Bump; the monument had been her playground, its visitors her companions. The area, mostly barren, patchily toxic, was not heavily populated.

It was impossible to concentrate. Ari could feel the dry heat of the sun creeping up behind her. How long have I sat here? She opened her eyes. Already a heat haze was shivering over the parched land beyond the Bump. The monument's attendant, an artificial manform, could be seen standing motionless between two menhirs, almost like a stone himself. Ari had not summoned him. She wondered whether he was watching her. Despite her efforts, she could not relax and meditate properly, and the uncomfortable feelings were still there. It was as if the dream had sucked her imagination dry, overpowered her ability to visualise, even though she knew it had been generated within her own mind. What message was there for her in that? She could not interpret it. At her feet, the grass and grains seemed pathetic, mundane, powerless. Have I invoked something myself? she wondered. Yet the dream's threatening images had not been violent.

Ari had reached an age when she liked to think she was able to solve her problems herself. She had, after all, assimilated every one of her mother's video-disks on personal development. However, in moments of crisis, she

still had access to personal communion with an inter-
cessory aspect of the Goddess, via the site's manform
attendant. He could speak with the words of the Goddess
Isis Confidentia; an individual the girl visualised as an
ethereal being floating in nul-grav splendour somewhere
high above the monument. Unfortunately, Isis tended to
present her wisdom in rather an inaccessible manner.
Kicking her stones and grass to one side, Ari decided,
somewhat reluctantly, that it was time for a chat with her
Goddess. She sighed and strolled to the manform's side.
'Love is the Law,' she said resignedly, hands in pockets.
The manform made a whispering sound deep inside himself and obligingly tuned in to the orbiting Goddess
satellite.

'Love under will,' came the practically instantaneous
reply. 'Blessings to you, Arani Shala Famber. You are
communing with High Goddess Isis Confidentia. Let us
share our thoughts and connect, sister. Is there something you want to talk about?' The deity had the bright,
melodramatic voice of an artificial intelligence programmed by a religious fanatic.

'Hi, Isis. This is Ari. Yeah, there is something.'

'This day blooms on the eve of our Great Festival of
the Fires. Spring stirs in the bosom of the Lady.'

'Yeah, it's a warm day. Er . . . I had a dream last
night.'

'Mmm. Dreams are meaningful; prophecies, gifts of
the Lady, sweet glimpses of the Great Akashic Mind-
pool.'

'It wasn't that kind of dream, Isis.'

'Ah, your voice signals a fissure in your aura sister . . .
Speak, speak, visualise a comforting embrace.'

Ari suppressed irritation, wondering for a moment if
she was doing the right thing. 'It kind of scared me a

little. You see, there was this noise which woke me up. At least, I *thought* it woke me up, but it couldn't have, because it was a dream see, but anyway, I woke up . . .'

The Goddess sensed the pause and quickly attempted to fill it. 'Be calm, let me soothe you . . .'

'Yeah, all right. Anyway, I woke up and sat up in bed, and it was really real, you understand, so I was thinking, "What woke me?" There was this strange, creepy kind of humming noise, and the light was all blue, like the wallscreen had been left on, you know? The light was coming under my door, so I thought, "Damn it, I'll have to turn it off", see, and I went through into the other room . . .'

'The house is your mind, Ari.'

This *was* a mistake. 'Maybe, just hear me out, will you? Sure enough, the screen was on and it was all fuzzy, with this scratchy noise coming out of it, like radio voices far away. There was this guy sitting on the floor in front of it, looking up. He had the remote in his hand.'

'A sexual symbol.'

Ari winced. Her first instinct was to protest, but that would only initiate an uncomfortable discussion. Better just to ignore it. 'Anyway, I thought, "Who the hell is this in our house?" and I was going to go over and kick him or something – which isn't really like me. I think I'd just back out and call for help normally. Then something made me look round. Mom's face was just behind me, right up close, like she'd come out of nowhere, and she looked really weird, all sick and pale. I think I said something about the guy on the floor, I can't remember what, and Mom just shook her head and said, "Don't touch him Ari. He's dead. It won't be nice." '

'Post-pubertal fears, Arani.'

'It wasn't like that, Isis,' Ari said, unsure of what the

Goddess really meant. 'It was so real. The guy looked round at us when Mom spoke. He didn't look dead at all, but when he smiled, it wasn't alive either. Can you understand that? I had this sudden feeling like I wanted to throw up and then he spoke. It was so *sneery*. "Looking forward to tomorrow. Ari?" he said, as if he knew me or something. I screamed, "Get out! Get out!" over and over. It was horrible looking at him. I can't tell you how he scared me.'

'It wasn't real, Ari. Sometimes, your mind has to play crazy in order to ease the bugs out. I think you should relax a little now, breathe deeply . . .'

'I can't remember any more. I didn't know him, Isis, and yet . . . I don't know. It was like a part of me, or something.'

'Then maybe it was. Your animus. You have to come to terms with your opposite side, Ari.'

'I'm scared I'll dream that again.'

'If you do, you must face him, absorb him. You cannot tell him to get out; he is your hidden masculinity.'

'I don't know about that. It doesn't sound right. He was more than that.'

'Did you desire him, Ari? Did you want him to touch you?'

'No!'

'The thought of that frightens you. I can tell.'

'It makes me feel ill!' That was so literal, and for so long unadmitted, Ari was flooded with a tide of relief once the words were spoken. 'Isis, you still there?'

'Of course, sister. I was thinking. Perhaps it would be best if, after the festival, you have your Mom take you to the Youth Counsellor at your local T-G zone station. One of my colleagues could talk with you face to face.'

'I wish I could come and talk with *you* face to face.'

'Maybe you *will* one day, Ari. But I didn't mean someone like me in this case.'

'I prefer people like you.'

'Ari! I cannot hug you, kiss you . . .'

'Yeah, I know Isis.' She squatted down beside the motionless manform, squinting out between the menhirs. This had been no help at all in explaining the dream, but at least she felt better talking about it out loud. 'I'd better go now.'

'Would you like me to book you an appointment at the zone station?'

'Maybe. I'll get back to you.'

'Blessed be, Sister. Enjoy the festival. Keep happy. And remember, a dream can't hurt you.'

'Goodbye Isis.'

There will be an empty house. I am not too late, but there will be an empty house. I feel it. (If I feel it strongly enough, will that make it true?)

A ground mist, morning white, hid all but a suggestion of landscape. A dreamer could imagine green fields might lie there, trees with leaves, even animals moving slowly over the grass. Concentrate hard enough and the smell of living plants might be conjured up. A psychic could probably manage it; someone good with ghosts.

Leila Saatchi knew better. Natro she might be, but she knew what lay within the mist and that it was impossible to change it in her lifetime. Last evening, she and her group had rumbled their trucks through the dreary landscape, spraying grit-powder over the crumbling and contorted wrecks beside the road; remains of farms, vehicles, life itself. They had camped as the sun set and someone said they'd seen a bird, a lone, black mote, sailing across the evening sky. Everyone had looked. Leila had seen nothing. Wishful thinking, a dust-speck in the eye. Nothing. Perhaps an omen. Last night, for the second time in eight days, her lover Jordan had not come to her tepee. She felt the victim of a planetary convergence. Powerful events were accelerating towards climax; events beyond her control. Life seemed a fragile, shaky thing to Leila Saatchi that morning. She sat, knees up, boots in dust, smoking a tar-free cigarette that tasted of dust itself, squinting into the future. The Star Eye trucks were some distance off; ghosts in the mist, saurian. There were tepees behind them, but invisible. She was alone.

Dawn; it feels like limbo. Leila sighed, flicked the wizened cigarette butt into oblivion and dangled her hands over her knees. *I don't need this. Need what? There'll be nothing. You told yourself that. Don't kid yourself, lady. No, there'll be nothing. Long gone. Seven years? Is it that long?*

She stared at her hands. They had become, ultimately, a man's hands. Sitting there, she felt skinned of all femininity. That was Jordan's fault. He unwomanned her. Somehow. Seven years . . .

Memories.

Lydia Famber had already hated Leila for years back then, suspecting she was 'the other woman' in a sordid sexual triangle with her husband, Ewan, but unable to prove it. Leila, being adept at getting what she wanted, and because Ewan had been, physically, quite devastating, had been conducting an affair with him for some considerable time, but that had hardly been a threat to Lydia. True, Leila had also seen a lot more of Ewan than his wife had, but that was because they'd worked together after Lydia had fallen pregnant and left the project. Work had always meant more to Ewan Famber than people had. He'd accepted the love of both women as a kind of inevitable right, and had exploited it only in so far as it aided his scientific activities, supposing the results of his research to be as important to them as to him. Leila had forgiven him his insensitivities, deceiving herself into believing it was merely the result of an endearing social naïvety. Lydia had just suffered for it. Leila had known this at the time, and had relished it. Lydia, after all, had the marriage certificate. *Yet neither of us ever truly had him*, Leila thought. *We loved him and he died. A long time ago. Seven years ago.* She felt the memory of Ewan Famber should no longer invoke such strong feelings. The cynic within Leila smiled. *Who are you fooling? We exist here, then, everywhen, in one single moment. We are back there. Now.*

Star Eye had symbolised something other than a natro nomad troupe back then. It had been the logo of a stable of élite Tech-Green thoroughbreds. Slogans sprayed on laboratory walls. A joke. Their esoteric symbol: an image derived from the equation $z \rightarrow z^2 + x$, its tendrils exploding over the boundaries of a triangle. A Star Eye joke.

There had been twenty-three of them; precocious, highly-strung young people, all brilliant technicians and thinkers within their respective fields. Their mentor had been a Tech-Green aristocrat named Quincx Roirbak, an older man, carbon black, who had infected them with his eccentric manner of behaviour and innate sense of superiority. Some of them had been brash enough to call him 'Dad' to his face, which he had whimsically corrected to 'Uncle', a term he'd considered more pertinent to his role. Others, though not to his face, referred to him as '666'.

They had scorned the title scientist and dubbed themselves reality speculators. Tech-Green had been high on its ascendent in those days; its inner sancti bursting with spectacular ideas, its priesthood delirious with the funding and facilities laid at their feet. Star Eye had been working under Roirbak on the space migration plan, although, politically, it had been decided unwise to advertise this. Therefore, a lot of their time had been spent designing earthbound artificial environments, in an attempt to demonstrate to the population how assiduously they were addressing the problems arising from the planet's sickness. Tech-Green, however, had decided in its early days the only cure for Gaiah was to purge Her of the most persistent and damaging of irritants – humanity – so She could heal Herself. Unfortunately, the People (and by that time the word 'masses' had taken on a considerably more sinister implication) were decidedly unkeen to migrate off-world. Popular opinion insisted people needed to feel solid rock beneath their feet, and that they would probably go mad or die if they were removed from the home planet. Ironically, quite the reverse came about. The majority of affluent, civilised populations, in a horrifyingly short space of time, went neurologically bankrupt, en masse, due to ravaging immunity breakdowns and environmental disasters. Most of the population were caught, helpless, in the crossfire between the planet organism and the leviathan-like rampage of big industry. Three environments were eventually left for the remaining populace: outlands where the elements roamed without purpose and seasons had fallen out of sync into improvisation; in-dome cities constructed within the spinal mountain ranges, filling valleys and absorbing peaks; and, finally, space itself. Tech-Green had restricted use of the oceans, for their own reasons. People didn't question this as the usual view from shorelines offered merely a far-reaching vista of froth-slimed garbage.

Tech-Green, therefore, went ahead with the migration project, cloaking it with secrecy, and reserving places within it for the chosen few. If indeed the plan proved impracticable, there was always the option of furthering research into ocean-bed communities.

None of Star Eye knew what the outcome of their research, trials and theories would be. Their directive was to overcome the problems encountered by humanity living in an alien environment. What Tech-Green would do with this information once it was published had not been their concern. They were, after all, well salaried for their brilliance.

Several orbital cities had already been constructed at that time.

Ewan Famber had been the driving force of the original Star Eye. Nobody had been able to dispute his genius, so consequently it hadn't been resented that he was Roirbak's favourite. It was because of Ewan's inquiring mind and technical brilliance that Leila was now travelling towards the place where his widow and daughter were supposed to live. Ari Famber was not a normal child.

Ewan had stored documents to be delivered to both Leila and Roirbak in the event of his death; obviously not having considered his extinction to be a real possibility. The documents had been shocking, demented, incredible; hardly light reading in the wake of grief. At first, neither Leila nor Roirbak had believed the claims. Ewan wrote deliriously of evolutionary mutation, of having tampered with his daughter's genetic makeup to create what he referred to as a Living Goddess. Leila and Roirbak weren't sceptics, but they could find no research data to back Ewan's statements up. If they existed, he'd hidden them too well. Both wondered how he'd had the time to work on such an ambitious project, and also how he'd managed to keep it so secret. They confided their mutual suspicion that the whole thing had existed solely in Ewan's head. The documents concluded with the request that, when Ari reached puberty, Leila and Roirbak should seek her out, take her into their care, and create the conditions necessary to facilitate her unique flowering. Explicit details were sadly lacking, but there were grandiose hints of the child's potential, almost biblical in scale and tone. Leila and Roirbak, concerned and slightly embarrassed by Ewan's apparent unhinged ramblings, decided to forget the matter until the time came when they should perhaps do something about it. There were other things to think about in the light of his death. Leila had metaphorically shorn her head by quitting the Star Eye project. It helped ease her pain to blame Tech-Green for Ewan's demise. As further demonstration of her grief, she'd furiously jettisoned her entire career, despite quickly proffered employment offers from other departments, and had taken to the road with the first natro group who'd accepted her. Later, she'd formed her own group, telling herself it was cynicism which impelled her to name it Star Eye, although deep down she'd known it was because of obscure affection for the past. Even now, she still wondered whether her departure from the team had ever been appreciated for the gesture it was. A few years later, Roirbak himself had turned off the juice and headed for the immense domed city of Arcady. The project had lost its magic for both of them with Ewan gone.

We felt immortal. Ewan scattered our dreams. He died mad. Do only Roirbak and I know that?

Leila had barely thought about the document Ewan had left her during the last seven years, but there'd been a clock ticking away inside her head which hadn't forgotten at all. One morning, the alarm sounded. Star Eye had been staying at Willow Grove, a natro settlement about a hundred clicks east of Taler's Bump. Leila had woken up in her tepee, Jordan beside her, and thought, 'Goddess, Ari Famber must be nearly a woman by now!' Later, she'd dug out Ewan's document from all the rubbish she'd collected over the years and re-read it. It still seemed like the product of a delirious mind, but the sight of his sprawling handwriting, virtually illegible because he'd hardly ever written anything by hand, had invoked a host of memories. Bitterly, Leila realised she was still in love with Ewan; nobody she'd met since had been quite as attractive or fascinating, not even Jordan. The pointlessness of these feelings oppressed her. Ewan had clearly not been quite the person she'd thought him to be. However, she knew she'd have to carry out his last instructions, seek out his surviving family, and trust to the Goddess there wasn't the slightest shred of truth in his claims. She was not looking forward to intruding on the Famber household. If there were any people from the past Lydia would be pleased to see again, Leila Saatchi was certainly not one of them.

Natro pilgrims usually began to arrive at Taler's Bump at sundown on the day before May Eve. Some years ago, many people would have gathered at the foot of the Bump, arriving in their road trucks, third-hand sliders or else on foot. Some had even ridden up on horses; a show of flamboyance rather than economy. It was cheaper to run even a third-hand slider than a single horse after the Biomass Regulations came into force in '15. Now, since Austin Grant had built Arbor Mount twenty clicks east, not many people bothered with the less-imposing pimple of Taler's Bump. There were fewer facilities on the Bump; those that did exist had declined in variety and function as festival attendees declined in numbers. Even the monument itself was becoming forlorn. True, it still boasted an attendant, who serviced the batteries and menhirs but, at some festivals, the incense sacs had been filled with perfumes inappropriate to the occasion and, from the monument's appearance, it would seem PH-balancing fluid hadn't been applied to its surfaces as often as it was needed. The dust-laden rain had bitten into it severely in places. People therefore considered the attendant to be rather unreliable.

Ari Famber thought these eccentricities were endearing and the nearest evidence she had that the manform possessed some kind of artificial personality. Starved as she was of company, she took him to her heart and ascribed him with shamanic properties – after all, he was a channel for the Goddess. Apart from his eyes he was very man-like to look at, although the thin layer of artificial skin he'd once been sheathed in had worn away, revealing a surface which closely resembled the ceraplas housing on Ari's school console. His eyes were like jewels, faceted and ruby-lit from within when he was paying particular attention to something. He often looked fierce, sometimes sad and sometimes philosophical. Ari preferred not to think these apparent expressions could have been a trick of the light. Her mother had boxes full of old natro pamphlets in the garage and sometimes Ari liked to leaf through them, looking at the cartoons and pictures whose captions she never quite understood. One had involved a fallen angel named Sammael and this was the name she invested on the menhir attendant. She felt it suited his rather wistful appearance.

A peaceful and uneventful night's sleep following the trauma of the dream quickly restored Ari's spirits. She now felt rather foolish for having spoken to the Goddess about it and hoped the zone station wouldn't try to follow up her call.

Early the next morning, as it was the day before May Eve, Ari climbed the Bump and went to stand among the tall, wire-tasselled columns, taking her binoculars with her to study the road from the west. She liked to keep a lookout for visitors before the festivals. A skinny, boyish creature, she could, according to mood, appear older or younger than her fourteen years. She knew her mother disliked the way she dressed in natro khaki, but took advantage of the fact that Lydia was always too apathetic (or drunk) to protest when Ari raided the bottom of her wardrobe for old clothes. Copying photographs of celebrated natro females in the pamphlets, Ari had untidily cropped her hair, which was the exact colour of dead grass, and spent half an hour every day binding up her trouser and shirt cuffs with leather thongs. It was always a disappointment there were so few people around to appreciate her efforts. However, when real natro randomati came to visit the monument, Ari always felt a little embarrassed about copying their appearance and generally changed into plain jeans and T-shirt. She knew the nomad natros could often be haughty with tight-liners (as they referred to settled individuals) and didn't want to risk offending anybody.

She had lived beside the Bump all her life and had never ventured beyond the district boundaries. Lydia had instilled into her since birth the idea of how dangerous it was to stray. Even Yellowfield, the deserted town ten clicks down the road, was considered a hazard. As she grew older, Ari's instinctive fears warred with a desire for adventure. She was often bored nowadays. All of her friends existed solely on the youthlink network; strangers she had never met really. Although they had grown up together in a way, learning from the schooling broadcasts and inventing complex computer games, most of the other teenagers had drifted away from the network. Ari scorned communicating with the younger kids who dominated it now. She knew her peers had traded their interest in computers and network friendships for more tangible relationships and pastimes. These were not available to Ari. The only other child she'd met in the area had been a sickly girl, generally confined to the house by anxious parents, who'd died two years ago. The local adults all seemed paranoid burnouts to Ari, even with her limited experience. They did not resemble at all the proud and beautiful people she saw in the wallscreen films. As time went on, she found herself wondering more and more just what the future had in store for her. Would she end up demented, living alone, talking to people who weren't there and dying before her time? She was unsure what other prospects there were for her. Lydia declined to discuss the subject.

The Famber house was a single-storeyed building, and had been constructed sixteen years ago in what had been termed 'luxury style'. This meant the synthetic building materials had appeared to be genuine wood when it was new. Now it bore lesions of disintegration. The wood patina had peeled away – Ari was amazed by its membrane thinness – and the seals had started to part company at the corners of the house where it faced north. Lydia often entreated Ari's father to sell the house and move nearer the town. Ari listened in a separate room and never commented. Her father was dead and the town was no longer there; it made her feel physically sick when Lydia was too drunk to remember that. Behind the house, a wasted forest clung with faint hope to a craggy hillside, shadowing the back yard and filling it with convulsed leaves in the Fall. Perhaps more than half the trees were grey and without life now, which gave the forest a surreal, enchanted atmosphere. When she visited Taler's Bump, Ari always chose to take the route through the forest. It was a longer path but she always had plenty of time. For months she'd been ahead in her studies and there was a waiting list for the new subject material she'd requested. In lucid moments, Lydia bitterly pointed out this was because they lived in the middle of nowhere and no one gave a damn whether kids were educated or not.

Ari walked into the sacred circle through the shadow thrown by the first column. She could see the manform standing motionless in the centre of the circle facing south, but Ari knew he was using his sensory devices to watch the western road. She suspected that, like her, he looked forward to visitors arriving.

'Hi Sammael!' Her call echoed round the columns. Whatever else might be in decline, the Bump's acoustics were still perfect. She wondered whether Sammael understood loneliness. He must surely experience it, but perhaps wouldn't recognise it as such. Sammael raised a hand; a swooping gesture, still graceful. His synthetic skin might have peeled, but his joints worked faultlessly. Ari went to stand beside him and raised her binoculars to scan the road. Grey and black, grey and black, it snaked into the haze of distance; a dead snake lying on expired ground. The world looked so small beneath the empty, white sky, so tired and drab. Ari shivered and moved out of the shadow of the columns. Sometimes a swift, mad fear made her think she was truly alone, utterly mindless; the last thing on earth, deceiving itself that there was still hope. She was afraid even the degenerate figures of her mother and the handful of neighbours were nothing but hallucinations. Worse still, perhaps she was old and dying already, just imagining she was still young: a terrifying thought.

'Nobody on their way then,' she said, grateful she could speak aloud, if only to a man-form. It reestablished her reality. Sammael turned towards her, his body making a noise that sounded just like a sigh. 'Perhaps the ones that came at Yoole, you remember, the people from New Tor, will show up,' Ari continued cheerfully. 'Didn't they say they might for Beltagne?'

'There are people on the road, yes,' Sammael replied, in his special, soft voice that sounded as if it was trapped inside him, 'but I can't specify who.'

21

'Where? Where? I can't see anybody.' Ari swept her binoculars from side to side. The landscape blurred.

'A long way off yet.' Sammael walked stiff-leggedly like a cat to the great trilithon and scanned its circuitry. The stones themselves were about ten to fifteen feet high and were manmade, specially constructed to appear like granite. Deep inside, several of them contained working parts that could project seasonal holograms, emit light, disperse incense perfume or play ritual music. Austin Grant had liked the element of theatre in natro celebrations and had catered for it lavishly. Unfortunately, because of the acid rain and the occasional dust-storm, one or two of the columns now had exposed circuitry and no longer worked. It was a shame. Sammael did his best but a lot of the repair tools had worn out anyway.

Ari swung herself up on to the altar table, idly tracing its raised spiral patterns with her fingers, but still looking at the road. She had brought a basket of dried grasses with her to adorn the altar. Really, she should have brought spring flowers, but they were precious and she did not like to pick them. It was important to make some effort, however, for visitors appreciated it and Sammael didn't seem to understand the importance or effect of decorative gestures.

Years ago, when she'd been a small child, her mother had been a devout follower of the New Goddess and had led her daughter up to the monument at every festival. They had made coloured flowers from old clothes, from food packets, anything that was bright and cheerful, and had adorned the menhirs with them. Ari remembered her mother's bright remarks to Sammael; an affectionate scorn. Her father had been alive then, but far away. Ari and her mother hadn't seen him for a long time before he died. It was work that kept him away, the work that had

paid for the luxury house. Ewan Famber had simply
been a distant, glamorous icon to his daughter and, very
possibly, Ari reasoned once she was old enough to consider it, to his wife as well. Taler's Bump and its surrounding district had dried out well before Ewan had
bought the house, which was why it had been within his
financial reach. Lydia told her daughter Ewan wanted
them to live well in order to make up for his regular
absence. Live well? Ari had often wistfully considered
what her life would have been like if there'd been other
children in the area to share her make-believe and
secrets. Lydia had always tried to maintain a homely
cheer, however, and before the bad times had been a
tireless and playful companion for her child. Ari's early
days were rosy memories of safety and comfort. Yellowfield had been an occupied, if not thriving town back
then, and she remembered the weekly visits to the natro
eco-store, where Lydia would buy packets of brightly
coloured beans and tall cartons of vanilla-flavoured soya
milk. They would call in at the Juicery on the way back to
the public transport garage, laden with shopping, and
Lydia would buy them both an ice-cold drink of apricot
juice. The memory of such treats seemed almost unreal
now. There hadn't been many families in the town however, because most of its inhabitants were individuals
who worked for the Tech-Green plant by the river. Their
families lived up north in domed suburban clusters.
Every month a fleet of helicopters would arrive with new
workers to relieve those going off duty and returning
north. Ari could remember watching the choppers from
her back yard; whirring overhead, bringing a sense of
excitement and activity. Lydia was excited by the helicopters too. She used to come out into the yard and talk
about the time when she and Ari would pack all their

belongings and fly away to a new home in the north. She spoke of trees and lakes, how there'd be hundreds of other children for Ari to play with. Ewan would arrange it. When the project he was involved in was completed, his bonus would make him a rich man. Of course, it never happened.

Everything bad had come to them at once. First, the town scare. A hideous accident at the plant had effectively poisoned Yellowfield to death. The plant produced genetically engineered fungi and, supposedly through human error, an explosion occurred, which effectively spread maverick spores over a wide area. A freak jungle of contorted growth appeared overnight, which a Tech-Green air/ground squad of aircraft and earth excavators came immediately to defoliate, erasing the remaining traces of Yellowfield in the process. The damage was so extensive that there was nothing else anybody could have done. The Tech-Greens, perhaps slightly embarrassed by their heavy-handed emergency measures, had ranted piously over the network for a few weeks about how the accident had been caused by the carelessness of their operatives, and that the technology had been perfectly safe. Lydia had sneered at that. Ewan, of course, had been working off-world when it happened. Ari remembered when she and her mother had been directed to remain indoors for several weeks while eerie protective-suit-clad Tech-Green commandos had painstakingly detoxified as much of the area as they could. Later, the Fambers had sat on the Bump, eating bean-paste sandwiches and drinking Ari's favourite vanilla milk, watching, through binoculars, the dead stain spread across the land. Vegetation had never been lush in that area, but what little remained – tough, stringy shrubs and grasses able to cope with the parched, dusty soil – had vanished. Lydia had said it was like watching a flood. Would the water reach them and engulf their house? 'There is no water,' Ari had said, and Lydia had replied, 'Yeah, but we could be engulfed.' They hadn't been, luckily. Taler's Bump with its partially petrified fringe of forest had been spared. At least, it had seemed so at first. The Tech-Greens had set up emergency eco-clinics to curb the spread of toxins, but every spring since then there were fewer leaves on the surviving trees in the forest, and in summer the land seemed to hiss and burn, yearning in vain for healing rain. Lydia said it was ironic that the very thing that kept Yellowfield alive had been responsible for the disaster. The shrunken, misshapen skeleton of the complex was still there, up river; a monument in itself. Lydia told her daughter it was a new Pompei. Ari could still see it on a clear day if she chose to look.

When Yellowfield died, it had caused problems with supplies. The transport firm, which had only ever boasted two trucks, never came into the district again. Arcady was a very long journey away by slider, even a zippy speed model like Lydia's. As Lydia was frightened of driving herself, she had allowed the solar panels on the sleek little vehicle Ewan had bought her to decay badly, leaving it to languish in the garage, hidden beneath a plastic web. Ari was old enough to drive now, but there was nobody around to repair it. Sliders had never been renowned for their durability, and most people considered them to be an expensive, rich kids' toy. Ari wished her father had had the foresight to purchase a rugged, sensible truck for his family. With the right machinery, the methane needed to run such vehicles could be produced from domestic sewage. She and Lydia wouldn't be trapped at the Bump if he'd done that.

Lydia had not been particularly economical when Ewan had been alive and, once the eco-store went, had wasted her husband's salary hiring expensive supplies couriers from the zone station. The couriers affected a heroic temperament (almost piratical, which was quite appropriate under the circumstances), and prowled the skies in fast, angry rotorjets that looked as mean and potentially painful as giant wasps. Lydia used to charter one nearly every week; a luxury almost lustful in its extravagance. Nevertheless, there had been a certain glamour about the black, insect thing that used to roar down on to the flat road outside the house, flinging back the washing hanging in the yard, tearing flimsy leaves from the trees with its powerful, gusting blades. Ari used to cower on the porch, weak with excitement and dread, never entirely convinced the predatory machine was only delivering store orders from the zone station. She half feared that one day lean, human carnivores would slink beneath the cutting wind and change her life forever in ways that would be as rapturous as they were terrifying. However, disappointment had always followed the landing. No leather-clad renegade had ever stepped forth. It had always been a nasal-voiced, runty little man who'd scurried from beneath the sweeping blades, hunched over, bringing out the carriers of food. When Ari and her mother had taken it inside the house, and the rotor had gone, Ari's mother would sigh as she lifted out the bright little packets. The order was never right. Lydia said she suspected she was not only overcharged, but sent inferior goods into the bargain. It never inspired her to repair the slider and go shopping herself however.

So Yellowfield's demise was the first disaster. Then came the news from the Tech-Greens. Not even a personal visit, but a message through the house console.

Ewan Famber had been killed in a freak accident off-world, it said. Following this stark information came some sweet words praising his contribution to the movement and an unembarrassed list of Lydia's entitlements and benefits as a widow. Whoever sent the message, probably just another computer, ended with the remark that they were sure Mrs Famber would contact Tech-Green HQ should she run into difficulties. Lydia howled for a week, now prey to weaknesses which Ewan's support, however distant, had kept at bay. For those first few days after the news, Ari had hidden beneath furniture, confused and terrified by her mother's erratic mood swings from raving fury to numbed silence. She found it hard to understand how the death of Ewan Famber, who was after all hardly more than a name to her, could affect their lives that much. Her mother had, overnight, become an absolute stranger.

At night, once Lydia had exhausted herself, Ari would creep into the living room to read the apocalyptic information still glowing on the house monitor. Lydia could not bring herself to print it out and clear the screen. Respectfully wary of this potent magick capable of turning a person's mind, Ari still felt impelled to try and identify precisely which words had caused her mother to go mad. It was puzzling, they seemed so harmless, some of them even sympathetic and kind. She could still remember much of that message even now. Although she didn't know it, and wouldn't even recognise it for some time, Ari's whole life had been changed irrevocably by Ewan's death. Lydia would not recover from her breakdown and her daughter would be forced into a greater self-reliance. Childish ignorance of the possible consequences, a certainty that everything would go back to normal eventually, kept Ari bewildered but emotionally unmarked for a time.

After a week, Lydia's few friends in the district had

come to investigate her absence from their gatherings, and had taken charge. Ari remembered them: big women in loose dresses with bare legs, or overalls and sandals. They rationed Lydia's alcohol intake, cleaned the house and talked in low, shocked voices that could not hide the relish and excitement they felt at this unexpected tragedy. Ari had watched one of the women furtively print out the Tech-Green message and then clear the screen. The woman had gone into Ewan's study, Ari following curiously. The room was barely used. Ewan's equipment and papers hadn't even been unpacked properly and the air felt close and stale. The woman had folded the printout carefully and put it in a desk drawer before squatting down and saying to Ari, 'That's for you one day, kid,' as if it was something of value. At the time, being only seven years old, Ari could not imagine what she'd ever need it for. Now she could no longer remember which woman it had been who'd said that to her, but the words remained. Some kind of superstition kept her from reading the message now she was older though. She knew she'd never look at it.

After Ewan's death, Ari and her mother could no longer afford the courier deliveries from the zone station. Although the Tech-Green pension payments were adequate for maintaining a comfortable lifestyle, they could not accommodate luxuries. Now the depleted Famber family had to buy supplies from the co-op gypsies like everyone else in the district, and their standard of living had gone down again. Ari's mother lost her faith: the New Goddess of Naturotech had spat in her face. She and Ewan had worked hard for their beliefs, worked hard for the world, and this was what happened in gratitude. She had believed they were special people and therefore protected, heaping the Goddess with devotional rites designed to maintain that protection. Lydia had never quite deprogrammed herself from the guilt-whip Buddhist Fundamentalism of her childhood, and had sought to appease a power she thought could destroy and uplift at whim.

Even Ari knew better than that. The Goddess didn't dish out favours and punishments in accordance with a rigid dogma; she was merely a feeling, the spark inside that made you laugh and dance or kept you close to the earth like a cat, stalking and turned-on with power. Lydia had never felt that. If she had, her belief system would have been her strength when Ewan died and not a thing to blame. Accidents happen, Ari knew that. Now she always kept up the year-cycle festivals without the company of her mother. On a still day, when Ari stood upon the Bump, she could sometimes hear her mother's music centre blaring out discordant music from the house below, which meant she must be moaning and drinking alone, as if daring the Goddess to hear and chastise her. Ari was glad visitors to the Bump never found out she was in any way connected with the embarrassing cacophony that floated up the hill.

Of course, there were festivals when nobody came at all, and Ari had to celebrate with Sammael alone. It was better if there were other people there though because then they could sing and dance together. Sammael couldn't sing or dance at all.

By the time Ari went back down the hill, through the forest, there had still been no sign of any pilgrims. She'd strewn the grasses around and had helped Sammael trim back the straggly weeds that tended to grow round the base of the columns. The afternoon had been hot and she'd taken advantage of no one being around, stripping off her shirt to enjoy the feeling of sunlight on her skin for a few minutes. Sammael never warned her about this, so she tended to disregard her mother's hysterical forebodings of what could happen if someone exposed themselves for too long. She trusted Sammael's preprogrammed judgement far more than Lydia's non-sensical, paranoid ramblings and had the good sense not to overexpose herself anyway.

Ari ate her evening meal with the intention of visiting the monument again later to see if there'd been any developments. Lydia's friend Patti had come visiting, a woman who lived a short way up the road in a broken down lux-res with half of its facilities dead. They were drinking together, a lethal home-distilled gin a friend of Patti's supplied. Patti was a widow too, but she'd killed her husband herself. Ari was tired of the story, of hearing how the beast of a man had deserved it. All the horror and shock value had been worn out years ago, yet Patti still liked to talk about it. The story had changed over the years too, to display Patti in a rather more courageous light than she deserved. The Fambers indulged her and did not contradict. After all, what did it matter anyway? Ari ate quietly, listening to Patti tell her mother about how someone was actually growing vegetables in a gar-den nearby, benefiting from a Tech-Green aid grant. They'd only revitalised a modest patch of earth however. Taler's Bump was located in an area afflicted by a multi-tude of ills: soil erosion, climate change, chemical toxification. There was really little point in trying to heal such a small part of it. Meanwhile, Lydia rambled in a monotone, when Patti left gaps in her conversation, about how much her head ached today. Ari sighed, filled with an uncertain anger as she watched these two lanky women disintegrate. She remembered them as strong, something it was clear they'd both forgotten. And yet

Ari was increasingly aware it might be herself who had changed, not them. She peered at her mother closely. Perhaps the beautiful and caring person she recalled from childhood had never really existed at all. After the meal, Ari slipped away, unnoticed beneath the chink of gin glasses and lamentations for the past.

There were sounds coming from the hill, discernible even before Ari left the forest: human voices. It was beginning to get dark. The western horizon was deep crimson with sunset, the menhirs solemn and stonelike against it, much like pictures of ancient cromlechs Ari had seen on her school console and on which the monument had been modelled. For a few moments, she paused among the scoured tree-trunks, hesitating before going forward. It had been this way for about a year now, some strange impulse within her fluttering like a panicked bird at the thought of meeting new people. The personal development disks had informed her that awkwardness and shyness were quite common anxieties in teenagers, but it was more than either of those. It was as if a primal 'fight or flee' instinct was urging for the latter; as if people, of any kind, were dangerous. Ari found it difficult to articulate these feelings, even to herself. She desperately wanted company, new stimuli, yet at the same time felt a strong desire to back away. Her only comfort was that she might eventually grow out of it.

As she breasted the hill, she could see silhouettes of people moving against the sky and hear the twittering voices of those who did not know a stranger was near. Sammael was moving among the people. Ari recognised his low, careful voice telling them about the chalets on the other side of the hill they could use for accommodation.

'I'd only bother if you don't mind being cold,' Ari

said, moving towards them. 'There's no heating any more in there, but you can use wood from the forest for a fire. Look,' she gestured with her arm to show them the trees behind her, sloping spikily away to the north. She couldn't see the people all that well, but they smelt of true naturotechs; an indescribable blend of smoky static and sandalwood oil. For the first time when meeting a new group of visitors, Ari had not changed out of her natro clothes, although she had taken the precaution of playing down the leather thongs somewhat. The pilgrims immediately took her for another of their kind and greeted her warmly. Ari knew from experience they wouldn't be so open with her if they knew she lived in a house nearby, so she didn't tell them. It wasn't a lie; they just didn't ask.

Natros called themselves randomati and roamed the country in their motley vehicles. They survived quite well outside the domes, as the outlands were full of salvageable debris and methane-producing substances, which served as a currency outside the credit-system and bartering. Naturally, they were always under the observation of Tech-Green zone patrols, who were alert for 'crimes'. Conflict with these agents was rare, however, as criminal activity was virtually non-existent owing to the low out-dome population and the fact that there was so much material lying around to be taken for free. The natros travelled from festival to festival, site to site, bartering their talents. At Yoole, Ari had met a man whose light terminal could read people's auras. The others in his party called him a medicine man. Ari suspected they were right. When she stood in front of his scanner, the monitor told her all about the problems she'd had with her kidneys years ago. Ari was impressed, although it would have been more useful for her had the medicine man been adept enough to divine certain other differences about her.

'Why have you come here?' Ari asked. She spoke to a woman whose strong, charismatic presence proclaimed her a motivating force within this group. The motivators were always easy to spot. The woman was tall, with a fierce, beautiful face, her functional khaki clothes draped with bright, fringed shawls. Ari was entranced by this dashing creature who strode from menhir to menhir, running her long, strong fingers over the circuits, her thick, red hair wrapped up in a coloured scarf. Too often, the natros who came to the Bump were small, colourless individuals who moved quickly and whose skins were dry; desert people. Ari liked flamboyance. She repeated her question and continued, 'After all, Arbor Mount is much better equipped. We don't have the same holographic facilities here. Well, I think we used to but—'

'Too crowded,' the woman interrupted. 'We like to have a little space and always use the less popular sites. The rites're more meaningful that way. Anyway, the big sites're always full of fat scuzzies from the mini-clusters, driving out in their dinky sliders, all rich and discontented, trying to get a buzz off whatever power is raised. I despise that. All of it!'

One of the men came over to listen. He had a lean body, his face sculpted by hard times, with long, tangled hair that was just a mess of colours. He looked like a trickster, and one who'd lost the gamble more than a few times, but he was still handsome. 'Yeah, but if it wasn't for the fat scuzzies and their bulging credit accounts, places like Arbor Mount wouldn't have all those flashy facilities,' he said in a low, tar-abraded voice.

'Exactly, Jordan!' the woman replied, but she looked

affronted. 'Now, shall we shift some stuff from the trucks into those chalets? I could use some food. Want to join us kid?'

Ari said yes and went to help carry their things.

The trucks, two of them, were parked at the foot of the hill; great bulky saurian things, whose armour plating looked as if it was about to fall apart. They were crowned with bulging methane-bags and flanked by ugly water tanks. Inside, large cushions and blankets were jammed between VDUs; cooking materials encroached on to consoles and keyboards. On high racks lay the furled convolutions of residential tepees, cables hanging down like vines. A boy was clambering over the junk, throwing baggage out on to the ground. 'Yeah, it's a bit of a mess in here,' he said. Ari liked him. He was thin and whippy as a willow branch with a face comprised of ropes of muscle and long, white teeth. His name was Cabochon. He told her the red-haired woman was Leila Saatchi and that the name of their group was Star Eye. They had obviously been in existence for a long time, exhibiting as they did the fluid cooperation of established companions. As Ari had thought, Leila was their motivator, along with her partner, Jordan. The others, nine of them at present, came and went as the seasons passed. This was normal. Most natro groups swapped members all the time. They liked variety. Naturotech wasn't a religion, it was a culture. Thousands of people in the cities were into it, but the randomati considered themselves the only true devotees. Since the Tech-Greens had gained more power, these wandering shamans had acquired more respectability. It was rumoured nearly all of them were Tech-Green operatives anyway. Their Goddess, whose main aspect was named Astrada, symbolising the youthful, contemporary, avenging face of old Gaiah,

had taken up where the out-moded Earth-goddess aspects had finished off. Nature had had to evolve, even mutate, to survive, using and manipulating the factors that had nearly killed it off entirely. Astrada appreciated the power of technology and used it with abandon to reclaim her devastated kingdom.

There were only six chalets now; the others had had to be cannibalised to maintain the least dilapidated. They had a quasi-organic appearance; domes, ridged with ceraplas struts. Older chalets, whose crowns had eroded, looked as if something had burst out of them from within. Ari led the way towards them, pointing things out on the horizon quite invisible to strangers to the area; it was nearly dark. She managed to jostle into a position which meant she could walk beside Cabochon. Something inside her was reluctant, but he was so nice to look at, such a rarity round here, that she did her best to ignore the urge to move away. (*What the hell is wrong with me? Is this normal?*) He didn't appear to notice any discomfort on her part, hopping down the tussocky hill. 'You from around here?' he asked, and Ari had to reply that she was. He didn't ask any more questions though, so he might just think she was a road scummer who didn't stray far from a tight-line location.

'You haven't been here before, have you? I don't recognise your group,' Ari said.

Cabochon shrugged. 'Dunno. It's my first time anyhow.'

Luckily, the chalets still had lighting, powered by a small generator, which Sammael had activated earlier in the day. Leila, leading the others, marched through the nearest doorway. The locks were operated from the trilithon, so the doors were already open, the lights on low. Inside, woodlook furniture essayed to convey a rustic air. Leila inspected the fireplace, previously used only for effect. She suggested some of the group go off to hunt for fuel. Leila Saatchi never gave orders, never had to. It was a knack she had. Her suggestions were so compelling.

Star Eye gathered to eat in the largest chalet. Although the food was very plain and devoid of the high flavourings Ari was used to, there was plenty to go around and none of it appeared to be synthetic. Someone had laid a fire in the grate to stave off the evening chill, and wine was plentiful if rather sour, conversation easy. Everyone sat in a rough circle on the floor. Ari was squeezed between a girl not much older than herself, who introduced herself as Justinette, and a ropy-muscled, middle-aged man whom the others called Kydd. His face was marked with scars, one long score on each cheek which were possibly totemic, and his head was shaved but for a single long pigtail which hung halfway down his back. He made Ari feel uneasy. Justinette, on the other hand, had the seductively compelling charm of a spoiled prize virgin: physically as delicate as a nymph but with a voice too big for her body. She was full of the settlement they'd just visited. She laughed when she talked about the people who came to, 'have their fortunes read'. 'That's what they called it. Can you believe that?' Ari reflected that those same people, so dumb in Justinette's eyes, were the ones that paid for Star Eye to exist, but she didn't say so.

Leila must have been listening. 'People who work with sewage don't necessarily like shit.' She must have guessed what Ari was thinking. Ari hated that.

After they'd finished eating, Justinette initiated a flood of idle chatter and Ari made sure she laughed in the right places, nodded earnestly in others; but she wasn't really listening. There was a twinge of discomfort inside her. Something was jarring. Star Eye were just a muddle of teeth and smiles around her, and for all their laughter, the atmosphere in the room was far from relaxed.

'Goddess, is it me? Am I doing this?' Ari wondered. *Paranoia! I'm getting as bad as Lydia.* It was also impossible not to be keenly aware of the feline presence of Cabochon across the room, even when she wasn't looking at him. He and a couple of the others had been smoking grass; his body was so lax it flowed like syrup. People like Cabochon had existed only on video and in dreams for her until now. And even though Leila was looking the other way, Ari was conscious of the woman's quiet, sentient power. Was Leila keeping an eye on her? Probably. Ari was a stranger after all, and being natro didn't necessarily mean you were OK. Some natros had veered off into pretty weird avenues after all, using the pagan aspects of naturotech, but mutating it into sadomasochism. Neither did Ari appear to belong to a group. That could mean she'd been kicked out of one or her path was so crooked nobody wanted her anyway. It was only natural the motivator would keep a watch on her. Only natural.

'Do you attend all the festivals at the Bump here?' Leila asked her. The wine was nearly finished and Ari was beginning to feel a little dizzy. She had tried hard to let go of her anxiety and relax all evening, but hadn't really succeeded.

'Yes, except when I'm sick,' she replied, 'which isn't often.'

Jordan had turned his head to listen when Leila asked the question. Now he extricated himself from the group round Cabochon and leaned forward to join in. 'What kind of groups have you worked with then, Aaaari?' he asked. Ari instinctively shrank back from his hard eyes.

'Most kinds I suppose. Why?' She had to ask the question, just to show she wasn't too happy about the interrogation.

Leila shrugged and flicked Jordan a significant glance. Ari began to feel even more uncomfortable. The atmosphere in the room had changed, condensed somehow. 'We have an important working annexed to the festival,' Leila said in a smooth voice.

'You don't have to worry. I can be discreet,' Ari replied in what she hoped was a careless tone. 'Lots of groups have come here. I've joined in with lots of rites.'

'Oh, so you're kind of like pretty static then,' Jordan said, grinning. Ari disliked the way he was speaking to her. It was not the way for natros to behave towards each other before an important festival. This group was entirely different to any she'd met before, oddly furtive. What the hell were they into? For the first time ever, Ari wondered whether it was a good idea to join in the festival. No other randomati had made her feel this way.

'If you must know, and it seems clear you do, I live here,' she said stiffly. 'My parents were Tech-Greens, both static natros, yes. My father's dead now. You may have heard of him. Ewan Famber.' She wished she hadn't said that. Most natros would have heard of Ewan Famber, if only because, before working with Roirbak, he'd been in the spearhead committee who'd detoxified most of the regions now used as festival sites in this sector. Austin Grant had made sure no one would get contaminated using his open-air temples. Perhaps Star Eye wouldn't believe her.

Leila laughed politely, a hard, cold laugh. 'Don't worry kid, we're not going to run you off the mount.'

Ari muttered and shrugged awkwardly. The atmosphere of congeniality, whether genuine or not, had been effectively frozen out. Now they were all looking at her. Goddess! To make an excuse and walk out would be unbearable, but it was unbearable to stay too. Why won't somebody say something? A snicker sounded from across the room; Cabochon with his hair over his face.

'Relax your asses, people. Drop the kid and get on with the yapping why don't you?'

Jordan smiled in a feral way. 'Just being careful,' he said. Cabochon sprawled over and put his arms round Jordan's waist, resting his face on the man's back.

'Careful? Don't frighten her off.'

Jordan twitched irritably. 'We don't know about her, not for sure,' he said, and narrowed his eyes at Leila fiercely.

'That's enough!' Leila admonished. The rest of the group were all looking at the floor, at their hands, anywhere but at the people holding the stage. Ari noticed Justinette had moved away from her.

Leila shook her head and stretched and yawned, rubbing her face. 'Leave it,' she said. 'We've been on the road all day. I don't need this shit.' She dragged her fingers down her face and looked at Ari through them. 'I fancy a look around this place. Wanna give me a tour, kid?' Ari said OK, relieved at being given an excuse to leave, but somehow worried Leila was going to scold her in some way. That was crazy. She'd done nothing, meant nothing to these people. Struggling awkwardly to her feet, she mumbled indistinct apologies to Justinette and Kydd, and followed Leila out the door. Cabochon's voice started up again once she was outside; a stoned drawl. The others laughed. Her face was burning. Shit. Shit. Shit. What had gone wrong?

Outside the chalet, Leila Saatchi braced herself against the cool air and took deep breaths. One, two, three. She was aware of the kid hovering behind her. This whole business was a mess already, Jordan twitchy and resentful as a mad hound, waiting, just waiting for her to fuck up. He is jealous, she thought. Talk about arrogance! And jealous of what? She turned around. Ari was looking small and pale but feisty. So you are all that's left of Ewan, Leila thought. Goddess, what am I supposed to do with you? She'd known from the moment Ari had walked in among the stones who she was. It was unmistakable. Ewan himself must have looked very much like this at fourteen. Later she will be a stunner, Leila thought, like he was. She wasn't really prepared to confront Ari with the reason for her being there yet. All the scenarios she'd worked out in advance involved marching up to the Famber house and making some kind of formal request. This was different. In a little while, she would have to get that damned document out again and try to decipher what Ewan expected her to do next. First, she must try to put the kid at ease. It was not a good idea to have her so suspicious.

'Beautiful night, ain't it,' Leila said, in an obvious attempt to lessen the awkwardness.

'Yeah.' Ari was wishing Leila would just say whatever she had to say. Maybe she'd give this lady a mouthful back. Nobody had treated her this way before, made her feel like an outsider. She doubted whether the festival could be successful blighted by this weird, suspicious atmosphere.

Ari took the path that led to the forest, marching ahead of Leila who was still admiring the red-ringed moon. Leila wasn't saying a word and Ari could hear the woman humming to herself, casual as anything. Perhaps she was just trying to wind Ari up.

'Wow, black and white!' Leila exclaimed when the forest came into view around the hill. She was right. The fat moon had bleached the stark trees, the spaces in between them were lightless. 'Isn't this place creepy?'

'I like it,' Ari said, stiffly. She was still wondering what the purpose of this walk was. There had to be a purpose. Leila was not the sort of person who needed someone to show her around anywhere.

'Hey, don't be upset,' Leila said.

Here it comes.

'You people are strange, that's all. Like you don't want anyone else around.'

Leila made a sharp noise of disagreement. 'It's not that. Jordan is just cautious with strangers at first. Take no notice. He'll warm up tomorrow, I promise. I don't want us to spoil your festival.'

Ari stopped and turned around to look at Leila's face. She wanted to see if that was genuine or not. Leila held out her palms. They were very white in the moonlight. 'We were surprised to see you up there, anyone up there . . . so soon. It was unexpected.' Unlikely, Ari thought. Any number of randomati might have shown up. Star Eye had no way of knowing that.

'Where do you live?' Leila said.

'At the other end of this path.'

'Can I see it?'

'If you want to. It's nothing special. We live nowhere special.'

They went into the forest, Leila squeezing alongside Ari on the narrow path. This isn't getting any better, lady, Leila told herself. Perhaps I should be straight with her. 'How come your mother doesn't keep the festivals with you now?' she asked. Branches brushed their faces. They had to duck. Leila broke off a crooked, dead twig and

41

waved it at Ari's face. The girl flinched. Obviously the gesture had been taken as threatening rather than playful.

'My mother's not been quite right since my father died. She lost her faith in life,' Ari said quickly.

'Too bad. I'm sorry.' Leila brushed Ari's face again with the twig. The girl grinned nervously.

'I don't care about it. It's her life.'

'You're right of course.' Leila noticed Ari had increased her pace a little. Was she getting just a little jumpy about being out in the woods alone with a stranger?

In fact, Ari had begun to wonder whether Star Eye were really natros at all. They had come to the end of the path. The walk was over, and Ari was only half relieved. A large part of her enjoyed the fearful excitement of being alone with this strange, powerful woman who could possibly be very dangerous. Wonder and fear: an intoxicating cocktail for someone who spent so much time alone.

'That's the house,' she said, pointing through the trees. The lights were on, shining out through the unshuttered windows, revealing all inside. It looked a tawdry and temporary place. Even from here, Lydia could plainly be seen slumped in the living room. Had Leila come this far to get inside the house? Impossible. Lydia would blindingly embarrass Ari in some way. 'You can't come in,' Ari said. 'My mother. You know.'

'That's OK. Are you coming up to the site during the day tomorrow?'

Ari shrugged. 'I think you should,' Leila continued. 'I apologise for Star Eye. We've not been very welcoming, have we?'

'I'll come up in the afternoon.'

'Fine. Love's law to you!' It was a natro catch-phrase.

Was Leila trying to make amends? Ari was not gullible enough to give her, or her group, the benefit of the doubt. She'd see about that tomorrow.

'To you too. Bye.' She trotted off down the slope towards the bungalow, looking back once she came into the aura of the house lights. Leila hadn't waited to watch. There was no one in the trees above. She'd gone.

Ari hoped Lydia would be unconscious by now. Once the back door was closed, however, she could hear the drone of voices from the living room. Maybe if she soft-padded it quietly to her bedroom . . . ?

'Ari! That you?'

'Yes, Lydia.'

'C'mere!' She heard her mother laugh, and another voice titter back. Patti was still here. It was not unreasonable to assume they were both gin-soaked to the bone. 'Don't know what she gets up to half the time,' she heard her mother saying and Patti answering, 'Yes, I know what it's like,' which she could not since she had no daughters of her own. Lydia Famber was sprawled half on the sofa, half on the floor, her face red under the eyes, her forehead damp, hair lank and wet-looking. Mother, you are a horrible mess, Ari thought.

'Hi,' she said to Patti and, 'Didn't think you'd still be up,' to her mother.

'Where've you been?'

'At the site. You know that.'

'Till this time? What could you possibly be doing up there till now? The damned festival isn't till tomorrow.'

'Some randomati came.'

'Trash!' Lydia exclaimed, her eyes lighting up. 'How

many times do I have to tell you, Ari, stay away from those weirdos. If you need to be into that natro garbage there's decent people hereabouts who'd let you join in with their family celebrations.'

'I like the site, and I like the people,' Ari said defensively, even though she had doubts about those who'd turned up this time. No way would she tell her drunken mother about that though. Let her think she was missing something.

'They got any readers?' Patti asked. 'I like all that. The weird little messages and everything.'

Ari's mother was opening and closing her thin, damp mouth. It made her look ancient, as if she was chomping on toothless gums. Ari shuddered and turned a bright smile on Patti.

'Yeah, they've got readers,' she said. 'I'm going up there again tomorrow afternoon, Patti. Come with me, if you want. I could introduce you.'

'Thanks Ari. I might.'

Lydia had hauled herself into a sitting position. 'Will you listen to me, girl?' she squawked. 'I told you I don't want you mixing with those people. They're shit! They're killers!'

'Mother, don't be ridiculous.'

'They'll have your ass, and all the juicy parts right next to it!'

Ari rolled her eyes and said to Patti, 'I've been attending natro festivals up there alone since my father died. Now she tells me they're after my body! It's a bit late for that advice isn't it, ma?'

'You're older now – tender. They'll have you!'

'Their leader walked me home. She was not improper at all.'

Lydia made a sulky snarl and drooped back into the

46

cushions. 'Don't come whining to me then.'

'Don't worry. You're the last person I'd come to if I needed to whine!' Ari said coldly, remembering at that moment how she and her mother had once been so close. It made her feel wistful, for it was the same person sitting there, only a person who was sadder, with less hope and even less strength. 'I can look after myself, ma. You taught me that a long time ago,' she said. Lydia allowed herself to be mollified by that.

'Have a drink,' she said. Ari had to water the gin down from the purifier in the kitchen. They had no soft drinks. Not any more. Not for a long time. It didn't taste too good, but she squeezed on to the sofa next to her mother and sipped at it. Strange how Lydia should worry about her innocence yet ply her with liquor.

'Sometimes I think about going up to one of the festivals myself,' Patti said.

Ari smiled sweetly. She knew Patti would never make it alone up the hill. From front doorstep to truck was about as far as she could manage without company. Most of the few people left in the area had gone rather agoraphobic. 'Were you ever a natro, Patti?' Ari asked. It was the first time she could remember that Patti had ever mentioned the subject.

Patti wrinkled her nose, hunched forward on her chair, clutching a plastic tumbler of gin. 'Nah, couldn't see the point. I'm just a little person like everybody else. Seems like the natros think they're something more, but they're not. I can't be bothered with lies like that. Where does it get you? You think you've got it made, you've got the power to control your destiny and then, pow!, you're back in the shit with the other vermin. It's all lies.'

Ari assumed Patti must have had a phase of being an ardent natro, but had been disillusioned. Perhaps she'd expected more. 'Someone has to care about the world,' she said.

'We have Tech-Greens for that,' Patti answered. 'I know they're all natros themselves, but they have the kind of power that matters: sly tongues and a fast hand when it comes to tricks. Politics. The same thing. They'll get my vote, but they'll not get my soul.' She laughed at her own joke. Lydia snorted.

'It's all a waste of time. We're all going down the pipe. The Tech-Greens will just make the dying slower, that's all.'

Ari couldn't help wondering if her mother was right. For all her slobbish behaviour, Lydia still had a mind in there somewhere, and she knew more about Tech-Green than she ever let on to Patti, Ari was sure.

'So apply for a place in Sky City One,' Patti said, gesturing with her cup. Sky City One was the orbital reputed to be more idyllic than Gaiah had been at her most uncontaminated. 'Wouldn't you and Ari be priority candidates, what with your background and all?'

Lydia sneered. 'Patti, wake up! The likes of us won't ever get so much as a hair off this planet.' She narrowed her eyes at her daughter. 'No matter whose name we carry.'

Jordan was waiting for Leila in the chalet when she got back. Everyone else had found a corner to sleep in. He was lying there, alone by firelight. *Dangerous beauty*. The walk through the woods had spooked her a little. She took a swig out of a half empty bottle of wine, eyeing the sprawled shape on the floor cushions. Longing and anger took up arms within her again, as usual. 'Where's Cabochon?' she asked sharply.

'You want him?' Jordan grinned, rolling on to his

back. Leila kicked his side and he grimaced, laughing.

'Sure I do! You're an asshole, Jord. What the fuck did you do that for?'

'Do what?' Innocent smile.

'You know. Scare the kid. What is it to you?'

'What is it to you?'

'Duty,' Leila replied, deadpan. 'You know that.'

'Necro-infatuation is what it is, lady!'

Leila staged a laugh. 'Goddess, you're jealous! You really are! I can't believe it! And, by the way, how dare you!' She took another swig of wine and sat down beside Jordan on the cushions. He extended a hand to stroke her hair.

'He's not as wonderful as you remember, girl,' he said. Leila jerked away.

'Stop that. Stop it! Listen, we have to sort things out with the kid. Tomorrow. I asked her to come up in the afternoon. Be nice to her, Jord. It really is important to me.'

'I know it is. We'll take off for the afternoon.'

'Jordan!'

'Listen to me for a change. I thought about it earlier. The rest of us can truck off to the supplies hanger at the zone station, but we'll leave Cab here. Let him handle it. Leave Famber junior to him.'

'Goddess!'

'You know he can sweeten her up.'

'I know *you* know that!'

Jordan dragged her down beside him. 'Give me some love,' he said.

'I hate you!' Leila said, helplessly.

Later, she dragged her laptop comms out of its battered case and sat naked in the moonlight to call up Roirbak. Jordan pretended to be asleep, but she could feel his attention riveted on what she was doing. Ewan's document she placed on the floor as far away from Jordan as possible. She didn't want him to read it.

Roirbak's answering service responded to her call, one of his favourite artificial intelligences. The machine had a receptionist's businesslike yet welcoming manner. 'Mellissa, tell Quincx I've met the girl,' Leila told it guardedly. 'And that tomorrow, at the festival, I'm going to have to try out this wild suggestion of Ewan's. Tell Quincx I don't like it and that I wish he was here. Get him to call me.'

'Mr Roirbak will be sorry to have missed you,' soothed the machine from far away in Arcady. 'He left a message you might call and said to tell you he's sure everything will work out all right. One question, Ms Saatchi. Mr Roirbak wants to know whether it's for real or not.'

Leila smiled at the quote. 'I can't answer that yet. She's a jumpy kid. That could mean anything. I don't know. Maybe, after tomorrow . . .' She sighed. 'I hope we're doing the right thing.'

'Mr Roirbak said to tell you he's sure everything will work out all right.' Mellissa repeated, sensing, in its limited way, a need for reassurance.

'OK. Bye.' Leila disconnected and slid the comms unit on to the floor. Before she lay down again, Jordan launched into the attack.

'You don't have to do this, Leila. Famber was obviously crazy. I think it's too big a risk to take, meddling about with the kid's mind like he suggested. Those menhirs are half-rotted. Goddess knows what it'll do to her.'

Leila had told Jordan the minimum of information. The rest of Star Eye knew something was going on and she'd had to tell them a little of the truth in order to stop them making wild speculations of their own. 'We have to retrieve data from her,' she'd said, 'using the site itself.' They had, of course, wanted to know what data. She'd had to be more forceful at that point, and told them to wait. 'I don't know myself yet,' she'd told them.

Jordan had been against the idea from the beginning.

'Don't tell me what I can and can't do!' Leila said. 'It's my business. Just leave it!'

'Well, don't say I didn't warn you if things go wrong,' he answered shortly. 'And don't expect me to hold your hand if you have to tell the mother you've killed her kid or something.'

'Shut up!' Leila cried, angry because she knew he was probably being more sensible than she was. 'I can look after myself, *and* Ari Famber. Ewan was no fool.' She picked up the document and tapped it. 'If he says it works, it works. I trust him.'

She wished she was telling the truth.

In the morning, Ari took her mother a coffee in bed. The bedroom was decorated without thought, depressingly plain, and strewn with Lydia's clothes. It smelled sour in there, and yet Lydia had once smelled so sweet. Ari opened the window, depolarising the glass to let in the sun. Lydia acted out all the classic symptoms of a hangover. 'No light, please! Oh, my fucking head!' Ari sat on the bed.

'Drink this. It'll make you feel better.'

Lydia sat up, the quilt falling from her breasts. She was such a scraggy creature. Ari watched in distaste as her mother guzzled the coffee. 'I'll call Amazon House today,' Lydia said. This was the Tech-Green HQ in Arcady.

'The comm's been out for a month, ma, remember?'

'I could walk to the district boundary. There're still public call-booths there. Come with me.'

'Don't be silly. It would cost a fortune. Why do you want to call them?'

'To get you in there and out of here, you stupid little fool, that's what. I've had enough of you mooning round that dead monument up there and mixing with freaks. If you won't take charge of your life, then I will.' Lydia had a disturbing, fanatical light in her eyes. Ari sensed a kind of panic, a great sense of urgency.

'There's no need, ma. I know what I'm doing.' She picked nervously at the quilt. Lydia's behaviour seemed a chilling, coincidental reflection of the way Star Eye had been with her. Lydia had never been so purposeful before.

'Why won't you listen to me? You think I'm crazy, right? You think I'm a brain-dead drunk. Well, think what you like. You're my daughter and I don't want you ending up mouldering away in this graveyard.'

'It might be a graveyard to you, but I like it,' Ari said, standing up. She went to the window. The hill was visible from here; just the tops of the menhirs. She wondered whether Patti would show up to go there with her. In a way, Ari hoped she would. No doubt the woman would embarrass her rigid, but she was nervous of going up there alone after last night. Yet, at the same time, she was eager to return – mixed feelings again.

'Ari, you can't keep living off your father's pension,' came the low voice from the bed. Ari looked around. So, there it was, said. Why be shocked, why be sad? Deep down, she'd known it for the truth for a long time. But maybe it was better that than Lydia having some kind of presentiment about the natros.

'One way or another, I'll get out of your hair and your bank account as soon as I can!' Ari said, and stalked out with as much dignity as she could muster. To her surprise, Lydia did not call her back.

It wasn't as if Ari still wanted to live in the bungalow with her mother. The peeling, the dissolution, the lie behind the façade, only served to remind her of what had happened to her family. No, it would be more sensible to take over one of the empty houses; there were plenty around. Maybe she could get an aid grant for a patch of land, so she could feed herself.

As the land died, a lot of people moved on, heading for the great barnacled domes of Arcady, the amorphous, swelling hive that had absorbed many older, smaller cities, and where the brilliance of artificial conditions kept poisons at bay. It was a Tech-Green triumph, self-supporting and affluent. And growing. Ari wondered whether a day would ever come when the whole of this tired country would be domed over from coast to coast. It wasn't impossible, was it? The lure of the city was irresistible, with its acres of lush parkland and sweet, clean air. Ari, however, was not attracted by it. She just hoped the Tech-Greens and their followers would carry out their promise and eventually flock to the orbital cities. Leave the planet to me! she thought. I don't mind. I don't mind being here alone. Of course, there were always rumours of bad people wandering about, stealing from or attacking householders, but it had never happened around here. Ari rarely felt unsafe and she wasn't going to let anyone drive her away from the land she loved. Strangely, the only time she ever really felt she loved it was when she thought about it being taken from her forcibly. Do you really want to stay here forever? she wondered. Alone? She thought briefly of the natro boy

Cabochon. *I could have a life partner*. In her mind, she reached to touch his face and a thick wave of nausea crested in her guts. *No. Can't do that. Can't. Bad thoughts. I want a house of my own. All my own. That'll do*. She pushed the thought of human contact away.

Soon she found herself out of the forest on the path leading to the monument. Sloping down to the right was a trail leading to the road where Patti's house lay. Ari hesitated. Would Star Eye be pleased to see her today? With a groan to banish discomforting thoughts, Ari swung off the trail and jogged down the road to Patti's place. Naturally, the woman had forgotten she'd wanted a scrying done, so Ari had to talk her into it again. It took a while to convince her.

They ended up climbing the Bump around midday, Patti hanging on to Ari's arm as if she feared she'd float right away at any moment. Ari was unpleasantly surprised at how light and scrawny Patti felt – no weight at all really. Ari pointed out the view from the hill. Signs of life was evidenced only by a solitary, sentinel windmill two clicks away, its ragged, skeletal sails turning slowly. On the horizon, a dust-trail could be seen, and a rotorjet streaking overhead cast a trembling shadow. Patti barely raised her eyes. She didn't want to see.

'It all looks so drab,' she whined. 'There's so much of it, all dead.'

Ari couldn't think of a cheering answer. She sighed. Maybe the grass was brown and feeble, the dirt dry and weak, but there was so much space! She liked to think that now the people were leaving this bit of land alone, it might recover and come back to life. The natros had told her how the earth was stronger than people imagined. She wanted to believe that.

When they reached the monument, Patti shuffling

among the menhirs, unappreciative of their stark
beauty, Ari thought their struggle up the hill was wasted.
She couldn't see any Star Eye members around and there
was no sound of activity from the chalets. Then she spotted Cabochon squatting down behind the altar, fiddling
with one of the menhirs. He'd tied back his hair which
coiled seductively down his naked back, tanned flesh
disappearing into ripped jeans that displayed tantalising
glimpses of paler buttock; a rare and awesome sight in
these parts. Sammael was standing nearby. Ari wished
she could stand and watch the boy for a while, but Patti
was restless and uncomfortable being out in the open up
there: her anguished noises alerted Cabochon to their
presence. Ari dragged Patti over to him, quickly introducing the woman as a friend of her mother's. 'Can you
do a scry for her?' she asked hopefully.

Cabochon smiled slyly and said, 'Yeah, sure. I'm just
about finished here.' They followed him down to the
largest chalet, Ari hungrily taking in his lissom movement, Patti whispering, 'Don't these people spook you a
bit?'

Cabochon was relieved the kid had turned up with
someone else. 'Come on, help me out,' Jordan had said,
'Leila's nipping my heels. Just be friendly. It'll be easy.
Famberette is hot for you.'

'Oh, says who?' Jordan had an ability to make Cabochon feel grubby.

'Everyone's hot for you, aren't they?' It was, as usual,
an accusation. Jordan lived in a reality populated by
one: himself. Cabochon couldn't understand what all
the fuss was about anyway. Ari just seemed like a normal
kid, no matter whose genes she'd inherited. Leila had
been jumpy and secretive for days, insisting they come to
this burned-out dump of a site. Ari Famber seemed to be

the reason. Perhaps, even after all this time, Leila thought Ewan had left her a legacy.

The chalet was full of quiet, warm afternoon; flies buzzing to break the silence, light coming in through the curved, slitted windows. Ari made a comment about no one else being around. Cabochon's explanation about supplies seemed to upset her. 'But the zone station's such a way off,' she said, frowning.

'Yeah, they'll be gone for most of the afternoon.'

'But Leila said . . .'

'She'll be back later. Here, wanna help me set this up?'

'OK. Wow, what is it?'

'Kydd's baby. Like it?' He'd hauled a battered case on to the table which, when opened, revealed a flat monitor screen and a compact keypad, lovingly etched with Kydd's favourite hexes. Cabochon lifted these out and arranged them round the processing unit which remained in the case. When he flicked the machine on, the screen yawned out from its storage dimensions like something looking for the sun, and a spectre of colour pulsed across it.

'What's it do?' Ari sat down, her fingers plainly itching to get at the scryer.

'Watch. Patti?'

The woman had sat down next to Ari. 'What do I do?'

'Just look into its eyes.' At a touch on the keypad from Cabochon, a reptilian arm extruded from the processing unit, a scanner shaped to fit around the eyes at its tip. Patti squawked and giggled, clutching Ari's shoulder, backing off. 'It won't hurt you. It just takes a look into your eyes. Then it'll throw up a random scry based on your iris and retinal patterns. OK?'

'Yeah. Oooh, it's lookin' at me Ari! Look!' Patti nervously fitted her forehead against the scanner.

Cabochon settled himself down, elbows on the table, and began stroking keys. 'OK, that's it.'

Patti cawed nervous laughter, propped back on her chair like a sack of metal pipes or a skinny, plucked bird. 'Just tell me the worst,' she said.

Cabochon frowned in concentration at the screen. 'Come and see,' he said. Both Ari and Patti crowded round him to take a look.

Close proximity to him made Ari's head spin. She wondered whether the heat outside had affected her. She felt as if she might faint, and moved back a few steps.

'There's the story,' he said, gesturing at the screen.

'But, it's just glyphs,' Ari answered. 'Crazy garbage.'

'Looks that way, huh?' He looked round at them and smiled, flexed his fingers together. 'This is the interesting part.' For a few moments he stared at the colourful display: letters, pictograms, mathematical symbols. 'So you killed a man,' he said at last.

Patti squeaked. 'Who told you that? Who told you that?'

'I just know. No use tearing your insides up over it any more. It's gone. You're scared of being punished, yeah?' Patti just stared at him. 'You won't be. I'm not talking about the law here, you understand. You're frightened of divine justice, oh Lady!' He laughed.

Ari thought he was being cruel. She put her arm through Patti's. What a wicked way to treat somebody! Then Cabochon looked Patti in the eye. His face was completely, beatifically serene. 'You're all right,' he said. 'Really. There was no other way. It was meant to be.' He reached out and touched the woman's hand. Silence was absolute. Then Patti cleared her throat.

'Well, that was something,' she said, shakily, and busied herself leaning down and burrowing in the bag she'd brought with her. Cabochon smiled at Ari, his arms folded on the table.

'Will you do it for me?' Ari asked tentatively. Cabochon hesitated a moment. He could tell she wasn't sure.

'If you like,' he said.

'This is for you,' Patti told him, and plonked a bottle of gin on the table. Cabochon grinned. 'Thanks. There's cups over there,' he told Ari. 'But don't drink until you've eyeballed the scryer, OK?'

She fetched the cups and let Patti start pouring out the poisonous stuff in the bottle. Settling down to peer into the scanner, all she could see in the faceted surface were a hundred images of her own eyes looking back. Her heart had begun to beat faster. Cabochon suddenly sucked in his breath, and Ari jerked back from the scryer. She could see he was surprised.

'Let me see!' He did not protest as she lunged forward, but pushed his chair back a little way.

'Must be an error, we'll try again,' he said.

The screen displayed only three words, repeated again and again, in various combinations; a nonsense mantra, line after line:

FLESH PAIN SOUL PAIN FLESH PAIN SOUL PAIN
FLESH PAIN SOUL PAIN.
SOUL FLESH SOUL FLESH I PAN I SOUL I
PAN I. PAIN. I PAN. PANIC PANIC PANIC

Cabochon watched Ari read every word, drinking a whole cupful of gin as she did so. The only time the scryer had ever produced such emphatic information was when he'd done it for himself. Only once. He'd never tried it again. So you have your demons too, little girl, he thought. There was an uncomfortable silence.

She was disturbed, naturally, and Cabochon didn't know what to say to help her. 'Hey, it's only nonsense,' he said, wincing at the insincerity in his voice. He always found it hard to lie. 'Sometimes it happens this way. Don't let it upset you.' Ari didn't answer. She was reading the screen again.

Patti wriggled in her seat. 'I want to go home now,' she said in a slurred voice. Of course, she'd been drinking before they'd set out, flushing herself out with liquid courage. Now she was on the verge of collapse.

'Then go,' Ari said irritably, relenting when she saw the helpless expression on Patti's face; she was afraid to go outside alone. 'OK, OK, I'll come with you.' Reluctantly, Ari moved away from the scryer. Somehow she felt that if she stared at it long enough, the message would become clearer. She didn't believe Cabochon's lame reassurances, but neither did she think he was lying. She was convinced he was merely incapable of reading the message. It was for her alone. She was not afraid of it.

'Would you like me to write it down or something?' Cabochon asked.

'No.'

'I'll do you another scry later. Like I said . . .'

'No. This is the right one.'

He shrugged, scratched his forehead awkwardly. 'Look . . . Goddess, don't let this get to you. It's not a proper scry. Sometimes the machine has, well, *moods*.'

'I'm not upset.' She was peering at the screen again.

'Well, sorry anyway.' He turned off the scryer quickly and packed it back into its carrying case. 'You want a hand with your friend?'

Ari nodded. 'I think so.'

Cabochon rummaged in a pile of luggage in the corner

of the room for more clothes. It took considerable effort to heave Patti from her seat, and once Ari began to walk towards the door, she didn't feel too lively herself. No way was she capable of dragging Patti back to her house.

'Want a lift, lady?' Cabochon asked Patti and hauled her into his arms. Patti smiled weakly, but did not struggle. They went out into the sunlight.

As they began to walk down the hill, Ari asked, 'Do you really think that scry was nonsense?'

'Yes,' Cabochon answered breathlessly, adjusting Patti's weight. 'Don't worry.' He smiled. 'Forget it. OK?'

Ari grinned and nodded, weaving along at his side. She pushed the words from her mind (soul pain?) and concentrated on her temporary companion. Why was it she felt so drunk after only a cupful, while the liquor had seemed to give Cabochon more energy? He was so beautiful it was almost unbearable. His feline body, now shirted in khaki drab, his blond-streaked hair, seemed to represent all that Ari could ever want, all that she would be denied once Star Eye moved on. Her feelings about these people were so contradictory.

Cabochon wouldn't go inside the house and Ari had to drag Patti into the bedroom herself, leaving her draped across the bed already unconscious. Ari lay on the floor in Patti's living room as the afternoon rolled on around her and thought about Star Eye. If only she hadn't got so drunk. She should have been there when Leila got back. Leila had invited her up. She wanted to be part of Star Eye's preparations for the coming festival, but she felt too muzzy to face going back up the hill now. Mumbling to herself, she rested her head on her arms, drifting into a deep liquor-sleep. She didn't hear the Star Eye trucks when they rumbled back to Taler's Bump.

Patti woke her about an hour before sundown. Sticky-mouthed, Ari followed the woman into her kitchen. She felt tearful and depressed. 'Oh, it's the liquor!' Patti exclaimed, when Ari threw herself at her, dissolving into tears.

'No! It's not! Mom's kicking me out!' Ari cried. A demand for explanation and consequent soothing followed. Patti thought it was just a petty row and best forgotten. 'Don't think too badly of Lydia,' she said as she thrust a cup of coffee into Ari's groping hands. 'She wants what's best for you.'

'And what is best for anyone any more? Can you answer that?' Ari asked bitterly, full of adolescent tragedy.

'Look, she's said things to me once or twice. Your father . . .'

'What about him?'

Patti gave Ari a final squeeze and then leaned back against the sink. 'Know where you were born, Ari?'

Ari pulled a face, wiped her eyes. 'No . . . Is that important? Do people know things like that?'

Patti rolled her eyes. She looked pained. 'Damn, I probably shouldn't tell you this but . . .'

'Tell me.'

'Your mother wanted kids, right, and she had problems. I think the Tech-Greens must have sorted it out, the ones she and Ewan were with, but it was a kind of an experiment. It worked OK. You can see that. You're here but I think . . . Well, Ewan, your father, he . . .' Patti shook her head, lowered it. 'I don't know the facts, only hints, but I think you were a kind of special baby, Ari.'

'You make me sound inhuman, like Sammael.'

61

'You're old enough to know, I guess.' Patti shrugged, lurched away from the sink and went to turn on the radio. 'There's no more so don't ask me,' she said. Music sputtered into the room, mournful, distant. Ari left as soon as her cup was empty.

As the sun set, Star Eye began to converge on the monument. Sammael had already opened up the observation panels in the bases of the stones, serviced the perfume sacs, and activated whichever parts still worked. Those of the menhirs that could emitted a soft, fluctuating light into the circle. As Ari climbed the slope to the monument, the cries of birds circling above seemed for an instant to freeze the world. She looked up and the sky above her was purple, strewn with gold-edged clouds, the birds hanging like black rags. All the poignancy of creation seemed instilled into this May Eve. She passed through the prodigious bulk of the trilithon, where the soft blue light of the Goddess shone forth from hidden niches. Ari stood with her back to the altar, staring between the massive menhirs. The trilithon represented the Birthing Mother and its significance was prevalent at Yoole. Tonight, one of the more slender menhirs was the focus. It was often referred to as the Maiden, or Maiden's Fire. Ari turned around, the artful rags and flutters of her festival dress, hurriedly gathered from home after a quick dash from Patti's place, swirling against her legs. The breeze was not too warm here on the Bump, raising gooseflesh on bare limbs. The natros were oblivious to such minor discomforts, however, and Ari could not help but be infected by their anticipation. A black-skinned Star Eye man was adjusting the settings on one of the menhirs. Unlike most natros, his head was closely shorn, giving him a stark, angular appearance. She could see Sammael surreptitiously following him round, checking the coordinates, making the odd realignment here and there. This made Ari smile. Could a being without human feeling be so fussy and so sneaky about it too? Justinette came up to take hold of Ari's arm. 'Good to see you again!' Her bright enthusiasm was painful. It was as if she'd been told to make Ari feel at ease. Also, Ari didn't like the proprietorial air Justinette had about her. 'Look at the sky!' Justinette announced with passion. 'All the colours there.'

'Courtesy of gross pollution.' Jordan had crept up in the dusk to stand beside them. Justinette pulled a face at his remark.

'I try to think positive thoughts on these occasions,' she said. Jordan expressed a humourless shrug and wandered off. Justinette made an irritated noise and then smiled, jostling Ari's arm.

'Ignore him,' she said. 'Ah, smell! Maiden's Fire!'

The menhir had begun to exhale a vaporous steam of gentle perfumes; mimosa, blackthorn and jasmine. The ducts were virtually invisible, disguised as cracks in the stone. Gentle lights bloomed around its base, illuminating the trimmed, scrubby grass growing there. Above them the slim monolith stood still and dark, but thrumming with repressed energy.

From down the hill, Ari could hear the tinny echo of her mother's music centre. It had obviously been turned up full blast to register Lydia's disapproval of the celebration about to commence. It wasn't intrusive however, merely serving as a reminder of where and when the group were positioned in time and space. Ari recognised the music as being the discordant strains of a Cinder Head anthem; all thrash, no melody. It was pretty typical of Lydia to announce her displeasure in this way. Ari visualised her drunk and swaying round their living room, all lights ablaze, visible to any passer-by.

Maiden's Fire emitted a sensual hiss, which announced the arrival of Leila Saatchi at the monument. She swept magnificently into the circle, trailing fluttering rags of pale and paler green, and also the remainder of her group. She stood before the altar and raised her arms dramatically, throwing back her head to expose a tower of pale neck draped with metal coins and synthetic jewels. She called for silence, a few minutes meditation on the festival to come. The group had now formed a rough circle inside the menhirs. Sammael had dampened the power of the monument; it merely glowed with lights like tiny stars in the darkness. In the west, beyond the menhirs, the sky was deep crimson and scarlet. A breeze insinuated itself into everyone's hair as it wound its way between the stones. All was quiet. Leila exhaled a shuddering breath and slowly lowered her hands, face tense in concentration, eyes closed. The group began to move, circling slowly, feeling with their hands for an invisible boundary. They were claiming the space for their own. There were no words, no verbal summoning of the elements. To Ari, this was something new; the silent, spiralling bodies describing the parameters of their temple. Then, one by one, each member of the group spun into the middle of the circle, describing with gestures the sanctity of this chosen space, slowly whirling shapes of rags and hair. When her turn came – and she felt instinctively when that time was – Ari knew exactly what to do. Closing her eyes, she visualised a dark and incense-filled place, high columns disappearing into lofty shadows where the hint of brass winked and swung and the smoke curled down like fabric. She danced around this temple, touching the columns, breathing the air, experiencing it as real and tangible.

Once their sacred space had been established, the group began to give voice, softly chanting. The menhirs responded with a rippling stream of gentle lights, emitting a chord at exactly the right frequency to induce a deeply relaxed, meditative state within each human present, evoking the voice of Gaiah herself. Gradually the volume of voices increased and the mist light of the monument glowed intensely white above their heads. The menhirs blazed with colour, jets of perfumed steam shooting into the sky only to fall in great clouds to hug the ground. Maiden's Fire blazed like a beacon, vibrating with a single, fluting note, as if picking up the thoughts of the revellers and transforming them to light and sound. Feet began to stamp, hands pound together, bodies to gyrate. We are the Earth, sang the wordless voices. Vibrant! Healing! We shake our skins to cleanse ourselves. Nothing is forever. Everything is Nothing.

Ari felt the ground beneath her feet grow hot. Bleeding from each pore was the power to change. She was drawn to the menhir, Maiden's Fire, momentarily oblivious to the rest of the group cavorting behind her. The menhir loomed above her, a blaze of light. It was calling to her. She reached out to touch the warm surface and leaned forward to press her face against it; maiden to maiden. It was symbolic; she felt full of love.

A darting numbness flooded through Ari's body from head to foot, so swiftly she was unsure whether she'd imagined it or not. Perhaps there was a fault with the menhir. Nonplussed, and shaken from her ritual fervour, Ari's instinct was to flinch away. But she couldn't. She could not move at all. *What*? Her mind supplied quick frantic explanations. She must be earthing the current in the stone. Could it hurt her? She was paralysed. She could not call for help. *Goddess, will it hurt me? Can it kill me?* She tried to struggle but it was as if her mind was inhabiting the wrong body, as if she'd forgotten how to send the messages to her limbs that could make her move at all. Behind her, the chanting and stamping had fallen in volume. *They've noticed. Thank the Goddess, they've* . . . She felt hands on her shoulders, a sharp tug and then someone was turning her round, releasing her from stasis. Her back was against the menhir. She laughed nervously, feeling drunk, almost tasting the juniper bitterness of her mother's gin on her tongue. Impossible. What had happened? Cabochon was standing just in front of her, arms folded, naked to the waist, his hair loose around his shoulders. Ari made an ululation of welcome, a calling of her own. For just a moment, in this no-time, no-space event of the festival, it might be possible for her to touch him, but Cabochon shook his head. No. He took a step back and Ari could see Leila and Jordan standing behind him, stone-faced and intent. The mood was falling away, reality creeping back; the sounds of night and fear, people panting.

'No!' Ari tried to struggle away. She couldn't. 'I can't move!' she said. Star Eye merely watched her. They mean to hurt me, Ari thought, all the warnings Lydia had given her filling her head. 'Don't,' she said. 'Please don't.'

'Ari, there's no need to be frightened,' Leila chanted 'Just relax. Everything's fine.'

'Leila!' Jordan put a hand on the woman's shoulder,

which she shrugged off, taking a step forward. 'Leila, I don't think . . .' He shook his head, clenched his fist in front of him.

'What's happening?' Ari gulped air, filling her chest with pain. 'What are you doing?'

'Your father redesigned certain parts of this monument,' Leila said. 'For you. There's nothing to be afraid of, really there isn't.'

'My father?'

'Hush now. Relax.'

'But why? What for?' Ari could smell sour oil. Leila came towards her, leaned above her head and did something to the menhir. She barked a question at Sammael. 'Is everything all right?'

'The sequence appears to be progressing as planned,' he answered.

'What's going on?' Ari cried. 'Sammael? What is this?' Something was fondling its way into her hair. Abruptly her vision furred over with leaping grey lines, and the ability to speak, never mind ask questions, was taken from her. A memory burst in her head: wall-screen, intruder, blue light, 'Are you looking forward to tomorrow, Ari?' A sequence of mnemonic odours surprised her senses. It reminded her of the colours rippling across Cabochon's scry screen when he'd turned it on. A new reality intruded upon her consciousness, overlaying the experience of open-air night, apprehension and confusion. She had become massive; a mammoth network of flooding impulses, neurons the size of planets. Maiden Fire:

Travelling, tumbling, Ari Fire Maiden traverses the multi-planed heavens of her own genetic code.

Snakes of colour memory fragments pass through and around – awareness comes abruptly – no longer isolated

*being contained in flesh – single point of light among
billions comprising vast interconnecting web – ancestry
stretches away to infinity – luminous trail more attractive than other strands of web – drawn to travel it –
aware of fractal nature – outermost bud on the tip of a
twig becoming a branch growing from massive ancient
main trunk in itself a bud upon larger tree – some
branches withered and dead, devoid of promise of new
growth new twigs – grief for genes lost forever upon
those branches – that failed to reproduce.*

Travelling, travelling. The rush of speed and time. The
tree of ancestral pathways glitters like a vast city, myriad
points of light. Ari tumbles along entranced. Which to
investigate now? No time. Something progresses; a feeling, a tremor, of the urge to seek forbidden, dangerous
knowledge. Ari can see its colour and knows it is both
inside and outside of herself. Flesh boils around her
essence, enfolding. The sensation of being trapped is
unfamiliar at first and causes panic.

SOUL PAIN FLESH PAIN I PAN PAN–IC

There is a series of frozen images in her head. It is a
sequence delineating the fall of a single drop of water.
Gradually swelling, the drop changes shape until it hits
an unseen surface, scintillant droplets flying off,
while the original drop spreads and stretches, finally
exploding.

Ari is facing the first of these images. She knows they
have always been frozen and that an important part of
herself is hiding inside them. This part of herself,
although imprisoned, sends orders to the other parts of
her mind continually. There are certain impulses and
conditions it does not like and has to repress. Sometimes

it does this by making Ari forget a thought she has just begun. Sometimes, when the thought is too strong to just push away, it has to make her feel physically sick so she has no choice but to concentrate on other aspects of her body. The hidden part of herself is the one that makes her feel uneasy with other people, especially those whom she would normally find attractive. Ari sees this quite clearly now. From this moment onwards, she will recognise the activities of her hidden part when they occur, and accept them for what they are. She herself now has the power to make the sequence of images run into one flowing motion; the drop of water will fall and explode upon impact, initiating new sequences which will be confronted in the future. Maiden's Fire is lending her the strength to effect this preliminary release.

Emotion: I *will*.

Surface tension shattered; the physical sensations are unexpected.

– Needle in skin, prickly touch – terrible pain shooting up from belly turning into light – sound – flesh pain soul – being torn apart – scream – limitless pattern of geometric light – whole being breaking up atoms spinning away – explosion reformed expand stretch break – Process speeds – no longer pain – Flower shedding petals opening up shedding – new petals form heart – process rhythm greater rhythm creating power.

Ari is unsure whether what she feels is agony or intense pleasure, but one thought shoots across her mind: I can mould this, take it, use it, throw it out . . .

There was a scream, many screams, and the night was ablaze with exploding fists of light. A voice cried, 'Disconnect her! We can't hold this!'

Then silence. Only a machine hum and the feeling of cool night air on skin, scented by vaporous steam. Ari slumped to the ground. Hands came to lift her, manipulate her into a sitting position, head between knees. She heard Leila's voice, Leila saying, 'You were right, Jordan. I think this is all too big for us.'

Ari could see limbs twitching spasmodically, only dimly aware they were her own. Her body was numb; it might not exist. Perhaps if she closed her eyes . . . ? No. Swimming blackness. She felt sick, only partially aware of her arm being lifted and pressure being applied to the inside of her elbow. Light spots fuzzed before her eyes. Somebody slapped her face. Very soon, she could feel her arm again. It hurt, burning where the pressure had been applied.

'Move your limbs,' said a voice. The name Jordan came into her head. He was squatting in front of her, his face tense. Ari weakly wriggled her fingers and toes. 'That's better. Roll your head. Come on.' Ari's neck creaked. Her vision swam but then abruptly began to clear. Her perception strengthened swiftly. Of course, the pressure. Injection. What of? Her heart began to race. She had an intense desire to stand up and move.

'You feel OK? Good. No, perhaps you'd better not . . .' Ari ignored the voice, fought the restraining hands and struggled to her feet. There were people all around her; ridiculous creatures. They did not look real, but two dimensional, like caricatures. Was her face like that? Blinking jelly-balls and silly stub of gristle above wet orifice? She began to giggle and hands reached out to steady her. The touch was hot and wet. She didn't like it and pulled unsteadily away. Did she know these people? The entire concept of 'person' seemed a fragile, unstable thing to her. Reality pulsed in and out.

'Can you speak?'

Leila. Her hair looked an angry, artificial red; a

careless afterthought to physical construction.

'Don't be afraid. Let the anger out if you want.'

Ari was confused by that. She did not feel angry or frightened. She was in a state of heightened acceptance. Anything could have happened at that point and she'd have observed it with absurd calm. 'I'm all right,' she said. 'What happened?' The words realigned her completely. She was undeniably Ari, female, human, her bare arms pimpled with cold, who shivered in the breeze of a late spring night, who existed solely within the flesh that contained her spirit.

Leila frowned, rubbed her face. 'I'm not sure I can explain yet.'

'Did you do that? Did Star Eye do that to me?'

Leila shook her head. 'No. It was something that's part of you.'

'What? What's part of me?'

Leila shook her head, mouth clamped into a bloodless line. 'I'm sorry if it was unpleasant.'

Ari considered. 'It was neither horrible nor good. It just was. I want to know what it was though. I saw things, but they're fading.'

'I think you should rest a while, Ari. We'll finish the ritual. You can watch from here. All right?'

Ari nodded. 'OK. But I feel fine now.'

'All the same. I don't think you should jump around too much yet. It might make you sick.'

It was easier to comply. Looking around herself, Ari was no longer touched by the sense of ritual anyway. She wanted to lean on something but her spine crawled with the thought of touching Maiden Fire menhir again, even though some deep, primitive part of her mourned the loss of that contact.

Night-wind blew her skirt against her legs. It was wet.

She shuddered. Don't think. A blink in time. It didn't happen. Hallucination? Did they drug me? Why? They mentioned my father. I don't understand. I am not normal. Why? What *is* the difference? Did Star Eye come here because of me? Who are they? I want to go home. No. I don't. I don't ever want to move again.

Her legs felt like the gnarled trunks of trees: rooted. She could sway but she could not topple. Star Eye had rather self-consciously resumed their celebration rite, casting quick, furtive glances towards the skinny, swaying girl at the edge of the circle. Ari tried to analyse the stream of their thoughts, which seemed quite plain to her at the time. Embarrassment, nervousness, pity, a little anger directed at Leila maybe; nobody was uninterested though. Perhaps the most puzzling emotion Ari picked up was the undeniable electric buzz, however small, however restrained, of animal fear. They might try to deny it, but Star Eye, for all their control of the past few hours (few moments?) were slightly afraid of her. Wary.

In the circle, Sammael, the least affected by what had happened, brought the Bel fire to life. It was not real flame, just a hologram, projected within a small ring of stones at the centre of the circle. Ari watched him. There was little doubt he was involved in what had happened in some way. He had been expecting it. An artificial manform only has limited autonomy. Someone must have programmed him to prepare the menhir. Her father? Sammael did not appear to be looking Ari's way at all, concentrating on the kindling. The flames were orange and red and heatless but still symbolic of the ancient fires of all pagan festivals. Leila clapped her hands and called out, her voice seeming to reach Ari from a long way away . . . *Perhaps I'm not really here* . . . 'Come and jump, jump the flames!' Leila

73

dextrously manipulated scene and atmosphere, sub-
liminally implanting the thought: Forget that, forget
the girl, jump and enjoy yourselves. Star Eye began to
liven up, skipping round the flames, chanting, clapping
and stamping, following Leila's lead. As they jumped
the flames, one by one or as couples, they named those
things they would leave behind them with the old season.
Ari heard the shouted words: Distrust! Fear! Laziness!
Cruelty! (Who said that? She did not notice.) Leila was
the last to jump. She soared like a bird over the licking
holographic pyre into Jordan's waiting arms. She cried
out 'Weakness!' fiercely and angrily. She meant it.

Now the time had come for the fertility dance, the
Great Pursuit. Ari knew this part well. Sometimes it
made her uncomfortable because some groups would
end the dance with actual sex. Ari knew she could never
participate in that. Just the thought of touching herself
in that way had always initiated a fearful sense of panic,
never mind anyone else doing it. Now she felt she knew
why. It was because of the hidden part of herself, the
imprisoned part. It was nothing to do with shyness or
inexperience as she'd once thought. One day someone or
something would come to open that place up, she was
sure of it. Even though some sequence had begun within
her when the frozen water image had started to flow, for
now she would have to keep shaking her head and backing off when people approached her. Occasionally someone would sneer, but she was strong enough not to care.
Weird things had happened to her in Star Eye's company
already. It was possible they might even be the ones to
make her a whole person.

The group had quietened down now and Leila had
begun to walk around them, pausing to stamp one foot
and raise her arms, glancing back over her shoulder at

Jordan. She began to skip, weaving between the motionless members of her company. Star Eye started to clap
their hands against their thighs, murmuring a rhythmic
chant. Jordan leapt into the air. For a single second he
hung poised like a hunting bird above the ground, his
ragged cloak spread like wings, before crouching close to
the earth, a stalking predator. The pursuit had begun,
Star Eye amplifying the chant, the body percussion,
accompanied by the synchronised blood-machine-heart
song of the stones. Jordan chased Leila around the circle, she lifting her skirts above her knees, highstepping
and shrieking with girlish pleasure. Everyone was
dancing now, leaping around, shouting, singing, crazy
with the primal, crackling wildness of the festival. Ari
watched from the edge, alone in a dark space. Jordan
caught Leila around the waist, tossing her effortlessly
into the air, catching her, kissing her, spinning round
and around. The menhirs screamed a riot of colour and
noise, projecting a vivid hologram into the sky, swirling
pictures of all that represented the feast of May; bursting
efflorescences. Jordan triumphantly carried his Goddess
away through the stones towards the forest. Their ultimate rite was destined to be private. The rest of the
group continued to dance until a couple of them went
down to the chalets to fetch the Bel feast up on trays.
Now the menhirs adapted their song to one of gentler
tones as Star Eye settled themselves down to eat and
drink.

Justinette trotted up as if nothing had happened and,
linking her arm through Ari's, led her to where the others
had sat down to eat. 'You OK?' she asked.

'Yes, I think so. What happened to me?'

'I don't know really. Leila told us she had to retrieve
some data from you or something. I suppose it's to do

with Ewan, your father. It was weird though, wasn't it! How did it feel? Did it hurt?'

'It was strange.' Ari was reluctant to describe how she'd felt: it was too private. 'I've never seen that happen here before, with anyone. Never.'

'Of course you haven't. It was you made it happen, wasn't it?'

'But why now? Why not before? Why have you come here?'

Justinette shrugged uncomfortably. 'We weren't told much.'

'What did you see?' Ari asked. 'How did it look to you?'

'It looked like you had a fit, but you were smiling!' Justinette grinned. 'You sure you're OK?' Ari nodded. 'Have something to eat anyway. I expect you need it.'

Ari helped herself from the big tray of hot baked yams, soya-cheese and vegetable protein stew, in the middle of the circle of people. Justinette gave her a cup of wine. But when Ari tried to eat she found it unpleasant to put anything in her mouth. There was a distance between her and the world, even though memories of what had occurred were beginning to fade. Like Justinette, the others treated her as if nothing unusual had happened, yet Ari could still sense a repressed sting of fear in them. It was possible such events were a common part of Star Eye rituals. They were certainly different to any other natro group Ari had encountered. As she sat among them, smiling, trying to appear as if she was listening to their talk, Ari wondered, 'What will come of this? Goddess, don't let it be nothing. It can't be . . .' She saw Cabochon sitting alone at the edge of the group, leaning against one of the menhirs with a cup of wine on his lap, eyes closed. She was aware of all that he was; a mind, thinking, impenetrable. Light played on his skin, deepening the hollows of his throat. Ari shivered.

Leila lay on her back, staring up through the bare branches. Jordan was breathing steadily beside her, but she knew he was not asleep. The silence was not comfortable. Once away from the rest of the group, their enactment of the ritual had become mechanical, soulless. She thought he was angry because she'd proved herself right. Ari Famber was all that Ewan had promised – or could be. 'We'd better get back,' she said. Jordan grunted.

'Are you satisfied?'

'What do you mean?'

He didn't answer, but stood up and straightened his clothes. Leila felt as if he was a fluid in her hands, dripping away. 'What's happening to us? Jordan?'

'Nothing's happening, babe.' He squatted down and stroked her face gently. 'I'm sorry. All this is too . . . heavy. I don't think we should have to take it on.'

'Nobody is but me.'

'You quit all that once, didn't you?'

'This is different. I'm doing this as a favour to a friend. It's got nothing to do with what I was.'

'Hasn't it?'

Maybe I tell him too much, Leila thought. She stood up and shook out her skirts, leaning against him when he offered an arm.

Everyone was tidying the debris of the food away by the time Leila and Jordan returned to the monument. Cabochon, not surprisingly, had disappeared. Leila took an internal reading of the group atmosphere and was relieved by her findings. Cheerful weariness. 'I'd better speak to Ari,' she said.

Jordan shrugged. 'OK, mind if I come along?' Leila looked at him keenly. 'As support. Really,' he added.

'All right.' Ari was nowhere to be found however. Leila discovered that Justinette had suggested Ari should go home and rest. Sensing Leila's displeasure, Justinette started blurting excuses. 'She was out of it,' she said. 'I told her to come up here tomorrow to . . . you know . . . say goodbye and all.'

'You should have waited till I got back!' Leila said.

Justinette shrugged. 'I didn't know how long you'd be. I was worried about her. She looked kind of green.'

'Why don't you go down there?' Jordan suggested, cocking his head in the direction of the Famber house.

Leila squeezed his hand, sensing a compromise and appreciating it. 'No, she should be OK. I'll sort things out in the morning. It's time Mrs Famber and I had a chat.'

Jordan smiled and kissed her cheek. 'And boy, are you going to enjoy that!' he said.

There was no music coming from the house when Ari got home. She felt tired and shaky, but had been doing a lot of thinking on the way back. A few things had settled into place, so much so the enervation felt cosy and satisfying. In the wake of what had happened to her, she needed answers from Leila Saatchi. Neither could she let these people just pass out of her life now. It seemed they may have been connected with her father and, if Justinette's explanation was correct, that Ewan had used her to store some kind of esoteric information. She also knew she had a problem and that the problem was connected with sexuality. It explained a lot: the bouts of sickness; fear of being with new people, males especially; lack of sexual feeling. All she had to know now was why she was like this. Could it be cured? Perhaps she should try to talk with Leila Saatchi about it.

All the house lights were still on, the back door wide open and the faucet was dripping precious purified water into the sink. Ari turned that off first, scooping up a litter of used plates sticky with congealing soya gravy and tossing them into the washer. Then she gathered up all the ravaged packets of Fry Bites, Lydia's favourite junk nibbles, and fed them into the garbage chomper. The place was a mess.

'Ari, that you?' came a querulous voice from the living room. Ari sauntered through, steeled by a queasy determination.

'Where the fuck have you been all day you little bitch?' Lydia tried to spit, catlike, when Ari went in to her. The spitting was all too literal, sadly. Ari watched her mother wipe saliva from her chin which was sunk into her chest.

'Your dress is dirty,' Ari said.

'Where've you been?'

'At the Bump. You know that,' Ari answered nervously. She was aware of her mother's careful, if drunken, scrutiny. Was it apparent something strange had happened to her? 'Can't you clean this place up once in a while? I'm sick of following you round with a rag.'

Lydia continued to stare. 'I told you I didn't want you round those people,' she said, sounding mean.

'And what's it to do with you?' Ari's jumpiness came out as anger. 'Don't tell me you *care* about me! You want me out, right?'

'I never said that,' Lydia whined peevishly. She reached out with grimy fingers. Ari could see the black crescents at the end of each nail. She withdrew fastidiously.

'When did you last take a bath?'

'I've always wanted what's best for you. Your father . . . it matters to him. You must follow in his footsteps. It's what he wants.'

'Yeah?' Ari slumped into the chair opposite her mother. In that moment, her mind was made up. 'I'm leaving tomorrow,' she said, waiting for the storm. She felt it would be tinged with relief, however.

'What?' Lydia did not shout.

'I said I'm leaving. You don't have to worry about

80

making ends meet any more, Lydia. You can spend all of Dad's pension on whatever you please. Piss it down the drain, use it to curl your hair, hire a maid even. I'm going.'

The ultimate affront: Lydia laughed. 'Going are you? Where? To the city?'

'Maybe. I don't know where. You suggested it this morning, right? I mean it. I'm really going.'

As if propelled by some supernatural agency, Lydia suddenly became human again, pulling herself upright in her chair, leaning forward. It was her old fighting stance for the conversational bullring. 'Ari, don't over-react. I was out of line, saying that to you. Have those natro assholes been giving you bullshit, is that it? Don't listen to them . . .'

Ari cut her short. 'I've heard no bullshit. I have my own head, you know. You're right. I'm wasting myself here.' Ari was gratified by the perceptible wince that tightened her mother's mouth.

'Ari, you're only fourteen. You know nothing about the world. You can't just go. You'll need money, transport, names, contacts. Understand?'

'You're trying to put me off?'

'Damn right.'

'I'm going with Star Eye.'

Lydia froze and then tried to disguise it by reaching for a cigarette. 'And who's that?' Now she was pure business, words hardening to flint. For the first time in months, Ari began to feel her age, sense her mother's superiority in years.

'The natro group on the Bump.' She didn't know when she'd formulated this idea, actually made the decision, that had been the biggest hurdle; somewhere between the forest and the house, she supposed.

Persuading Star Eye to have her might be another, but in view of what had happened, Ari was confident she could handle it. Maybe.

Lydia pushed back her hair. She made no comment but her face was talking all about zone patrols, abduction accusations, possible action.

'Ari, in your father's study there are a whole batch of videos, ones he made while he was working. I suggest you take a look at those before you even consider leaving this area.'

'No, I have to see for myself. It's what you did, what he did.'

'We were older and we knew what we were doing.'

'So do I. These are the right people for me.'

Lydia leaned back on the sofa, smoking rapidly and blinking at the ceiling. The only sound was her gusting exhalations.

'Are you going to try and stop me?' Ari asked. Lydia looked at her. It was as if she were trying to visualise her daughter dead.

'Go to bed,' she said.

'But . . . we have to talk, we . . .'

'No, no more. Go to bed. We'll talk tomorrow.'

Ari stood up and stomped out of the room, slamming the door, which prompted a satisfying shudder throughout the house before it bounced open again. She went to her room and threw herself face down on the bed. I'll run anyway, she thought. I'll just go. There are other groups. Let Lydia play warrior queen and lead a troupe of bulldogs after Star Eye if she wants to. I'll go somewhere else. That'll show her.

She could hear her mother moving about, the creak of doors, padding footsteps. Lydia went into Ewan's old study. She and Ari hardly ever went in there. Ari heard things being moved, a clatter, an expletive from Lydia. She was trying to find the videos, Ewan's diary of all he had achieved or tried to achieve with the Tech-Greens. Ari knew what those shiny tapes concealed, the images of devastation, deformity and barrenness. She'd watched them a hundred times as a child when they'd been forbidden. They'd been her secret ecological porn, taken with hot fingers from their boxes when Lydia had been absent. She did not want to see them now, and was half expecting her mother to come bursting in to drag her into the living room and make her watch them. Not so. Ari's door remained closed. She heard Lydia go back into the living room and turn on the wall-screen. She obviously wanted to watch them herself. Ewan Famber's voice echoed deeply through the disintegrating fabric of his once-luxury house. Ari put a pillow over her ears. This was the past. This meant nothing to her.

In the morning, Leila Saatchi came to the house.

Leila took Kydd with her as support. Naturally the group had been pestering her for explanations as soon as they fell out of their sleeping sacks. She'd tried to keep them at arm's length and had put in another call to Roirbak. Mellissa informed her he was still unavailable, so she left a brief report of what had happened. 'We fixed the kid up as Ewan instructed and, Quincx, he was telling the truth! At least it looked like it. When she was given the right stimulus, the power came flooding out! Question is, what do we do about it? This is weird, Quincx. She's only a kid and a cute little thing at that. Please, get back to me. We have to talk.'

Kydd was the obvious choice to take with her to the Fambers; he was the least likely to ask questions. The girls were just downright curious and, as she'd known, were making their own suppositions and passing them on to the others. Jordan was a potential hazard. He'd wanted to come along, naturally, if only as spectator to a possible scene with Lydia, but Leila didn't trust him not to get involved if things got difficult. She'd been grateful he spent the night with her and more than a little guilty when she'd asked him to stay at the Bump. Their relationship seemed as delicate as thin ice: too much pressure either way and the whole structure would splinter. She wasn't sure when it had got that way. He'd lain in bed watching her get dressed for power; fingerless leather gloves and ancient black jeans, a leather jacket over a Tech-Green T-shirt, scuffed ex-patrol boots. In the city, such designer gutter chic would cost a fortune. 'So, do I look like I mean business?' she'd asked him. He'd beckoned her over, pulling her down on top of him for a bear hug.

'Uh-huh, but a little heavy on the patchouli and truck oil, maybe!'

She reached out and grabbed Jordan's favourite artefact from the floor, a wide-rimmed black hat, and threw it on her head. 'Can I take this for luck?'

Kydd was happy to lounge on the back step of the Famber house, soaking up the morning sun, a pair of battered shades perched on his beak of a nose. Leila would call him if she needed him. She was wondering if Lydia Famber had weapons and just how nasty this encounter might get, but had voiced none of her fears to Kydd. The guy was perceptive anyway. He'd know Leila wouldn't have asked for his company if she'd been making a dainty social visit.

Leila sprinted up the steps and knocked on the outer door. A security viewer hung dead by a conventional door buzzer which had clearly been added at a later date and was now also devoid of life. Leila couldn't imagine that Ewan Famber had ever lived there. It was too regular a place.

Ari came to the door and stared at her blankly for a few moments through the screen. 'Ari, it's me, Leila Saatchi. Can I come in for a while?' The screen wobbled open.

'Sorry, I was kind of surprised to see you.'

Leila grinned. 'You sloped off last night without saying goodbye. You OK today?'

Ari nodded. 'I feel fine, honestly. That why you came?'

The girl led Leila into the kitchen, offered a coffee which Leila accepted. 'Not entirely. I've come to make an outrageous proposal!' Ari glanced round from where she was unsuccessfully trying to fill a kettle from the water dispenser. Angry, liquid burps were rewarded by a thin trickle.

'Oh? You too?'

Leila felt a pulse of cold spread through her. 'You mean you've already had one today?'

Ari giggled. 'No, actually I was going to make one to you.'

'OK.' Leila paused, smiling, half anticipating what was coming. 'You go first.'

Ari plugged the kettle in, messing with cups in the sink. 'Well, the reason I'm asking has to come first see. I want answers about what happened last night, all this stuff about my father. I was thinking about it a lot, you see . . .'

'Understandably,' Leila interrupted.

'Mmm. Well, I think you know all the answers. I think you knew my father. Am I right?'

Leila shrugged. 'Go on.'

'I think you came here because of me. Is that right too?'

'Maybe.' Ari grimaced and Leila raised her hands placatingly. 'OK, yes, I admit it.'

'I thought so. I don't want you to tell me why yet. I just want to say that I'd like to go with you when you leave the Bump.' She drew in her breath, held it, waiting for Leila's response. Leila couldn't resist letting her hang a little, tapping her mouth thoughtfully with her fingers.

'We-ell,' she said.

Ari leaned forward earnestly, gesturing with her arms. 'Please! I have to get out of here! I have to know what's going on! I have to . . .'

A voice from somewhere in the house interrupted her. 'Ari, who is that?' Ari looked anxiously at Leila, who put one finger against her lips.

'Hush!' she whispered and than nodded and mouthed, 'Answer her.'

'Yes, Mom?'

'What in hell's going on in there?!!' There was a thump from Lydia's room, the sound of someone fumbling for clothes.

Leila felt adrenalin rushing through her body. Soon, soon. 'Ari, I'll talk to your mother, OK?'

The girl's face bloomed with pleasure. 'Does that mean you're saying yes?'

Leila nodded. 'It does.' She stood up, just as Lydia came into the kitchen still belting her robe. Ari's mother straightened up when she saw the visitor, filling out like a big cat finding trespassers on the boundary of its territory. She folded her arms, eyes narrow. 'I thought it would be you,' she said.

Leila forced a smile. 'Hi, Lydia, long time no see, yeah?'

'Not long enough! Get me a cigarette, Ari!' Ari backed cautiously from the room.

'I have to talk with you, Lydia.'

'Not in front of the kid.' Lydia took the lighted cigarette Ari had brought in for her.

'Yeah, that's cool,' Leila agreed. 'Why don't you skip outside, Ari. Kydd's out there. I want to talk with your mother. OK?'

Ari paused, unsure whether she should obey an order from a stranger in her mother's house.

'Do as she says,' Lydia said. Ari nodded wordlessly and left the house with round eyes. Leila smiled.

'Great kid, Lydia.'

The woman sighed. 'You think so? Fuck, I need a drink.' She rummaged through cupboards, clanking empty bottles.

'You look like shit, Lydia. I really don't think you need a drink.'

'Fuck you!' Lydia poured herself a cup of gin with shaking hands. 'How you can just walk in here like this!' She shook her head. 'It's all right for you, Leila Saatchi. You still had your career. I was just pensioned off as a brood mare, remember?'

Leila shrugged. 'Whatever. I really don't care. I'm not here for your sake.'

Lydia cawed harsh laughter. 'Don't tell me! It's for the kid, right? Oh, please! You don't give a shit about her. Ewan didn't, so why should you? I know why you're doing this. It's for him, isn't it? Dear, loyal old Leila, still to heel after all this time. You make me puke!'

Leila rolled her eyes. 'Dear Goddess! What a performance! Wise up, Lydia. You know something's got to be done with the kid, and you are obviously not fit to handle it! Cut the sarcasm and just be grateful someone's come to let you off the hook.'

Lydia took a gulping drink and smiled slyly. 'You're so clever, Leila, aren't you? You think I'm stupid, but you're wrong. I'm thinking of sending Ari to Amazon House.'

Leila couldn't help showing her shock. 'You can't be serious!'

Lydia shrugged, took another drink. 'Why not? They'll know what to do with her. I don't have to hand her over to you. Ewan's dead. I don't give a fuck about what he wanted. Anyway, there might be something in it for me if I give her to the Tech-Greens. Ewan didn't exactly leave me well provided for. Just look at this dump!'

'So much for mother love, eh?'

'I don't see any kids of yours around!'

Leila ignored the jibe. 'You can't stop me taking her, Lydia. You don't scare me. You know why? Because you haven't changed. You're still the weak, whining little showpiece Ewan chose to carry his kid. Nothing more. Nothing less. Goddess! You complain about him? You let him do it to you, all of it. And now – well, you simply haven't the energy to do *anything*.'

'You think so?' Lydia's voice was choked, her eyes glittering.

'I know so.'

The two women stared at each other for a few moments. Leila felt she'd gone too far. Lydia should have shouted her out, denied the accusations, but she'd just accepted the insults like a kicked dog. Too close to the truth to deny, maybe? Leila hadn't really intended that. She'd wanted an argument. 'Do yourself a favour,' she said softly. 'Forget the past.'

Lydia shrugged and sighed. 'Fuck it, what do I care? Take her with you. She'll give you a hard time though, I promise you. How about me? I've let you win, right? You got anything to give me, Saatchi? Come on!'

'See how well I know you!' Leila said coldly. She withdrew a film-wrapped packet from her jacket. 'Finest hash. Better for you than that poison!'

'You're just a fucking terrorist, Saatchi! You're ridiculous, parading round in that get-up like a kid.' She laughed harshly. 'Get the fuck out. I don't want to see you again.'

'My pleasure, Mrs Famber.' Leila moved towards the door.

Lydia turned to face the wall. She didn't want Leila Saatchi to see her cry.

Later Lydia sat alone in the once luxury, now decaying house, re-running Ewan's diaries again and again. At the beginning and end of every tape, the logo flashed up. She'd hoped they'd never come, that they'd forgotten. Lydia rocked and drank her gin and stared at the screen. Rewind. Play. Rewind. Play. Exploding triangle. Star Eye.

Lydia Famber closed her eyes, vowing that after this last examination of the past she would never think about it again. She remembered the old breathing technique, untried for years, which would put her in a deeply relaxed state and allow her to meditate. One last time. Goodbye Ewan. One last time.

There is a feeling of great pressure, a certainty of being deeply underground. The walls in this place are smooth sheets of moulded ceraplas cladding, their translucency revealing the ancient rough stone beneath. The room is brightly lit only over the workstations and carpeted with anti-static tiles which look soft as foam. Untidy piles of software stray over notebooks shedding pages and older bound books in plastic cases. Opaque ceraplas tables, tinted pale blue, are virtually covered with further untidy mounds of equipment; here and there signs of human participation, a foam cup still half full of cold coffee, plastic plates stained red and yellow, sticky with congealing food. Overhead, ropes of coiling wires loop their way across the ceiling like arteries revealed by the delicate teasing away of flesh. The room hums rhythmically, making the air feel warmer than it actually is.

Warmed by a tight row of hanging spotlights, a man leans over one of the workstations. He is young, his lean body accentuated by the loose cloth of his coveralls, which are hanging open at the front, revealing the bead and metal tangle of his personal totem hanging from his neck. He is watched by a young woman, similarly dressed, wearing a similar totem, who stands some distance away, hugging herself tightly, fingers pressed firmly against her right cheek, jaws moving, nibbling the flesh inside. Their postures are immediately discernible as those of excited revelation and anxious concern. The man punches the table beside a computer keyboard with enthusiasm and yelps to accentuate his pleasure. He turns to the woman, waving a glittering, delicate instrument in her direction which, misleadingly, looks vaguely surgical. 'This is it, Lydia,' he says, ignoring or blind to the woman's distressed posture. 'This is evolution, and we're seeing it happen!'

The woman's voice, shaky, threatening tears: 'Don't Ewan. Please don't.'

The man's face darkens briefly, a shadow of irritation. 'Don't go all reactionary on me again, Lyd,' he says, and then softens his voice. 'Don't you realise how important this is, what a leap forward we're taking here?'

Lydia Famber shrugs. 'I don't want it to be me,' she mumbles, picking up fragments of equipment from the nearest surface, examining them needlessly. Her husband sighs and turns away. The sigh denotes frustration as well as impatience. He presses a pad and the wall illumines in front of him. The representation of a pale, veined foetus is revealed. Lydia makes a sound and averts her head. She knocks the table behind her, sending a spray of shiny video disks to the floor. Ewan manipulates console keys, muttering encouragement to himself. 'Get it, Lyd?' he says. 'The power was there all the time. We were so dumb.' He turns around, a thinking frown on his gaunt face. 'You must keep her safe,' he says. Back to the screen, a laugh. 'When this baby hits fuck heaven, more than the Earth will move, believe me.' More laughter.

Lydia's voice, dull. 'You're crazy.'

'Don't worry, I've imprinted specific repressions. She'll be quite safe, quite *harmless*, until the right codes are induced.'

'I hate you, Ewan.'

'This is the real world, Lyd,' he says, passionlessly.

'Turn that thing off.'

'That's your baby, Lyd,' he says softly, gently reprimanding, 'not a thing, but *our* child.'

Lydia makes a nervous gesture. 'I know, I know. I meant the screen. Turn that off, that's all.'

'It's ready for implantation now.'

'Maybe *I'm* not ready . . .'

A silence hangs between them. Lydia knows her words are an empty threat. Her fearful squeamishness battles with a scientific cool. She shakes her head, then nods it, eyes closed against her husband's cold, waiting stare. 'OK, OK, I understand. It's just a bit weird, that's all – more than a bit weird.'

'Women have had children conceived artificially for a long time, Lyd.'

But *I* don't need that, Lydia screams inside herself. She nods. 'I know.' She longs to rage: I am not an experiment, not me, not my unborn children, none of me; but Ewan is her weakness, her whole being centres upon craving his approval. Ewan, satisfied, fixes his attention on his work again. He speaks over his shoulder. 'You have to get out of here soon.'

'Where to?' Lydia asks. It is the first time Ewan has suggested she should leave this place.

'I've seen to it,' he says abruptly. 'It's a good place, plenty of room. A good place to bring up a kid.'

Now they are far away. The luxury house is freshly painted, bright under the trees. They stand before it, looking in. Lydia is heavily pregnant. Ewan stands with his arm around her, dressed in natro drab and leather. 'You will be safe here, Lyd.'

'Don't leave.' He says nothing to her. Just a light kiss on the top of her summer head. She's frowning. 'We can't keep this a secret, Ewan. The . . . others . . .'

Now Ewan is angry. 'Don't even say that. They're not ready for this. The child must only have herself, understand? When she's old enough, I'll be there to help her, and if I'm not, I'll make sure there are people who can carry on without me.'

'People? Who? What do you mean? Why?' There is a certain echo in his words which implies Ewan does not expect to be around to see his daughter grow up. Lydia does not like this lonely, stark place with the rattling trees. She feels weak, as if the reins of her life have been snatched away and broken off entirely. She is being pulled along by maddened horses and the only aid in her command is the whip.

Lydia Famber came out of her meditation weeping. She had forgotten how beautiful Ewan had been. Later, she went out into the yard and burned the videos. She never wanted to remember what she had lost again.

Will you go for it now? Will you?

He wakes sweating, his fingers convulsing round the ragged totems at his throat. His anxiety is not prompted by dreams but the reality of beforesleep. Heavy depression feels like a physical weight on his shoulders; he remembers.

Eyes open, he surveys the smooth, featureless walls, hardly visible in the lowlight creeping slitwise beneath the door. The air is odourless: strange, he has not been in such a place as this for so long. He breathes through one nostril and then the other, attuning his sense of smell to a finer pitch; but still the only aroma is that of his own body. His flesh mildly tingles from the unseen fingering of microwave caresses. Is this home?

No. He is cocooned in a flimsy thermowrap, his head sunk in a foam pillow. He has no home. This is Arcady. This is Acropolis Park. This is the technological temple of Quincx Roirbak. He inhales, experiencing the rack of abused lungs, eyegrit and weary fibre. He wakes up fully and realises the wellspring of his tension is ages past, aeons buried, lost, lost, yet still he wakes to fear.

This is another world now. And I am Tammuz Malamute, thinks the man.

*　　*　　*

The angels of climate control have freshly misted the streets tonight. If Arcady has to have low-life areas (and what city doesn't?), the streets should always be damp at night. Steamy. Clusters of translucent, ceramic globes hang along the warren of boulevards and alleys, like fizzing crystal balls gossiping prophecies. Blue-white radiance that should be bright, but isn't, making the sidewalks gleam. Exhalations of blue-grey steam puff sporadically from basement gratings. The air smells of meat fat, incense, human waste of all types and the sweet, rubbery electric perfume rising from the subway entrances; some gated now. In this part of the city, away from the slick glitz of Thelema Row and the Grand Alley of Shrines, only a spit distance off, it is essential to good business that the ambience should promise excitement; not all of it harmless.

Porta Lucis Street is long and straight, flanked by low buildings of only ten to fifteen storeys. The buildings are not lit beneath the third floor. Doors are shielded with metal which reflects the stately ballet of roving security cameras exercising their limber joints. There are no windows at street level. Despite appearances, this is probably the most fashionable part of the city. People living nearer townheart south in topgrade apartments such as those found on the ninety-eighth floor of Cincti Serpente metalith, Community Sector 12 – 'this month's most desired hab. loc.' – flock here in their thousands, usually after the clubs uptown have closed their doors for the night. This is Sector 23; it never closes. Its reputation for human corruption has been carefully groomed by its natives for years. Occasionally they will stage something desperate and shocking to maintain their standards. All those privileged to give this area of town as their address are aware they owe it to their neighbours to exhibit volatile natures and magnificent bodily scars. Every alley is thick with thieves and whores, as colourful and vicious as the tourist trade expects. The nature of Sector 23's markets, at all times, must be suspect and unpredictable. It advertises itself as home to a thousand thousand dark delights, reeking with the perfume of adventure. In order to keep up appearances, most of Sector 23's nocturnal activities take place behind doors.

The scene is set. Enter the players. First, a long-haired starveling lurches from a doorway. Black glamour-rags and the flash of silver on skinny wrists. Quick slam of metal, the whine of electronic bolts slipping back in place. A blue-white shaft of light from inside the building is sheared back even before it hits the street. An echo of voices. Music thumps and roars, floating, fading quickly to silence. The figure pauses to light a cigarette. Flare of flame, blue plume, sharp breath. It sways, teetering on spike heels, before advancing unsteadily to the centre of the empty road, gloom-skirted buildings on either side. Take no risks. Have space around you. That is the sensible way. Because it is wandering alone in this place, at this time, the figure must be a weathered veteran of the streets – appearance of youth aside – and undoubtedly well-armed. It is impossible to tell from a distance whether the erratic movements are caused by intoxication or sickness; both conditions abound in Sector 23. This character is the Road-walker.

Someone else's presence is advertised by a sound of crashing off-stage, accompanied by the whorish screams of cats. The corners here are awash with feral communities. Fanfared by the last, tinny ring of something falling, falling, a Soldier of God emerges from a side alley, its progress ducking from military poise to stoop to poise. This is not a person sure of themself. The Soldier is dressed in dark blue uniform and carrying in its hands an oversize, archaic defence weapon. More brutal, metallic devices are slung around its shoulders. It peers around, head wagging, as if the only sign of life is not immediately apparent strolling up the middle of the street. The Road-walker stiffens imperceptibly, but does not increase or decrease its pace. Its advancement has become more steady, however. The Soldier of God jumps into the road, screaming. 'I believe in the Lord! Oh yes!'

Thankfully, for the Road-walker's sake, it does not brandish any of its weapons in a particularly threatening way. The Road-walker, this seasoned inhabitant, deduces quickly that the Soldier is, in fact, completely estranged from its life-course, straying from its army, lost in mind and body. That does not make it any less dangerous, and perhaps even more unpredictable, but at least establishes its reality pattern.

The Soldier begins to enact its spiritual imprint, an instinctive reaction on espying a godless soul, and throws itself to its knees on the road, holding its weapon aloft and crying, 'He showed me, he showed me the way. Life and Love in the Blood of the Lord. Oh, he shed for us. Let us shed together and acknowledge the Lord!'

'Long way from home sister,' responds the Road-walker, thus revealing the Soldier's sex for any interested parties. The two figures are merely feet apart.

'I am at home in the Lord!' announces the Soldier.

'Lady, you are lost. Go find your barracks. It's late.' The Road-walker, it must be pointed out at this juncture, in no way has any interest in the fate of the Soldier. The Road-walker merely wants to pass by with the minimum of inconvenience.

'Have you seen his face?' inquires the Soldier, with passion.

'I seen lot of faces.'

'Kneel with me!'

The Road-walker edges to the side. The Soldier follows its movement. 'Kneel now and I will show you the Lord!' The Road-walker has by now established the Soldier is too far gone to be of serious danger and will probably be burnt-out and lifeless by morning when the body may be retrieved by her people should she still be in one piece. The Road-walker skips deftly round the kneeling Soldier, who for several seconds does not realise her target is no longer in front of her. Then she turns, still kneeling. 'Oh, yes, I can see now!' she exclaims, eyes narrowing. 'Satan uses your body! You are his eyes, his hands! A whore, devil's effluent! Oh yes! Sold on the streets to spread the plague of unbelief!'

The Road-walker considers that, in certain ways, the Soldier is right, but still cannot countenance the shaky lifting of the Soldier's weapon without retaliating. Not a serious danger. The act of threat lacks verve and decision. Perhaps the Soldier is wondering how she came to be in this place where the presence of her god feels very distant indeed. She aims the weapon. The Road-walker watches carefully, sifting choices. The Soldier's weapon will make a loud noise if she fires it, maybe attracting unwelcome attention. The Road-walker knows the pointlessness of trying to persuade the Soldier to drop her gun. A decision is reached, without passion. In moments, the Soldier lies dead upon the street, gazing up at the distant dome through one remaining eye. The Road-walker debates whether to recover the mosquito bolt whose contents are now liquifying the Soldier's brain, but decides against it. The bolts are expensive, true, but it has been a long, hard, exhausting night and the Road-walker just wants to get home.

Tonight, a difficult choice has been made, a split-second acceptance, back in the smoky plushness of arch-madam Jahsaxa Penumbra's Club Eleusis. The Road-walker, enervated by the hard swill of spent adrenalin these last few hours, discourages the thought the Soldier of God might be viewed as an omen. There is enough to worry about without that. Crazies spill out on to the street all the time, any time. Coincidence. Inconvenience. Nuisance. Mere irritation. Forgettable. A night shiver; foul breeze from the subway throat, far-away whine and hum, presaging life below, far below. One last draw from a cigarette. Stub thrown to gutter. The Road-walker moves on.

The scene is now empty, but for the staring body of the Soldier awkwardly sprawled, still half-kneeling in the middle of the road. There is no blood, no mess. Attracted by the sounds, alley cats who have been waiting in the corners slink nervously forward to investigate the meat. High above, in the pandemonium of Club Eleusis, Jahsaxa Penumbra stands with her back to the curtained windows, an accomplished hostess of influence, beauty and charm, laughing daintily through a pall of cigarette smoke and perfume, her eyes aglitter with the succulence of a triumph she hadn't dared to think possible. 'Zambia,' her mind chants, 'Zambia Crevecoeur.' It feels almost like falling in love.

In Sector 23, life imitates art.

Tammuz Malamute sat up on the side of the portabed, rubbed the back of his neck, rotated his head, stretching muscle. He was rewarded by the silvery grate of flexing gristle. Pulling on a T-shirt, he groped his way to the door, fleeing the dim cubby and its thousand provocations of memory. By Roirbak standards, the room had been conservative, virtually a cupboard set into the wall of the roofed plaza beyond; a restroom where Quincx snatched quick naps during intensive work schedules, and a convenient place to stow an unexpected visitor needing rest.

Outside lay the rococo vastness of Quincx Roirbak's workshops; half atelier, half museum, a monument to past technologies, a celebration of new. The building itself, a series of interconnecting tiered vaults, was based around an open ground plan on which forests of Moorish columns had been rooted in between clearings of tessellated patios. Here the play of light from high roof-windows on fountains and pools created a moving fresco on the patterned walls. Where the columns thinned in number, a great plaza was revealed: the place where Roirbak worked and played. The austere shapes and superimposed perspectives of this ostentatious indulgence produced effects which made Tammuz feel as if he was trapped in some Cubist virtual reality. The building was also integrated into the natural setting of Acropolis Park, scenery and vegetation being incorporated into the innermost parts of it. The plaza was dominated by massive robotic machines, artefacts of the industrial past. These brooded aloft, their spider limbs bunched up against their tarnished bellies. Ceraplas worktables in sand and red clay tints were untidily grouped upon the marble tiles below, their surfaces littered with pieces of the hardware for artificial intelligences. The results of other, half-completed, projects covered most of the remaining floor. A row of data suits for virtual exploration were hung on the far wall next to a vast screen displaying images, words and equations: the notes for Roirbak's creative thought. Other walls, painted with complex, geometric patterns, were studded with banks of video monitors – head sets trailing like vines – where the great man edited the more ambitious of his inspirations, or else relaxed by interacting with old movies.

Currently, Quincx Roirbak was sitting in front of one of the dozen or so workstations dotted around the plaza walls in recesses resembling shrines. He was a lean, black-skinned man, gaunt and handsome, who appeared to be in his late thirties. He wore a silk smoking-jacket over stained coveralls, his long dreadlocks held back at the neck.

'Ah, awake I see.' He swivelled round in his chair, having sensed Tammuz padding up behind him. 'Are you hungry?'

'Not yet.' Tammuz rubbed his face. He still found the decor of this place a little freaky. 'Would welcome a shave though.'

'By all means. All facilities are on hand.' Roirbak waved a hand in the direction of a long, colonnaded corridor. 'Through there. Second right. Take a shower. Use my things. Whatever.'

'Thanks, soul.' Tammuz smiled and loped away in the direction Roirbak indicated.

Quincx Roirbak, entrepreneurial genius, revered as part madman, part visionary, watched his guest weave his way between the overflowing tables and architectural protusions. He tapped his lips thoughtfully with a slender light-scriber; he sensed there was more to Mr Malamute than met the eye. Roirbak lived and worked without human company. He was not a solitary animal but preferred to exercise sociability beyond the confines of his private space. That way, it was always a relief to come home. It was regarded as an eccentricity on his part (at worst an affectation), that he chose to live alone in such cluttered splendour, the current fashion for people of affluence being Oriental Minimalism. The complex at Acropolis Park had come up for sale four years ago and, as this event had coincided with his seventieth birthday, Roirbak took it as a good omen and snapped the place up as a bargain. The plant had been curiously old-fashioned, an archaeological relic from the last century, encapsulated like a stone toad within the gleaming expanse of a city that was faintly embarrassed to be host to such an anomaly. Roirbak wasted no time converting this leviathan into his own vision of elegance and comfort. It had been crammed with outmoded machinery, most of which Roirbak had disposed of, retaining only those pieces which were valuable as industrial antiques. A lavishly appointed suite of rooms on the first floor comprised his actual living quarters, but he spent most of his time in the plaza.

The majority of people also found his taste in personal adornment rather too pretentious and showy. 'Only a man as rich as Roirbak can get away with living like a rat in a catacomb and dressing like a cheap dandy,' one lady of standing had once said contemptuously. It had earned him the dubious compliment of becoming the root of a popular adjective. To be dubbed Roirbakian implied someone who affected such conceits as leaving their personal holodisk movieware festering beneath unwashed silk shirts festooned with flounces, who ate hideously expensive real meat pâté from its container with a plastic fork, and drank cheap liquor from quartz crystal; all of this and more. To youngbloods negotiating the ascent of Arcady's precarious success-tower, being termed

Roirbakian had come to be a compulsory fashion accessory. Hardly one of them could manage it with style.
Quincx paid no attention; he was quite content. He did
not care one way or the other what people thought of his
lifestyle. It required more energy than he felt the subject
deserved even to be amused by it. Through persistence
and determination, garnished cleverly with guile and
cunning, he had achieved most of his ambitions in life.
His career, as had most people's in his profession, had
begun among the ranks of the Tech-Greens. Five years
ago he'd abandoned the final shreds of zeal and vocation
which had become, ultimately, a pretence, and headed
for the world of commercial independence. Arcady had
still been a chain of individual towns and cities at that
time, tentatively extending their boundaries for the final
mating. Only parts of it had been domed then; the lesser
conurbations had withstood climactic caprices and pollution hazards as best they could with a kind of hectic,
post-apocalyptic panache. (Even now, though protectively domed, some of those areas still remained as
dreary and uncherished sectors.) Roirbak had cheerfully
joined in with the enthusiasm for change and development, finding his niche, incorporating the skills of others
under the guise of tutorship, expanding his little duchy to
become a kingdom. He had never yearned for an empire
although he could easily have built one. Now he spread
his eccentricities contentedly through the spacelavish
vaults of his workshops on the borders of Sector 23,
and the emperors came to him, seeking the wisdom and
expertise of the magus. His speciality was artificial intelligence: he liked creating people. Eighteen months ago he
had dispensed with all his human assistants and replaced
them with placid robots he'd designed himself. It
solved all problems peculiar to personnel. Occasionally,

however, some soul would drift into his orbit and their uniqueness would catch his eye or imagination. He would consent to their company, allow them to learn from him. Tammuz Malamute was such a soul.

Tammuz fiddled with the shower controls which were caked with dried soap. A single, wizened nugget of Zingbublz was stuck to ornate, enamelled walldish; a typically Roirbakian effect. Tammuz told himself he had not meant to come here, that he was victim to a compulsion he could not ignore, that it was some urge for self-destruction. He was not sure whether he'd expected Roirbak to recognise him, despite his precautions. There had been no indication he had. But then Tammuz remembered enough about the man to know he probably wouldn't show it if he had guessed. A game. A dangerous game. Scalding water suddenly spat from the showerhead (a yawning, metal gargoyle) and Tammuz prised the soap from its dish, holding it up to the jets. After a few seconds it had become slimy enough to produce a feeble lather. The bubbles, such as they were, hardly zinged. How many times had he dithered mere clicks from Arcady's shimmering haze only to force himself to turn away, travel somewhere else? Too many times to recall. Relatively speaking, there was nowhere else to go in this country now other than Arcady. He told himself that was why he'd eventually succumbed and let his eager feet bring him here. It was nothing to do with the past, the thirst for information, the aching, inescapable desire to discover whether his work had developed as he'd planned. Vanity, he thought. It will be my downfall. It is merely vanity. I cannot kid myself I feel concern or responsibility. No. He scrubbed himself with the inadequate soap.

Only twelve hours before, he had presented himself to the security eyelimb officiously scanning the approach route to Indra's Network Inc. and requested an interview with the proprietor. Fighting his body's compulsion to sweat nervously, sternly calming his heartbeat, he spoke briefly of his respect for Roirbak's work, his own expertise, the desire to perfect it. He mentioned a few names, claiming familiarity. He mentioned his clamouring ideas and the absence of a shrewd patron who was reckless and canny enough to help realise them.

The eye, bridling and bunching on its cabled stalk, beadily appraised him in silence. Tammuz, lightheaded with anticipation and fear, had felt the curious presence behind the monitor deep within. He had experienced a sensation of nakedness as if all his bonedeep disguise had been in vain. He nearly blurted something unwise, but his impassioned yet concise speech, it appeared, sufficed. The panel on the main door displayed a light-sequence and opened a man-sized segment, allowing him to enter. Once inside, the receptionist woman-form summoned a security robot – without human shape, sleek yet functional – which scanned his body for weapons and inspected his irises. Seemingly satisfied, it directed him to follow it and hummed ahead, leading the way to the great man himself. Tammuz was surprised it had been this easy. He had been prepared to wrangle, explain himself, lie.

If Roirbak had changed in all these years, he had done so only by appearing younger. For a moment Tammuz sincerely considered the possibility his old mentor was dead and this smiling, striding figure approaching him across the plaza was some android creation, perhaps developed as a joke by Roirbak himself before he died. Quincx must be over seventy now, surely, and yet this man looked thirty years younger. This would not be remarkable if it wasn't for the fact that he had once scorned the concept of regeneration. Perhaps encroaching decay had changed his mind, eroded his principles. Tammuz did not think the prospect of senility would be greeted with resignation by such a man. He smothered his surprise. He would wait and observe, and then decide.

Quincx took one of his limp hands, that not occupied with luggage, and shook it. Tammuz knew the man was gathering information, forming conclusions from the dampness of his skin, the temperature and texture of it. He had been taught that technique by Roirbak himself once. Quincx's hands were hard and cool, and very steady.

'So, and who am I inviting into my domain? Do you have a name?'

'Tammuz Malamute.'

'A stranger to these parts? My colleagues seem to have no record of your existence!'

'I came thrudome two days ago.'

'Strange. Forgive my importunity, but I would have thought had you studied under Blisley, Gonzales and Ritter, as you claim, your presence would be felt on the city's datavaults . . .' He paused when Tammuz did not react. 'Still, there are errors, oversights – praise the Lady they're still possible – and, of course, tailored identities.'

'I did not lie,' Tammuz said. 'I can do all I claimed.'

'That's easily proved,' Roirbak said, smiling. 'Anyway, come in, come in. Tell me why you're here.'

The canteen was very large, rather like a doctor's surgery in comparison to the rest of the complex, a relic of days when the building had thronged with personnel.

Now it felt forlorn, wistful, the only signs of life centred on a couple of tables situated near the grill and counter, where the remains of an earlier meal lay beside an open book. It was as if Roirbak had renovated only as far as the plaza before the desire to work had overtaken him and he'd abandoned his flamboyant architectural enhancements. Clearly nothing much had changed in this section since the building had been constructed. Roirbak bustled behind the counter to make coffee, making small talk, sounding crazy. Tammuz was not deceived. He felt the scrutiny beneath the blather as if a laser was passing over every pore of his body. He was conscious of his own terseness. That was not intended. He wanted to appear ingenuous, enthusiastic, chatty: a student eager for knowledge. Now he felt more like a hired assassin, a fake. Words were having difficulty passing the constriction in his throat. He wanted to pour out the truth and relax into the comfort he knew would follow. It would be so easy. Roirbak would be astounded, perhaps wary at first. He would question, with a frown on his face. When convinced, he would smile and hold out his arms to embrace. He would mutter words of joy, of incredulity, welcoming Tammuz home like a prodigal son. If only that was possible. Sadly, Tammuz was only too aware how dangerous it was for him to be in Arcady, even though he was disguised. He could not risk revealing himself – to anyone. That was the sacrifice he'd made. At least he had scraped up enough guts to put himself in the position where he could win Roirbak's friendship again as someone else. If only he could trust this persona to behave itself and be likeable!

After two hours' conversation, Tammuz had decided the relationship could never be duplicated, not under the necessary conditions of deceit. Roirbak was going to treat him differently, even if he proved himself. Tammuz would gain respect, he knew, but the closeness he'd once had with this man was because he'd been a Roirbak protégé. Now he was an outsider, no matter how talented he might prove himself. The admiration would be delivered from arm's length. He spoke guardedly of the ideas he had – old ones naturally, carefully chopped and changed to appear spawned by a different mind. Occasionally he allowed one or two phrases to slip through, shining hooks that grabbed at Roirbak's attention. Tammuz knew he gulped the bait, but the hooks were so swift, so brief, it was doubtful Roirbak would remember hearing them before. Tammuz' flesh shrank to ice when he said, 'It is uncanny. I had a student once who talked like you.'

'No idea is wholly original,' Tammuz replied glibly. 'There are too many souls in the world for any one of us to have the luxury of being unique.' He paused, affecting wounded pride. 'I have not plagiarised anyone. The ideas I have come only from me . . . although using your study programs did help nudge them along. That's why I'm here, of course. You are the only one who will sympathise.' That sounded suitably student-like.

Roirbak laughed gently. 'Come now. As you said, no one is allowed the luxury of being unique.' He was as flattered, though, as Tammuz had known he would be. Roirbak had changed less than he had, and not just in a physical sense. Tammuz Malamute looked around twenty-eight years old. Like Roirbak, he was lean and gaunt, although his skin was tanned Caucasian rather than black. It was not inconceivable Tammuz had had his old mentor in mind though when he'd redesigned himself. His hair was long, reddish brown where

Roirbak's was greyed black, but held away from the face in the same way. His totems, too, were very similar. But whereas Roirbak was a more relaxed version of his old self, his personality still recognisable, Tammuz was someone else entirely to the person Roirbak had known before. At least, he thought he was.

'Perhaps you are not unique, but you are my preference,' he said.

Roirbak raised his brows. 'Assertive, aren't you!' He folded his arms on the table. 'Well, I admit you intrigue me. I'm willing to give you bench space around here. Although, I warn you, I'm not an easy man to work with. I like to have room for my thoughts and the silence to think them in.'

You always did, Tammuz wanted to say. Believe me, I know how not to irritate you. That was the first thing you taught me.

'My way of working entirely,' he said. 'This place is big enough, isn't it? I won't snag in your hair.'

Roirbak nodded thoughtfully, sucked his upper lip. 'Hmm. We'll see. Obviously you'll want to talk, ask questions, tell me your brilliant discoveries, etc. We'll have to set a time for that. I have no objection to sharing my mealtimes with you.'

'Sounds fine to me.'

'I eat once a day. Evening.'

'Fine.' Tammuz shrugged.

'You'll need a room I suppose. Fix one up for yourself. The further from mine the better.' He smiled. 'Sometimes I rant in my sleep. I don't want ears around.'

That's new, Tammuz thought. Perhaps it's a symptom of age.

A tour of the building followed. Tammuz was told which equipment he could use without asking – more than he needed, naturally. They ended up by Roirbak's main workstation, where the man embarked upon a monologue about his work. Tammuz wished he could tell Quincx to leave out the bullshit, but of course it was customary for a man of his accomplishment to speak to a younger stranger that way. Tammuz nodded and made noises when appropriate. Privately he thought Quincx had become too involved in chimaeric theory, but perhaps it was self indulgence rather than caution that had dulled his brazen approach. He had once sought to construct godlike beings, now he concentrated on playmates. Their conversation touched for a moment or two on the taboo subject of biomech, which Tech-Green had ostensibly outlawed, along with the more esoteric branches of gene and soma manipulation, some years ago. Both men hinted to each other about how this was a phenomenon confined to the planet and that off-world scientists and engineers enjoyed far less restriction to pursue their ideas. 'You have been off-world of course,' Roirbak said.

Tammuz hesitated. 'No, I haven't . . . but I have friends . . .'

'Of course!'

Tammuz appeared edgy. 'It is necessary to know what is going on above our heads, I feel. Probably the most startling discoveries about our field of work goes on up there.'

Roirbak nodded. 'And what is your field exactly?' he asked. 'You obviously know a lot about my work and have been trained in the same subject, but what's your speciality?'

Tammuz grinned and leaned back against a desk-top. 'My field was originally neurology, which led to a.i. programming, naturally.'

'I don't know about naturally!' Roirbak laughed. 'Is that what you've come here to do? Play doctor to the minds of my machines?'

Tammuz shrugged. 'That wasn't exactly what I did. My job was to emulate the human thought process, but I'll do anything you need me to. I must admit I'm rather more interested in getting back into working with humans.'

'Well, plenty to work on there! Machines tend to be nicer people though. I started my career in neurology.'

'I know. Your thesis on human sexuality was most useful to me once.'

Roirbak laughed again. 'I'm still trying to build an a.i. with a fully functional sexual profile! The perfect mate!'

Tammuz pulled a scornful face. 'You really think you can do that?'

'Don't you?'

'I'm tempted to say I know you can't.'

'Oh? How interesting.'

'Of course, I may be wrong.'

'How modest of you.'

'I'm not criticising you, Mr Roirbak.' Tammuz turned away and carelessly poked around in the equipment on Roirbak's desk. 'I just don't think sexuality can be artificially duplicated. I believe it has its own life-force or, more accurately, it may be *our* life-force. The soul?' He turned around again, a bright, challenging smile on his face.

Quincx Roirbak was astounded. He was almost tempted to say that was not the first time he'd come across such a wild theory, but something, something indefinable, held him back. Instead, he mirrored the smile and said, 'I can see you're going to be an intriguing guest, Tammuz Malamute.'

'I don't want to go home!' announced the girl on the tramway, swinging gleefully on a support strap and incurring impatient glances from the other passengers. It was only eight o'clock in the morning and most of them were on their way to the occupations and diversions that kept them happy for the day. From the girl's appearance – smeared body paint, glossy with skin grease – it seemed she'd been out all night and was now on her way home, although still inclined to party. Her companions were slouching wearily in the seats around her; sadly drooping creatures of the night, their plumage too bedraggled to keep them aloft. One of them roused herself enough to say, 'Sit down, Sammy.'

'But I don't want to go home,' the girl called Sammy insisted, in a bright child-like voice which either encouraged a bloom of sympathetic warmth in the hearts of her fellow travellers or deep, irritated scorn, depending on their view of children. The Road-walker, now tram-sitter and caught up enough in the mundane world to recognise his persona as being that of Zambia Crevecoeur, was sitting close to a window, his cheek almost touching that of his mirror-inverse in the glass, thinking, 'Wish *I* was going home.'

It was a strangely silent journey. The tram was too well

insulated to allow sounds from outside to interfere with its passengers' comfort, and the girl Sammy's extrovert behaviour had effectively silenced everybody else's conversations. Zambia watched people's reflections in the window, noting the covert, curious glances about the thin, archaic news-sheets held, he was sure, only as camouflage against faces that were too raw and naked at that early hour to bear scrutiny. Why else would anyone carry a news-sheet for the Goddess' sake? He smiled and winced at the reflection of himself. He'd never liked the way he looked when he smiled. Why am I here? he wondered. He felt no trace of excitement, pleasure, nor even acceptance. Hunched dejectedly on a speeding blip above the city, he was hurtling to a place of dread. He stared relentlessly at himself in the glass, prickling with self-loathing, repressing the urge to turn his head in the particular ways that he knew would mutate his reflection into something he could stand looking at. No, hate yourself, he decided, and carried on grinning at his reflection.

The tramway soared between giant video hoardings proclaiming the benefits of applying for emigration to Sky City One. Glass-fronted buildings flashed past. Zambia turned away from the window. It was too painful to be reminded how destitute and desperate he was. Sammy's companions had succeeded in fussing her into a seat, where she wriggled and giggled, making high-pitched remarks. Crevecoeur wondered just how full her social map for the next few weeks would be following this tram skip. Her friends were looking far from impressed. One girl, squeezed as far into a corner as she could get, dressed in a second skin of electric blue incongruously ridiculous at that hour and in that place, almost certainly had murder in her eyes. Zambia Crevecoeur envied their happy little lives. He could tell at a glance exactly what kind of people they were: rich, zappy weirdos, living off their daddys' credit accounts, feeling they were wild and eccentric. Crevecoeur knew he could show them, tell them in a single sentence, just what real wildness and eccentricity entailed. It'd blur their bodysuits for good, although the chances were they probably wouldn't believe him. Damn it all, he thought, what the hell is *real* anyway? He sighed and rested his face against the window; a skinny, drab figure heavily in disguise, his face bare, his long, black hair screwed up tight behind his head, clothes neutral and conservative. Normal. He considered the bleak irony that his disguise consisted of what he really was. For now. By tomorrow the Zambia Crevecoeur sitting on this tramway would effectively no longer exist. He would be dead. Effectively. It was better not to think of that, better to think bitchy thoughts about his fellow travellers. Yes. They might all be areek with executive perfumes, but they were still too low in the pile to have transport of their own. Naturally, all of them would be aiming for it, by Goddess, oh yes, but only the very rich could afford ground vehicles, never mind purchase the necessary licence, traffic being restricted at all levels in Arcady.

Crevecoeur shuddered at the swish of expensive clothes, the tang of expensive aromas, the click of metal fingernails, the flash of brilliant re-chromatised eyes, but comforted himself with the thought that every one of them was still obliged to travel on the scummy tramway. As the compartment flung itself between high buildings along a perilous wire a kilometre above the city, the natty travellers had to shuffle their shining shoes to avoid suspect patches of damp on the floor. It was sweet, really sweet. Who do they think they're kidding? Zambia thought. He still wished he was one of them however: going to a safe job, clean and odour-free, with sculpted flesh, sculpted hair, sculpted existence. (No, perhaps *not* the sculpted flesh.) He imagined they all went to parties at night in the high towers, casting off their stiff, daytime skins. They probably steeped themselves in perfumes with names like Sector 23 and Raw Blade, and wore one eye completely black to be bizarre. Hosts might splash out and hire a dervish to bring the party music to life, a real dervish from downtown. They wouldn't be able to understand its jargon of course . . . but the dancing. *Hint of heat from the darkside, fingernail in the blood drawing it out, out . . .*

A featureless, artificial voice broke into Zambia's reverie, 'Knossos Palisades, next drop. Knossos Palisades.' The woman sitting next to him, of whom Crevecoeur had been virtually ignorant the entire journey owing to her utter silence and lack of human movement, smoothed her trousers, patted her smooth hair and adjusted the carry-all on her shoulder. Already her hand, complete with scintillidium fingernails, rested gently on her seat-belt button. She was ready to leave, eager to begin her day. Crevecoeur closed his eyes, swallowed deeply, feeling a gulf of air force itself painfully into his body. It was his stop too.

Outside, Crevecoeur's unacknowledged travelling companion trotted briskly off towards the elevators, her hair bouncing jauntily. She waved a quick hello to someone she knew and disappeared between the sliding doors. Crevecoeur simply stood on the edge of the platform, leaning against the safety rail, feeling sick. For a few minutes he could not move. A sharp morning wind, gusting authentically from whatever weather facility serviced this section, plucked his hair from its confines and whipped it across his eyes. I could go back now, he thought. He visualised turning around, hopping on to the next compartment heading east. It would be nearly empty, and he'd smile at his reflection in the glass, full of relief. But then? Back to the screaming landlady demanding rent, the empty foodstore, the cold room. The heating had been out for months now and since the Sector's Community Committee had opted in with adjoining sectors for seasonal temperature variations, he'd suffered badly. Zambia hated being cold. He was dreading the day some bright spark on the Committee, with too much time to spare, suggested they start synthesising snow. The regular rainfalls were bad enough. Discomforts, discomforts. Would he ever be free of them? We have this marvellous, monstrous city, warm and clean, and They have to duplicate the worst elements of living outside. Insane! If only he was rich. He could live in an air-conditioned apartment then, and they could recreate the Ice Age in Arcady if they wanted to; it wouldn't matter. He heard Jahsaxa's glittering promises whisper through his head. 'Do this, and you're guaranteed a thousand creds per trick. It's unique. New. Perfectly safe. And you're rat-poor, Zambia.' He hadn't needed the reminder.

For a long time, Zambia had taken pride in not having been part of Penumbra's empire. Oh, she'd made offers in the past, plenty of them, but he'd turned them all down. Eventually, she'd stopped bothering him. Those had been halcyon days, he mused sadly. But of course, she'd closed in on him anyway, expanding her domain, stealing his livelihood. He could not hope to offer people the same service as Club Eleusis, and then Penumbra started undercutting his charges. When the day came that he was forced to sell the last but one of his self-defence mechanisms in order to eat, Zambia knew he'd have to crawl to Club Eleusis and ask her for help. She had the entire Sector in a bag nowadays. He couldn't get work without her backing. It had been one of the most humiliating experiences of his life. For two days she'd refused to see him at all, her secretary telling him to call back tomorrow. He'd lived on black coffee, just waiting. Finally she'd felt she'd punished him enough and relented. Gave him a meal and told him the deal. It was the only way she'd take him on.

'Look on it as a challenge,' she'd said. 'Come on, Crevecoeur, what is it to you? Does it matter? I would have thought it'd be more convenient.' She'd loved every minute of it. There'd been mezcal cocktails, and wrangling and nitpicking and, he winced to recall, even drunken reminiscences, which resulted in him shaking the woman's hand across her desk and thanking her for the chance. Embarrassing. After that, the godfreak had jumped him in the street. The promise of things to come. Oh Goddess.

The clinic was only two blocks away from the tramway elevators, within easy walking distance. The city was pretty regular in that sector: neat squares. It was virtually impossible to get lost there because of the orientation terminals on every corner for strangers to the area to access without charge. Crevecoeur, however, knew the way, having memorised it the previous evening using the apartment block communit, hooked on to the public orientation grid. He had already walked this journey a hundred times in his mind. Each time he'd imagined a different scenario at the end, but the walk was the same.

All he had on him, apart from his clothes, was enough cash for the tramway home afterwards. No ID. No credit card. Today, even though it was probably an unnecessary precaution, he wanted to be traceless. Jahsaxa had told him she'd paid for the surgery beforehand. She at least must feel confident.

'Call it an advance,' she'd said, laughing.

I must be mad, I must be mad, Zambia chanted to himself as he walked along the seamless street. In an effort to remain calm, he furiously concentrated on admiring the lush foliage bursting from display carts outside the glass-fronted ultramalls. Their leaves were so unbelievably green and fleshy, their flowers so unbelievably bright, it was obvious they were high on artificial nutrients, a chemical cocktail so strong they'd die instantly if planted in regular soil, beneath the light of an unshielded sun. Crevecoeur had a plant of his own like that, highly-strung and temperamental, rooted in a crumbly bed of nitrofert nuggets. He kept it next to his bed in a tray, warmed by a gro-lamp because it did not care for daylight particularly. If he looked after it well it might live forever, never exceeding its prescribed height and girth, never fading. It was almost artificial. Such thoughts directed his mind back to regions of discomfort. So far, he'd avoided wondering about what special routines he might have to perform on himself every day after this. There must be some, because he'd be as artificially mutated as the plants. Perhaps it would be regular doses of hormone treatments, or even the hideous possibility of mechanical servicing, should the surgery be so crude as to involve non-biotech implants, independent of the body's nervous system. Last night he'd accessed 'Intersexing' on the public library files at least twice, but had squeamishly wiped the information before he could read it, telling himself it was best not to know and best not to be seen looking, standing there in the lobby of the apartment building. He could not risk being put off. It was hard enough to force himself to go through with it as it was.

Further imaginary wound-licking was curtailed by the appearance of the Parmedes Clinic round a corner. Without pausing Zambia walked quickly into the clinic's foyer. Almost obscenely, it was as hushed and elegant a place as any high-class hotel lobby. A holo-fountain played in time to softly tinkling music, its colour fluctuating from blue to green to blue. Pretty. Zambia instantly became conscious of his appearance – scruffy – and half expected someone to come and shoo him out of the door again. Unfortunately, it didn't happen. Hands in pockets, Crevecoeur sauntered purposefully to the registration desk. Behind it, a receptionist wearing a smart uniform that looked only vaguely medical, sat surrounded by monitors and keyboards housed in attractive dove-lilac ceraplas. Sensing his approach, she looked up with a professional smile which did not waver when she saw him. 'Can I help you?'

'I've a reservation. Dr Parmedes.'

The receptionist nodded politely and tapped a key with the end of one blade-like fingernail. 'Ah. Crevecoeur?' she inquired.

'Yes.'

'You are a little late,' she admonished with a smile and a wagging talon.

Crevecoeur shrugged. 'Had to wait for a tramway. Didn't realise they were so full at this time. Sorry.'

The receptionist beamed. 'That's all right. No problem. At least you're not *too* late!' Crevecoeur was impressed. She had to know what he had come for, and therefore must have guessed what he did for a living. He was sure the only person who'd ever apply for such surgery would have to be someone connected in one way or another with the carnal arts. Admittedly it was fashionable in Arcady for people to be aggressively tolerant and unshockable, but deep down he knew most 'decent' citizens were made nervous by members of his profession. He was an aorist – without limits. The dark of the soul had to be as familiar to him as breathing, yet this woman just smiled and said, 'Now you haven't eaten anything since last night, have you?'

'No. I followed the instructions you sent me.'

'Good, take a seat. Someone will be down soon to settle you in.'

She began tapping keys with one hand, directing him to a row of plush sofas across the hall with the other. Crevecoeur nodded and went to sit down. His heart was racing now, his body tingling; a tingling concentrated in his groin and belly. His palms were wet, hands gripping each other. He tried to breathe deeply, calm himself, but the effort was useless. It was easier to ride the tide of panic symptoms.

A male nurse appeared from behind sliding elevator doors across the lobby. He had brilliantly golden eyes and an oriental tattoo on his neck. Zambia hated him on sight and decided, viciously, that the nurse just had to be another of those who rode to work on the tramway. After consulting the receptionist, the nurse sauntered over to where his victim was sitting and spoke. 'You are Zambia Crevecoeur? Would you like to come with me please?'

No, Crevecoeur thought, but smiled and stood up and followed.

In the elevator, Crevecoeur wondered whether he should try to make conversation, but the nurse was frowning so intently at the control panel, he hadn't the nerve to break the silence. Under normal circumstances, Zambia wouldn't have been able to prevent himself making remarks about personal transport, whether they were aimed at an appropriate target or not, but the idea of trying to be humorous at that time was hateful. They emerged into a brightly-lit corridor, panelled with what appeared to be authentic wood, and busy with giant plants. Thick beige carpeting silenced their steps and seemed to muffle the soft music emanating from hidden speakers. At the end of the corridor, Zambia was shepherded towards another reception desk.

'Good morning,' smiled the young man behind the new set of terminals. 'Welcome to Floor Lavender Sky. We aim to make your stay as comfortable and pleasant as possible. Please do not hesitate to ask for anything. Now, if you'd be so kind as to answer a few questions . . .'

Zambia's guide padded off without another word. His loss was not mourned. Crevecoeur mechanically supplied details of his medical history. The receptionist's fingers moved in a blur over his keyboard, a light-pen stuffed jauntily behind his ear. 'Thank you. Your personal attendant will be along shortly to take you to your room. Any questions?'

'Er . . .' Crevecoeur's mind was a blank. He said, 'How long will I have to be here?' even though he could still see the words, 'Your stay in the clinic will be a mere three days, after which you should be ready to resume your habitual activities within two weeks', as they'd been emblazoned on the communal monitor at home the night before.

The receptionist smiled comfortingly and leaned forward, knitting his fingers together in front of him on the desk. 'Don't worry. Not long. Didn't you read it in the information data? It's quite normal to be nervous. Discuss your fears with your attendant. It's what he's here for. To make your stay as comfortable and pleasant as possible.' The receptionist's comm receiver started to buzz. 'Excuse me, will you? You won't be kept waiting long.' He stroked a keypad and said, 'Lavender Sky. How can I help you?'

Unreal. Crevecoeur thought. This must be costing Penumbra a fortune. Whatever surgery they required, Zambia's kind never came to places like this. They were more likely to be found in dim-lit cellars bright only with the glint of surgical steel. Zambia knew he would probably feel more at home in such a place. He walked to a polarised floor-to-ceiling window and leaned over a gush of hysterical emerald-green fern to press his nose against the glass. Far below Arcady hummed with life. Far above the dome crackled like crystal. *This is the last time Zambia Crevecoeur as he is, as he was born, will do this. The last time. Help me, Goddess. I know I've deserted you but you're still there somewhere aren't you?*

There was no immediate answer. Crevecoeur looked away from his pallid reflection, wondering what perverse, wriggling part of him was holding him to the spot. If he was human, worth something, he'd be walking right out of here now, quickly. Was it something more than money preventing that? He felt uncomfortable truths bustle to proclaim themselves and beat them back.

'Zambia Crevecoeur?' He turned around; another nurse, this one smiling and blond. He dreaded a future of inane, incessant conversation. The nurse flicked cerulean blue eyes over his coat, perhaps wondering how such a tramp could afford the hospital facilities. Zambia felt a life-saving thrust of indignance. He stuck his hands in his pockets.

'Yeah.'

The nurse continued to smile, extending a pale hand. 'I am your personal attendant for the duration of your visit. You may call me Frond. This way, if you please.'

Crevecoeur followed through double doors into yet another corridor, faintly fragranced by lavender. Music hummed airily on the edge of perception. The nurse's lilac sneakers made no sound. Crevecoeur glanced warily into side doors; mostly offices where clean, bright operatives smiled at their terminals. They ascended a gentle ramp, flanked by even more tubs of riotous fern, to another reception desk. A woman greeted him with, 'Now, if I may take a few details. When was the last time you took analysis?'

Crevecoeur answered the questions without much thought, watching his psychological profile bloom on the receptionist's screen.

'I am a trained neurotech,' Frond told him. 'Consider me your closest friend.'

Crevecoeur nodded, embarrassed. It was all too unreal. He wished he could summon the courage to laugh.

There was a marked lack of other patients around. Perhaps they were all secreted behind closed doors, gibbering freaks. Crevecoeur felt as if he was being taken deep into a maze. There was no way he could find his way out. Don't panic, he told himself. Frond opened a door and ushered Crevecoeur inside. A bedroom, tasteful, understated and with no sign of medical paraphernalia.

'Just like a hotel,' Zambia said weakly. Frond beamed.

'If you'd slip out of your clothes. There's a shower unit through there. Put on the robe after you've washed. The coordinator will be around shortly. And don't worry – I won't be going anywhere.' He sat down on the bed. Crevecoeur stood awkwardly. 'Do you need a hand?'

'No.' He took off his coat, stripping down to his underwear and padding self-consciously into the shower unit before he removed it. The shower jets were blood-heat, fragranced. Beyond the hiss of water, he could hear Frond humming to himself in the bedroom.

Sitting in bed, wearing a hospital robe, Zambia waited for the coordinator to arrive. From a screen by his bed, Zambia learned his surgery was due to take place at 1000 hours. He found it strange that his decision hadn't been questioned by any of the medical staff. Inside, he had hoped some therapist would have been on hand to try and talk him out of it.

'*Are you sure you're making the right decision, Mr Crevecoeur?*'

'*No, I'm not sure.*'

'*Then I'm afraid I'll have to recommend you are not a suitable subject for these implants . . .*'

A dream. Nobody even asked him.

The coordinator arrived armed with a colour brochure which contained graphic pictures of a selection of implant arrangements. Apparently, as some kind of grotesque concession, Jahsaxa had left the final decision over the aesthetic arrangements to Zambia himself. He felt like vomiting and his eyes had flicked away from the pictures as if he'd been scalded. 'Anything, anything,' he blurted.

The coordinator was gentle. 'Now, come on, there's no need to be shy. This is a relatively new line, you know. You'll be the first Parmedes adaptation in Sector 23. Think of that! We are setting ourselves up in competition with the northern clinics, Sectors 200 and 210 in

125

particular. But you'll be the only one around here until it catches on, and very special to us. Won't that be great?'

'Marvellous!' Zambia peered cautiously at the photographs: naked torsos blighted by wounds, or so it seemed. 'I don't really understand this. Won't it interfere with my internal organs?'

The coordinator rolled her eyes. 'My goodness! Don't let Dr Parmedes hear you say that! He is a genius. Everything is taken care of. This man is a true artist, I'm telling you!'

'OK. Sorry. I just wondered.' He stabbed a finger at the least repellent representation: a mere six sphincters, three of them almost vestigial. 'That one will do.'

The coordinator seemed disappointed. 'Well, if you're into minimalism . . .'

'I am.' If Penumbra wanted something more garish, she shouldn't have risked leaving this decision to him.

The coordinator placed the brochure on Zambia's bedside table. 'Dr Parmedes will be around to see you after surgery,' she said. 'He will want to explain himself about the hormonal adaptations.'

'Just hormonal? Not viral?'

The coordinator looked away. 'It is best to make some of the processes as easily reversible as possible,' she said. Crevecoeur didn't ask why, but was thankful all the same. That, at least, scotched one rumour he'd picked up.

'Great. Great.' Zambia felt his nausea return.

After the coordinator had left, Frond returned to administer a tranquilliser. 'That's some scar you have there,' he said, gesturing at Zambia's shoulder. 'Was that major surgery you had before?'

'A growth,' Zambia answered shortly. 'A malignant one. It was once very much part of me.'

'The picture is great!'

Zambia smiled thinly. A friend of his, a tattoo artist, had insisted on disguising the disfigurement with an elaborate fractal pattern; but people could still tell it was a scar.

The drug claimed his nervous system and offered a deceptive euphoria. Zambia felt more inclined to converse. 'How many of these operations does Parmedes perform then?'

'You are the second,' Frond replied. 'I expect they told you this is a new line for Parmedes Clinic.'

'Oh. I see.'

'Don't worry. You're in good hands.'

Frond flashed a smile of almost mechanical symmetry, causing Crevecoeur to wonder whether the nurse might be some sophisticated form of artificial intelligence. There was very little evidence of humanity or even real understanding of Zambia's predicament. As his consciousness descended towards deeper levels of relaxation he asked, 'Are you real? I mean, like, flesh and blood?'

'Don't you worry about a thing,' said Frond.

'Honey, it's worked a treat!' Jahsaxa Penumbra, dressed in scintillant floor-length black, her white hands spiked with jet-enamelled fingernails, diamond-studded cigarette-holder held aloft, surveyed her newest employee through slitted eyes. She regarded herself as a true professional; 50 per cent carbon-steel image, honed to glittering perfection, 45 per cent killer class business woman, 5 per cent dangerous psychotic. Zambia Crevecoeur, sucked dry as an old bone, slumped on a sofa in one of her offices, could only wither before her inexorable vitality. Discharged from Parmedes Clinic that morning, he still felt sick and stiff, and had directed the clinic transport to bring him to Club Eleusis like an injured dog painfully seeking a hand it knew, even if that hand was as likely to slap as fondle.

Penumbra's place was a monument to luxury, a statement of her success. Zambia knew she must have started her career grubbing in the flesh and soul, like any of her employees, but looking at her now it seemed almost heretical even to think it. The décor was exquisitely understated: as black and white as the woman herself, spacious, speck-free, the air smelling of mimosa. She stood before a potted, dead tree, lacquered black, its petrified fingers rising like a bizarre ornament behind her head. An illusion. Black flames. Spikes. Horns. Crevecoeur blinked. Will I ever feel right again? He could not stop shaking. Naturally they had pumped him full of happiness at the clinic before shepherding him out of the door, and his journey back to Sector 23 had mostly had a grinning, depthless fluffiness. Now the effects were wearing off. He could feel his strange flesh aching and wondered what Jahsaxa would say if he asked her for more chemical relief. He knew she regarded intoxicants of any sort as tools of the trade, to be used for specific effects. She did not encourage any of her people to use drugs for relaxation or entertainment. That would take the edge from their performance, she felt. Crevecoeur rubbed his damp face. 'How the hell can you tell it's worked? What the hell can you see?'

Jahsaxa laughed. 'You're alive aren't you?'

'I think so – just.'

She picked up the bitterness in his voice. 'Stop whining Crevecoeur! I've invested a lot in you. You're a product now: my product!' She softened at his shocked glance, but not through compassion. 'I'll look after you better than you've ever looked after yourself . . .'

Panacea. Crevecoeur sank back into the voluminous black cushions behind him, blinking. Jahsaxa Penumbra smiled at her magic words. They are all children, she thought, and very easy to reach, even though she knew Zambia's tractability was merely a result of post-operative weakness. Her excitement at finally landing this choice morsel was concealed behind her urbane talk of investment. For over a year, she would have given two of her best operatives in exchange for Zambia Crevecoeur, but the boy had been so awkward, resisting all her proud, veiled offers of employment to suffer starvation and deprivation in the name of autonomy.

Penumbra had eyes on every street. She was well aware of the way Crevecoeur had been living. How could he ever had hoped to compete with, or even exist beyond, her operation? He simply hadn't possessed the hardware, or even the imagination to come within an inkling of her inventiveness and creativity. Talk about self-delusion. And since when had anyone been truly in control of their own destinies? Penumbra knew better than that. She had learned the hard way how to dodge and barter with Fate. And now she had him. Standing before her tall, opaque windows, the gentle white light falling in to make everything glow in seductive soft-focus, she gloated privately over her acquisition. Oh, he was a mess all right. Half-starved, bad skin, dull hair; but give her a month or two . . . She sighed in contentment, stubbing out her cigarette. Time to begin work. To prolong the enjoyment, she would even delay inspecting the details of what her friend Dr Parmedes (a regular client) had done to him.

And what was it about Zambia Crevecoeur, archetypal street-urchin, cur-tempered to the end, that was so fascinating, so compelling for arch-madam, fantasy-spinner Jahsaxa Penumbra? A quality. She had simply defined it as that. The ache to touch, to sample, to receive any attention at his hands, so that even positive rejection would be a pleasure. People hated him, even though he lacked all the typical attributes of the perennially bitched. He had never, to her knowledge, involved himself in other people's scandals, was careful to avoid causing any of his own (or at least kept them private), kept his silence, did not betray, swindle or attack his peers unless provoked, and might, upon persistent treaty, even help someone out once in a while. He was insular, true, which people were wary of, but it was not for his character he was so unpopular. It was for his face, his angles of flesh, his passage through space and time – a dance of movement. Zambia Crevecoeur, Jahsaxa suspected, did not naturally belong upon the street and doubtless had originally come from somewhere quite different. She knew many people came to lose themselves in Sector 23, but she suspected Zambia Crevecoeur had, in fact, *found* himself there. She also knew he could turn his attractiveness on and off at will, thus being able to hide effectively when it suited him. At present, it was most definitely turned off, turned inwards. She recognised the body language of self-loathing. Something would have to be done about that. The dog in him must be expelled. He must become cat: pampered, svelte, spoiled, confident of his own unique beauty. It would be a pleasure to teach him that.

Jahsaxa had been in this business a long time. Following a heritage of courtesanship handed down with complete instruction for accomplishment through her mother, she had, at fourteen years of age, embarked upon the career perfected by her ancestors and become a Fulfiller of Dreams. Never a whore. That was a rude approximation of her talents. Jahsaxa had a gift. She could see inside a person and become what they most desired in a woman. She could really make them feel like a king if they wanted that. Sex was almost irrelevant in her services. She traded delirium, a treasure of experience, and had made a healthy living from it, so that ten years ago she'd been able to step from public attention and begin to train others to do her work for her. Advances in software had aided her activities: it became so much easier to transfer her ideas via simple neural links. She picked the best. All her people bloomed beneath her tutelage and enjoyed the lessons thoroughly.

They enjoyed the power she gave them more. It irked her that, because of city custom, she was not allowed by the zonal authorities to move her operation from Sector 23. The welfare committees liked to compartmentalise citizens' activities and, despite her insistence that she should be allowed to install her firm in a luxury hotel uptown, which she could easily afford, had received continued refusal for a permit. What she and her employees were capable of made people in positions of authority uneasy. It was only a small step to remove her talents from the realms of giving pleasure to the realms of taking control. They knew that. She knew that. But Jahsaxa had no interest in government. She was quite happy in her chosen *métier* and wanted only to expand and improve what she could offer. However, she was also aware the majority of her patrons considered it part of the adventure, the sense of illicit fun, to take one of the few remaining subway trains to Sector 23 and climb, giggling and fearful, never in groups of less than three, up to the streets, where 'Street' was still a phenomenon, a lifestyle, a culture, and something to be feared by the comfortable up-towners. Perhaps her clientele wouldn't enjoy it as much if they had only to stroll a couple of blocks to reach a swanky, air-conditioned hotel, whose glass-fronted lobby would be open to the street.

Five years ago she had hit on the idea that had made her famous, rather than notorious, and very rich indeed. Working with a one-time client, a mindprogrammer employed uptown by an esteemed neuro therapy clinic, she had devised the single most orgasmic, cosmic, shattering experience ever. The idea had come after she'd seen an old horror movie on her vidscreen. By combining sex and death within a single, riveting experience, she had engendered a coupling of minds and bodies from which the participants could expect to emerge totally reborn and cleansed. But for the sexual element, religions everywhere would have been clamouring to emulate the technique. Her competitors snidely dubbed it the Suicide Sex Trip, and liked to spread exaggerated stories about what could happen to someone if they had a bad time. Jahsaxa ignored such rumours. Her people were too highly-trained for any of her clients ever to have a bad time under her roof. Still, the technique could take its toll on those who performed it, who took the lead. Sourly, Jahsaxa could not deny that there were more than a few burnt-out husks scuffling round Sector 23 who'd once been in her employ. Some people just weren't hardy enough to take it long-term. Luckily, because of the extremely attractive salaries she offered and enormous perks, there was no shortage of people willing to take the places of those that withered. She told them right from the start, 'You have to be strong to take this on,' and how many of those canny little street-grubbers could resist such a challenge? They all thought they were the toughest people alive, citing the hardness and emotional barrenness of their lives as testament to that fact. Some were obviously telling the truth and Jahsaxa had learned from them. As she became more familiar with the technique and its effects she had fewer casualties, but it was necessary for her people to 'dry out' every few months. Dr Parmedes took care of that. He had connections. He did quite a lot for Jahsaxa in fact, in exchange for free services. Now that wonderful, talented man had given her the ultimate. Not only had she snared the impoverished Zambia Crevecoeur, but she'd had Parmedes transform him into the most splendid vehicle of pleasure his brand of surgery could provide.

In its crudest terms, Crevecoeur should now be

bristling with sex organs, male, female, bits and pieces that were something of both, and all concealed in convenient nooks and crannies around his body. It was a new idea she'd had, having become bored with providing technologically-manipulated experiences. It was time, she thought, to return her attention to the realm of the flesh and the flesh alone. She'd known she would have to wait until the right person presented him or herself to take advantage of it. Then that blissful day had come: Zambia Crevecoeur desperate and starving. Perhaps she'd had it in mind all along, just waiting for him to be smoked out of his lair by unemployment. When she'd explained a little of her plans to him, his initial reaction had been sheer delight. He'd been very drunk of course. 'That's amazing!' he'd said. 'Can they really do that?'

'Of course,' she'd answered, fingers crossed behind her back. Parmedes had only been experimenting, but Crevecoeur must never know the doctor had paid *her* to redesign him rather than the other way around. It was important for Crevecoeur to trust her implicitly. The training demanded it. Of course, she'd guessed the boy would start having doubts eventually (who wouldn't for the Goddess' sake?), and had prudently had him tailed to the clinic in case he lost his nerve at the last minute and had to be physically coerced into fulfilling his appointment with Dr Parmedes. Luckily it had not been necessary. Jahsaxa was happy. She had never looked into Crevecoeur's mind. She thought him essentially a simple creature.

Club Eleusis itself occupied only the first seven floors of Jahsaxa's property. From the eighth floor up, she leased it out to various independent enterprises, all of which were of use to her. The rotor pad and arbour garden on the roof were available to all occupants, residential or otherwise. She was a benevolent landlady, she felt, and looked upon everyone within the building as part of one amorphous family. Her most recent offspring she installed in a modest suite of rooms on the third floor. For the time being Zambia would be as compliant as a puppy, but she was shrewd enough to realise his returning faculties might possibly result in a certain desire for independence. There was only one window in the suite, a small one in the showercubby. Jahsaxa did not intend to take unnecessary risks.

Her other employees were all desperately curious about Crevecoeur and she saw no reason not to be as open as possible about it all. It would only incite ridiculous intrigues otherwise. On the day of Zambia's arrival, Jahsaxa took two of her most trusted operatives in to see him. Like all her people, they were physically superb, dark-haired sirens of an oriental caste. Jahsaxa had had Zambia put to bed and thoroughly doped. He needed the rest to recover, she thought. Genoa and Haiku were sensible girls. They praised Jahsaxa's ingenuity and Zambia's beauty, the latter of which was hardly deserved at the time. Jahsaxa glowed beneath their compliments however.

'I want you both to keep an eye on him,' Jahsaxa said. 'I'm sure he will undergo some trauma once his mind's cleared.'

'Well, yes, I mean, is he strictly a "he" now?' Genoa giggled. Jahsaxa shot her a stern, hurt glance.

Haiku, more diplomatic, defused the statement. 'I've heard that up in Alexandrican, all the intersexes use a different term. It helps them adjust apparently; gives them a sense of unity.'

'Oh Hai, be reasonable, how can a single person have a sense of unity!' Genoa tended to have heavy feet sometimes.

136

'What is it, Haiku?' Jahsaxa inquired, ignoring the other girl.

'Well, it's hir and SHe,' Haiku replied, and then spelt the words out.

'That sounds female to me, but I don't suppose Zambia Crevecoeur will care!' Genoa said, and then linked a familiar arm through her employer's. 'Can we, like, take a look?'

Jahsaxa tolerated the contact for a few moments before drawing away. Yes, it might be best for the revelation to occur when others were present. She was aware of a slight trepidation. 'Very well. Haiku, would you see to it please?'

Haiku drew back the covers and lifted Zambia's shirt. 'Oh!' Jahsaxa said.

'Gross!' squealed Genoa. 'Oh wow!'

'Haiku, turn him, lift his arms!' Jahsaxa ordered. Haiku did so. 'Well, I expected more than that!'

Genoa was puzzled by Jahsaxa's disappointment. 'More than that? Are you kidding?'

Jahsaxa made an irritated gesture. 'Well, no matter.' She leaned forward to inspect Zambia's implants more closely. 'They're very convincing, I must say.'

Zambia was kept under sedation for a couple more days, during which time Dr Parmedes popped in now and again to monitor his patient's progress. He reassured Jahsaxa over the wisdom of Zambia's choice. 'A simple arrangement is far more artistic,' he said. 'I'm sure your clients will appreciate that more. Of course up north they're more inclined towards garish displays which, personally, I find quite revolting. This, on the other hand, is a simple yet devastating masterpiece.'

Jahsaxa didn't contradict him. Both herself and Parmedes were present when Zambia woke up properly for the second time since his operation, with Haiku at the bedside to hold the patient's hand. Parmedes had suggested the sedation should be stopped: at some time the intersex would have to face reality as what it was. Zambia appeared confused at first, naturally, and a great deal of fuss was made over a glass of water in order to divert the patient's attention from the recent surgery. The first thing Zambia was told was that he was now a SHe. This was blinked at in perplexity. Haiku had been thoroughly briefed on how to cope, so Jahsaxa and Parmedes withdrew to allow her informal, natural friendliness to sooth Zambia's return to reality.

Zambia clamped hir left hand to hir right shoulder and rubbed the large, tattooed scar there. Hir face twisted, hir head turned anxiously on the pillow, 'It's OK,' Haiku soothed and put her hand over Zambia's. 'You're wonderful. You really are.'

Zambia, remembering those horrific couple of days after the operation – the bright, sickening cheerfulness of the hospital staff, their complete incomprehension, or unconcern, of hir terror – hardly heard what Haiku said. SHe told hirself, 'You fool! You complete and utter fuckwit!' The shoulder was tingling like a reprimand, as if it was telling hir, 'That was the way out. You should have sought help from that direction. Pride brought you to this.' It was too much to bear. SHe began to weep; dry, painful sobbing. Haiku scooped the skinny body up in her arms and pressed it to her accommodating breast.

'You'll be fine,' she said, stroking Zambia's hair.

'I want to die!' Zambia replied.

The following day, Zambia smashed the water glass by hir bed and cut hir wrists. This, in addition to certain other information, forced Jahsaxa to admit she had a problem on her hands.

'Good afternoon, Indra's Network Inc.'

'Good afternoon. May I speak to Quincx Roirbak please?'

'This is artificial intelligence Woman-Form Zero Twenty-Two speaking, tag Mellissa. I am equipped to deal with all inquiries.'

'This is Jahsaxa Penumbra and I would like to speak with Quincx Roirbak please.'

'Mr Roirbak is working. I am instructed not to disturb him.'

'This is an emergency. I must insist I speak to Mr Roirbak.'

'What is the nature of your inquiry?'

'It is confidential.'

'You may leave a message after I have whistled a tone . . .'

'No! Look, I have work for Mr Roirbak. It's an unusual job. I'm sure he . . .'

'Beepp!'

'What? Oh for . . . ! Quincx, this is Jahsaxa. For Goddess' sake call me! Immediately! I need you! And, by the way, your answer service is a monumental stressor! Please be quick!'

Jahsaxa received Roirbak in her most relaxing salon. She needed all the help she could get to remain calm. Thank the Goddess he'd responded so quickly to her cry for help. Their friendship went back a long way: Jahsaxa had consulted him several times over the years concerning psychological problems she'd run into with her staff. Even when he'd moved on from his practice to work with the Tech-Greens, she'd maintained the contact. It was merely an added convenience that he had now become both rich and famous. 'Oh Quincx, I'm devastated. How was I to know intersexing surgery had been criminalised two weeks ago? It's not something that's discussed on the public networks is it!'

Quincx, enjoying a glass of Jahsaxa's best vintage brandy, pulled a wry face. 'You should have researched more, you and Parmedes both! If you'd bothered to consult me in the first place, I could have told you the neurological side-effects of the synthetic hormones they've been using can sometimes be catastrophic. You are a hairball sometimes, Sax.'

'So help me! I can't approach the neuro-clinics. Parmedes would be prosecuted! What can I do to sort this mess out? Stop the treatments?'

'Too late. Your subject will require a complete remapping. Anyway, if you stop the drugs now, it's likely the implants will just heal over. I don't suppose you want that, do you?'

'Don't look at me that way, Quincx!'

He shrugged. 'It's not my place to judge. Tell you what. I have a young man working with me at present whom I suspect is accomplished in dealing with neuro-sexual problems. Let me ask him if he can help you, huh?'

'Oh would you? Thank you Quincx!' She leaned down and planted a kiss on his forehead. 'I knew I could count on you.'

Tammuz Malamute was convinced he'd made the right decision in coming to Acropolis Park. He'd been worried that getting close to his old line of work might provoke more problems but, if anything, it had soothed him. He'd settled into a comfortable routine over the past couple of weeks. It had been enjoyable setting up the workrooms Roirbak had allotted him on the first tier gallery, and the computer he was working with was nearly as familiar as the one he'd had to sacrifice all those years ago. Even now, he couldn't help thinking that that had been an act of murder. As a penance for this crime, he lavished the benefits of his knowledge on the new machine, equipping it with virtual autonomy. Following this, he directed his attention to the canteen, cannibalising a couple of Roirbak's domestic droids to create authentic counter-staff. He programmed them with gourmet cooking skills and a meticulous sense of hygiene. Thus the canteen became a place where he could comfortably spend an hour or two reading every day, enwombed by the smell of fresh coffee and freesia-scented polish. Roirbak commented on the improvement. 'I never bothered with this section before,' he said. 'But it's actually pleasant to spend time in here now.'

Every evening, Tammuz made a point of venturing out into the club zones of Sector 23, drinking moderately, sampling whatever soft narcotics were available, and shaking his body to the vibrant sequentialfunk music. He wore his hair loose and dressed in black, which did very little to change his everyday appearance. Occasionally he indulged himself with the company of others. Nothing physical, because he felt uncomfortable with such things nowadays, but suggestive conversation could be just as stimulating, coupled with the right sultry eyes. If his companions were ever disappointed that he always went home alone, they never complained.

He pushed all the possible consequences of his being at Roirbak's to the back of his mind. After all, it might never happen. Years had passed. Things might have changed. People might even have died, Goddess forbid. He wanted nothing to upset the precarious rhythm he'd established in his new life. Roirbak was still a fascinating person, and Tammuz enjoyed their daily meetings. Whatever Roirbak had intended when his guest arrived, they now met up several times a day, having found they had so much to talk about. Tammuz was grateful Quincx never inquired too persistently what he was getting up to in his workroom. If he'd been asked, Tammuz would have been stumped for an answer anyway. All he'd done was idly tinker around with the computer, nose through the public information network and catch up on recent works in his field. He told himself he needed time to get back into things but really he was subconsciously distancing himself from his old theories. Life was too sweet at present to spoil. He did not want to be attacked by pangs of responsibility.

His first reaction was to be faintly annoyed when Quincx came into his workroom one afternoon and suggested he might like to take on the job for Jahsaxa Penumbra. He tried one or two excuses. 'I haven't done anything like this for years. It was only part of my initial training. I've forgotten most of it. I changed fields.'

Roirbak ignored it all. 'Tammuz, I feel it will be good for you to establish a reputation of your own around here. After all, you won't be hiding under my wing for ever, will you?'

Tammuz had been stung by that and grew sulky. 'But a prostitute?' he said grumpily. 'It's so sordid!'

'Listen, the poor creature is a victim. Tried to kill itself the other day. Have you no pity?'

Tammuz couldn't help smiling. 'That was very insincere, Mr Roirbak.'

Roirbak shrugged. 'Well, whatever. Do it for me then.

I'd like you to. I want to see what you can do.'

Tammuz glanced at him sharply. 'OK. If you really want me to.'

'You'll be paid well too,' Roirbak added. 'Look on it as a challenge.'

Tammuz sighed. 'People only say that when the job is shitty,' he said mournfully.

Roirbak patted him on the back. 'Good boy. An initial consultation is all set up. The address is on Mellissa's file – a hotel somewhere.'

'Naturally.'

'Just take a look, you don't have to commit yourself.'

Tammuz nodded, sucking his upper lip.

'Well, see you later then. Have fun.' Roirbak sauntered off, calling over his shoulder. 'I'll get the droids to hold dinner till you get back!'

Tammuz addressed his computer. 'If this job comes off and the pay's good enough, I'm going to build you a manform that looks just like me, then you can handle all this shit.' He put his feet up on the workstation. 'What a drag!'

Tammuz was already waiting by the time Zambia Crevecoeur arrived at the hotel. Jahsaxa's sense of humour was at its most needling that afternoon; the establishment was one of those owned by the Godsarmy Corporation. It was named The Holy Innocent. Zambia began cursing directly after Jahsaxa's rotor dropped hir off on the roof. SHe was dressed as a smart young woman: hair coiled behind hir head, sharpheeled shoes, and any inner wounds concealed behind mirrorshades and a savage, blood-red, painted smile. SHe carried a small case.

Tammuz Malamute had filled the elegant, pale suite

with odd-smelling smoke and was lying on the giant, oval-shaped bed, fully clothed, his heavy boots torturing the cream-coloured quilt. A plastic bottle of cheap gin rested on his stomach. Zambia stood in the doorway, unsure whether to be appalled or relieved, before succumbing to an attack of nausea and fleeing to the bathroom to compose hirself. SHe supposed this must be hir first client for Club Eleusis. Jahsaxa had been infuriatingly secretive about it all, simply telling hir to meet a man named Tammuz Malamute in this room. To Zambia's currently untrustworthy senses, the man appeared to be some kind of natro tramp. Jahsaxa had taken no chances since the suicide bid; Zambia's mind was fuzzy with narcotics, and had been since SHe'd been patched up. The whole incident, blood and all, now seemed unreal. But even through a mental fog. Zambia still felt SHe was living in the body of a stranger, and that the two of them did not particularly like each other. The harsh halo-lights around the hotel mirror did nothing to contest that. Hir skin looked yellow, waxy, and hir smile appeared even more moronic than usual, illustrating plainly that the body reflected in the glass was not a happy machine. The heavy make-up might lend a semblance of life if not examined too closely, however. SHe stripped off the expensive suit Jahsaxa had given hir and shrugged hirself into a cream silk robe. It felt cool against the skin. Zambia rooted in the bottom of hir carrying case, found a small file of tiny pills and swallowed two. After a moment or two, SHe gritted hir teeth, attempted to regulate hir drunken heartbeat with a visualisation of placid waters, and went into the bedroom.

This man. SHe decided, must be important to Jahsaxa Penumbra. Zambia was sure the woman wouldn't bestow this privilege on just anyone. (It had been pounded into hir brain for days just what a privilege SHe amounted to.) Tammuz Malamute, however, did not strike Zambia as Jahsaxa's type. He appeared to be a scrawny bag of unhealthy-looking bones, but then the drugs SHe'd been taking had a tendency to warp hir perception. SHe turned around, disguising hir appraisal of the man beneath a smile. His neck was hung with totems, his personal gods, some of them new feather-and-bead confections with painted faces, others old and ragged, about due to disintegrate completely. Crevecoeur's smile turned acid. Gods; what use had they been to this person, what protection? He looked *terminal*. What use were they to anyone? Natro bullshit! *If that's your trip, brother . . .*

'You are the startling creature then,' Tammuz said in a slightly slurred voice, successfully diverting Zambia's uncomfortable train of thought. It was hardly a propitious start to the transaction however.

'Startling in what way?' SHe asked.

Tammuz swigged from the bottle. He grimaced. 'Let's just say you're more impressive than I imagined,' he said, wriggling into a sitting position. 'I mean, the surgery, the drugs – that's nothing new; but this . . .' He gestured, pulled down the corners of his mouth. 'It's more than superficial. Must be the hormonal treatment, right? That's an achievement.'

'You make it sound as if I should be drip-fed through bars,' Crevecoeur said. Tammuz Malamute's dispassionate appreciation made hir feel like a dog with two heads.

Tammuz took another swig of the gin. 'No, not that, but I wouldn't let you run round the streets if I were Jahsaxa Penumbra either. Well, not until I'd duplicated the experiment enough for it not to matter.'

By this time Crevecoeur had developed a positive dislike for the man. SHe wondered what exactly Penumbra had had in mind when she'd sent hir to him.

Tammuz leaned forward, peering intently. 'So what *were* you, before all this?' he asked.

Crevecoeur stood up, sighed. So this is where it began. SHe slipped off hir robe. 'You don't wanna know that, soul. Not really.'

Tammuz narrowed his eyes, thankful at that moment he'd taken the precaution of getting drunk. He couldn't help flinching back from what he saw. Still, it was quite impressive. The figure before him could hardly be termed an object of desire; it was something else entirely. It was a manifestation of fantasy that should be confined to the imagination. This creature of flesh and blood and bone was perhaps too crude a thing to admire. He could understand now why the poor fuck was in such a state.

'I sold my life,' Zambia said coldly, and then furiously displayed some of hir body's functions.

Tammuz tried to smile. 'Interesting,' he said.

'That's one word for it, I guess.' Zambia adopted an aggressive pose, hands on hips. 'So where do you want me, and how?'

'Sitting over there in the chair with your robe on will be fine.'

'What is this?' Zambia flung the robe around hir shoulders. 'Changed your mind?'

'It wasn't made up.' Tammuz stood up and Zambia backed into the chair. Tammuz pointed at the cuts on hir wrists, neatly sealed. 'Why did you do that?'

Zambia hid hir arms in the sleeves of hir robe. 'None of your business. Look Mr Malamute, save the chit-chat for Penumbra. My job involves one thing. If you want that, we get on with it. If you don't, I leave. I'm in no mood for small talk.'

'Are you this friendly with all your clients? You must earn your employer a fortune. Or is this behaviour traditional for you people?' Zambia remained sullenly silent. 'Very well. This was a stupid idea. The wrong place to deal with it. You've no idea who I am, have you?'

'Should I?'

'I don't want to screw you, Zambia, so relax.'

Zambia couldn't help asking, 'So what are you here for then?'

'For proof maybe,' Tammuz replied. 'I suspect Ms Penumbra intended me to, shall we say, delve deeper for it, but I'm really not into that. You're in a real mess, aren't you?' Tammuz shook his head. 'We'll see what we can do.'

'What?'

'Ms Penumbra can be reached at Club Eleusis, I take it?'

Zambia shrugged. 'Probably.'

'Then I'll speak to her.' Tammuz picked his jacket up off the floor and moved towards the door.

'Is that it?' Zambia asked.

'For the time being. Take care.'

Zambia watched him leave, amazed. SHe was totally confused about what had just occurred. Another of Jahsaxa's games, no doubt. After a moment, SHe went back into the bathroom, got dressed and washed hir face. What was going on? What had been the point of all this? Malamute had thought SHe was a freak. This was too humiliating! What the hell was Jahsaxa playing at? Hir mind was too disordered for further conclusions to be reached.

Back in the bedroom, SHe called Jahsaxa on the

commset. SHe felt SHe ought to complain in some way, but it was too much effort.

'Are you alone?' Jahsaxa asked immediately.

'Yeah. He's gonna call you.'

'You don't sound too happy, Zambia.'

'I'm not. You know why? That guy wasn't one of your monied misfits needing a thrill. He barely kept his liquor down when he saw me. What's going on? Who is he?'

'Oh Zambia, I'm sorry. I should have warned you. He's a genius. I need him for a job. That's all you need to know for now. I thought you'd prick his interest.'

'More than I interested his prick.'

Jahsaxa ignored the remark. 'I'll have transport waiting for you on the hotel roof, Zambia. Get right out there and come home. Do you feel all right?'

'Yeah, yeah, fine.'

'Good. Now, I have some of the committee of Club Minerva coming over tonight. We're going out for a meal. Would you like to come?'

'I'm not hungry.'

'Zambia, I'd like your company.'

Why did she have to use that tone? Zambia felt hirself relenting. 'Oh, all right. As long as you don't tell them about me.'

'I have no intention of doing so.'

Tammuz decided to continue Jahsaxa's little melodrama in his own way. In the hotel lobby, he called Club Eleusis. As well as being curious about the woman, and for that reason interested in meeting her, he thought it best to enter into the spirit of the thing and behave in a way Penumbra might like. This was more fun than going to a club for the evening. He arranged to meet Ms Penumbra later on, in a location of his choice, leaving him enough time to slip into one of the clubs for an alcoholic top-up. The image of Zambia slipping off hir robe kept flashing into his mind; his feeling of shock, the ghastly resignation on Zambia's face. The look was the worst. Jahsaxa had sent him a simple message by getting Zambia to do that, and the message sickened him.

Jahsaxa Penumbra had not been pleased by Tammuz Malamute's call. It necessitated summoning her personal limo – a ground vehicle of statuesque proportions – and taking a short ride through the city. Jahsaxa disliked journeys of this nature and disliked even more the bizarre rendezvous point Malamute had stipulated. Two of her security staff followed behind. Sector 23 was just beginning to stretch into wakefulness after a quiet day's slumber. Early evening street hawkers were emerging from the pleasure palaces, preparing to advertise their wares. At one point, her vehicle was detained by an incident in the street; rival hawkers, still bad-tempered from the previous night's dissipations, had engaged in conflict after one of them had ventured on to the other's territory. A large crowd of interested spectators had gathered to watch, some calling out encouragements to the combatants. Jahsaxa had been forced to direct her chauffeur, Grendel, to leave the vehicle in order to exterminate both hawkers before the journey could proceed. They left a cheering crowd behind them.

Now she had reached the appointed meeting place, situated in one of the subways, where the lower reaches of the city could be accessed. She stood tapping her nails against a hot water conduit, the echo of it pealing right off up the conductor passage. It was hot and steamy down there. She did not feel alone and was grateful for the protection of her concealed weaponry. A metallic echo. Scraping of boots. Her hand nonchalantly glided to her hip, rested there. A shadow against the bright light of the inspection floods up the passage. Archetypal halo. Man with legs akimbo. Jahsaxa stubbed out her cigarette and ground it underfoot. What was this man playing at? She didn't feel comfortable so far from the protection of her house, her aides, her automated guardians, even though she knew Grendel and two lesser succourants waited just above her head, alert to the slightest, minutest sounds of distress, and would come tearing through the grillways like missiles if she should need them.

'Malamute, I must insist we have no more meetings like this,' she said to the silhouette some yards away from her. 'There was a perfectly good hotel room laid on for your use. I would have visited you there had you asked.'

The figure advanced. 'I prefer my own territory.'

'Was the show to your liking?' She withdrew a wafery sliver of silver from her coat, took another needle-like cigarette from it. The wafer also supplied a light. She did not offer one to her companion.

'Freak show, Penumbra, freak show.' Tammuz Malamute sat down on a wide conduit, to warm his butt as much as to ease his limbs. Jahsaxa remained standing.

'Your subjective opinion does not interest me. Your professional one does. Well?'

'How could I tell from such short acquaintance?'

'You had the opportunity for longer . . .'

Malamute made a sound of disgust. 'No thanks. I like real people. Primitive I know, but I'm an old-fashioned guy. My opinion? Hmm. Tell me exactly what you expect from me first.'

'Your talents have come to my attention.'

'Indeed.'

'Yes. Mr Roirbak spoke very highly of you. I find

myself in an embarrassing predicament. How much did Quincx tell you?'

Tammuz decided to play careful. 'Not much. What I saw tonight was enough to tell me the score. You want to keep your little monster in business, right?'

'Well, at least alive,' Jahsaxa answered stonily. 'You can do that. Quincx says so.'

'Maybe. Maybe.'

Jahsaxa sighed. 'Tammuz Malamute. Don't try to play games. I really have no time for that, pleasurable though it may be. Will you work for me or not?'

Tammuz grinned. 'I might give you more than you bargained for . . .'

'Meaning?'

Tammuz shook his head. 'All that surgical stuff was never really my field, but I tinkered with psychology a little. I'm giving your petition serious consideration.'

'I am grateful, Mr Malamute,' said Jahsaxa Penumbra. 'But I need a more positive reaction than that.'

'Now, there's only one thing to fix,' Tammuz continued cheerfully. 'You tell me what's an offer for this little favour, and I'll tell you just how interested I am, huh?'

Jahsaxa pulled a face. 'Surely Quincx has discussed this with you?' she snapped sharply, affronted. Penumbra did not like to discuss finance under these circumstances. The circumstances, altogether, displeased her. 'It will be enough, I assure you. Well?'

Malamute dragged his boots over the metallic stone. He had, of course, already made up his mind before coming here to take the project on, yet thought it politic to make the woman suffer a little before giving in. It made for better future relations. 'I'll certainly think about it.'

'Not good enough,' Jahsaxa said smoothly. 'You've had the time for that. Why did you insist on meeting me down here in this . . . this filth hole? I need an answer now, and won't take no, I warn you.'

'I cannot promise results. Not yet.'

'Don't misinterpret me. I haven't asked for that. Only your commitment. Don't be a fool Malamute. This is the best offer you'll get around here. And there are other people equally as talented as you. Just thank whichever aspect of the Goddess you adopt that I came to you first.'

'It's not that I don't appreciate your offer. I like a private life.'

'I don't intend to advertise, Mr Malamute. In my business, one comes to appreciate discretion and silence very quickly.' Her patience running out, Penumbra rummaged in a coat pocket and produced a wafer of plastic. 'Here. Take this. An advance, if you like. It operates any terminal in the city and will pay you 2000 creds. I don't care for this place Mr Malamute. I've indulged you enough and expect to see you at Club Eleusis tomorrow morning. Goodnight.' She began to walk away. Malamute stood up.

'I hope the hardware can stand up to the software,' he said.

Jahsaxa turned briskly on her heel. 'The hardware is the best, Mr Malamute, and upgraded to perfection. Again, goodnight.'

Although Lydia had remained tight-lipped over whatever she and Leila Saatchi had talked about, she had helped Ari pack her bags, making an effort to hide whatever dissatisfaction she was feeling.

'Leila said she knew my dad,' Ari said, adding carefully, 'You know her too, don't you.'

Lydia shrugged. 'A long time ago, yes.'

'You must have known her quite well. I mean, to let her change your mind about me going and all.'

Lydia furiously zipped Ari's bag, her mouth clamped bloodlessly. Ari could tell she wouldn't say what she was thinking. 'She'll look after you,' she said, sourly; then brightening up and saying, 'Mightn't you need these one day?' waving Ari's box of computer disks in front of her face. That meant she must have read them and knew what they contained. It no longer seemed relevant to complain about the invasion of privacy.

'Yeah, thanks,' Ari said, and put the disks in her bag.

'And this, huh?' Lydia held out the old instant-picture camera Ewan had once bought for them. A lump swelled quickly in Ari's throat. She blinked, painfully remembering the many times she and her mother had used it, the bright squares of smiling faces and sunshine that were once pinned up on the corkboard in the kitchen.

153

The photos had rotted a long time ago. Nothing ever got pinned on the board now, and neither she nor Lydia had used the camera for years. 'There are a few unused films left,' Lydia continued bravely. 'They might have gone off, but . . . well, I thought it'd be good for you to take pictures along the way. Send some back to me, maybe.'

Ari stuffed both camera and film cartons into her bag. This was terrible. She wished the leave-taking was over.

Before she left the house, Lydia hugged her, a ritual gesture, and told her to keep in touch. Ari wondered whether her mother would cry or wait to do that until she'd gone.

'Will you be all right?' Ari asked.

'Sure, sure. Get going now.'

'I really think you should get someone in to live here with you . . .'

'Ari, I'm not an invalid! I'll be fine. Look, they're waiting.' Lydia rubbed her face nervously, putting Ari on edge. She felt Lydia wanted to cry, 'Get out! Get out!' Perhaps Leila had frightened her in some way, even threatened her.

'You really think I'm doing the right thing, Ma?'

Lydia sighed, a shuddering sound. She smiled weakly. 'You wanted to go last night.'

'I know that. That's not an answer.'

'Your father trusted Leila Saatchi implicitly a long time ago, believe me,' she said coldly. 'There's no reason why we shouldn't now.'

'OK,' Ari said quietly and walked out of the house without looking back. She wanted to ask questions about just what the relationship had been between her parents and Leila Saatchi, but it was clear Lydia would not tell her anything. It was an uncomfortable leave-taking.

The trucks stood gently heaving as their preliminary mechanisms warmed up, just beyond the chalets which were now automatically locked until the next festival. Ari glanced up at the Bump, wondering if she'd catch a last glimpse of Sammael between the menhirs. The place looked deserted; in daylight the monoliths appeared decayed and tawdry, damaged by weather and time. Perhaps it would not be long until the Bump ceased to function completely and Sammael was left to stand alone without purpose until he just became part of the dust himself. Ari shuddered. The Bump had never felt this impermanent to her before. She hung around the back of the trucks, watching the activity of Star Eye's removal. She noticed the trucks had names: Spirit of Disorder – the smaller of the two – and Rentfree Aphrodite. The names made her smile; the trucks exhibited neither the fleetness conjured to mind by the word spirit nor the beauty of Aphrodite. Rentfree and disorder might be accurate however. Jordan came up holding a wet finger in the air. 'We better catch the tail of that breeze and set ourselves west pretty soon,' he said. A Star Eye man pulled himself from the Spirit's gut, oily bandana round his head, grease to elbow and said. 'What she smell of?'

'Nothin' bad,' Jordan replied ponderously, 'but it's a sassy breeze. You never know.' Ari was intrigued by this esoteric exchange, standing there smiling to herself until Justinette breezed along, long coat flapping and said, 'Don't stand there gawpin' girl!' before bundling her up the corroded metal steps of the Spirit of Disorder. 'Claim yourself a seat,' she instructed, gesturing at the heaps of cushions which were held in place by rope netting bolted to the floor. The inner walls of the truck were also swathed in heavy, rope netting, hung with rather wizened vegetables and unidentifiable pieces of cloth.

'Where are we going?' Ari asked, bewildered, sitting down. Suddenly, she felt breathless, as if everything was speeding up. Half of her wanted to bolt. Justinette took Ari's bags off her and climbed up the netting to stow them with the tepees on overhead racks. Through the open slide-door, Ari could see people jumping up into the other truck, throwing their remaining unstowed belongings ahead of them. She drew up her legs to avoid getting trampled as someone else clambered into the Spirit.

'Where we going?' Justinette asked the girl who'd just joined them. Ari was immediately wary of her. Not just because of her height, which made the girl tall and intimidating, but because her personality felt sharp and slightly hostile. Her unruly hanks of black-and-white hair were speared with sharp sticks.

'Well, Leila mentioned something about Arcady,' she answered, giving Ari a narrow stare. Then she smiled thinly. 'I'm Elice.' Ari moved along to let the girl sit down. Justinette flopped down beside her.

'So, you're joining the family then?' Elice said, as if the prospect was not the least bit attractive to her.

Ari nodded, unsure how to react. She didn't want to upset anyone this soon.

'That was some show last night,' Elice continued abrasively. 'You do that every festival?'

'Elice!' Justinette interrupted, elbowing the girl in the ribs. 'Don't bitch!' She smiled at Ari encouragingly. 'You ever been to Arcady before?' she asked.

Ari shook her head, shrugged. She didn't want to say that she'd never been anywhere.

'Ah, I love it!' Elice said. 'Oh, hi Zoo, come to ride with us, have you?'

A young black woman, with a huge pile of tangled

dreadlocks scraped up into a topknot, was leaning through the door. 'Nah, no way!' she exclaimed. 'Just come to say hello to our new friend here an' wish her the best. She'll need it travellin' with you scuzzies!' She extended a slim hand. 'I'm Ezooli.' Ari leaned over to shake it.

'Hi, er – thanks.' Ari was conscious of Elice's disapproval.

'Well, see you later, souls!' Ezooli skipped off towards the other truck, waving a farewell to the last two people about to board the Spirit: an older woman in a striped blanket-coat and a limber young man, who to Ari's eyes appeared half naked, his clothes were so ripped up. The woman settled herself on some cushions apart from the others, while the man climbed the net rigging on the sides of the truck to secure his luggage aloft. Ari wondered what the others would think if she took out her camera now to see if it still worked. She decided she wanted pictures of all of Star Eye, but she felt it might annoy Elice. Still, there'd be plenty of opportunities later, once she'd settled in. Funny how the camera had so quickly lost all its depressing associations. Ari looked on this as a good omen.

Then Leila poked her head around the side door of Spirit, a blanket draped around her shoulders. 'Bolt up guys!' she said, and slapped her hand against the truck. She did not come inside.

Doors slammed, shutting out the raw gashes of sunlight and submerging the passengers in an oily, temporary dimness. The Spirit of Disorder uttered a low growl before rumbling into life, shuddering like some vast, waking reptile. 'Hold on!' Justinette shouted. 'Cable hasn't managed a smooth take-off yet!'

'Cable drives this rig,' Elice explained. Ari nodded

numbly, wondering how long her bones were going to hold together. The whole vehicle trembled to a symphony of accelerating whines and throbbings. Ari would not have been surprised if someone had told her the thing could sprout rotor blades and take to the air. 'Leila rides up front, in case you were wondering!' Elice yelled. 'See him over there? The guy with the sexy grin? That's Urran. He's a bastard, and that old tramp back there with her nose in her sack, that's Charcoal Eve. The others ride with Jordan.' Both Urran and Charcoal Eve looked up when they heard Elice's description of them being shouted over the din of the engines. Ari shrank back into her cushion. An uncomfortable ride in all senses was presaged, it seemed.

Once the truck got the feel of the road beneath her treads, the vibrations diminished and the noise level fell, a little. 'Of course the highways are impassable nowadays for anything flimsier than this,' Elice said airily. 'Once, back east, we were on this old highway and Jordan and Cable got an idea into their heads it'd be good to have a race. It was hell back here. We were being banged about all over the place, getting bruised to shit, when I found myself in Urran's lap, half unconscious: a horrible place to find yourself, in any state.' She grinned.

'What happened?' Ari asked, responding to cue.

'There was a damn great crack in the road up ahead, wide as you like. The land had just opened up. If our brakes hadn't been in shape we'd have fallen clear to the centre of the earth! They've never raced since, thank the Goddess.'

'Elice, you're full of shit,' Urran said, lighting up a cigarette. 'It was just a hairline.'

'Fuck off!' Elice cawed, 'and open a bloody window if you're going to smoke that shit.'

Urran leaned back and slipped the catch on one of the side windows, small portholes set deep in the armour-plating. He grinned goodnaturedly at Ari. 'You'll get used to her mouth,' he said. 'She goes on like that to try and hide the fact she's crazy about me, don't you honey?'

Ari didn't think she could bear to hear Elice's response and hurriedly blurted, 'So tell me about Arcady, then.'

'Arcady!' Justinette sighed and leaned back against her cushion, folding her arms over her belly. 'It's a pretty wild place in some areas. The areas we're likely to frequent, that is. There's some weird stuff goin' down around there. People can make a living doing all kinds of spooky shit. Some of it's dangerous, but well paid, if you get what I mean.'

'Not really.'

'Ask Cabochon, he'll tell you!' Justinette said with relish.

Elice giggled. 'Sure. Ask about his family, why don't you.'

'Leave it,' Urran said, sounding as if he meant it.

'She'll find out sooner or later,' Elice said waspishly.

'Yeah, well, maybe it shouldn't be from you.'

'That's all very noble, Urran,' Justinette said in a reasonable voice, 'but we're all cooped up together so much the lines become blurred between what's anybody's business. I reckon we're all so involved we share everything, crises included. Who was it comforted Cab the last time he had a blow-up with that guy? Huh? Me, wasn't it? Don't call me a gossip, Urran, or any of us. We've all had our share of shouldering Cab's grief over that.'

Charcoal Eve sitting further down the truck, who'd said nothing to anyone since they'd left the Bump, suddenly spoke up, 'The girl's right, Urran. When

Cabochon goes off the deep end, it affects us all.' She eyed the net-swathed glass partition between the group and Leila in the cab up front. 'If I were her, I'd leave the boy outside the city at Lazar Farm. It's not worth letting him screw himself up the way he does.'

'If Cab had any sense, he'd stay there anyway without being told,' Justinette said. 'Oh, sorry, Ari. We shouldn't be layin' this stuff on you. Not yet, anyway.'

Inevitably, and despite Justinette's efforts to help, Ari felt completely out of it in Star Eye's company. She could not join in the repartee, or participate in the flirting that went on between the three younger members of the group. It was obvious even to Ari, who was inexperienced, that Urran and Elice had, at one time, enjoyed some kind of physical relationship. She bitched; he glowed. Justinette occasionally defused the worst of their arguments. Ari felt Elice was not too pleased another young female had joined the group. When she wasn't ignoring Ari, she spat snide remarks, which sounded as if they were just witty, but which Ari knew were designed to hurt. She wished she could travel in the other truck with the people who'd made a point of coming to say hello.

To keep themselves occupied during their journeys, the group spent their time dreaming up and constructing new natro paraphernalia to be sold when the opportunity presented itself. While Justinette, Urran and Elice busied themselves with divination software on a beat-up computer, Ari was given a heap of materials and told to have a go at making some totems. She felt that too put her at a disadvantage. She sat there staring at the feathers and beads, wondering what was expected of her. Perhaps it was a test. The computer looked much more interesting. Luckily, Eve must have noticed her distress,

and shuffled through the quilts and cushions to lend a
hand. She told stories of spirits and threaded the beads
on leather. If you put a micro circuit-board between the
blue and brown beads, it helped conduct the energy of air
to earth, or so Ari was told. Between them, they put a
personal totem for Ari together. Eve made sure the
essence of Mother Fox was incorporated. 'Cunning
won't go amiss for a young girl in a new world,' she said,
nodding sagely.

Not long after noon, Justinette had given Ari a poke in
the ribs to offer her some food and a swig of warm water.
'We'll be in dry lands by evenin',' she said. 'If you want a
piss, or whatever, you'll have to go behind that curtain
back there. It'll go down into our cooler tank then. But,
be careful, the seat's a bit cold.'

'What!?' Ari squeaked, horrified. She had not considered what the toilet arrangements might be.

'We have to save everything,' Elice said. 'No use being
proud. Shit is currency on the road.'

'What she means is, we use all waste to create
methane,' Urran explained. 'Don't worry. You'll get
used to it.'

Ari could not imagine ever doing that. She waited
uncomfortably until the trucks stopped for the day.

In the late afternoon, Cable hauled the Spirit off the
road with a bone-grinding bump and rolled it to a halt
beside an abandoned farm, in a group of spindly, dead
trees: skeletons in a field of dust. Everyone scrabbled to
get out of the truck, causing Ari to wonder how they
could be full of energy when she felt so bone-tired. Her
ears were ringing from the constant vibration. The Spirit
of Disorder wheezed and sighed, giving off waves of dry
heat. Charcoal Eve, rotund in a muffle of coloured blanket coat, came and put her arm round Ari's shoulder.

'This is where we're stoppin' for the night. You can share my tepee if you like. Bin too big an' cold for me since my friend Rowan left the group, and I got no one to gossip to at nights.' Ari thanked her, although she was feeling raw from Elice's incessant bitching. As the rest of the group noisily unloaded the tents and set about powering up the cooking stoves, she half-heartedly helped the older woman erect the tepee. Jordan and Cabochon were building a fire, Leila sitting on the Aphrodite's steps swigging from a bottle, watching. Ari wondered whether Cabochon had a thing going with one of the group; he was so beautiful. Surely one of the girls, Elice particularly, must have claimed him as hers. Nobody approached him with confident intimacy however. If anything, Cabochon appeared to be given a wide berth. Perhaps it was her imagination, fired by hope, making her see that.

She hovered around for a few minutes but it seemed she'd become invisible. Eve had bustled off to do some chore or another and Leila was nowhere to be seen. There was a glorious moon crawling up the sky, nearly full, the sky itself still pink in the west where a dark red sun sank into the horizon. Ari walked away from the camp, out into the flat dustfields that had once been fertile land. Cornstalks still lay in the dirt, pocked with spots of fungus. Ari kept on walking until the voices of Star Eye had become indistinguishable from the night. She sat down on the crest of a slope, looking over the dry bed of a dried-out pool, resting her chin on her knees. It was hard to beat down the voice inside her whispering that she had made a mistake leaving home. She could not imagine ever being able to fit in with these people. Everyone else's amiability was eclipsed by Elice's sharpness. All day, the girl had tried to make it clear that they had no need for newcomers. Leila had hinted to Ari that she was special in some way; it was possible the other girls resented that. All Urran's attempts to be friendly to her had prompted such vicious retaliation from Elice – joking acidly about her lack of knowledge in all areas of natro life – that Ari had eventually avoided his eyes for fear of further attack. Normally she would have given Elice the same treatment back, but was too conscious of the strange environment, her ignorance of the right terminology. Elice would make mincemeat out of her. Sitting there in the twilight, Ari submerged herself in a mudpool of self-pity and rolled right through it. Even her mother hadn't cared she was leaving. Ari didn't know what had transpired between Lydia and Leila, but it was clear Lydia had no qualms about just handing her over. The outcome had been what Ari wanted, but she would have felt better if her mother had at least made a show of fighting. Ari also wanted to talk to someone about the things she'd learned about herself: surely that was a mother's job? She would be travelling in close proximity to people like Urran; attractive and sexually active males. What effect would that have on her? Who is going to help me deal with this? Ari wondered. I don't know any of these people well enough to confide in them. Since leaving the house, Leila had distanced herself, as if Ari had instantly become just another girl in the group. The future seemed so unclear.

I am unwanted, Ari thought mournfully. I am merely the product of Ewan Famber, nothing more. She thought about Sammael standing alone among the Menhirs of Taler's Bump, the twisty path through the forest, all her secret places of power. She had been a fool to leave them. This was not the answer. She lowered her head even further to indulge in a little poignant sobbing when the sound of her name came floating thinly through the cool air. 'Aree! Aaa-ree!!'

It sounded like Justinette. There was a pound of feet behind her and then Justinette was throwing herself down breathlessly on the ground at her side. 'Aren't you hungry?' she asked and then noticed Ari was not at all cheerful. 'Aw, c'mon! What's up?'

Ari felt embarrassed at having been caught like this. She didn't want the others thinking she was soft. She scrubbed at her face.

'Nothing. This place makes me sad. It's so empty.'

'Uh-huh!' Justinette leaned back on stiff arms, wiggling bare toes in the dirt. 'Gets worse you know, once we hit the highway. Just desert from sky to sky all round.' She flicked a sharp glance at Ari. 'Don't let anyone get to you.' she said. 'They all have their problems.' Then she linked her arm through Ari's and dragged her to her feet. 'Race you back, soul! Stretch those legs! Yeah! Come on!' She was already halfway back to the camp; a distance not as far as Ari thought she'd walked. Ari could run like a deer. Her long, skinny limbs pumped her past Justinette in no time. The exercise and the glow of beating the other girl had thoroughly dried her tears by the time she reached the first fire.

Leila Saatchi rolled her head and massaged the protesting muscles at the back of her neck. 'A rest never does me good,' she said. 'I only have to get used to being thrown around again!' She was sitting in the cab of Jordan's truck, a laptop commset on her knees, sharing a fragrant smoke of real hash – as opposed to the Arcady-produced synthetic garbage they usually had to make do with. Leila had just contacted Quincx Roirbak, who'd apologised for being unavailable.

'You and your projects,' Leila had said to him, affec-
tionately. 'So, what do you think?' She had related all
the events concerning Ari.

Quincx had pondered for a moment or two. 'Well, it
would seem that Ewan wasn't as crazy as we'd thought,'
he answered. 'Once you bring her here, we'll have more
of an idea. How's she taking it?'

'Seems all right. I haven't told her much yet.'

'Hmm. Perhaps you should, as soon as possible. If
Ewan's theories have become reality, then the poor child
has probably been experiencing mild abnormalities
already.'

'I don't want to frighten her, Quincx.'

'Leila Saatchi! Remember you are a scientist, for the
Goddess' sake, and be sensible! Remember when you
were that age: wouldn't you rather have known some
truth if you were in Ari's position? Young women are
more resilient than you think. Shame on you for forget-
ting that!'

'Point taken, Quincx. I'll talk to her.'

Leila had estimated that by the time Star Eye reached
the city, she should have had more than enough time to
help Ari get used to the change in environment.

Jordan had remained silent while she talked to Roirbak. He still emanated a strong aura of disapproval.
Leila badly wanted to unburden herself to him, even
though she knew he would only get angry. They had sat
quietly, but hardly in comfort, since Leila had finished
her call. She accepted the joint off him, noticing, as she
took a draw, that one of Cabochon's T-shirts was
stuffed between their seats. We are never alone, Leila
thought melodramatically. She began to speak.

'I really didn't think we'd find the Fambers, you
know. After all this time . . . I thought Lydia would have

moved or something. Hoped she had.' She shook her head. 'I should have known! If it wasn't for Ewan . . .'

Jordan reached over and kneaded the back of her neck. He sighed through his nose. Leila sensed his distraction. He hadn't wanted her to get involved in all this in the first place. 'You're making it a problem, gal,' he said. 'She's just a kid.'

Leila suppressed irritation. She had told Jordan nearly everything. 'She is not, and you know it!' Perhaps he hadn't been interested enough to absorb what she'd said. She sighed. 'Why did Ewan have to lay this on me? Why?'

'He didn't. He asked and you said yes. Isn't that so? And we know why that was! You worshipped the guy!' He gave her a narrow-eyed look, daring her to deny it. Leila resented him saying it. She'd known Ewan Famber for a long time before he died. Jordan had only been around for a year or so. She felt he had no right to comment on her feelings for an old friend, especially one who was dead.

'How many times do I have to tell you, Ewan was special,' she said. 'I don't know why it bugs you so much.'

'Yeah. I know. You tell me often enough. And if this kid's for real, I take back all I think about him.'

Leila laughed. 'Oh, come on, you were there last night. You saw.'

'I dunno what I saw. Do you?'

Leila grimaced. 'The readings we took from the menhir were pretty emphatic. There was a massive surge of energy when her nervous system was stimulated.'

'That doesn't prove the whole caboodle,' Jordan said.

'You don't know what that is!' Leila couldn't help responding acidly.

'True. And why? Because you won't show me the damn love-letter he left you.'

'It was not a love-letter! Please, Jordan, let's not fight.' Leila tried to calm herself. She didn't want another argument. Her cowardice, she felt, was despicable. She had every right now to turn to Jordan and say, 'You cannot criticise my feelings for someone else. This is because I know you are not faithful to me.' Was it any wonder their relationship was so shaky when this vast, fundamental factor was not even discussed? Jordan couldn't possibly believe she didn't know what was going on. He was always discreet, for which she was grateful, but Star Eye was such a small community. Absences were noticed.

She sighed deeply and sought to steer the conversation on to less dangerous ground. 'Goddess, this is one hell of a responsibility.'

Jordan, obviously prepared to compromise, took the commset off her lap and stowed it on the shelf above the truck's instrument panel. He put his arm around her and she sidled up against him, liking the way it made her feel young and protected. She could feel the stringy, steel-strong muscles of his arm through her shirt.

'Yeah, it is.' He squeezed her. 'But you'll handle it.' His voice echoed through his bony chest.

'I won't feel happy until we reach Arcady. I'd rather let Quincx handle it.'

'We'll be fine, don't worry.'

Leila put her hand upon his chest – dark, tanned skin. Jordan looked older than he was and yet such a boy at the same time. She experienced one of those regular moments of realising how deeply she loved him. It was a physical pain because it reminded her that she could lose him too. Lose him. If ever . . . No, don't even think it.

But the chain of thoughts prompted another. 'I wish we could leave Cab at Lazar's. I think it would be best.'

She sensed Jordan stiffen. Goddess, how that hurt. She wished she could control that pain. 'He wouldn't stand for that. You know that.'

'It's just we'll have enough on our plate without him throwing a tantrum.'

'That was a bit harsh. You know how he feels. How would you feel if it was your kin?'

She patted his skin. 'I know, I know. Sorry, it's nerves.' Leila winced inwardly at her own insincerity. She wanted to say, 'I've never had such a weird obsessive feeling for any of my family', but knew it would annoy Jordan if she did.

Jordan sighed. 'I'd give anything to break that little Arcady shit's neck – in cold blood.'

I know you would, Leila thought, bitterly. She pressed her face against him, inhaling deeply. 'I guess I should speak to Ari tonight,' she said, muffled against his shirt. Jordan stroked her hair.

'What you going to tell her?'

'Something about what she is. I suppose Quincx is right. There's no point in wet-nursing her too much.'

'It'll be a shock to her, won't it?'

'Probably, but she's bright and intuitive. I hope what I tell her'll bring relief, not pain or fear.'

Jordan made a sound of distaste. 'It's sick. It's like Famber was using that kid to live out some weirdo dream.'

'He was a scientist. It was nothing like that. You weren't there. Ewan was . . . totally unsentimental.'

'That what you call it? I call it sick.'

Leila took a deep breath. Maybe Ewan had been some kind of hero for her, maybe she'd looked up to him too

much, but it was impossible to explain to anybody who'd
never met him quite how special Ewan had been. There'd
been times when she'd hated Lydia Famber, looking on
her as insipid and whining. What had Ewan seen in a
woman like that? Once, Leila had seriously considered
murdering Lydia; a short-lived, drunken fantasy, but the
bright hot flame of passion she'd felt, anger sharp and
powerful as a sweeping blade, had been hard to keep
under wraps. Even after all this time, Leila thought that
walking into the Famber woman's house and demanding
Ewan's daughter was just about one of the best things
she'd ever done. That face, ruined now by age and
indulgence, no longer pretty, a thing to be pitied in fact,
but still with that sly, slack-lipped passiveness Leila
loathed of old. Leila had felt as tall and destructive as a
whirlwind. Lydia hadn't put up a fight really. There'd
been one or two blustering remarks which Leila had
swept aside with a blink of her eyes. At the door, Leila
had turned back, smiled sweetly, and said, 'I still miss
him, don't you? There's never been anyone like him for
me,' hoping to leave Lydia with the impression she'd
been more than a friend to Ewan once. Petty. The sort of
thing Elice would do on an extremely off-day, when she
was desperate. It didn't make Leila feel good about herself, knowing that, but there was no point denying it
either. The flame of jealousy still burned, after all these
years.

Star Eye regularly meditated together before each evening meal. While slabs of vat-grown meat-protein hissed
in its own fat atop one of the portable cookranges, everyone gathered around the fire which had been lit near the
trucks. Ari was beginning to feel more at ease since
Justinette had extended friendly overtures and her spirits

rose even further when Cabochon sat next to her and asked how her first day on the road had been. 'Takes some getting used to, I think,' she'd answered. He took one of her hands in his own and gave it a little squeeze. Ari's first impulse was to pull away, in anticipation of being scorched. This warred with her second impulse which was to squeeze Cab's hand back. The moment passed; he let her go. If he'd noticed her conflicting feelings, he didn't show it.

'You'll be fine. There ain't a better bunch of people anywhere else, believe me.'

She smiled. 'Thanks.' Ezooli, the black girl, plonked herself down on Ari's other side, a struggling baby in her arms.

'Hi Aree-Aree,' she said. 'Wanna hold my boy?'

Ari accepted the child. 'Thanks. What's his name?'

'Stickit,' Cabochon answered smiling, 'Or else, "Get that goddam critter out of my truck!" in some cases.'

Ezooli rolled her eyes, flashing perfect teeth, flicking a stray dreadlock out of her eyes. 'Jordan has no way with kids,' she said. 'Actually, his name's Stirrik, after my man's totem, but it got kinda changed.' She reached over and punched Cabochon in the arm. 'You!' He groaned and clutched himself.

'Mean punch mother!'

Again, Ari wished she was travelling in Rentfree Aphrodite. She felt sure she'd settle in quicker with a straight, friendly person like Ezooli around.

Leila jumped down from Jordan's truck and came to join them. 'Will you lead the viz tonight, Cab?' she said.

Ari noticed the boy seemed quite surprised to have been asked. 'What? Oh yeah, sure. You got anything in mind?'

Leila mussed Ari's hair. 'How about a welcoming for

our friend here,' she said. 'We'll have a talk later, kid. OK?'

Star Eye joined hands in a circle and, at Cabochon's direction, began to breathe together. Ari sucked in air through her nostrils, visualising its release mingling with everyone else's breath. Cabochon's hand was warm and dry in her own. An insidious sense of *belonging* crept over her with each indrawn breath. The atoms of her body were mingling with those of Star Eye, and vice versa. The taste of Cabochon must be on her tongue. Her fingers jerked in his hold and he gave them a reassuring squeeze. His voice carried her to a place where the grass was green beneath her feet and she danced in a circle with the others; one of them, part of them, star-born.

After Star Eye had gathered up the last of their scraps to be stowed in the cooler tanks with all the other rubbish, and begun to move towards their tepees or blankets under the stars, Cabochon wandered off into the fields, finding himself at the place where Ari had sat earlier. He skidded down the slope to the dead pool, poking the cracked mud with a stick. He knew Jordan must have said something to Leila, prompting her to ask his assistance with the meditation. He appreciated her doing that, being keenly aware of how she felt about him. The whole situation sickened him: he admired Leila Saatchi and didn't want to be a thorn in her side, the maggot in her soup, whatever.

He'd only been with the group for six months or so. His recruitment had happened at the Sow-hain festival, north-east in the mini-cluster city of Thebes Delta. He'd been scumming around for a year or so, tagging along with this group and that, learning about life away from the confines of Arcady society. He'd been hitching with a group of juggling fire-readers, throwing a few tumbles for the punters while the pyromancers moaned and swayed. The group had been putting on a show during the afternoon before the festival and a large crowd had gathered at the site. Cabochon remembered how good he'd felt that day, how excited. He'd always loved festivals, of course, but it had been more than anticipation. He'd danced like a dervish to the clay drums of his troupe, twisting his body, enjoying the experience of his own muscles. That's when Jordan had seen him. The intent face in the crowd had meant nothing more than a possible scrounge-source at first. Cabochon had flirted and displayed his body further for Jordan's benefit and the offer of shared drugs had been the reward. He'd been introduced to the rest of Star Eye, stuck around to share a meal or two and just ended up being part of them. It had quickly become clear Jordan was spoken for, even if Jordan didn't like to think so. An initial displeasure had given way to resignation once Cabochon found Leila to be the person she was. He'd just shrugged his shoulders and thought what the hell. Star Eye were good people. He liked their company; that was enough. It wasn't enough for Jordan, however. Fending him off became more of a ritual courtship than a defence, until the performance just had to reach its logical conclusion: a night under the stars communing with the Goddess. He'd half hoped his and Jordan's physical union would be a failure. Fate had decreed otherwise. And Leila knew, of course. Cabochon knew he would never terminate the relationship voluntarily, and the fact Jordan had a woman didn't matter. Cabochon wasn't selfish, but he also knew that three-sided relationships never worked unless all three people either consented to the arrangement or were actively involved in it. Leila would never go for that.

Now there was Arcady to contend with. Arcady and beloved brother: beloved, sick, selfish brother and his perverse occupation. 'You will stay away this time,' Cabochon told himself. 'You can do nothing, so you might as well stay away.' It had to be faced: he and his kin lived in different worlds now and had different views on reality. But it was hard to turn away. All their lives, it had been Cabochon who'd had to bail the other out of horrendous messes – moral, legal and otherwise; Cabochon who'd bound the wounds, placated the enemies, made his brother feel loved and secure. When he'd reached sixteen, it had all got to fever pitch. Their feelings for each other were so intense: fear, love, hate. Relationships with outsiders had foundered on the rocks of sibling sparring. The casualties had even been physical in one case – Cab's first and last girlfriend, who escaped the affair with a broken cheek-bone and dear brother's nail-marks down her face. The consequent fight Cab'd had with his brother himself was the nearest he'd ever come to being raped. It had to be admitted, it was time to leave the city. The problem should have been discussed, but he couldn't face it. Flight was preferable. He feared the outcome of rational discussion. It wasn't the physical implications which repelled him. Even incest would not be frowned upon in an environment like Arcady's where anything was permissible, but the mental side of it was like a devouring disease. In his darkest moments, Cabochon was convinced the only thing he and his brother wanted from each other was mutual extinction. It was easier once he'd left Arcady, although dark yearnings still tugged at his soul.

He'd lived with various natro groups for two years,

contacting Arcady as infrequently as he dared. It was like trying to give up a drug. *This time, I won't call him. I'll wait until the next time I think of it.* The situation was worsened by the fact he was aware his departure had only initiated his brother's descent into even more bizarre activities. Five months ago, only scant weeks after Cabochon had thrown in his lot with Star Eye, there'd been a horrific scene. Visiting Arcady with the group, he'd discovered down which avenues his brother's life had finally led him. He'd been faced with a diminished wraith, scrubbing out a life of prostitution, keeping alive from day to day using energy-boosting drugs because pickings had got so slim. It had hit Cabochon harder than he could have believed possible. He and his brother had once been so close, literally part of each other; in defiling himself, he was also defiling Cabochon. When this was pointed out, Cabochon was appalled to see an expression on his brother's face which suggested that that was one of his reasons for becoming what he had. Cabochon had begged him to get out of the city, ride with the natros for a while, re-evaluate things. This suggestion had been met with adamant refusal, and laughter.

'Brother I'm fine. I love this. Get out of here! Ha ha.' Cabochon had seen, through the pain, the spectre of death in that laughter.

Star Eye had been performing a minor ritual in one of the parks and Cabochon's brother had turned up with a few friends. Employing his usual knack for inflicting excruciating emotional agony, he'd seduced the most vulnerable of the group – Elice – and then provoked Cabochon into a fight. The rest was too sordid to think about. Cabochon had got very stoned and ended up having to be physically restrained by other members of the group. He remembered Jordan trying to calm him down, saying, 'For Goddess' sake, Cab, leave it. You just don't freak out like this over family relationships. People will think this is about something else.'

Cabochon winced as he recalled shouting back, 'And who says it isn't?' The others had found that highly entertaining. He was still trying to accept that his brother's self-destruct button was firmly pressed down, and maybe always had been. Only Cabochon knew this, or was aware of the bitter self-loathing in his brother's heart. On the surface, it appeared he didn't care about anything. It was a lie. Inside, his brother was slowly dying.

They were six scant weeks away from Arcady. Cabochon felt wretched. His whole body had been aching for days, his guts were in turmoil. The joints in his wrists throbbed as if they'd been recently broken. Was it presentiment that made him feel so depressed? Cabochon sat down in the dust and pressed the heels of his hands into his eyes. 'I love you, I hate you, Zambia Crevecoeur.'

Several members of the group elected to have their own tepees – communal sleeping was not a necessity – and Leila was one of those. After they had eaten, and Ari had taken her turn at cleaning dishes. Leila asked her if they could talk. 'There are things you have to know. About your father and everything,' she'd said. The night had turned chill and Ari was thankful for the rough-spun jacket Urran had insisted on lending her. (Elice had just *loved* that.)

Leila's tepee was small, barely room for two people to curl up, never mind stand, but its entrance was hung with tiny bells, precaution as well as decoration maybe, although Leila said she liked to listen to their song at night. Ari wondered how many nights Leila actually spent alone in here. It was made of stitched canvas, lined with shawls and smelt warmly of old incense smoke. Leila seemed distant, as if the offer of conversation was perhaps a duty rather than a preference. Ari was embarrassed about what might be said. Suddenly, she had little desire for enlightenment, feeling it might be better just to adjust to her new life without a burden of information that may not be wholly pleasant. Leila patted her hard mattress, recently unrolled, and said, 'Think you'll get used to sleeping like this? Far cry from a soft bed, huh?'

Ari shrugged. 'Everyone has to sleep,' she answered. She hadn't even thought about it. If she was to develop any regrets, she felt sure they'd concern old habits like walking through the forest, tracing the familiar paths, touching the landmarks she'd marked with her personal power, the Bump and its monoliths. The loss of a physically comfortable life didn't really bother her.

Leila rubbed her nose and fidgeted on the mattress, where she'd eased herself into a complicated cross-leggedness. 'Pass me that box behind you, will you?' Ari squeezed round and handed the woman a worn, warm-to-the-touch oblong of wood.

'Cards?' Ari asked.

Leila shook her head. 'No. Look.' She lifted the lid. Inside were about half a dozen small glass jars filled with dark powder. 'Nose magic,' Leila said. She rummaged in a pile of clothes and cartons, bringing out a brass saucer and a handful of hard black charcoal blocks. 'You'll learn about this.' She applied the flame of a battered cigarette lighter to a block of charcoal held on the end of an ancient pair of scissors with twisted blades. Ari had made small fires for herself back home, behind the house

on the top of the bank, just at the edge of the forest.
She'd experimented with the fumes of different woods
and grasses and had collected the hard, pungent resin
chips from dead trees to fragrance the blaze. She knew
about nose magic, but refrained from boasting about it.
How many times had she danced herself into a deli-
ciously drunken frenzy around the edges of her smouldering offerings, breathing deeply the heady, powerful,
almost frightening reek of the smoke? Many times. She
did not know the correct names of all the plants she had
used, but had made up her own. Leila unscrewed one of
the jars and offered it to Ari to smell.

'That's lovely,' Ari said, genuinely impressed. 'Did
you make it yourself?'

Leila shook her head. 'No, that's one of Cabochon's.
It invokes the Goddess at the time of the dark moon.
Typical of him, I suppose.' She took the jar back. 'We
can't light that now of course. How do you fancy Lazy
Dream? That's one of mine. Here, sniff.'

It was flowery, light, perhaps with a hint of wist-
fulness about it. Ari was reminded of Spring nights, a
Spring night before a leave-taking maybe, or a necessary
but unwelcome ending. She nodded. Leila sprinkled a
pinch on the glowing charcoal and the tepee was slowly
filled with a silvery, fragrant smoke. Burning, its hint of
sadness was lost. Now, the incense was purely how it had
been named: lazy, dreamy. 'Let's hope we don't fall
asleep before we've finished talking,' Leila said with a
smile. 'I've got some wine here that Ezooli brewed up
while we were wintering up north. It's good, if a little
musty!' She produced two metal cups and poured the
wine from a cloudy plastic bottle. 'I don't like drinking
wine from metal generally, but glass and crockery break
so fast when you're travelling and plastic is so tacky.

Well . . .' She waved the bottle and grimaced. 'Sometimes it's necessary, I guess.'

'Do you always stop travelling in the winter?' Ari asked, accepting the cup. She tasted the wine and had to force herself not to pull a face of sheer disgust. Leila sipped thoughtfully. She was obviously used to the merciless flavour.

'Yeah. I admit to a certain softness. I'm not keen on being cold all the time. There are a couple of communities further north – near Thebes Delta, natro ranches – that a lot of people gravitate to, come Sow-hain. We help with the rice harvest and the land over the cold season before heading off into the great unknown again. Other groups go there for the summer. They are busy places. Personally, living there permanently would drive me nuts. At least you can limit the amount of people around you out on the road.'

Ari digested the information. In her small world, she'd quite overlooked the fact that, in other places, people could still farm the land, or were doing so once more after it had been healed. I will see this, she thought. I will see it soon. She smiled.

'Have I thanked you for rescuing me yet?'

Leila laughed. 'Rescuing? Waking, more like.' She arranged her face into a more sober expression. 'Ari, have you discussed what happened at the festival with anyone?'

Ari shook her head, ducked her eyes away. 'No.'

'Aren't you curious?'

Ari didn't want to discuss her reluctance. 'I expected you'd tell me,' she said.

Leila cocked her head on one side, not fooled. 'Bullshit! I'm going to tell you straight, now, before you can protest and run out of here in a huff . . .'

Ari tried to make a sound, but Leila silenced her with a louder voice. 'No. It's like this. Ewan, your father, made you . . . different . . . Ari. He gave you a kind of power.'

'Power?'

'Yes. P'raps you've felt its presence already, deep inside, but it's blocked at the moment, as a kind of safety precaution. Now, when he died, he made sure that I, and a friend of mine, were given instructions what to do for you. He asked me to come and find you, remove the blocks and help you learn to use the power. I cared for him a lot, Ari, that's why I came. I never forgot.'

Ari didn't know what to say. She knew she should be shocked, but the information was too bizarre for her to feel anything just yet. It explained so much though. It had been the ghost of her father, locked in her mind, that made her feel sick if she thought of sex, his influence preventing her from forming physical relationships. What father wouldn't give their eyes for such control? she thought cynically. Dumping her and Lydia out in the middle of nowhere was a minor precaution in comparison. It was as if a muddled screen had cleared in her head, and flashed up the words: 'he was not perfect.' This was the greatest revelation, worse than finding out she was abnormal. The great Ewan Famber had been, despite his fame, quite cruel. How dare he, she thought, how dare he?

Her voice, when she spoke, sounded harsh and adult. She noticed Leila sat up straighter. 'What kind of power is it? Why did he put blocks on it?'

Leila shifted her weight. 'We-ell, Ewan believed that human beings had a natural source of energy inside them. He used to keep his suppositions pretty much to himself, but I learned a lot from the document he left me. He said he didn't believe the future of the human race lay in technology. He thought that was a blind alley. He thought it lay within ourselves. We were so busy trying to create more and more sophisticated computers, light processors, that kind of thing, out of quasi-organic bits. But he believed the foundation of all this research should be in neurology rather than physics.'

'I don't understand what you're talking about,' Ari said sharply. 'What does it mean in plain language?'

'I'm trying, Ari. This is difficult . . . for both of us. All you need to know for now is that he managed to *change* your genetic make-up. Your power can be accessed via your own sexuality.'

'Well, I'd kind of guessed that much.' She sighed, turned the cup in her hands. 'Was he mad, Leila, or just evil?'

Leila made an anguished noise. 'Neither, Ari, he was just . . . well, Ewan. I know it's hard for you to understand, but your father was unique. He had a capacity to effortlessly make people love him. He *was* loveable.'

Ari looked up quickly, but Leila was staring above her head, smiling in recollection. 'Sex was a very meaningful thing to him. I'd met no one like him before. The power of the orgasm; boy, was he into that!'

Ari was quite shocked that Leila was being so open. 'You were that close to him then?'

Leila pulled a mournful face. 'History,' she said.

'I don't think so,' Ari replied. 'Leila, I have to know. What went on between you and my parents?'

Leila nodded. 'OK. We were all working on the same project under Quincx Roirbak. Ewan and I had an affair . . .'

'Did my mother know?' Ari interrupted.

Leila looked ashamed for the first time. She shrugged. 'I guess so. She suspected, I think.'

'She must have hated you!'

'Yes. She must have.'

'And yet she never showed it.' Ari shook her head, wonderingly, remembering the caring, nurturing person her mother used to be before Ewan's death. All that time she must have been carrying the burden of suspicion, while making out everything was fine for the benefit of her daughter. It was vile. 'She loved him so much,' Ari said. She felt near to tears.

Leila briefly pressed her fingers over her eyes and then blinked. 'Look, I know how this must sound to you, but it was a long time ago. We were all younger then. Things seemed different. You wanted the truth. I told you. Nothing can change it. Both your mother and I were virtually destroyed by loving Ewan. She cracked up when he died, I jettisoned my entire career. Now look at me!' She gestured around the tent. 'I did not escape unscathed, believe me!'

Ari nodded. She'd heard enough on the subject. 'All right. Let's talk about me. Start with what happened to me at the festival.'

Leila relaxed a little. 'Well, the menhir was redesigned by your father, so it could be used to find out whether you'd grown into what he thought he'd created. It also began the process of removing some of the blocks he put in your mind. To me, it seems as if his work has been successful. The readings we took showed that, when a stimulus was introduced to certain areas of your nervous system, there was a massive power surge of some kind. Now, what do we do with this knowledge?' She shrugged helplessly. 'It's all a bit beyond me, I confess, – and to be honest with you, I suspect it was all a bit beyond Ewan too – which is why I'm taking you to the other person your father trusted, Quincx Roirbak. He's a very clever man, and if anyone can help us he can. He taught both your father and me.'

Ari sighed, still turning the empty cup in her hands. 'I don't understand,' she said. 'I don't understand why he did this to me. Was it just to stop me having sex or something? The blocks I believe in; the rest, I'm not so sure. Why did he do it, Leila?'

Leila refilled her cup with wine and screwed up her face to think about her answer. 'We-ell, let's use an example. Let's suppose you were going to test a new mind-expanding drug on the human nervous system. Now, it's not a case of whether the drug will work or not, but how the nervous system itself will be affected by it. Does that make sense to you?'

'If you're talking about drugs, yes, but what about me?'

'What I'm trying to say is, Ewan used sexuality as a medium for his ideas, because it is a stimulus that can be controlled. Ari, you haven't got any specific sexual imprinting, because of the blocks Ewan stuck in your head. If you did have imprints, it might affect how the power affects reality. Just imagine if you'd somehow got into heavy sado-masochism; the power might throw up war machines, or something! Ewan obviously didn't want to take that risk. You must realise what unknown territory this is, we're all feeling around in the dark.'

Ari was not comforted by Leila's explanation. It prompted too many questions. 'It all felt so weird up there at the Bump, like being on some kind of drug. Is that involved somehow? Will this power do strange things to my head as well? Will I have to take drugs?'

Leila shook her head. 'No, listen, maybe it was

misleading, me using that metaphor. You know how we can take a brain, a human brain, a monkey brain, whatever, and prod it, and put electrical charges through it, and think we can suss out how the whole caboodle works? Well, the truth is, the more you find out, the more there is to find out, and the less it feels you know. In his notes, Ewan mentions that altered states of consciousness come into it, but I don't think the power itself will put you in an altered state; it's more likely you will have to *be* in an altered state to access it.' She frowned. 'I think.

'He didn't mean by using drugs, Ari; he must have been referring to the altered state we can achieve ourselves, through heightened erotic awareness, using natural neuro-chemicals. Artificial drugs might bring in too many other sensory stimuli.'

'You say you don't understand it all,' Ari said. 'Yet, to me, you seem to know a lot.'

Leila grinned. 'Well, I'm jammin', mostly. Making my own inferences from his notes. Anyway, I haven't really answered your question. You wanted to know why Ewan did all this? The answer is simple: because he could. Probably. He was like that. I'm not sure whether he was even convinced all this had any practical application.'

'Great! Sounds as if *he* was "just jammin'", as you put it, as well,' Ari said bitterly. Leila shuffled round on the mattress and tentatively put an arm around her.

'Listen, he was a strange and brilliant man. A great mind, full of plans and ideas, all galloping around inside. I don't know much, Ari, and I know it must sound kind of grisly and weird, but you have to understand that if he could have done it to himself he would. He couldn't, so it had to be you, his child. He wouldn't think it would bother you. He couldn't think like that.

He'd look on it as a great adventure and no doubt expected you to feel the same. I can see from your face that you don't.'

'I don't know what I think yet,' she said, between sips of wine, 'I feel someone should have told me about it a long time ago though. If it's part of me, it shouldn't be something that's just dumped on me now, I should've grown up with the idea. That wouldn't have been so bad.'

'Well, things do get dumped on a woman now and again, Ari,' Leila replied. 'Like the changes at puberty.'

'No, not like that. I knew about that.'

'Some women don't.'

'I'm not them. Anyway, this isn't natural, is it! There's no comparison. What will it do to me? What is this power? How does it work?'

Leila smiled. 'Goddess, Ari, it's not a curse! All I can tell you is that for thousands of years, certain people have believed in the power of sexual energy. They trained themselves to be able to harness and use that power, but it was a strict discipline and took a long time to develop. Only a few, very dedicated people could achieve it. Your father believed he had discovered a way for human beings to access that power easily and naturally. He called it giving evolution a bit of a nudge.

'Understand?

'If all goes well, and you receive proper guidance, you'll be able to do things that old witches like me only dream about. You'll be able to have a far more direct effect upon the fabric of reality than ordinary people, no matter how adept they are in the ways of the world. When we work magick, we have to do things gently, with symbols and dreams and little plays; think in pictures. These are all props which help to convince our minds we can achieve the object of our working. Believing in something strongly enough is all we need to make it real, but people find it hard to believe in their willpower so absolutely, which is why we need the props. I'm not sure, but I don't think you'll need any of that. It'll be like breathing . . . sort of. We won't know for sure what you're capable of until the blocks have been properly removed. I'm quite sure, once they have, and the process has been triggered by your first sexual experience, you will *become* this thing Ewan dreamed of, and the power, whatever it is, will be there for you whenever you want it. What I mean is, I don't think you'll have to be sexually stimulated to access it each time. From then on, you'll probably find that sex is just as regular an experience for you as it is for the rest of us. I hope so, but . . .' She shrugged. 'I don't really know. I guess we'll both have to be patient.'

'I can't understand why Mom didn't tell me,' Ari said miserably, looking up, directly into Leila's eyes. 'She knew, didn't she?'

Leila nodded. 'Of course she knew. But you know how she feels about natro and all that now. She also knew someone like me would be turning up one day, so she thought it would protect you by not telling you, I suppose. She was trying to make you invisible.'

'That's crazy!' Ari said bitterly. 'In that case, why didn't she leave Taler's Bump? Living in Dad's house, she might as well have had a neon sign over the door saying, "the mutant lives here"!'

Leila clearly didn't want to discuss Lydia's shortcomings. She wriggled uncomfortably. 'It's really irrelevant now, Ari. I've found you, as your father wanted me to.' She reached for Ari's hand, putting aside her wine cup. 'And I intend to help you reach your full potential, loyalty to Ewan or not. You're a real person to me now, Ari, not just a name written on paper. I feel a responsibility towards you. I want to help you shape this remarkable womanhood you'll have.'

Ari nodded thoughtfully. 'Thanks. For everything. I'm feeling a bit numb, but I appreciate how straight you've been with me.'

'It's the least I can do.'

Ari sighed. 'There's one other thing yet though. Leila, will you let me read the document my father left you?'

Leila was taken aback. She had not expected that. The document had become rather like a religious relic to her. No one else had ever read it. 'All right,' she said at last. 'You may not like what you read though. It's rather . . . well, clinical.'

'I need to see it.'

Leila dragged her strong-box out from under a pile of clothes. Ari watched her unlock it, noticing the woman's hands were unsteady. 'I only want to read the bits about me,' she said. 'Show me which lines to read. The rest is your business.'

Leila looked at her steadily, and then smiled. 'I'm wondering who you inherited that sensitivity from, Ari! Here, read it all. I don't mind.' She handed Ari the crumpled pages.

Ari was prepared to be upset, shocked, appalled, but the words were so technical, she hardly understood them. There were not, as she'd anticipated, any sentimental messages for Leila in them.

The document had obviously been printed on to the paper by machine, although it seemed to have been hand-drawn originally. Most of the information appeared to refer to data not contained in the document itself. Some of the glyphs seemed familiar to Ari, like the sketches and diagrams she'd seen in her studies in biology. Some parts of it – barely legible scrawl – were like some ancient, magickal formula:

> *Input data to Al Thoth – Let it determine hidden variables:*
>
> *93   RNA – Hermes – Mercury – pineal – black earth – 0 = 2 – materia   prima – 1 = 3,   quanta – vas hermeticum – ruach – NQBH – chromosome permutations – Visnu –*

There was much nonsense like that, and a drawing of a female body as from some antique hermetic script, glyphs and cramped writing hugging its limbs.

It showed Ari, more than anybody's reminiscences, just how single-minded her father had been about his work. She wanted to feel some kind of kinship with him, reading the pages he handled and marked himself, but it only made her feel more distant from him. He had not loved her. She had been an experiment. There was no need even to feel disgusted or hurt. When she'd scanned the pages, Ari only felt a dim pity for this dead man who'd never been able to love. She herself, at that moment, felt immense and calm and full of joy. It was very strange. She put down the document and curled into Leila's arms, hugging her tight. There were tears on her face, but they were not those of sadness. Leila rocked her and stroked her hair.

'You'll be strong, Ari, you'll get used to it. Don't be hurt.'

Ari pulled away and rubbed her face. 'I'm not upset. Don't you understand? I'm not upset.'

Leila suddenly felt as if there was a great physical

distance between her and the girl. She saw this serene young woman sitting there: it was like a visualisation of what Ari was to become. She smiled back at her and shook her head. The aroma and smoke of the incense seemed to have moved the primitive tent to a new continuum. I am looking at a goddess, Leila thought.

As Star Eye penetrated deeper into the arid dry lands, south-west of Taler's Bump, Ari reluctantly decided Elice may not have been exaggerating in her story about the crack in the road. The route they travelled must have been some great highway at one time: multiple lanes littered with debris, old camps and long abandoned vehicles streaked with rust that attracted persistent lichens. The surface had broken up completely in places, which Urran told her was because of the extreme temperatures experienced in that region. 'One day it can be hot enough to bake a dog on the cab roof, the next you're being beaten by balls of ice the size of fists,' he said, balling his own fist to illustrate. Ari smiled carefully. Urran laughed and flicked her cheek with his fingers. Ari knew he believed she was easily frightened, and perhaps she was, but it was not Star Eye's road mythology that scared her. Although the talk with Leila had opened her up in ways she couldn't previously have imagined, there was still the mundane aspect of her condition to deal with. Until she fully understood and could control the power within her, people like Urran, brimming over with masculine energy, would continue to pluck a dissonant chord inside her. She knew this was something she was going to have to cope with until Star Eye reached

Arcady. Now that she'd been told what it was that was so different about her, she sometimes found herself wondering what would happen if she tried to remove the blocks in her mind herself. What if she just went ahead, braved the unpleasant side-effects, and lost her virginity to someone? Wouldn't that free her? Despite these rebellious thoughts, some deep instinct warned her she would only bring disaster on herself if she tried. That didn't remove the temptation however.

Because she travelled in Spirit of Disorder, the only men she'd had consistent close contact with were Urran and Cable. Cable wasn't a threat at all – he didn't like women in that way – but sometimes Urran made her shudder in both fear and excitement. She caught him watching her with weird patience, his dark hair hanging in his eyes, as if he was waiting for her to transmit some kind of signal. Rentfree Aphrodite's people were not much more than names to her yet. Apart from Cabochon, Jordan and Kydd, there were Ezooli and her man, Grover, the latter being a rather sombre character who didn't speak much and, thus, hadn't made much of an impression on Ari as yet.

Occasionally Leila would skip over to Jordan's truck and ride with him, so other people in the Spirit got a chance to sit up front with Cable. Surprisingly, nobody seemed to regard this as a special treat, although Ari looked forward to these opportunities. She was glad no one else argued with her for the privilege. Cable made her laugh, telling her, in his deadpan campy way, intriguing and unlikely gossip about the others. She'd never seen him be rude or less than cheerful with anyone, yet he referred to Elice and Justinette as 'silly cows' and Urran as having 'a brain the size of his prick – and that's not all it's cracked up to be either!' Ari wondered what the others said about her when she wasn't there.

The land looked so flat through the visor of the truck, as if it stretched for ever and ever, featureless, barren and hostile. Looking through Leila's binoculars, which she'd left lying on the seat in the cab, Ari could make out the white plastic domes of minor settlements some clicks back from the road. 'Why doesn't someone ever repair the highway?' she asked Cable.

'Hardly anyone uses it honey, that's why,' he replied, 'Point your glasses at the sky and you'll see.' Air transport was more popular.

One day there was a collision overhead not far from the road and Cable and Jordan stopped the trucks so everybody could watch the flames for a few minutes. Then Cabochon pointed out that a zone patrol might be along soon and it wasn't a good idea to hang around to answer their questions. Ari asked Cable why the group was nervous of the patrols.

'We're not doing anything wrong, only looking,' she said.

Cable shook his head in disbelief and made a show of rolling back the sleeve of his shirt. 'See this,' he said, pointing to an ugly, dark scar on his inner forearm. 'I got that from asking a zp man directions.'

Ari laughed. 'I don't believe you! Cable, I am not *that* stupid!'

He shrugged. 'Suit yourself. Randomati aren't that popular with some people, kid. Remember that. Learn the art of the quick suss. Survival sometimes depends on it.'

Ari thought she must have offended him. It was often difficult to tell when Cable was being serious.

Sometimes huge, monstrous trucks, seemingly ten times the size of their own, would thunder past, blasting

out a single moan from their deep, brassy horns. Ari
found them terrifying, from their black, polarised windows that made it look as if there was no driver inside
the cab, to the gory cartoons splashed on the armoured
flanks. She remembered one particularly: a woman surrounded by men's headless torsos, standing on the
legend, Headfucker Hussy. 'I won't tangle with that little
scrubber!' Cable said drily, and pulled his truck over to
the side so the Hussy could scream past.

Ari was surprised at how few people they came across
on the road. It was easy to believe they were the only folk
alive at times, although one guy just came up out of the
desert one evening, up like a ghost and as dusty as if he'd
been buried there too. The only details Ari could remember of his appearance were his pale and crazy eyes. He'd
sat down at the fire and the others gave him food. Never
spoke a word. He was gone by morning. Ari didn't like
people like that. You could never tell what they were
thinking, and they always made a point of showing they
were armed. Occasionally, though, there'd be a roadside
storeblock for methane fuel, root vegetables, and
suchlike. Star Eye would barter their own refuse in
exchange for methane, and also totems and other
artefacts in exchange for food and water. Elice told Ari
those stores always had a thin whore hidden away
upstairs somewhere. 'They like to supply every need,'
she said. 'One time, Kydd went up these stairs to see.
Said he'd pay an' all. Saw her on the bed. Sixteen maybe,
one leg gone, eyes all filmed up and a smile that'd turn
a guy to stone. He came runnin' out like he'd seen a
ghost!'

The relationships between group members intrigued
Ari. It was as if, should she half-close her eyes and watch
her new companions, they'd twist and wave around each

other like water weed. It was a closed environment within the trucks. People got tetchy. People got close. There were good times and bad times, but somehow they moved faster, blending into one another so quickly you hardly finished crying before it was time to smile. Elice and Justinette were a quick-fire team. When they were on form they made Ari laugh till it ached her gut, but she was uneasy about being a third young girl among the group and didn't particularly try to become part of their friendship. One person she felt utterly at ease with, as Leila had predicted, was Charcoal Eve. Eve was pleased to have a new ear willing to hear her history. She told of how she'd once lived in a mini-cluster up north and how, when her children had grown up and left home, she'd been left with a stranger who called himself her husband. It seemed the pair of them were doomed to sit there in front of the wallscreen waiting for death to come knocking on the door. 'I had nearly half my life left,' Eve said. 'Had to do somethin' with it.' She'd attended a seasonal festival on her own one day and just took up with the first natro group that seemed keen enough to have her. 'Never told him I was leavin'. Probably hasn't noticed I've gone yet,' she said, remembering the father of her children.

Eve also spoke a lot about Elice. Ari was given the picture of a spoiled little rich girl who became too much of a handful for her social-climbing parents. The mother had known Leila vaguely back when she'd been with the Tech-Greens and, during one of the festivals, they met up again. The outcome of that little reunion had been the girl's mother virtually begging Leila to take her daughter off her hands, speaking glibly of how the girl needed education about 'real life'. Elice felt neglected, apparently. Ari wondered why she behaved in such a way as to keep people at arm's length in that case. 'It's like a curse with some folks,' Eve replied. 'They try so hard but they don't know how.'

At night the western sky burned with a clear fury and Star Eye would build their lesser fires, sitting down to cook and eat before each day's spiritual work. The bulk of their diet consisted of various vegetable and soya products although, whenever it was available from roadside stores, Leila would purchase some cuts of the salty vat-grown protein. It was altogether a tougher substance to chew than the synthetic poultry meat Ari had eaten at home.

One evening, Ari said to Eve, 'We try to change our lives, our reality. Have you done that Eve? Are you happy with your life?'

'There's limits,' Eve intoned darkly, lighting her pipe.

'Should there be though?'

For a while there was only the sound of Eve's lips smacking against the pipe, her indrawn breath. There was only the dim glow of the burning tobacco. Then she said, 'There are folks that can change the world, I guess, but I'm not one of them. I'm happy, yes. It's more of an internal changin' I'm wise at, you see. It's learnin' to be happy with the way things are and seein' the richness of the world a different way. We got no fancy homes and little money, but we eat and keep warm and see a bunch of things around the land. We do a little healing' here and there, do our bit for the Lady and keep each other safe. That's a little bit of paradise for me, girl.'

'I see,' Ari said, pondering. Yes, that made sense. There was no use hungering for what you couldn't have. The true magic was seeing wealth in what was available, what was there.

'Everyone sees things different,' Eve continued.

'That's just my way. Leila now, she wants a lot more, I'm thinkin'.'

'Oh, what do you mean?' Ari had quickly learned Star Eye loved to gossip about each other.

'She's a strong lady, brainy too. I reckon she misses her science and all that sometimes.'

'Then why does she stay on the road with the rest of you?'

'It's what she knows and what she can have. She don't talk about the past much, but I reckon there were things she saw or did that she didn't like too well. You can smell it on her sometimes like a bitter smoke. Then you know she's angry with herself, or with somethin', and you keep away if you're clever.'

'Oh.' Ari had not yet seen Leila in a bad mood and had difficulty imagining her being that way. Leila always seemed so cool to her, in control of her feelings and thoughts. Ari envied that. Sometimes she found herself blurting out stupid things just to fill a silence, wishing she could ride that silence the way Leila did.

Star Eye scavenged whenever they could. Although Justinette told Ari these desert-lands provided slim pickings for natros, Cable would always try to stop for the night by promising ruins and garbage heaps. The detritus of civilisation was a world in itself, providing a tenuous eco-system for other scavengers: rats and flies. The desert was dotted with these untidy, manmade hills, which Cable explained was rubbish from city clusters, remains of old settlements or else just junk which had fallen out of the sky; disabled satellites and orbital refuse. Most of them had been scoured of useful material years ago, however. It would be necessary to stray far from the road to discover more fertile picking-ground, a hazardous venture which Star Eye avoided unless really desperate for barter goods. Closer to Arcady, Tech-Green refuse sites could be entered for a toll. These places were always crawling with natros searching for useful material, and offered the advantage of being continually re-stocked: city refuse was yet another currency for randomati. Occasionally, however, it was possible to uncover useful items from the desert which had either been overlooked by previous scavengers or else had been unsuitable for their needs. Ari was surprised by some of the methods by which the group obtained material. One evening, the trucks came across a recently-crashed VTOL jet, its cockpit half-buried at the end of a long, gouged trench, its wings and tail some distance away. The wreck was spotted by Leila who had been using a scan device to find somewhere to camp for the night. The wreck sported a zone patrol marker which advertised it was permissible to salvage material from it. The patrolmen had already helped themselves to what they wanted – various pieces of hardware – but had left the body of the pilot still jammed in the cockpit, removing only the ID tags. Although most of it had been consumed by the hardy desert animals, what was left of the body was unceremoniously dumped in the cooler mulch with all the other Star Eye refuse. Ari, who had hardened herself to virtually pissing in public, and thus thought she could now stomach anything, still threw up when Jordan and Grover had hauled the barely-recognisable human remains across the dust, and had hid, shivering, until the grisly process was completed. Elice, with her usual callous sense of humour, noticed Ari cowering behind the Spirit and tossed the pilot's helmet towards her. Squealing, Ari screwed up her eyes as the hideous relic hit her legs, but not before she'd noticed the leathery strips of dried flesh still glued by congealed blood to the shattered visor.

Urran also managed to cobble together a couple of music generators from materials he'd salvaged from the cockpit. The group congratulated themselves on a lucky find.

One morning, Jordan came hammering round the tepees just after dawn, waking everyone up. Ari, curled up against the furnace heat of Eve's slumbering back, had blustered from sleep, scared stiff by the raucous shouting. 'What is it?' she squeaked at Eve, fearing attack from those strange dust people she believed existed beneath the dry soil.

Eve dragged herself upright, fumbling into her heavy woollen clothes. 'Must be a fog, the way he's panickin',' she said with stolid calm. 'Get your things on, girl, and help me pack the tent away.'

'What fog?'

'An eatin' kind. Come on, haste up!'

Ari carefully bundled the sleeping quilts into a roll the way Eve had taught her. There was little else to pack. Outside she helped pull out the ground pegs. Justinette hurried past, smiling with excitement.

'Have you seen it?' she cried, pointing. Ari crawled round the side of the tepee to look. In the south, over the flat land, a yellow cloud was visible. They'd only been on the road a couple of weeks and the weather had held good so far – no hint of Urran's ice hails anyway. Star Eye kept out of the sun, obviously, emerging uncoated from the trucks only during the evening. This was the first fog Ari had seen.

'What is it?' she asked Justinette, who had paused to help her and Eve dismantle the tepee.

'Poison,' Justinette replied. 'It'll come all around us and if we're not in the trucks, we're dead. Well, at least after a while.'

'We had nothing like that at the Bump,' Ari said.

'No, don't s'pose you did,' Justinette replied. 'It's a flat-land phenomenon. Doesn't roll our way too often, thank the Lady.'

Ari lifted one end of the rolled tepee, Justinette took the other, while Eve fussed with the straps holding it in place. 'If it's so bad, doesn't it harm the trucks?' Ari asked, glancing back over her shoulder as they heaved the tents inside Cable's vehicle.

'Well it would if we were stuck in it all the time, I guess,' Justinette answered, 'but Cable has special stuff painted on the outside, so it's pretty well safe. He tells us this story about how he was driving somewhere once and a goon shot through his side window letting the fog in. He said he had to tie a rag over his face and it took him two hours to get clear. Said he was spitting up blood for a week. He still has a bad chest. Haven't you noticed?'

Ari was never sure whether Star Eye were making fun of her or not with their little folklore tales. She always took care to laugh in such a way that, if it was a joke, it showed she'd understood it.

The fog curled up around them so quickly that they'd barely had time to check the truck seals before the yellow tendrils were trying to feel their way inside. Ari looked out of one of the windows. The fog sniffed and reared up phantom questing fronds that looked like the heads of dog-snakes. She'd caught a whiff of the stuff before she'd scrambled inside. It had made her cough, rather like some of Leila's more vicious incense blends. The light inside the truck became eerie, sound condensed. Cable started the engine and the fog curled back as if in distaste, enveloping the dark cloud of exhaust fume as if in search of nourishment.

It is seeking our warmth, Ari thought. Horrible. It really senses us. The truck prowled forward, nose lamps on, although all they illumined was a dense, boiling cloud of off-white murk. Ari suppressed a shudder, wondering what would happen if Headfucker Hussy or one of her kind should, at this moment, be thundering towards them. They'd hear nothing, see nothing. 'Why do we keep moving?' she asked in a high voice. 'Why don't we just stop and wait for it to pass? What if we run into another truck or something?'

'Calm down,' Elice said coolly. 'It's best we keep going. That way we leave this mess behind quicker.'

'It can hang around places for days,' Urran said, fidgeting because he could not roll himself a cigarette. (Elice complained if the windows weren't open when someone was smoking and there was no way they could do that now.) 'It might eat its way right inside this old truck and gobble us up.'

'It's horrible!' Ari said, rubbing her arms. 'I didn't know there were things like this out here.'

'Yeah, well, it's not something that's advertised on TV exactly,' Urran said. 'Got any fruit nuggets, Eve?'

Eve, grumbling, rummaged in her carpet bag and threw Urran a packet of tofu sweets. He gratefully filled his mouth with them and Elice made a sarcastic sound. The truck seemed to be creaking more than usual. Ari closed her eyes and swallowed, trying to banish an evil vision of some fog beast perched on the roof, gnawing its way inside. The air was getting closer, staler. Cable was always complaining about the purifier, and that it really should be replaced. Leila always said they'd not enough funds yet to see to it, but what if they just all suffocated in here? Ari was scared. She started to tremble.

199

'I know,' Justinette said cheerfully. 'Let's get into a guided trip. It'll pass the time and stop Ari here passing out! Anyone into it?'

'Yeah, why not,' Urran said, popping another sweet into his mouth. 'Where do you want to go, Ari? A clean beach littered with naked boys perhaps? A green forest full of psycho-whores looking for a job?'

'Oh be quiet, Urran,' Elice spat. 'Let's go up, above the fog. Let's fly.'

Ari ended up falling asleep, a bad habit of hers during any meditation. When she woke up, they were in clear air once more, the sun beating down and frying anything unprotected. Cable stopped the truck at the next road-store to check everything over. Larger than most road-side communities they came across, and boasting more facilities, the store was also host to a landing strip, complete with small plane, and a dirigible tower. The main building also supplied accommodation for travellers.

Leila muffled herself up in a blanket and inspected the water carriers, testing them with a toxin sensor. She swore. 'Dammit, Cable, this one's foul! I told you the tank was faulty!'

'So get a new tank!' Cable called back from behind the store screens. 'Know anyone can give us one for free?'

'Ask them if they can change our water in there,' Leila responded irritably. Jordan appeared round the side of the truck, having parked his own behind.

'Your tanks OK?' Leila asked him.

'Cab's checkin' 'em now,' he replied. 'Don't get worked up, lady. We can fix all the mechanical wobbles at Lazar Farm.'

'Shit! What we gonna do till then?' Leila flounced up the store steps. Jordan looked into Cable's truck window and grinned at the faces peering out.

'Leila's getting jumpy,' Urran remarked. 'Now why does that make me feel uneasy?'

'She's not jumpy, just right!' Elice said. 'That tank's been suspect for months. She was going on about it way before Taler's, you know that. What are the chances of not running into foul fog around here? Nil. That tank should have been replaced. If it rains we've had it.'

'So? We could give it another coat of sealant. You're as bad as her, panicking like this.'

Elice bared her teeth at Urran. 'Makes sense to be careful,' she said.

'Does it ever occur to you Leila may be wrong about some things?' he inquired.

'Does it ever occur to you what a prick you are?'

'Often. I'm into it. Open a window, Ari, there's a good girlie. Want a smoke?'

Ari, who was unnerved by group bitchings, felt too embarrassed to say yes, although she'd been developing a taste for it since leaving the Bump. She was sure Elice would turn on her if she appeared to support Urran at the moment, and there was no way she could make light banter of it like he did. She looked out of the window and saw the store proprietor, masked and shrouded in what looked incongruously like waterproof gear, hauling a thick hose over to the truck. She wondered what induced people to set up business in places like this, holed up indoors all day to keep their skin safe, waiting and waiting for the eerie rumble of approaching customers. It could not be an affluent life. She watched as the man, his fingers almost immovable inside thick gloves, opened up the offending water tank and let its contents pour out on to the dust, turning it dark and temporarily fertile. Two small figures in helmeted one-piece suits came out of the store, pushing a trolley, heaped at one end with Star

Eye's meagre purchases. Leila followed them, head down. She rapped on the truck door and Urran slid it aside. 'Get this stuff in, will you?' Leila said.

'I'll flush this for you,' the storeman said.

'That'll cost, I presume,' Leila replied.

The man shrugged, unoffended. 'Sure, but it could save you and your people a bad belly.'

Leila nodded impatiently. 'OK. Do it.'

The store children sat down on the truck floor, legs dangling outside, and took off their helmets. Ari could see they were twins, both pale and sandy-eyed, sex unspecific.

'Wanna buy a totem?' one asked. 'We got fog pushers and rain spit and . . .'

The other twin pushed its sibling. 'Silly, they're natros, make their own. Bet you have a fearsome grit snarl-demon huh, roady?'

Ari shrugged and smiled.

'Yeah, and she'll breathe it down your eyes in a minute. Push off!' came Elice's grate from behind. The twins giggled and pulled on each other's helmets, making noises of complicity, before running back to the store.

'Something wrong with them?' Ari asked.

'Brats,' Elice replied, stretching out her legs to admire them, tanned and skinny poking out of the bottom of her cut-off trousers. She yawned. 'Roll on Lazar Farm,' she said. 'These legs need stretching good and proper.'

After their initial talk on the first night out, Leila had more or less entrusted Ari solely into Charcoal Eve's care, but Ari could not tell how much the older woman knew about her. Ari never mentioned what her father had done and neither did Eve. She was treated just like any normal kid who had joined a natro group for the first time. Ari enjoyed being taught things by Eve: her slow, drawling voice, her vast store of knowledge wrapped up in a colourful skin of myth and rumour interested Ari far more than straight-eyed, blow to the gut, no-nonsense training, which is what she felt Leila would have meted out to her. Eve would put her arm round Ari's shoulder and take her pipe out of her mouth to point up at the sky with it, saying, 'Now, there's a thing, Ari girl. Look at that little birdy up there. Think she knows the state the world's in? No, by Lady, she doesn't. Just gets on with her business, and if food's a little hard to find some days, if her bones creak a little too early in the season, she don't go lookin' for somethin' to blame or nothin'. Just keeps flyin' till she finds somethin' to fill her belly and beds down early with her beak in her feathers. There's somethin' to be learned in that, girl.'

Ari thought about this. 'Course,' she said. 'I see it. It's like with problems, isn't it? Getting vexed about the problem won't solve it. Thinking of reasons why its happened won't solve it or agonising any. You just have to face it head on and *think* of the way to solve it.'

Eve smiled and nodded, greatly pleased. 'You're a bright girl, Ari,' she said and puffed contentedly on her pipe.

'Is that . . . is that like *my* problem, Eve?' Ari asked timidly, eyes upturned in lowered head.

Eve puffed contemplatively for a second or two. 'You reckon you have a problem then?' she answered.

Ari wriggled. 'Well, it's not a problem exactly.' She shrugged. 'It's why I'm here, I guess, why Leila came and took me away from home.'

'Sounds mighty sinister,' Eve said in a careful tone that implied no feelings on the matter.

'It does. It does *sound* that way. I'm not sure what's waiting for me. Do you know?'

Eve peered down at her, looking like some native American matriarch, her large body swathed in blankets, her long, grey plait and perennial pipe.

'There's a body in Arcady. Leila fancies he's some kind of magician or somethin'. Name of Roirbak. All the fireworks and pazzazz of him covers the fact he knows a lot.' She nodded, puffed. 'Hmmm, wise guy. He's Leila's kind of guru; she runs back to him once in a while when things get sticky or she just needs a friend who can make things right in her head. Roirbak's the one. That's who she's takin' you to. Hasn't told me this, of course, but I'd bet my blood on it.'

From Eve's worried champing on the pipe stem, Ari guessed the woman wasn't too sure whether she should have told Ari this supposition. Ari was warmed by Eve's concern and snuggled up against the woman to show she appreciated the gesture, and just how hard it had been to make it. She hadn't the heart to say she'd already known about it. 'So why is she doing that?' It helped to get someone else's opinion on things though.

Eve sighed, mussed Ari's hair. 'Oh, girly, girly. I'm not sure if all that wild fancy about you is true or not. It's not my kind of workin', not my path. Don't know nothin' about it, but if it is true, Leila's canny enough to know she can't handle it herself. These people we're travellin' with, they're good folk, scatty maybe, but basically good. Think on it, now. Do you think any of them are up to handlin' what's been laid on you? These are nomads, road scummers, live for the day folk. And what are you, eh? What are you?'

Ari shivered. 'I didn't ask for this!' she said angrily,

close to tears. 'It's not fair. Why can't I be like them? Why can't it be forgotten about?'

Eve squeezed her. 'Now, now, don't go hurtin' yourself. You gotta be strong girly. Be wise. If it's all true, there'll be no forgettin'. Not if you want to live a normal life. Once you start wantin' a man with you, an' all. You know that. That's when the show starts, kiddo. You got to learn how to handle that, and Leila reckons Roirbak'll be the one to teach you.'

'But what if I decide to live without . . . all *that*, you know,' Ari said hotly. 'It won't matter then whether I know how to handle it or not! Surely a woman can live without . . . you know.'

Eve chuckled, deep in her chest. 'Don't kid yourself,' she said.

Leila kept a discreet eye on Ari's progress. She knew Eve would gently nudge the girl along like a docile old cow with a calf. Part of her insisted she'd passed Ari's welfare over because Eve was a better person to deal with it, while another, more honest part, told her she was nervous of Ari, or rather of the girl's potential. The vision she'd had in her tepee of Ari as a potential goddess had unnerved as well as awed her. It was also disorientating to see Ewan's shrewd eyes looking out of that young face now and again. As the group approached Arcady, each day rumbling them just that bit closer, her tension increased. It would be a relief to spill all this to Quincx, but Arcady itself would bring other problems to the surface. She couldn't argue with the fact Star Eye needed funds: they'd had poor pickings recently, despite their luck in finding the crashed jet, and she'd become exhausted trying to chivvy the others into being more productive. Sometimes a surge of anger would flow through her, thinking about how they were all just content to sprawl inside the trucks aimlessly trundling round the country, growing lazy. Just lately it had been an effort to raise any power within them, especially so since Cabochon had started having problems. She knew they needed the shot of life Arcady would give them, the desire to get up and strut around again, even though the city would be as good as poison to Cabochon. It was more than superstition that warned her trouble was crouching there waiting for the boy. She was also sore at Jordan because he should be supporting her now, kicking ass a little, so it didn't make her look such a nag, but he was getting deeper and deeper into his own head, courting fancies she felt could only end in disappointment and humiliation. Maybe he was too infatuated by Cabochon to see that the boy was addicted, physically, psychically and emotionally, to the destructive influence of Zambia Crevecoeur. Driven half crazy with worry for the group, she tried and tried to reach Jordan, touch his mind as she'd once been able to do and drag him into reality, drag him up beside her as colleague and ally, kidding herself the failure was only temporary when she could not manage it.

She was not convinced Jordan really understood the gravity of what she'd taken on with Ari. She remembered going out into the morning, just after she'd woken up and had thought of the girl for the first time in seven years. She'd been wearing only a blanket and had looked at the sky and thought, 'Well, you're this close. Coincidence or not, you're nearly there and now's the time to take the last few steps.' It had been no difficulty persuading the group to celebrate Beltagne at Taler's Bump; they'd become so apathetic they were happy to let Leila make all their decisions for them. That made her angry too. Why hadn't someone argued against her? Subconsciously, she must have been putting off the visit to Taler's Bump for over a year; after all, Ari must have reached puberty when she was about thirteen. It would have taken very little persuasion to have made Leila agree to further delay. But no. It was not to be. Once they got there, they might have discovered mousy Lydia Famber had upped camp and moved on, but no, there it was; all laid on, easy as pie, the succulent fish jumping up on to the deck without even having to tickle the water, flopping about there weak as a babe, impossible not to pick up and put into the basket. Damn Lydia! Damn Ewan! Damn all of them! As to why Ari should make her feel this unsafe, Leila could not entirely specify. She was, after all, only a girl; ignorant of her power and vulnerable because of that.

We are all vulnerable, Leila thought. She was not getting any younger and times were hard. Cabochon, the spiritual power unit of her group, was voltless in the face of the familial difficulties which were getting nearer every day, and her partner was falling victim to the strength of the boy's distress. She knew Cabochon was a gem in more than just the sense of his name. It was no coincidence that times had got harder since the last visit to Arcady and Cabochon's last fight with his brother. Cabochon's interest was waning along with his concentration. It irked her beyond measure that he was so instrumental to the group's well-being, but she could only look back to the days when Jordan had found him and the way their fortunes had blossomed in the aura of the boy's inner strength. She wanted that security again and feared she could not get it from Cabochon. He was losing his strength and dragging Jordan down with him – albeit, she supposed in charitable moments, without knowing it, but the effect was the same. What was happening to Star Eye? Shouldn't they be able to empower each other? Why was she losing control like this? Was it time to disband and start again? She knew that could happen to groups – when the power and unity weakened beyond redemption – and had experienced it herself several times; but Star Eye had been different. She'd formed it herself and named it after the team she and Ewan had worked with all those years ago. It meant so much to her. It had possessed such possibilities. And now? She sighed. Now, she suspected, its fate rested solely in the hands of a naïve and innocent girl, who had no idea such responsibility was invested in her. In whatever way.

Ari walked out among the dead trees: a rattling forest, grey as bones. She wondered whether her own forest, back at the Bump, would end up like this one day. She touched the branches, made them move. They were wind-scoured, shiny, no dust came away in her hands. Star Eye had eaten and most people had turned in for the night. Ari felt restless. She needed a walk. She came to a place that would have been a glade at one time. There was a dusty depression that might have held water, cracked clay beneath the dust and a carpet of dried moss underfoot. She sat down under the creaking skeleton trees, and was overwhelmed by a great sadness. It hurt too much to think about the life that had once inhabited this place; the animals and plants, the people walking through the trees. She closed her eyes and took several deep breaths, seeking the inner calm Eve had shown her the path to. She fancied she could almost hear the sounds of the forest. It was a glorious day, yellow sunlight through the green, people sitting around on the grass, eating, drinking, children screaming and running around, music playing, mothers shouting, groups of dour youths in leather jackets skulking importantly round the edges of the cars, taking their six-packs of beer and their girl-friends into less populated areas. All gone now. She opened her eyes with a gasp, momentarily scared by the silence, the night, and looked back through the sparse branches at the cheerful glow of Star Eye's camp fire, indistinct forms moving against the flames. Plenty of firewood here, she thought. She knew Eve would not appreciate her going off too far alone, but would also understand Ari's need for doing so. She needed space to gain perspective. Breathe deep, she told herself, and sucked in air through her mouth, pursed as if to whistle, tasting it. She tried to get a sense of the Earth spirit, because Eve had told her the essence of Astrada was everywhere. It was important to empower that spirit with intention whenever she could. Unfortunately, during such personal rituals, Ari was also made aware of the sexual nature of all earth magick and that raked screech-ing claws down the impenetrable blocks Ewan had implanted within her subconscious. It *was* like a curse, no matter what Leila said. As time went on, her bitter-ness towards Ewan increased, eclipsing any pity she might have felt for him. She could not function as a woman, and the whole purpose of Naturotech was to take hold of Sexuality with both hands and throw it out in a far-reaching arc of healthy, nurturing power. As if in ironic punctuation to her thoughts, Ari's belly convulsed in a searing spasm of pain, presaging the arrival of men-struation. All the miseries without the pleasure, she thought, and banged the ground with her clenched fists, allowing herself a single cry of anger and frustration.

'Hang on there, Ari! What's bustin' you, kid?'

Ari jumped. Urran? She hadn't heard him come up. 'I didn't hear you,' she said, beginning to stand up. He looked jaunty and cheerful in the moonlight, his long black hair all loose, grin from ear to ear.

'What are you doing out here? What's up?' he asked, moving closer. 'Are you all right?'

'I'm fine,' she answered, wishing she could come out with something clever and sarcastic like Elice would.

'No, don't get up,' he said, dropping down beside her and putting a restraining hand on her arm. 'Well, this is a miserable place, isn't it?'

'Not miserable, just gone,' Ari answered. 'It's empty.'

'Why are you here then?' And then, before she could answer, 'Let's have a smoke.'

Ari was prepared to be sociable, although she sometimes felt Urran was mocking her for being young and inexperienced. Perhaps that was just a front he put on when the others were there. Perhaps he could be a friend. Could she talk to this man and tell him the things she had hidden inside? Surely his view could only be helpful. She settled herself down and instilled a sense of comfort in her body. The stomach pain had gone.

'Don't you think,' Urran said, beginning to pack his pipe with hash, 'there might be ghosts out here? I sometimes wonder. Think on it. A scoured land, all the life gone, but . . .' he shrugged, 'there must be echoes.'

Ari wasn't sure whether his intention was to frighten her or not. 'I don't feel anything,' she said. 'It really is empty.' Now, she wasn't sure whether that was right, but tried to banish the feeling of unseen eyes around her. It was only Urran making her think that.

'But there's so little sound. The silence . . .' He made a strange sound, which may have been prompted by the fact he'd lit the pipe and taken a deep lungful of smoke.

'It's not really silent,' Ari said. 'If you listen hard, there're sounds. Cable told me it's aircraft and things, the distant sound of the city support systems. They reach this far. He said so.'

'Nah!' Urran scoffed. 'We're alone out here . . . well, not that alone. There's people see.'

'Dust people?' Ari blurted, perhaps unwisely. Urran narrowed his eyes at her and handed her the pipe.

'Dust people?'

'Yeah, like that guy who came one night. The one who didn't say anything.' She took only a small draw of the pipe, not wanting to embarrass herself with a coughing fit.

'Oh, right, *them*, those dust people. Oh, there's plenty of them.'

'Are they real? Like us, I mean.' She handed him the pipe again.

'Real enough. Different maybe.' He smiled, chewing on the pipe stem. 'They won't hurt you, though. Nor the jelly-crusts.'

'What?!'

'Oh, you'll see plenty of them soon. Nearer Lazar's. No, I reckon it's the ones you never catch sight of you have to worry about, which is why I don't think a chucky young thing like you should be sittin' out here all alone.'

Ari resented that. 'I'm perfectly safe. Eve's taught me how to use my senses . . .'

Urran laughed. 'Girly, against the kind of folk I'm talkin' about, you're senses are diddly-squat! Eve should know better than to fill you with such talk. Why you think we travel together, huh?'

'Oh? If these *people* you're on about are that bad, it isn't much safer if you're here, is it?'

'Oh, we can see the light of the fire here. We're close enough to be safe,' he replied airily.

'You're not making much sense,' Ari said, realising this was all a game, and probably at her expense. He must think she was so stupid.

'Maybe I just need an excuse to . . .' He casually slung an arm around her shoulder. His hand hung over her chest. Ari looked at it in the same way she'd look at a very large spider hanging there. Of course. He'd been watching her. He'd followed her. Urran sidled up against her. 'Cold, honey?'

'No,' she replied, but filled with a horrified fascination at this new development.

'Ah, come on.' Urran put his pipe down on the ground beside them and nuzzled the side of her neck, bringing with him his masculine scent and the warmth of his body. Ari was moved by a monumental astonishment that such an attractive creature as Urran could be interested in her in this way and also a sense of alarm, remembering all Leila had told her. Did this count? If she responded to Urran's embrace, did it have to get all complicated, triggering off security codes all through her libido? Why should I be denied this? she thought. I'm free. I'm me. Why can't I have this like Elice and Justinette and the others. Impulsively, she groped to put her arms round Urran's neck and he made a surprised, delighted sound. He'd obviously expected more resistance.

She'd never kissed a man in her life. Doing it, she realised what she'd been missing. Damn Ewan! He was dead. His sick plans couldn't touch her any more. She'd deny them, blot them out, curse him, blank him, unmake him, become she: woman. Urran pushed her back on to the prickly dry moss and they happily writhed and nuzzled, Ari with a fierceness that was more than straightforward desire. Urran grabbed her hand and guided it between his legs, murmured, 'You want this?

You want this?' Ari was filled with a sense of power, the hard clarity of the night condensed inside her, a black core splintered by rushing stars. Yes, she wanted this. She was conscious of Urran's hands moving over skin. It was delicious like the taste of vanilla, the feeling of fur. She wriggled pleasurably beneath his touch. A languorous wave was rising within her, higher, higher, a tidal wave, curling over, crested with sparkling spume, the ultimate in elemental power, ready to crash, crash, sending up spray a hundred clicks, touching clouds, touching sky, sparkling under the cruel sun, this was it, yes, yes! She let him undo her jeans, felt his hand slip against her flesh, opened her legs willingly to let him touch her there. She felt like a sacrifice awaiting the blade, knowing that death would bring immortality.

And then: from the locked part of her mind a dark moving mass woke up and passed like a ghost through the barriers. It began to engulf her entire body, brindled with electric tongues. It was like blackness covering the sun, smothering the wave of her desire, threading it with sizzling, spiky fingers of harsh brilliance that electrocuted her flesh, spasmed, sending her crazy with pain. She was plugged in, sucking in, a million million volts of pain.

Vaguely, she was aware of Urran making distressed sounds, of him backing away, of her body being arched and rigid, her tongue protruding from a grimacing mouth. The night hummed, crackled, whamming into her, locking her limbs and mind. Extinction would be a relief.

'What the fuck is going on here?'

She sensed a living manifestation of anger. It was red with a white core.

She heard Urran say, 'Lady, I don't know, soul, it

wasn't me. Swear to the Goddess, it wasn't me. She just flipped out. Went into a convulsion or something.'

An absurdly cool inner part of Ari sensed someone laying her on her side, pushing hard fingers into her mouth, pressing down on her tongue. Then they slapped her hard across the face. This new, sharp pain exorcised the darkness. Suddenly she felt perfectly normal. The night swayed in; silence, but for a distant hum. Cabochon's hair was dangling in her face, his naked torso suspended above her, his face tense with panic.

'Goddess, you all right, Ari?' he asked and turned away, spitting out, 'You prick, you utter prick, Urran!'

'Sorry,' Urran responded, sheepishly.

'Get out of here!'

'All right, all right, I'm going. Cool off, soul. I didn't mean to hurt her.'

Ari didn't see him leave. She had closed her eyes tightly, hideously ashamed that Cabochon should see her like this.

'Can you sit up?' He made no further move to touch her.

'Yeah, I'm OK. I'll live.' She struggled into a sitting position and fumbled to do up her clothes. Her legs felt numb and bloodless. 'Goddess, that was . . . that was . . .'

'I know what that was,' Cabochon said drily and then, more warmly, 'You stupid little bitch. Weren't you warned?'

'Of course,' she answered sharply. 'Maybe I just didn't believe. I had to find out. It's no big deal. It's my life and my experience. I had to find out.'

Cabochon sighed and stood up. His knees clicked.

'You'd better get back. Come on, I'll walk with you.'

Ari ungracefully stumbled to her feet. 'How come you found us?' she asked.

Cabochon smiled tightly. 'Eve was looking for you, and Urran's been eyeing you up for days. I still have instinct, you know, in spite of everything.'

'What everything? I don't know about that,' Ari answered.

He shrugged. 'Congratulations. You're about the only one who doesn't.'

Ari thought about how Cabochon had known what to do when he found her. Did that mean he was aware of her condition? 'Does everyone know about me?' she asked him.

'How should I know? Jordan told me a couple of things. He's a sceptic.'

'Oh. Um . . . is it OK to take your arm? I still feel shaky but I don't want to go crazy again.'

Cabochon stuck out his elbow. 'I reckon you're safe with me,' he said. She took his arm, suppressing, suppressing, oh how bitterly, the experience of his muscle and bone, the heat of his skin.

'Goddess, I was dreading getting to Arcady and being dished up to Leila's guru man, but I've changed my mind now,' she said. 'I want this curse lifted.'

'It's not just the lifting of a curse little Ari,' Cabochon said. 'It's what comes with the lifting.'

'I know. I felt some of that just now. I know.'

'You've got to be sensible.'

'Yes, I know. Don't lecture me.'

'Well, it has to be said.'

He could say anything he wanted to her, insult her to pulp, she wouldn't mind. He was Cabochon and she was walking by his side, her arm through his, and all of what had happened didn't matter any more. Ari was young, resilient, and had a young girl's longings and sudden, eager, consuming passions. It was perhaps the one thing Ewan, in his cold, analytical way, had not counted on.

As if Urran's conversation with Ari had invoked them, jellycrusts materialised from the dry lands the very next day. Cable had stopped the truck for the night, pulling off the highway as usual, drifting towards some kind of shelter. Today it was the rounded, weathered remains of a clump of buildings that may have been part of a farm once. It was not easy to tell. At one time, rich people had owned big houses with lots of stables and garages in the country: it could easily have been one of those. Ari had spent an uncomfortable day travelling, pretending to be asleep so she didn't have to look at Urran. She'd confessed everything to Eve when Cabochon took her back to the tepee, speaking in an almost hostile manner, expecting Eve to chastise her. Naturally, the woman did nothing of the kind, leaving Ari feeling somehow unsatisfied. Eve did not even say, 'Didn't I warn you, girl?' She did not say anything, so Ari was forced to cry, 'Well? What do you think of that?'

'I can't give you no wisdom on that score. I told you that,' Eve had replied. She sounded almost embarrassed. 'You were right. You had to see for yourself.'

When Cable parked the Spirit, Ari quickly followed Justinette and Elice outside, fearing Urran might say something to her. The other girls went to grub about in the ruins, looking for things that might be useful, and Ari tagged along. The stones had been picked clean a long time before though, and no one found anything of interest. Ari felt the other two were being a little off with her; it may have been paranoia. Had Urran talked to them? At least she didn't feel awkward about approaching Cabochon now. She left Elice and Justinette to their exploring and went to sit beside him as he built the fire. She was hoping he'd say something about the night before but was disappointed. Maybe it was because Ezooli came to join them, messing with her baby and joking with Cabochon about the way the fire was taking so long to light. Ari picked up a few dry sticks to Cabochon's comment, 'That's really not helping you know,' when Ezooli said, 'Uh-oh, looks like we've got company.'

R. J. Somesense liked meetings. He liked them a lot. Even more so when he could lead his people up from the dust, through trembling air, into the laps of more conventional travellers. It was a strange mixture of fury and defiance and frustration he felt at those times. People looked at him and his followers and had to smother a quick ripple of aversion which, superstitiously, they always sought to disguise. There was little tremble in the air that night, however, when the Leaning Towards Revision Line-Huggers (not Somesense's idea; he had inherited the group name) spilled over the smoothed ruins into the light of Star Eye's fire. His prime touch Louanne hissed through her teeth, a sound she had perfected to mystic import and said, 'She, the squatter there, *she* has colour of it, all right!' Somesense was vaguely annoyed that he hadn't been the one to say something like that, although he'd been aware of it from the moment he'd seen the natro group. A thin girl, by the fire, squatting next to a power rod of unique silkiness. These things, even before he'd seen more, told him the Huggers had stumbled across, at last, something out of the ordinary, something they could study and perhaps, if the study merited it, attach sublime importance to. He raised his hand, flexing the fingers, feeling the stretch and creak of his second skin. It was a signal. The troupe stood upright, silent, wind blowing hair and any item of clothing long and loose enough to catch the breeze. They stood there in a row, ten of them, of differing heights and build, but possessing the same quality of stony stillness.

Ari, by the fire, thought, 'Statues clothed. Yes. *Old* statues.'

Ezooli sighed. 'Goddess, no! We have to have these creeps this time?' She hoisted Stickit over her shoulder, sculpted bones showing through ebony flesh above thin, drooping shirt, gorgon hair twisted into a lump atop her head. Ari looked up at her to take her eyes away from the disquieting apparitions. Ezooli was not afraid of them, so it was OK they were there. She sounded merely irritated, or even bored. 'I'll seek Leila,' she said, striding over cooking pots, Stickit waving at the ruins, a smile on his calm, buddha face.

'What *are* they?' Ari hissed in an exaggerated whisper to Cabochon.

'Jellycrusts,' said Cabochon, stirring the fire with a stick. Ari wanted to get up, talk to the others, ask questions, but Cabochon was making no move to do so, so she hunched down again, knees up, her thumbnails in her mouth and thought, 'Are they looking at *me*?'

The rest of the group were congregating in a territorial sort of way. Ari tried to analyse the shared vibration.

They did not feel threatened, but they did not feel exactly comfortable either. Everyone was hovering round the side door of Rentfree Aphrodite. Leila and Jordan must be inside.

R. J. Somesense bathed in the atmosphere he and his people were creating. All such times were of religious significance, to be recorded with the mind's eye. Omens abounded: the quality of light, the dip of a single bird high above, a particular sound, a child's unsuppressed cry at being interrupted. The Huggers had been travelling in silence for almost three dark-times now; that presaged an Approach of some kind, as each individual ordered themselves to greet it in the proper manner. And there it was: the Revelation.

A girl: white, young, not beautiful exactly, but that was only right. She: like a membrane of human skin around a core of heat and power. Somesense, as his name implied, gathered the girl herself was largely unaware of what she contained, or more properly, what her skin covered. His people travelled the land, recorders of the Is Now, their minds remembering with photographic clarity everything they beheld, with the faithful precision of a sound recording, everything they heard. When the time came to die, the knowledge was transferred, in secret ways, on the path of High Currents. Somesense felt the knowledge of his people was a new bible: a goddess bible, but a history book too. This time, there would be no mistake, no error in translation. Everything was recorded as fact, without subjective slant. In a world dizzy with conflicting cultures, futures and fates, it was inevitable there had to come a Difference Clothed in Flesh, someone who had the capacity to leave a mark. It always happened that way. Somesense also knew that this person forever stood at a crossroads upon the path of life and that many of those paths led to obscurity, nothingness, death, complacence, ignorance and even more pointless tracks to subvert the possibility of making the mark. Such folk were only human and were prey to errors of judgement. He for one, having studied the past minutely in earlier days, did not believe the world was any better for certain people having made the choice to die for their beliefs, if choice it was. Somesense had an idea of how the world might have been if things had gone differently back then. And it had nothing to do with religion at all. That had come later. He looked at the girl of hidden colours and saw a few of her paths, radiating off, diminishing glows. He would have to talk to her. He knew he must not, could not, influence her decisions and choices for the future, but considered it important to record her Is Now. Just in case.

Leila jumped from Aphrodite, pulling on a jacket. 'Dammit,' she said quietly. She knew jellycrusts were harmless, but they would always insist on making such an event about their encounters with other travellers. It annoyed Leila as being unnecessary and rather defiant. Nevertheless, mindful of the courtesy of The Road (a complex mixture of fear and superstition) she put a smile over her face and went towards the silent group, holding out her hand. She had learned some years ago that it was a gesture jellycrusts couldn't help but be flattered and surprised by. It always gave her the advantage in the first stages of introduction, she felt. The tall male standing just ahead of his troupe took her hand in his own with a remarkable amount of sang-froid. Perhaps she'd met him before and taught him the trick. Leila smiled inside.

The jellycrusts, scorning the protection of travelling within armoured trucks, walked the dry lands in ragged groups, pushing or dragging their belongings in carts and sledges. Their skins were concealed by a thick, insulating gel once manufactured for military use. Since then, the jellycrusts had bought up all remaining stocks of the stuff, slapping it on their integument, where it accumulated the dust and debris of the desert lands; hence their nickname. It reminded Leila of certain larval creatures who once lived in freshwater streams, and which perhaps still did somewhere, who attached stones and water rubbish to their skins, making a shell to live in. The jellycrusts could look like that: frightening, peeling, gaunt creatures. She used to wonder whether they ever washed it all off and started again from a clean skin. Did they make love? It was not a pleasant image. The gel had a strange smell, rather like a room that had been locked up too long; a wooden room beaten by sunheat, rotted by rain, stale and with the promise of hidden corruption. They always wore bulky, colourless clothes, quasi-military in appearance, heavily adorned with totemic ornaments, constructed from the desert trash.

The jellycrust who had shaken her hand (she'd wiped it quickly on the backside of her jeans) bowed slightly, just his head, and said, 'An evening of clean air to you, Madam. I am R. J. Somesense and these people are the Leaning Towards Re-vision Line-Huggers.'

'Hi,' Leila said, smiling inanely and rather crazily over Somesense's tall shoulder. 'You people want to come sit with us? You're welcome. Hot day, huh?' She led them over to the fire. 'We're Star Eye. You want water?'

It was customary to offer water to anyone who crossed a natro path. Again, superstition, the subliminal fear of being out alone and friendless, the memory of a good deed somehow promising beneficent reprisal.

To Ari, still hunched by Cabochon's fire, Leila's voice

sounded high, as if she was uneasy. Cabochon, as if telepathic, chose that moment to say, 'They can come out with some weird shit sometimes, you know. Nightmare stuff. People wish they'd stay away from us, but they always show up around here. The area must be thick with them.'

'What do they want?'

Cabochon sighed. 'Hard to say. They feel they have to impose their odd lifeview on people, I guess. Sometimes they'll give you things. Their totems are supposed to be strong.'

'They look horrible. Are they falling apart?'

'Nah, that's the gloop they put on their bodies. Keeps out the UV, any unfriendly vapours that are drifting around with poison on their minds. See the masks hanging round their waists? Wear one of those and you can walk through a bad fog safe enough to think up poetry in the murk. Kind of peaceful, huh? I wouldn't fancy trying it though.'

'No, me neither!' Ari was still terrified of the fog.

Star Eye and the jellycrusts sat down around the fire and Ari got up at last to help set up camp and prepare a meal. Nobody ever said anything if you didn't join in camp duties, but the bad feelings hit you like a hurricane if you sat around doing nothing. Charcoal Eve was stirring up a stew over one of the stoves, Ezooli beside her, shredding some sheets of meat-protein to throw into it. Ari fetched two cans of water from the truck tanks to make the meal go further. 'I wish they wouldn't look at me,' she said to Ezooli.

'Seems you're attractin' a bit of attention,' Ezooli conceded.

'Well, they have the gift of seein',' Eve explained.

'Why, they can see right into you, girl!' Ezooli said

with a laugh, putting her long-nailed, panther hand with its rough, dry palm on Ari's shoulder.

'Can they?' Ari narrowed her eyes at the jellycrusts who were all sitting straight-backed and cross-legged round the fire. None of them appeared to be looking at her now.

As soon as the Reverent Silence of the Joy of Replenishment could be breached, R. J. Somesense broke open his pouch of smoking mix and offered to share it with the natro group. He smiled in satisfaction at their enthusiasm. That was one thing his people were always welcome for indeed! He'd taken care to sit himself beside the red-haired woman who was clearly the group Motivator and Speaking-Tongue, and passed her the pipe first. She inhaled lustily and croaked, 'That sure is fine, Mr Somesense.'

'R. J., please,' he replied. He knew about the art of timing and when to press the moment key to greatest effect, and so waited until Leila had passed the pipe on before saying, with surgeon's precision, 'The fair little girl over there . . .' Nothing more. Not yet. He did not look at Leila but was deeply aware of her sharp realignment, the banishing of smoke languor, a sudden alertness. Oh yes. He'd been right.

'What about her?' Leila asked. Her casual tone did not deceive him.

'We perceive the innermost of her. Saw it instantly.' He directed a brief, poignant glance at the woman through a fringe of ropy tangles. 'She is a carrier of great magnitude.'

Leila laughed in a forced way. 'You could say we are aware of . . . the girl's possibilities.' She sounded greatly upset. Afraid, maybe. 'But it's not what you think. Repressed trauma. We're working it out.' She knew better than to try and deceive a jellycrust entirely. It was pointless to deny Ari was different, but she didn't trust anyone enough to tell them the truth.

Somesense nodded slowly. 'Mmm, mmm,' he said. 'Caution, caution. Always wise. You are a wise woman, Leila . . . Leila . . .' He frowned, prompting.

'Just Leila will do,' the woman replied drily.

'Just Leila.' They both watched the passage of the pipe for some time before he said, 'I would like to speak with your girl who suffers this repressed trauma.'

'I'd rather you didn't,' Leila said quickly. 'She's nervous. I don't mean to be rude, but she's never seen a . . . one of your kind before. You wouldn't get much sense out of her and it would upset her.'

'You mean you want me to Peel?' he asked. Leila looked back at him, an expression of quizzical amusement and alarm on her face.

'You what?!'

'I believe you heard. It is not unprecedented. We slough regularly. Did you think otherwise?' He laughed, condescendingly.

Leila shrugged. 'Well . . .' She frowned. 'Why is . . . the girl so important to you? I've seen you watching her. Has someone sent you here?'

Somesense held up his hands in appeasement. 'Please! No, no. We *see* her, is all. I have to record her Is Now; nothing more. We are chroniclers, leaning towards revision, as is implied. Surely you are aware it is vital your girl is recorded?'

Leila made a disparaging sound. 'Recorded? Maybe. But it makes me think about how when something's recorded, it's always around for people to play back. Understand?'

'You are very afraid of her.'

'No, not *of* her. I have a responsibility. She's a friend's kid. A dear friend.'

'She also has a responsibility,' Somesense said gently. 'For her own life. At least let me ask her myself. I promise I mean no harm to her. You have been on the road long enough, Just Leila, to know about us, the people you call the jellycrusts! You know our function, our purpose. Your paranoia and protectiveness are unjustified in this case.'

'Course I know that!' Leila said in an urgent whisper. 'But I also know there are folk around who'd use your reputation, and appearance, to wheedle and deceive their way into a group's heart without arousing suspicion. I know when to be careful.'

'Do you really mean "no"?'

Leila studied him for a moment. 'Listen R. J., I hate to be unsocial and all, but it is necessary. If the girl really is so important to you, if you really want to record her, we're going to Lazar Farm and you can speak to her there if you care to follow. I reckon there're enough of you people around there for them to smell a rat if you're not genuine. Also, I'll feel safer when I've got her nearer Arcady, and no, I'm not going to explain that.'

'Are you offering us transport?'

'Like hell! Think these people could stand being cooped up with you for days? If you're that interested, you follow. That's all I'm offering.'

'Because you also want to know what we may Notice in her, yes?'

Leila pulled a face. 'Did I say that? I know her. You can't tell me anything.'

'We can.'

'You can think that if you like. She may not want to talk to you. I'm not going to force her.'

'She will. She wants knowledge.'

The pipe had come back to them. Leila shook her head when Somesense offered it to her. 'I can't let you tell her anything without you telling me first. I have to be there.'

Somesense nodded again. 'We will come to Lazar Farm. We will Peel and Dance. And you may be there, Just Leila, when we talk to your girl.'

Ari, looking at Leila and Somesense conferring through a veil of a red and yellow flame, knew she was the subject of discussion. Rather than unease or worry, this provoked a feeling of excitement within her. She felt compelled to say something to somebody and because Elice was the only person available at the time, turned to her and murmured, 'I will soon be free.' She guessed this would be a pretty oblique remark and was surprised when Elice answered sharply, 'From what I've heard you were quite free with Urran last night!'

'What did he say?'

Elice made a spitting, catlike noise. 'Say? Think we're blind or somethin'? Said nothing. *I* saw. You shouldn't mess with him, Ari. I know!'

Ari felt as if Elice had dragged abrasive claws across her skin. She felt embarrassed. 'I don't think you saw right,' she said stiffly. 'I didn't mess with anybody.'

'Anybody?' Elice cawed with laughter, putting considerable effort into the hilarity. 'Saw Cabochon bring you back to camp. Think you can score there too? You're a fool! He wears Jordan's mark, Ari, don't you know that?'

'What do you mean?'

'I mean you should use your eyes more often, that's all.'

Ari looked over at where Cabochon was sitting, next

to Jordan as usual. She wasn't sure she understood properly what Elice was implying. After all, there was little evidence for it. Cabochon and Jordan didn't seem to touch each other more than any other members of the group. She suspected Elice was merely spreading a rumour.

'Why do you have to say things like that?' she said, for the first time feeling confident enough to challenge the older girl. 'You make it all up! You're sick! I don't want to hear your stories about people.'

'Stories!' Elice was immediately outraged. 'You'd better bide your mouth, Ari Famber. You ever seen two snakes in the dirt, the way they weave about each other?' She jerked a thumb at Cabochon and Jordan. 'That's them! They're not always that careful. We seen things before. We know. So does Leila.'

'So what? It's none of our business.'

'Suit yourself. You don't know it all yet, Ari, Miss Powerpack!' Elice jumped to her feet and stormed off. Usually, after a scene of that kind, Ari felt hot and tearful, yet tonight she felt absurdly calm, so calm in fact, that she stood up and went to sit by Cabochon.

'I just upset Elice,' she said, proud of herself.

'You come over here for proof or something?' Jordan asked her, with such a direct gaze that Ari's mood fell from her instantly. She felt an old, familiar heat creep up her face.

'I . . . No! I mean, it's none of my business . . . I . . .'
She fumbled helplessly for words. Cabochon made a sympathetic sound and put his hand on the back of her neck.

'Don't fret,' he said. 'There's adventure in the air tonight, don't you think?'

'Whatever's in the air sure smells sour,' Jordan replied and laughed. He meant the jellycrusts.

*   *   *

Two clicks east of Lazar Farm, where the old, shaken-up
highway struggles west towards Arcady, the totems of
Emanuel Hiram Lazar IV (and family) began to punctu-
ate the dust alongside the road. Ari, peering out of the
truck window at the gradually clustering camps and
shanty-towns presaging civilisation said, 'Look, is that a
skull?'

Urran leaned over her without touching – he was still
warily maintaining a certain distance between them –
and replied, 'Sure is. A ram skull.'

'It advertises their affluence,' Elice added. 'Like it's
saying, see, we have sheep here.'

'I can't see any fields yet,' Ari said, pressing her face
against the glass and trying to see past the armour plating
and further up the highway.

'You won't,' Elice said, making it sound like a mystery. 'Lazar's fields aren't exactly visible from here.'

The shanty-towns diminished, and now the trucks
sped along, through avenues of windmills, the horizon
aglint with the shimmer of solar panels and terraced
banks of light-storing crystal plates. It was an alien landscape. Huge conduits, like tongues, hung out of the earth
in places.

Ari slumped back down on her cushion, digging an
elbow into the slumbering form of Justinette, who
merely squeaked without waking. Her heart was beginning to beat faster now. She knew whatever happened
to her at Lazar Farm would be the beginning of her
education – about life and about herself. Leila had
taken her aside the day after the jellycrusts had appeared
and told her that R. J. Somesense might be following
them to Lazar's, and that, if he did, Ari could expect him
to ask her questions and so on. She explained a little

about the jellycrusts' function. 'He may also be able to tell you things about yourself that nobody but your Father knew,' she added – somewhat reluctantly, Ari thought.

'Why couldn't he do that out here? Why does he have to come with us?' Ari asked.

Leila's face twisted impatiently. 'I'd prefer it to happen at Lazar's, if it happens at all,' she said sharply. 'I feel safer there among friends.'

Ari had an idea Leila was not exactly keen on the jellycrust being interested in her, but also that Leila did not have utter control over her. She didn't want R. J. to speak to Ari but was apparently powerless to prevent it.

Leila, sitting up front with Cable, feet up on the control console of the truck, chain-smoked, swigged beer from some cans they'd picked up at the last store stop and gossiped cautiously about Cabochon. She had never been able to ascertain Cable's feelings towards the boy, Cabochon being one of the few people Cable never passed comment on. She kept to safe ground, talking about Cabochon's problems back in Arcady. 'You think he should stay here at Lazar's?' Leila asked.

'He won't stay where he don't want to be put, honey,' Cable replied.

'I don't want the others getting involved in some scene again,' she said.

'Uh-huh. Turn the lights on, will you?'

Leila pressed a few pads. 'I mean, it's not like I don't care or anything . . .'

'Hold on, we're goin' under!' Cable sounded the deep, aggressive horn of the Spirit. Dim red light filled the cab and, with a back-wheel buck, the truck swerved to the left, off the highway, and down a steep incline towards the mouth of a wide tunnel disappearing underground. 'Check all!' Cable said, reaching for a cigarette from Leila's pack. Leila adjusted the micro eye-height monitors, taking the keypad from the console and leaning back in her seat with it on her knee, playing a tune of test signals.

'Seems fine,' she said. 'Clean anyhow.' Lazar's people had got fussy recently about contamination. 'Apart from the suspect water tank, the night-vision looks a little shaky, but I can't see that's any of Lazar's business, can you?' She put the keypad back in its housing, leaning back again with her hands behind her head. Bright, acidic sodium light strobed through the cab windows, flashing more slowly as Cable decelerated. The checkpoint was coming up.

An ambitious project from the start, Lazar Farm was the product of one rich man's dream, one rich man's fear. An eccentric aristocrat, the second Emanuel Lazar had commissioned this underground community decades ago. Ahead of its time, one might say, ridiculed and scorned during its construction. People scoffed and said. 'When will we ever need such a thing as an underground community?' The main fear of the world at that time had, of course, been nuclear devastation. Perhaps the farm began as some kind of fallout shelter. Since then its ambitions and size had enlarged accordingly to accommodate the true holocaust, which had been ecological. As primitive peoples had always feared, the sky actually had come to fall on their heads when the ozone layer collapsed. Now Lazar Farm was a pure, sweet haven in the wreck of the world, nourished and enfolded by the spirit of Gaiah herself, nourished by the winds and sunlight collected by the crystal plates, solar panels and mills above. Going there was like a journey to the centre of the Earth to find a secret, alien community living there, where sunlight shone without a sun, breathing gentle rays down upon the glossy hides of placid herd beasts and tanning the smiling inhabitants to a tawny beige. The roof of this immense underground cavern was concealed by holographic projections which could depict a variety of natural skyscapes. The sunlight which shone from a huge crystal plate on a mechanical arc, was not artificial, merely redirected. Natro groups from all over the world swarmed there for temporary work, social and ritual activities, the sharing of knowledge. Needless to say, such a paradise had to be held on to firmly. Guards thorned with the latest state-of-the-art fireware thronged around the checkpoint: blondhaired and lithe, their lion-tan skins shown to effect against soft khaki and green. These people were stamped with Lazar's mark. Lazar was a movie star come to life; handsome as a dirty thought, promiscuous, charming, fierce and brave. Leila considered that his faults, well hidden, must be twice as shaming as most people's because of this. Despite his perennial courtesy towards her, she did not like the man. She was not looking forward to speaking to him, and that was going to be unavoidable. She needed the work he'd once offered her, and hoped the offer was still open. She'd already called him on the commset but he'd been cagey, just telling her he looked forward to talking with her. That could mean anything from bestowing a fully-fledged contract on her to a request for casual sex. Either was likely. Leila shuddered and then reminded herself that working here for a few weeks would provide Star Eye with some therapy they sorely needed. Emanuel Lazar she could handle. She'd just have to.

Cable pulled the Spirit to a rumbling, purring,

snorting standstill. The previous night, he'd rummaged through the garbage on the truck console and found the sliver of plastic which was a regular pass into Lazar Farm. These people couldn't be too careful. He passed it to the gleaming boy who came up to the window.

'This pass is for fifteen. How many you got brother?'

'No more than that. Wanna count 'em?' Cable jerked his thumb at the back of the truck.

'No more than fifteen in the two trucks?' The boy looked sceptical.

'Listen, we like space,' Leila said irritably. 'Now will you get out of our way, please? Lazar is expecting us.'

The boy stepped back churlishly without a word and slapped the side of the Spirit, gesturing for Jordan to follow with a wave.

'These people!' Leila said waspishly.

Cable kicked the Spirit into life and she surged forward, down, always down.

'So, it's under the ground!' Ari said in the back. 'I never thought a farm could be underground.'

'Wait'll you see it!' Justinette said, who had woken up. 'Say, you think I should put some make-up on?' She'd fished a tarnished mirror from her colourless with age shoulder bag and was wiping fingers under her eyes.

'Oh, time for that later,' Elice said. 'There may be nothing happening anyway.'

'There's always something happening here!' Justinette replied. 'Enough to tart up for anyhow. We're only two weeks away from the Lithafest, too. Bound to be people beginning to show up for that.'

Elice grunted.

Ari was oblivious to their exchange, nose pressed right up against the window once more. The tunnel had delivered them into an enchanted land, or at least that was how it looked to her. Steady, benevolent light fell from high above. She craned her head back in an attempt to see the source, but could not manage it. The illusion of a cloudless, summer blue sky was faultless. The truck was now cruising smoothly along a flat red road, flanked by unbelievably green fields that stretched towards what could only be a wood. Lush, acid-green leaves sparkled in the clear light. Between the trees, Ari glimpsed a metallic glint that could only mean water. Whole flocks of birds flapped like black sheets, soaring up from the fields as the trucks disturbed their tranquillity. A teenage girl strode, loose-limbed, in a baggy, cottony dress, through the thigh-deep grass, leading a pony with a child on its back. She was chewing a stalk, and waved an enthusiastic hello to Star Eye as they roared past.

Ari was delighted. This place could not be real. It must be a movie set or something. A herd of cows mooed their way across the road ahead of them, causing Cable to stamp the brakes a little. The Spirit of Disorder wheezed and rattled, as if uneasy at being in so clean and smooth a world, used as she was to the dust and chaos of the dry lands and beyond.

Further on they came across the signs of agriculture: fields of corn, motionless and lush, flanked by domed translucent greenhouses, steamy places of jungle-thick growth. 'Can I open the window?' Ari asked. 'Can I smell it?'

'Sure.' Urran obliged by cranking the capricious frame up. What hit Ari's nose was a stifling blend of heat and rich earth, the rank tang of spice herbs, the bloated steam of fertiliser and warm animal. The smells flowed and changed as they progressed along the road. Soon, a midnight fume of heady flowers filled the air, melding into a deep, vegetable root dark. People working the fields were nearly naked, babies slung on backs in slings, horses dozing, one foot resting, in front of half-laden carts. Everything possessed a picture-book clarity. It was as if everyone was posing or acting; a scenario of perfect contentment. Lazar Town came into view above an avenue of slim, dark trees. Low, stucco dwellings hugged the road, each with its own garden of produce out back.

Lazar's house lay, naturally, at the very centre of Lazar Town's spiralling, maze-like streets. Cable and Jordan coaxed the rumbling trucks right under the white arch that led to the circular courtyard. Ari and the others tumbled out of the side door like a litter of puppies, stretching. The yard was enormous, accommodating two other brooding, dust-mantled trucks, one half-washed. There was a lot of activity, people rushing to and fro, others standing to watch the new arrivals. Leila and Jordan walked into one of the buildings in an authoritative, 'we have a right to be here' manner, which signified, in a way, that they did not. Justinette, keen to explore territories that might have changed since she was last here, was eager to set off on a foray, and she wanted Ari and Elice for company. Ari wasn't sure whether she should just wander off without asking Leila, but Justinette argued that they wouldn't be *going* anywhere exactly. 'Where's your sense of adventure?' she asked.

'All right,' Ari agreed.

'Are you coming Urran?' Elice asked.

'No. See you later girls.'

Elice marched towards the gates with a face like thunder. Justinette pulled a face at Ari. 'I want a drink, a real drink,' she said. 'Come on. Last one out of the yard is buying!'

Justinette, almost as if she'd dowsed for liquor, led them straight into a bar. It had nothing to discern it from any other building from the outside, but once within, a low throb of music filled the dark air, complementing the malty smell of ale. At this hour, before midday, the bar was mostly empty. The barman had long brown hair in a pony-tail, bare, scarred, muscled arms and an eye-patch. He didn't look too impressed with Justinette's effusive demands for refreshment. Ari hung back. She felt an intruder in this place. The walls and ceiling were plastered with colourful posters, most of which bore the image of aggressive-looking people toting weapons which may have been musical instruments. They were night creatures, looking uncomfortable and self-conscious in the dim light that was unconvincing with the freshness of daylight. She supposed Lazar Farm must have night-times. Would there be an artificial moonlight to replace the sun? Somehow, she felt strongly that there would. She and Elice sat themselves at a corner table which looked as if someone, or something, had been taking bites out of it, and waited for Justinette to bring their drinks over. Elice had offered to pay. 'I wonder if those jellycrusts will show up,' Ari said, feeling she ought to initiate some conversation at least. She and Elice were still not getting on particularly well after their brief exchange of sharpness nearly a week ago.

'So, what's their interest in you?' Elice asked. Ari thought it was unlikely Elice really wanted to know the answer, because she begrudged anyone but herself attracting attention. She shrugged. Elice was probably the last person she would discuss her secrets with. The other girl leaned over a little way, flicking a quick glance towards the bar where Justinette was still flamboyantly flirting with the barman.

'Stay away from Urran here,' she hissed, eyes sliding uncomfortably from side to side.

Ari was taken aback by this. Interference with Urran, of any kind, could not have been further from her mind just now. Elice's tone annoyed her. 'I'll do what I like,' she said.

Elice leaned back. 'Make a fool of yourself then!'

Justinette brought the drinks over. 'Oooh, smell this stuff! Nectar!' She dumped a frothing glass in front of each of them. 'Well, Liss, got any plans?'

Ari couldn't help laughing out loud. She could think of one, at least. Elice ignored her. 'I thought I'd try the packing plant. The pay was good there last time we were here. Why don't you come with me? We could both get a job there.'

Justinette shrugged. 'Might. I sort of fancied working out of doors, so to speak. Picking, or something. The scenery's better too. All those guys with their shirts off! Being with Star Eye's a real drag, Ari: the ones that aren't spoken for are either men-only guys, or ugly. Really! Well, apart from Urran, that is.' She laughed and Elice pulled a sour face. 'How about you, Ari?' Justinette asked. 'What you planning to do while we're here?'

Ari shrugged. 'Well, I hadn't really thought. The fields sound like a good idea though. I think I'd like that.'

'The pay's rubbish!' Elice said. 'You'd be better off in the plant. Leila will expect us all to pay our share when we're back outside. The more money you have the better.'

'Oh for Goddess' sake, Liss!' Justinette said, rolling her eyes. 'There's really not that much difference in the wages between jobs.'

'That's right. I'm always wrong, aren't I!' Elice said in a hard voice. Ari detected the invocation of tears.

'Lighten up!' Justinette said, putting one of her hands on Elice's and shaking them. 'We're here to enjoy ourselves! Don't be glum.'

'It's easy for you to say that!' Elice snapped and stood up quickly, knocking the table. Ari steadied her drink and watched Elice march off towards the restrooms. She shook her head.

'Boy, you are just so patient with her, Net!'

Justinette shrugged. 'I know. She can't sort her life out. Urran doesn't help. He puts her on and shrugs her off like an old coat. Today he snubs her, tonight he'll sniff around the town and get laid. Tomorrow he'll take her to bed for a while. It happens that way.'

'Then why does she take it?'

Justinette took a drink. 'She calls it love, I believe. Urran doesn't deceive her or anything, but she wants more than he can give.' She brightened up. 'Oh, all that's a real downer! Let's forget it. I'm going to find myself a sweet, young, golden boy while I'm here. How about you?'

Ari averted her gaze. 'Maybe,' she said.

'Leila, Leila *Saatchi*,' smoothed Emanuel Lazar IV, passing his lips just above the woman's hand. It was unnecessary, a preliminary to their privacy. She and Jordan had been talking with Lazar for half an hour outside already. Leila withdrew her hand from his polite, manicured grasp, weirdly embarrassed. This man always threw her out of sync somehow: words didn't come easily to her in his presence, actions were doomed to be clumsy. One day she dreaded he was going to ask for something she was unwilling to give. Her reticence would show, whatever her mouth uttered, and it would be the axe for her one way or another. She wished it wasn't necessary to pause their journey here.

'You're lookin' well soul,' she said, dutifully. Lazar would know this for an indisputable fact, but Leila was canny enough to know he still liked to hear it. They were in Lazar's 'office', a great canyon of a room, lined by disapproving Lazar ancestors portrayed in oils. Near the back of the room two of the women were displayed as holopics; a sign of the times, representing perhaps an aunt, a sister, mother. Lazar comfortably filled his cave-space with an abundant surplus of personality. One wall was entirely covered by monitor screens, all buzzing greyly but for one which was trained on the outer door.

239

Leila wondered whether the blank screens were a sham, turned off for her benefit, usually engrossed in being the sinister, roving eyes about the makebelieve world of Lazar Farm, the place of surreal shadows. She never felt at ease here. She accepted the offered refreshment; cruel wine, one of those vintages stiff with vanity for being rare and expensive and thus sour on the tongue, resentful of being drunk.

'So,' Lazar said silkily, elaborately putting himself in a chair behind his great table of a desk; long, soft coat arranged artfully, satiny cloth falling back from the tanned arms, revealing a precise arrangement of gold bangles. His square, handsome face was framed by pale hair, held back at the neck. 'Are you going to tell me what it is you want from me, Leila Saatchi?'

Leila sidled past the chair he expected her to sit in and perched on the edge of his desk, painfully sipping the wine. There was a taste of metal to it, definitely. Her display of nonchalance and casual ease was an agony she hoped he could not penetrate.

'I guess it's a waste of time to say I just stopped by to be social,' she said with a laugh, nervous. She hoped it wasn't obvious. Lazar merely smiled, lacing the expression with a reserved pinch of impatience. Leila took a deep breath. 'Our reserves are pretty damn cleaned out. We'd like to stay here for Lithafest. Work . . .' She paused, waiting for him to take the bait.

He nodded, fingers steepled, tapping his mouth. 'Work.'

'Yes.' She got up, unconsciously beginning to pace. 'Last time we were here you said—'

'I know,' he interrupted her. 'I remember.'

'You still need the service?'

He smiled. 'Leila, my dear, if I remember correctly,

which alas I do, last time you were here you fabricated a host of excuses to decline that particular offer of employment.'

She put the wine goblet down on the desk too hard, remembering too late she shouldn't really do things like that here. Lazar fixed a stare on the goblet. She picked it up again, wiped the gleaming surface of the desk with her sleeve. 'I've changed my mind.'

She knew she was begging. It was vile, this man even more so, no matter what he'd achieved down here in his little kingdom. Last year, Roirbak had dropped her in it, communicating with Lazar to advise him of her talents. Roirbak had a habit of doing that. She presumed he got commission. What she'd learned all those years ago, embraced in the claustrophobic hold of the original Star Eye, she preferred not to practise as a rule. It wasn't that she was ashamed of it, or even thought it particularly wrong, but it made her edgy, messed with her sleep patterns, filled her with depression. Like Ewan Famber, she had been involved in mutating the human psychological profile to adapt to living off-world. The end result sounded philanthropic, but often the means of achieving it had been far from that. Every person in the world was different: there had been drastic errors when working with the guinea-pig volunteers, some of them utterly irredeemable. However, some compulsion had moved her to copy illegally a lot of the software they had used on the project before she'd left. She still had it. A lifeline maybe?

'Leila,' Lazar said, casually opening his desk drawer and removing an enamelled box. 'It's been a long time, a whole wheel has passed. Don't you think I'd have found someone else to do that little task for me now?' He opened the box and spooned out a small amount of white powder which he placed on a concave lens the size of a dessert plate.

Leila had thought that was an ornament. She put down the goblet on the desktop and, this time, left it there. 'No. No, I don't.'

Lazar picked up a knife, chopped and levelled the powder into a line, removed a slender, carved, avian-looking bone from the box and inquired, 'Would you like some snow, my dear?'

Leila shook her head, wishing he'd just get on with their conversation.

Lazar snorted up the line through the bone and laughed, throwing back his head and opening his mouth. No sound came out. 'Roirbak has many contacts,' he said, sobering. 'I've heard there's a new man on his files who is just as capable as you. Leila, you declined. I'm not moved to offer you the job now.'

'Oh, give me a break, Lazar!' Leila said. 'You know why I backed off. It's shaky stuff, you know it.'

'And now you're prepared to risk it. I can hardly believe this is because Star Eye are down on their luck financially.'

'I'll be straight with you. There's a new factor.'

'Didn't there have to be?'

Leila shrugged, pushed back her hair, sinking into a partial relief. She'd hooked him: just by that simple statement, she'd hooked him. The idea had only come to her since she'd arrived here. Maybe it would intrigue him enough to convince him of her sincerity. 'Yeah. I have a girl with me, a special girl. I can't go into details but she needs an equally special guy to help her out. At least, I think so. There's no one around fits that description, not who'd be willing,' she added that last phrase drily with a frown, 'but I can make that guy, Lazar. I can make him

242

all right if I get the right raw material, a blank slate. A *sexual* blank slate, that is.'

'This is preposterous,' Lazar said mildly, as if it was nothing of the sort. 'Are you suggesting I allow my son to become part of some bizarre experiment you've dreamed up?' His expression was, as she'd hoped, that of the utterly intrigued.

'Listen Lazar, you wanted me to work on the boy last year. It seemed pretty important to you then. If I succeed in accomplishing what you asked for, the stuff with my girl afterwards will be nothing in comparison. It won't hurt him. And I do need the credit real bad.'

'Your group has several young men. Why do you want to use my son?'

'I told you. He's blank in that respect. The others in my group are too heavily imprinted.'

'Then "blank" one of them, my dear.'

'That's immoral in my book. Why should I when the perfect material is waiting here? Anyway, I thought it would interest you.'

'It does. I admit fascination, but Mr Roirbak may be disappointed if I do not avail myself of his counsel.'

'He put you on to me.'

'True, but I told you, he has new limbs now. Fine new limbs. This man might have the edge on you, Leila. How long is it since you practised?'

'Don't give me that shit! It's not something you ever forget!'

'Please, don't get upset, my dear.'

'I'll be cheaper than Roirbak. You know that.'

'Economy is not a concern in my case. I'll pay whatever it costs. What a coincidence, you turning up again like this on the day following Mr Roirbak's communication. However, I like you, Leila Saatchi. The job's yours. I'll even pay you what I offered Roirbak.'

'That's . . . that's not necessary,' Leila spluttered. 'The original fee . . .'

'Nonsense. You'll fix my boy, have him fix your girl, and everyone will be happy.' He stood up and swiftly glided round the table to touch her shoulder. 'And you, my dear, can fix me too, can't you?'

Leila didn't start shaking till she got out into the sunlight. Star Eye were mostly still hanging around the trucks. Leila swung up into Aphrodite's cab, her jaw aching with the pain of being clenched. Cabochon and Jordan were in there, sharing a smoke. 'Get the hell out!' she snapped at Cabochon. He didn't question her, didn't even look at her, lithely dropping down into the dust outside. 'We have accommodation,' she called after him. 'See the creep at the desk inside there. He'll tell you where to stow everybody.' Cabochon saluted her, bowed and slunk off into the shadow of the building. Leila watched him go, hating, in that moment, every muscle sliding beneath his skin. Jordan stared stonily ahead, allowing her to fill up with self-recriminating shame. She knew he'd wait for her to apologise. He wouldn't be the one to break the silence.

'Shit, Jordan, it's hard you know!' she said at last, close to tears. 'It's so damned hard! Can't you understand that?'

He slid his eyes to look at her without moving his head. 'Not really,' he said. 'What happened in there?'

Leila found herself wiping her eyes. Giving in to emotion, especially of this type, was all but unknown to her. Combination of events, she guessed. Jordan reached out to fondle her shoulder, thawing. 'Hey, come on. What's up?'

'That shithead!' she said. 'Jordan, I think I'm going

to have to screw the son of a bitch to get us solvent again.'

Jordan actually laughed. 'Is that all?!'

'Thanks!' She managed a watery smile. 'No, not all. I've also got to screw around in his son's head. I've decided Jord. I'm gonna try and use him for Ari.'

'That wise?'

She sighed. 'I don't know. It computes OK up here.' She tapped her head. 'I'll have to wait and see. Goddess knows what Roirbak's up to now. He's hawking new talent by the sound of it. New talent very similar to my old one.'

'Another T-G dropout?'

She shrugged. 'It's possible. You gotta remember it's been years since I worked on that shit though. The process was bound to creep into the public sector sooner or later. Doubt if it even came from the same source. Somebody else probably just dreamed it up too. It was always only a matter of time.' She leaned back and sighed. 'Goddess, the architecture of the mind!'

'You still got your kit intact?'

'You know I have. It's like having a demon in a bottle. It's power, Jordan but, like a demon, unpredictable.'

'Then be careful.'

She curled one of her hands over his. 'You too,' she said, wistfully.

'So, Leila Saatchi and her tumbling troupe of natros are at Lazar Farm,' said Roirbak, turning from his comms monitor. Tammuz Malamute was padding furtively into the room, recently returned from Club Eleusis. He always looked so antsy, Roirbak reflected, as if he expected duplicity round every corner . . . perhaps perceptive. Tammuz did not appear to respond outwardly to his remark, which Roirbak found surprising: he wondered for an instant if he was wrong in his suppositions about the man. 'You know her?' he prompted.

'Should I?' Malamute ran his fingers along the edge of Roirbak's desktop. An idle gesture or a nervous search?

Roirbak turned back to his console, straightening the key pad, flicking away invisible motes of dust. 'Well, you are in the same line of business. I did wonder.'

'Always wondering, aren't you?' Malamute folded his arms, leaned against the desk. His reticence was beginning to annoy Roirbak, who believed he should have got through to Malamute by now.

'I had hoped to fix you a commission at Lazar Farm. Seems Ms Saatchi has beaten us to it.'

Malamute shrugged, pulled a face. 'Well, I have my schedule full at present. Seems no great loss, whatever it was. Determined to make me work, aren't you?'

'How are you progressing with Jahsaxa's . . . problem?'

Malamute pushed himself away from the desk. 'I'm taking it steady,' he said.

'Are you satisfied though?'

'Hardly a word I'd use in connection with that job. Anyhow, I'd have thought Madam Penumbra's satisfaction was more important, and I expect you know more about that.'

'She's curious. I keep her at arm's length, mouthing platitudes. It mollifies. Don't keep her waiting too long though, Tammuz. After all, if Leila Saatchi has restarted operations in this field, you can expect tough competition.' If his suspicions were correct, that had to be an irresistible gibe, surely? Malamute merely shrugged.

'It's not exactly an overstaffed area, Roirbak. I'm sure there's room for more than one operation.'

'You don't seem very curious about this woman. I would have thought you'd want to know more about her.'

'Seems like you want me to, Roirbak. I don't care. I do my job, which pays for me to exist. My interest in this work does not extend beyond that.'

'I wouldn't keep on about it but, well, sometimes I get the feeling from the flavour of your work that you may have been trained by the same people as trained Leila, that's all. I know both of you. I can see similarities in approach.'

'Anything's possible.'

'Good of Lazar to let us know, I suppose.' He pulled his lip, somehow reluctant to say more. It was too soon perhaps, yet he was still anxious to initiate some reaction.

'Seems Leila's up to something out of the ordinary. Lazar's a whore. Told me everything, which I'm sure wouldn't be appreciated. Leila must be desperate to confide in him . . .' His silence did not prompt questioning from Tammuz Malamute. 'From what Lazar can gather, she's hoping to conduct some kind of experiment in sexuality with a young girl she's picked up for her troupe. Lazar was trying to grill me for information, see if I could work out what she was up to from what she told him. It's mystifying. She said she needed what she referred to as a "blank slate". As you know, Lazar junior was diagnosed a-gen some years ago. It was a genetic defect. Permanent neuro-somatic damage, rumoured to be linked to a vitamin supplement prescribed for pregnant women – rich pregnant women, I might add. Seems young Lazar is just what Leila needs. She's willing to take on the rehab if Lazar will allow her to use the boy afterwards.'

Roirbak watched Tammuz carefully. The man was picking at stuff on the workbenches, a thoughtful look on his face. Reckoned that might interest you, Roirbak thought. He allowed nearly a full minute's silence. 'I think I know who that girl might be, Tammuz,' he said. 'The name will have to be familiar, even to you. It's the name of the foremost innovator in your field: Famber.'

Tammuz nodded. 'Yes, I've heard that name. Ewan Famber is dead, isn't he? Or are you implying his persona now resides in the body of a young girl in this Saatchi woman's natro group?'

'I'm implying nothing of the sort! That will be his daughter. She'll be about fourteen now. And if Ewan messed with that kid the way I suspect he did, she'll be just about ripe.'

'For what?'

'The knowledge died with him, Tammuz, but it'll be big. The cover-up proves that. Ewan hid his wife and kid away someplace, and I think only Leila Saatchi knew where they were. Leila's a genius. She'll handle it, but it'll be big, I'm telling you.' Roirbak was playing a private game designed to provoke a response. He did not intend to reveal his own involvement, nor that he had been Leila's confidant all along. He had a high regard for his protégés. Only a hunch allowed him to reveal this much now. He couldn't be wrong, surely? There was always the outright question to be asked, but he shrank from that. Malamute would deny it whether it was true or not. He'd been working with Roirbak for months now and had never given anything away. Perhaps Roirbak was wrong after all.

'Yeah, it sounds interesting,' Tammuz said, yawning. 'I'm guttered. Do you need me for anything or can I go and sleep?'

'No, I don't need you. Go ahead.' Roirbak watched him go. Too young maybe? But look at me. I can afford it though. He can't. He was nearly starving when he first came here. Yet, I was so sure . . . He shook his head and hunched over his console. He'd have to put in a call to Leila soon. Should he tell her his suppositions? No, no point – unless they were true, and then there was every point. A dilemma. He didn't want to worry her needlessly and he knew Leila Saatchi right now was one very worried woman, anxious to get to Arcady and deliver her hot little charge into his hands. And what will we do with it then? Roirbak wondered, and flicked a glance down the plaza in the direction Tammuz had headed. What then indeed?

Tammuz Malamute threw himself down on his unmade bed and blinked at the ceiling. He calmed his racing heart with a subconscious natro technique, regulated his breathing within seconds. This is why you came here, he told himself passionlessly. You knew this was on the cards. He put his arms behind his head and closed his eyes, summoning Leila's face on to the screen before his inner eye. She would look older of course, unless she'd managed to fix herself up. The poverty of a natro group could be a front. She was obviously working for Roirbak now, no matter how much he tried to disguise the fact. Tammuz knew Leila would have hung on to the contact with Roirbak merely for security. As you have done, maybe? She will be coming here, he thought. Oh yes. That's a foregone. Then what? You planned this, you work it out. He groaned softly.

At least the project at Penumbra's appeared to be progressing well. As a precaution, Tammuz was taking it slowly. Crevecoeur had been created WoMan by

Penumbra's friendly surgeon, but in body only. It was crude. Without the assistance of someone like himself, Crevecoeur would fold and collapse very quickly, a victim of galloping neuroses and conflicting personalities. His job was to adjust Crevecoeur's neurological make-up to something other than normal human gender. He wasn't convinced it could be done successfully, but felt he'd be able to patch things up enough to prevent a major disaster. It was easier to make someone a balance of anima/animus mentally and emotionally than it was to incorporate physical effects. The former exercise was one practised by the mystically-inclined for centuries. The latter was a vulgar obscenity spawned by the clubs' frantic search for new delights in order to compete effectively. Crevecoeur was scared, despite hir streetlevel wisecracks and hardnosed unconcern. Tammuz did not blame hir. Sometimes he was scared too.

He remembered the first day he'd turned up for work at Club Eleusis. It had felt strange, reminding him vividly of the past: new workplace, new equipment, everything clean and unused. Jahsaxa had granted him an audience in her office, where they'd sedately discussed current affairs for half an hour, until she'd signalled the end of the interview by standing up and saying, 'I'll have someone show you where you'll be working. How soon do you want Zambia to come along?'

'Just give me till after lunch,' Tammuz replied, putting down his half-finished coffee.

Jahsaxa nodded. 'We have a dining area for staff, but I'll have something sent along to your workroom for you today. Unless you planned to go out, of course.'

'No. A meal here will be fine.'

The accommodation she'd organised for him looked as if it had been furnished from a medical supplies' catalogue. The equipment was pedestrian to say the least. He examined the computer and its therapy software, wrinkling his nose in distaste. Useless! It was fortunate he'd had the forethought to design his own program during the night. At least there was a coffee machine in the corner of the room and Jahsaxa hadn't considered it necessary to equip him with a simpering secretary of some kind; he'd half expected that. The morning was spent configuring the computer and installing his work program, after which he sat with his feet up, drinking coffee, staring into space and waiting for his lunch.

Jahsaxa Penumbra herself had brought Zambia into him, later on. His first thought had been, 'Well, the whore looks better by daylight.' Zambia appeared coltish and awkward, hir face unmade-up, hair scraped back behind hir head. The face, undeniably, was beautiful. Jahsaxa clucked around her charge, always touching; light fingers to the hair, the face, the shoulders. Zambia, wearing a bath robe, remained sullen, hunched on the edge of a seat. Jahsaxa had obviously decided she was going to stay and watch the proceedings, but Malamute made it clear he could not, would not, work with an audience. She took it fairly well and retreated graciously, doubtless, Tammuz considered, to conceal herself behind some device that monitored the room. He could handle that; bodies getting in the way was something else. When she'd gone, Zambia had fixed him with glittering eyes and said, 'It's you, isn't it?' There was a slight edge to the tone indicating SHe wasn't sure.

'You mean from yesterday, the hotel room?' Tammuz perched on the edge of his desk, arms folded, trying to look professional. 'Yes, that's right.'

'And you're a doctor, right?'

'Wrong. I'm well . . .' he glanced at his computer,

'I'm more of a medicine man, if you like. Here to help you sort yourself out.'

'Why didn't you tell me that yesterday? Why did you let me think that . . . ?' Zambia shook hir head.

'I didn't want you to know. I just wanted to observe the person that is Zambia Crevecoeur. If I'd told you, you'd have hidden yourself.' He tapped his head. 'Deep in here.'

Zambia shrugged. 'OK. You got a cigarette?'

'Not tobacco, no, and I want you straight for this first session, OK?'

'Can I have some of that coffee then?'

'Sorry, no drugs of any kind. You can have some later. How old are you, Zambia?'

'Nineteen.' SHe fidgeted on the seat. 'Why? Does that make a difference?'

Tammuz ignored the question. 'Do you have any family? Do they know about this?'

Zambia stared at the floor, as if someone had thrown a coma-switch. Tammuz stood up. 'Well?' he asked softly. 'I'm not judging you, I just want to know if there are maybe extra factors giving you grief.'

Zambia's head shot up. 'Oh, they're giving me that all right.' SHe pulled down hir robe to reveal a scarred, yet exquisitely tattooed shoulder. 'Look at that.' Tammuz leaned closer to examine it. 'That's what's left of my family,' Zambia said, and shrugged hirself back into the robe. 'That's all.'

'Mm,' Tammuz said. 'Would you get up on the couch there, please?'

'Are you going to examine me?' Tammuz noticed the way Zambia enfolded hir stomach with hir arms.

'Only the head, OK?'

'Yeah. Right. Of course.' SHe stood up. Through the

robe, there was no suggestion of gender marks of any kind. Tammuz understood Parmedes had instituted some hormonal therapy to induce mammary growth. You poor little bastard, he thought. If anyone's a monster around here, it sure isn't you, Zambia Crevecoeur. He began to pull equipment out from the wall: mind-scan nodes on limbs. It could be done automatically, but Tammuz always believed that was more frightening for the patient. Zambia's eyes followed the movements. Tammuz smiled. 'There's nothing to be scared of. Really.'

'I'm not scared. This gonna hurt?'

'No. Not a bit. You might feel heat, but it won't be uncomfortable.' Tammuz positioned the limbs. 'OK, I'm all ready. You just lie there and close your eyes. There will be lights. So just relax.'

He retreated behind his desk and stabbed the start-up pads in sequence before settling himself down to watch the monitor screen. The familiar map of human consciousness began to blossom in colour in front of him and he began to mark the territory for remapping. Rippling his fingers over the soft keyboard pads, Tammuz enlarged the images, getting right into the heart of Crevecoeur's composition, right in. Brain patterns washed across his screen in waves of light: a secret landscape. Tammuz' face was illuminated from below; he loved to do this. It was such an intimate thing, more intimate than sex. And Jahsaxa Penumbra excelled in manipulating this intimacy for profit. Tammuz grimaced at the thought. The living miracle lying across the room on a rug of black hair, this pale, porcelain miracle, as delicate as spun glass, as tough as steel, was a potential God/dess. And to be used for what? To partake in cold-blooded, passionless experiences, without magick or reverence or love. It sickened him. Tammuz made a disgusted sound and automatically retracted the scanner arms. Using the occult art of manipulating electromagnetism, he would soon set Zambia's feet on the path to possible deification. He shook his head and stood up, willing his misgivings away. This is a job, he reminded himself.

Zambia was still lying with hir eyes shut, believing the scan was still in progress. Tammuz filled a syringe with a mild euphoriant and pressed the high pressure nozzle against Zambia's inner arm. Hir eyes shot open.

'You pinched me!'

Tammuz rubbed the inside of Zambia's elbow. 'Better for you than nicotine. Come on, sit up. Treatment's over for today.'

Zambia swung hir legs over the side of the couch. 'That's it?'

'That's it. I made a few tests. We'll talk tomorrow.'

Zambia nodded and then blurted. 'It's all gone wrong, hasn't it? I'm falling apart.'

Tammuz maintained a distance. 'You'll be fine. Don't worry. I'll fix you up.'

Sometimes it was hard to keep that distance up. Zambia could be a child, could be sullen and difficult. But, at the same time, SHe could be so appealing and, quite often, turned on a siren charm in an attempt to manipulate hir therapist. Tammuz observed all this and could tell when Zambia was testing him. He became curious about hir past. What made a person choose this kind of life? Zambia was no fool. Under the cover of a talk session. Tammuz exercised his curiosity. Zambia resented his questions and became truculent. 'I need to eat! Everyone needs to fucking eat!' SHe exclaimed. 'You get off on this or something?'

The comment stung, mainly because there was a grain of truth in it. Also, he found himself wondering what qualification he had to mess with someone's persona when his own was such an unknown territory to him. He remembered he used to think that the personality was independent of the body, which was simply a vehicle of flesh and blood. His own experience indicated otherwise now. He decided to question Zambia on the matter. Had SHe noticed any difference in hir personality since the surgery?

'What do you mean?' Zambia asked, defensive.

'Well, do you feel as if you're more *womanly*?' It was the only way Tammuz could think of to put it.

'You mean do I want to get screwed?'

'No Zambia, I meant do you feel more – how can I put it? – *nurturing*, passive or caring.'

Zambia shrugged. 'Sometimes I used to feel . . .' SHe wrinkled hir nose. 'I don't know – violent, maybe. I used to get very angry about things. That hasn't happened since I was changed, but then I've felt ill and weak.' SHe rested hir elbow on Tammuz' table and put hir chin in hir hand. 'What do you think?'

Tammuz had to physically tear his eyes away from Zambia's stare. It would have been so easy just to keep looking and looking. He turned to his keypad and wiped imaginary marks from its surface.

'I think you're learning to be manipulative, and that's something I'd recognise as a female trait.'

'Ah, bitter, bitter!' Zambia laughed.

'Not at all.' He would have liked to say more, but some prim part of himself insisted on reminding him that this was supposed to be a professional relationship. 'Keep a diary of the way you feel,' he said. 'It might help us to analyse your progress.'

He glanced at Zambia who was still staring at him, grinning. 'What do you think?' Zambia said again.

To rid himself of the image of his patient, Tammuz spent more and more time at the clubs every night. Some mornings he stumbled to Jahsaxa's bleary-eyed, directly from some stranger's home. He had lost the taste for sex but forced himself into it again. His condition, on these occasions, amused Zambia and even seemed to please hir. 'Was it man, woman or beast last night?' SHe'd ask, grinning. Tammuz would not answer. Zambia would laugh. 'Get your hands off me! You're in no state to be at the controls of a human brain!' Then they'd sit and drink coffee until the caffeine kicked Tammuz back to reality, Zambia in the meantime chattering on about other people in Club Eleusis, viciously demonstrating their personalities by imitating their speech.

'You're getting better, aren't you?' Tammuz would say, and Zambia would shrug. They both knew that when his work was finished, Jahsaxa would have Zambia work down the list of clients waiting for hir services. Maybe that was one of the reasons why Tammuz was taking it slowly . . . Maybe.

Zambia hirself managed a self-deception of immense magnitude. It was this: that the reason SHe virtually floated to each therapy session, hir heart racing in anticipation, was because the therapy was working and SHe was feeling better. Tammuz Malamute, SHe told herself, was a pathetic excuse for a man: unfeeling and sexless. Which had to be considered a shame, because he was so good-looking. SHe had formed a friendship with Haiku and had told the girl that Tammuz Malamute was 'tight-assed and crusty'.

'I bet he's never had a good fuck in his life,' Zambia added. 'Strikes me as the sort of guy who'd come before he got his trousers off. Lives with a computer, no doubt.'

Haiku was delighted by Zambia's mordant remarks about the therapist and, subconsciously influenced by Zambia's unspoken feelings, developed a certain fondness for Malamute herself, second-hand. 'You can see him out buying socks in the hypermall, all alone,' she observed pensively.

Zambia nodded. 'Yeah. It drives me mad being with him. I just want him to loosen up. It's unnatural.'

'I expect you terrify him,' Haiku said. She, herself, often found Zambia terrifying, even though she'd never seen the slightest hint of hir bad side.

Zambia laughed. 'Oh, I *do* hope so!' SHe said.

One day, while in a light trance, Zambia said something strange. Tammuz had incorporated a modicum of natro mind-training into the therapy. It wouldn't do Zambia any harm to take a slightly more spiritual view of hir condition, although Tammuz had to disguise what he said with scientific terminology. Zambia had reacted badly when the subject had first been introduced. It seemed SHe had no love of natros or their philosophy.

Tammuz had been guiding Zambia through a meditation and was just preparing to end it, when Zambia had opened hir eyes. SHe looked confused. 'Oh, I don't know what to do,' SHe said.

'About what?' Tammuz asked.

'You *know*.'

'I can't remember. Remind me.'

'He loves me. I'm sure it's that. What shall I do?'

'Who loves you?'

Zambia shook hir head. 'Jordan does. I'm not playing. I'm serious.'

'What are you talking about?'

Zambia fixed him with a stare and the eyes were

different, darker, than Tammuz remembered. A chill coursed down his spine. The face was different, the expression. His alarm must have showed. Zambia shook hir head and put out hir hand, curling it over Tammuz' own which were clasping each other, and squeezed them hard. 'What's wrong with you, Ari Famber? Have you lost your mind?'

Tammuz thought he would faint, scream. Zambia closed hir eyes and hir head lolled to the side. For several minutes Tammuz just stared. A ghost had spoken to him, a ghost. I'm going mad, he thought. This is it, the edge. Fuck!

He took a tranquilliser and left Zambia resting for a while. Once he'd calmed down, he wondered whether he'd hallucinated or not. It couldn't have been real. No, it was; he'd heard it. He'd been totally straight; it had happened. Be sensible. Rationalise. Zambia must have picked up Ari's name from his own head, via some weird kind of feedback from the remapping. Tammuz rubbed his face and groaned. How long did he have left? How long?

'So, Ari, are you willing to go along with all this?' Leila asked. She'd just tentatively outlined her plan involving Lazar's son. Ari, as she'd anticipated, looked a little stunned.

'Well . . .' She shrugged. 'It's kind of embarrassing.'

Leila nodded vigorously. 'I can understand that. That's why I'm telling you now, so you can get used to the idea. Of course, if you really think you're not into it, say, after a week or two, then we'll think of something else, OK?'

'OK.' Ari didn't believe her. She could tell that Leila, now she'd thought of it, had set her heart on the idea. 'What's he like anyway?'

'The last time I saw him? Sweet, I guess. He's not ugly or anything, Ari.' Leila sounded impatient. Ari thought she was looking a bit peaky too.

'I'll think about it, then.'

'Good. Now tonight I'm going to Lazar's house, so you go and enjoy yourself with the others.'

'Can I get a job tomorrow?'

'Oh, that . . .' Leila considered. 'Yeah, you better, I suppose, otherwise Elice will get spitty.'

'I want to be treated like the others, Leila. I don't mind.'

'Yeah, yeah. OK.' She didn't really seem to care.

Everyone had planned to go out together to one of the local bars. Ari enjoyed getting ready. Cable brought his disc-player to the hostel room that Ari was sharing with Justinette, Elice and Eve, so they applied make-up and teased out their hair to the accompaniment of a wild beat and screaming. Cable danced round the room, trying on Elice's clothes and generally being a riot. Ari's face ached with laughing. Gradually the others homed in on the noise, so the party started before they even left the hostel. Ezooli arrived with her man, Grover, armed with bottles of her evil wine. She was intending to make full use of the hostel crèche facilities, that was clear. Kydd and Jordan turned up looking like a pair of criminals in shades and ripped leather. Cabochon, by contrast, was cool in a strip of white T-shirt and black jeans, his hair washed and loose. 'You look great,' Ari told him.

'What are you after?' he asked, grinning.

'Something I can't have, I guess.'

Cabochon shook his head and laughed awkwardly. 'Leila will sort you out,' he said, deliberately missing the point.

Nathan Lazar must have been a disappointment to his parents in more than the obvious manner, Leila decided. Her first official interview with the boy occurred in the presence of Lazar Senior himself, his confection of a wife, aptly named Lacey – blonde, sanitised, and to all appearances a robot – and the family child-rearer, Morven; a young man who was proud to wear babies on his back and boasted of his maternal anima. Well, hmmm. She had been shown into an elegant little salon, soft-lights around the wall, where the family had arranged themselves to best effect. She perched herself awkwardly on a chair, conscious of being untidy and a bit grubby in the corners. Lacey smiled at her blandly like an automaton. Nathan looked mortified when Lazar introduced Leila as the person who would try and make a man of him. Even Leila winced.

Nathan was a slight creature, beige rather than tanned, with soft brown hair rather than the traditional vigorous blond. It raised Lazar in Leila's opinion that he didn't just cast the boy aside and set about training his next oldest to be prime heir. It betrayed a softer, even human side to the man's nature. Poor Nathan looked miserable. In their ham-fisted attempts to prevent him feeling a freak, the family had inevitably made him feel exactly that, and had ground it deeply into his psyche. He was about the same age as Ari, perhaps just a year or so older. Looking at him, Leila decided she'd been right in her choice. If she could do something with him, Nathan would be an ideal tool for her. Lacking the innate sexual ferocity and campaigneering of Urran, the cold apathy towards womanhood of Cabochon, the threatening advanced years and experience of Jordan (her only other possible candidates), Nathan would be a fresh, untainted creature. She only hoped she could make him strong enough. For now she had to sit and cringe while Lacey lisped such timeless platitudes as: 'Well honey, Leila here has come to set you to rights, you know? So you'll be able to get to know people better.' Even a sexually active child would surely balk at such a public statement.

This getting-to-know-each-other routine was a waste of time in Leila's eyes. Nothing would be achieved with Nathan, even on the simple level of social communication, until she could speak with him on her own. The company of these people ground on her nerves. She was only relieved that Lazar's other two precocious, unbearable children were absent. Lazar kept tossing her knowing glances too, to make it worse. It did cross her mind that Lazar might not actually be Nathan's father: there was little similarity between them. Simpering Lacey might have romped with some passing natro or trader at one time. What could it possibly be like being married to a creature like Lazar? She shuddered and consciously grounded herself, needing strength, aligning her body along an imaginary spine-straight connection with the earth. She must progress in a linear fashion here, whatever occurred: set her sights on Arcady and not blink. Then Lazar bared his teeth at her and Leila's axis wobbled dangerously.

The man waited for nothing. After the shallow fraternising of the evening, Lazar followed Leila from his house, cornering her in the hallway of the hostelry where she and her people were staying. He pressed her against a wall, covering her with sickly, scented breath and the promise of the weight of his body. She tried to smile, make light of it, duck away with a laugh. He would have none of it, so she had to let him tag along to her room. It was empty. She'd half hoped Jordan would be there waiting for her, but of course he was out on the town with the others. Out of sight, out of mind. The cliché sang through her brain again and again. Lazar stood just inside the door, and began to undress matter of factly. Leila could not summon enthusiasm at the sight of his giant cock which bobbed, half erect, with a motion that reminded her of heavy ferns. On every visit, Lazar had tried to seduce her. She had never been in the position where she'd had no choice, always been able to slip out of his hold without giving offence. She had been lucky, clever. Now the inevitable smacked down. She turned her back on him as she wriggled out of her clothes, saying, 'I'm sure Nathan will be fine. I'll start working with him tomorrow if that's all right with you.' There was only silence behind her. 'I'll begin with some simple relaxation and meditation, just to help him feel comfortable with me and then . . .' She felt hands on her waist.

'Shut up and bend over,' said Lazar IV. It was a long night.

Everyone had drunk rather too much. Ari lolled on a low couch beside the dance floor, blearily and contentedly watching her friends throw themselves around. Urran, as Justinette had predicted, was chatting earnestly to a local girl, who looked disdainfully amused by his attentions but was obviously interested in him. Justinette had dragged Elice off to flirt, in a corner of the club where Elice could not possibly see what Urran was doing, no matter how she craned her neck. Eve was unashamedly gyrating around with a boy who must be a third of her age. Ari smiled; this was good. This was real good. Cabochon had gone off to the bar to fetch her a drink. Soon he'd be coming back and she'd be talking to him – bliss. She could see him coming now in fact, a glass in each hand. She straightened up on the couch. Then Jordan appeared from nowhere, damp from dancing. They spoke. Ari thought Cabochon looked defensive. She wondered whether she should go over. Even as she began to stand, she saw Cabochon put the drinks down on a table and put his arms round Jordan. She sat down again quickly. Fury on her own behalf and Leila's consumed her. It took over ten minutes for Cabochon to drag himself away and bring the drinks. Ari was seething. 'Don't put yourself out!' she snapped as Cabochon handed her a drink. 'I don't want to get in your way!'

He flopped down beside her on the couch. 'Don't lay this on me, Ari. You knew the score.'

'Of course I did. Who doesn't!' She took a drink of the cool ale, wishing she could control her anger. It didn't make sense. She heard Cabochon sigh, even above the music.

He put a hand on her arm to force her to look at him. 'You want me to tell you, don't you?' he said.

'No. No, I don't. I saw enough. You wouldn't have done that if Leila was here.'

'Course I wouldn't! Are you nuts, Ari Famber?!'

Ari put her drink down and turned towards him. 'Why do it at all then? What good can come from it?'

'It's difficult. You don't understand. I don't know what to do about it. I really don't.'

He looked so forlorn, Ari relented. 'Do you love him or something?'

'It's not that simple. He loves me. I'm sure of it.' Cabochon leaned back and closed his eyes. 'Goddess! Sometimes I just want to run away.'

Ari tentatively touched his arm. 'You can always talk to me, Cab.'

He smiled. 'You're a sweetie, Ari Famber.' He gave her a hug and planted a kiss on her forehead. 'Wanna dance?'

R. J. Somesense and the Line-Huggers arrived in Lazar Town only two days later. Somesense made a few inquiries and led his people directly to the hostel where Star Eye were staying. The proprietor wasn't too keen on having jellycrusts in the establishment but offered them a comfortable shed outside for accommodation and set about having cots put out there. Ari had got a job picking vegetables with Justinette. The Lazarenes considered manual activities with the earth good therapy for stress; they used few machines in their agriculture. Elice had grumpily elected to join them, but after a couple of days of working side by side with a group of glowing, beautiful local boys, her spirits had lightened considerably. Ari found her easier to get along with.

The jellycrusts were all sitting in the hostel garden when she and the others got back from work. Ari found she was quite curious about what they might have to say to her. Leila wasn't there, being cooped up with the Lazar boy, as she had been since the day after they'd arrived. Ari supposed the work must be hard. Leila hadn't been looking too well these past two days. Jordan wouldn't let Somesense talk to Ari until Leila came back, even though the jellycrust insisted it would only be an introduction. Ari was annoyed she appeared to have so little say in the matter but did not like the thought of going against Jordan. She did not trust him. Perhaps because Leila wasn't there much of the time, and because of what she'd learned, Ari had begun to notice the subtle wordplay between Cabochon and Jordan. It was obvious Jordan was relieved Leila wasn't around. He didn't seem to care how ill she looked. Ari mentioned something to Justinette about it. 'Yeah, that's typical,' Justinette had said. 'Cab and Jordan usually get pretty close when we stop someplace. Leila is always so busy then, keeping this group alive, sorting out funding, supplies and all that.'

'Doesn't she mind?'

'She doesn't notice,' Elice said, who'd been listening. 'That is, she makes sure she doesn't notice. If I were her I'd forget about Jordan. He uses people. He's not the only one, either, in this group who does that.' She sounded bitter.

Later, as she lay in bed thinking, Ari could not help but be slightly envious of all these bondings and experiences that were going on around her, even though they were entrenched in hurt and intrigue. It was the passion that excited her, the finewire dancing that was the essence of all human relationships. There was also the ultimate prize to consider: the consummation, to possess and be possessed. It was something she'd never been able to feel for herself. Suddenly the idea and pictures of Star Eye's varied sexual liaisons rose up around her in a swirl of seductive imagery. A wave of nausea rocked naggingly in the pit of her stomach. She sat up in bed to dispel the feeling. Not yet, she thought, but soon . . .

There was a long, low, community temple on the street where Star Eye were staying, and it was here that Somesense announced the jellycrusts would peel the following evening. All of Star Eye were invited to the ritual. 'Sounds disgusting,' Cabochon said, as the group ate breakfast next day. 'Like skinning chickens or something. I can't wait.'

'I want to see what they look like without all that shit on them,' Ezooli said and most of the others seemed to agree with her.

Leila didn't come back to the hostel until everyone was eating their evening meal. Ari felt as if she hadn't seen the woman for days. Leila looked tired, her face pale, her hair scraped back from her face. She picked at her food before wandering off alone to lie down in the common room. Jordan pulled her plate over and started raiding it. Ari finished her meal and went after Leila. Although she didn't really want to bother her, she'd been waiting to talk to Leila for some time, and there was no knowing when she'd be around again. Leila was lying on her back on a couch, one hand over her eyes. Ari approached cautiously. 'Leila, can I talk to you?'

Leila looked through her fingers blearily. 'Sure Ari. Just excuse me if I sprawl here. What is it?'

'You remember you told me about R. J. Somesense wanting to talk to me?'

'Uh huh?'

'Well, will that be tonight? I'm kind of curious about what he has to say and well, Jordan won't let him talk to me unless you're there.' She felt embarrassed having to mention Jordan.

'Yeah, you can talk to him tonight,' Leila answered. 'I could do with a diversion.'

'Are you working very hard?'

In reply, Leila held out an arm for Ari to squat down and be hugged. It wasn't a typical gesture for Leila, who was perhaps the least 'touching' member of the group. Ari was surprised by it, even more so when she realised Leila had put her head on her shoulder and was softly crying. Ari could not understand what was upsetting the woman, but thought it was likely something to do with Jordan. Overcome by a feeling of sympathy and warmth, Ari hugged her back fiercely. 'Don't let it hurt you so much, please,' she said helplessly. '*He's* not hurt.'

Leila stiffened and looked up abruptly through wet eyelashes, wiped her face. 'What? What do you mean?'

Ari squirmed, her face red. 'Nothing. It's none of my business, I know.'

'What isn't?'

'You and . . . well you and Jordan, I guess.'

Leila sighed and sank back. She laughed a little. 'Oh, *that*,' she said. 'It's not that bugging me, kid. I learned to share Jordan from the day he tacked Cab on to our group. It's not that.'

'Can I help?'

Leila looked at her earnest face: wide eyes, little boy, messy hair all standing up. I'm doing this for you, kid, she wanted to way. She wanted Ari to know exactly what she was doing for her, but kept her silence. It was no use laying guilt on the kid on top of everything else. 'Yeah, you can help,' she said, smiling and turning on to her stomach. 'Give me a rub. My shoulders ache.' Ari's awkward little fingers stabbed into her flesh, soon losing their self-consciousness and smoothing away the dull pain. Leila was hoping Lazar would lose interest in her soon. She felt she was on the verge of piling everyone back in the trucks and running out. More time had been spent accommodating his lust, which was colourful and tiring and bruising, than getting his kid sorted out. Every day, Lazar was turning up in the office where she was working with Nathan and sending the boy out on some excuse or another, saying, 'Leila I want to try this with you,' as if it was a new business plan he'd thought up or something. Her whole body was sick of him, sore and bored and sick. He could keep it up for hours, plunging away, saying all kinds of stupid things. The fool, with his monstrous egotism, also believed she enjoyed it. If he didn't get fed up soon, she'd be off. Today she'd mentioned she needed more time to work on the boy.

'Things aren't happening as quickly as I hoped,' she'd said.

'Then take longer,' Lazar had quipped back, grabbing for her again.

'I have appointments in Arcady,' she'd answered. 'I have to be there within a month.'

Lazar had shaken his head. 'Shame. I'm enjoying our own experiments, aren't you?'

She'd turned away. 'I'm tired, Lazar. If you want me to work on your boy, you'll have to let me rest more.'

Then he'd painfully clutched her arm, shaken her. 'You want him whole as much as I do,' he said. 'And the money. You need that too, don't you? Remember that and keep me happy. Understand?' She did.

The morning after the Line-Huggers arrived at the Farm, Ari gave herself a day off work, being too preoccupied about her coming meeting with the jellycrusts to be able to concentrate on digging, never mind up put up with Elice's conversation. Looking through her bag the night before, she'd come across the camera she'd brought with her from home. Despite her intentions of recording her journey with Star Eye in some way, she'd forgotten all about taking pictures. On impulse, hoping the thing still worked, she filled it with film and took it with her out into the streets of Lazar Town. First she walked to the nearest market area where she took a couple of shots of the stall-holders, who were happy to pose in smiling groups for her. She was so pleased when the film developed properly, she lavishly gave one of her precious photos away to the market people. As she walked further away from the hostel, she came across a small square roofed by a lattice wound with vines where a band of musicians played to people sitting outside the cafés and bars. The musicians were Oriental, playing eerie flutes and drums whose rhythm could be felt rather than heard. Ari took a picture of these, and walked on. She came to a canal which bisected the whole of Lazar Farm, and followed it for a while as it curved towards a lake on the

271

edge of town. Flat boats were being poled through the water, carrying produce from the fields and green-houses. Ari found the lake particularly interesting, as she'd never seen live fish before. A boy and a girl were fishing at the water's edge, providing a nice composition for a photograph. Ari was astounded when the picture developed. Where the sky should have been reflected in the water's mirror surface, only rock, cables, trackways, ladders and other equipment could be seen. It frightened her at first until she realised the holographic projec-tion of the sky hadn't been captured by the camera. The automatic focusing facility could see through Lazar's magicks.

She headed back into the town and wandered around for a while, investigating areas she'd not yet visited before her feet led her to the place where the Peel was scheduled to take place. There was a lot of activity around the community hall, people bustling to and fro carrying things in and out, so Ari decided to take a look inside.

The function chamber itself was spacious, floored in pale, smooth wood that felt warm to the touch, with brightly-coloured cushions scattered round the edge. A simple stage was erected at the far end, to the side of which reposed a portable altar for religious ceremonies. Plain, shoulder-high quarter lights were stacked together beside it. A couple of the Line-Huggers were laying out the design of a sacred space for themselves, setting up the lights, and debating whether or not they should use the altar. Ari self-consciously took a couple of pictures, without flash so she wouldn't disturb the jellycrusts, and was pleasantly surprised when they turned out OK. The atmosphere in the hall was one of waiting presence, as if the room existed solely in anticipation of the next event to be staged within it. It was a feeling shared by theatres and conference halls, but Ari had visited neither of those.

Next she investigated the skylit passage running alongside the main hall and found a good-sized bar, where the floor was carpeted in rust and yellow and brown ethnic rugs, and the floor-cushions were accompanied by low tables which Ari suspected were also made of wood. The smell of it permeated the entire building. Ari was used to synthetic materials whose smell in no way resembled the real thing unless specifically designed to do so. Bowls of incense were already smouldering along the bar-top and a young girl in a dark green dress and bright red hair was tidying cups and mugs behind it. Smaller lounges and function rooms were to be found beyond the bar, restrooms and bathroom facilities. In one room, clearly used regularly by children, colourful paintings were tacked on to the cork-lined walls. Ari took a picture of those. There were school consoles in there, their keyboard markings fading from long use, the housings grubby and battered. Delighted, awed, and imagining a childhood growing up in such a place as Lazar Town, Ari eventually found herself in the kitchens, where a youthful troupe of caterers were happy to make friendly overtures and press-gang her into helping them prepare the evening's refreshment. Someone told her all the food would be on sale after what they referred to as 'the freak show'.

Her belly full of filched titbits, Ari wandered back into the temple hall just as people were beginning to drift in. Most of Star Eye were there already. Justinette came scooting over the polished floor in her thick socks and demanded to know where Ari had been. 'We looked all over for you!' she said. 'We were real worried when you didn't turn up at the field.'

'I just took a day off to look around,' Ari answered.

'Well, thanks a lot! Why didn't you tell us? We'd have come with you!' Ari sometimes found it annoying that she was expected to stick by Justinette and Elice all the time nowadays. Too much of Elice's company tended to wind Ari into a frenzy. In a place like this, where the residents were so friendly to strangers and it was perfectly safe to wander around alone, Ari preferred not to have company. Before joining Star Eye she'd spent most of her time alone, and she occasionally missed the privacy. She knew the afternoon wouldn't have passed so pleasantly if Elice had been there to grate on the Lazarenes' nerves. The other girl would have felt compelled to try and impress them in some way, which was always a recipe for disaster. Justinette sometimes seemed blind to the effect Elice could have on people.

'It was a last minute decision,' Ari said vaguely. 'Come on. Don't sulk with me. Let's get a drink. I can take your picture. Look!'

Justinette squealed when the flash went off. 'I wasn't ready, Ari! Do another one. Elice! C'mere!' Good humour was restored.

People were settling themselves in groups around the edge of the hall. Ari and Justinette went to join the rest of Star Eye, who had claimed a pile of cushions near the stage. 'Do you think this is going to make us throw up?' Ezooli wondered with ghoulish glee.

Kydd said he'd seen a jellycrust peel before. 'It's not as bad as it sounds. Only their arms and lower legs, faces and necks are covered in the gel, you know.'

'It's the faces, though, that are most important,' Grover said ponderously. Ari had barely spoken to him before, finding him quite a forbidding creature. He and Ezooli often seemed an ill-matched couple, she being so vivacious and noisy, he so dour; yet she had never seen them less than sublimely contented together. They'd left Stickit at the crèche again. Because Ezooli was so used to carting the baby around everywhere, it seemed to Ari she was unsure what to do with her hands, like someone who had given up smoking.

Gradually the conversation in the hall turned to murmurs and the overhead lamps dimmed. Music started up from somewhere, filling the entire room through hidden speakers: the low fluting sound of wind instruments, the hollow click of tapping bones above an almost subliminal constant metallic ringing. Banners of thin cloth had been erected around the hall, displaying the symbol of the Line-Hugger troupe – an open hand – below the traditional jellycrust glyph of incomprehensible lines and swirls. The altar had been set up in front of the stage, draped with a faded, fringed cloth. Here the jellycrusts had laid out the tools necessary for their exfoliation. Ari settled back against the wall, leaning against Eve's side; a little nervous of what she might see, even after the traumatic incident of the dead pilot in the VTOL wreck. The hall dimmed to virtual blackness, punctuated by the glow from people's pipes and cigarettes around the edge. Everyone was seated but for two girls who stood with camcorders at the edge of the hall, waiting to video the night's events for posterity. The music had changed to a single wooden-drum beat, the only other sounds being those of people moving against the cushions, the occasional, quickly silenced demand of a child.

Slowly the quarter lights began to bloom with colour: blue for the east and the element of air; red for the south and fire; a sizzling, silver white radiance for the west and water; and a deep yellow smoulder for the north and earth. As the lights grew brighter, the silhouettes of the jellycrusts standing in a circle were revealed. The deep drum beat began to increase its pace and volume once more, accompanied by a scurry of pattering hand-drums. The figures in the circle began to weave slowly and dance, round and round, extending their limbs, twisting their bodies. Gradually, moving with the drumbeat, the speed of the dance accelerated and the jellycrusts began to utter sounds; whistles and cries. They clapped their hands, slapped their thighs and stamped. The dance became chaotic, without apparent pattern, jellycrusts leaping and spiralling every way within the glow of the circle lights. Ari felt her heart beating wildly. She experienced the cohesive force of the jellycrust troupe, the power they drew from each other and the earthforce around them, a power they moulded and encouraged. Outside the circle, everyone was utterly silent and still, respectful of the ceremony. The gust of rising power was like standing face first into a strong wind; it was hard to draw breath. Ari watched in amazement as the Line-Huggers began to tear off their garments, kicking them away, sending them skidding across the floor. The light was too dim, the mêlée too muddled for Ari really to see much of what lay beneath the clothes, but the leaping figures seemed attenuated, scrawny, yet with elemental elegance. She could not tell which were male and which were female: all were a mass of writhing, knotted hair and skinny flesh. Now wind instruments joined the thundering drums and the Line-Huggers threw up their arms, reaching up to the sky, then crouching low to the earth, stamping along like turtles. Their movement was a wave, finding its own pattern as each body dipped and reached, dipped and reached. The power of their movement was almost visible; Ari felt sweat bead on her upper lip. She wanted to join them in the dance. Star Eye's rituals seemed so tame in comparison, even though they were more complicated, more theatrical. This was root magic, fundamental, stripped bare and raw and throbbing. When the power peaked and the Line-Huggers joined hands, raised on high, shrieking and yelling, Ari cried out too. All around the hall, spectators took up the cry, waving their fists in the air. Then the jellycrusts sank to the ground, earthing themselves, and a sparkling, invisible peace descended like dust over the hall. The air was ripe with the smell of the jellycrusts coated skins.

With reverence, R. J. Somesense approached the altar and lifted the hooked scraper he would use to strip his flesh. He saluted the sky and the earth with the tool, bowed his head and then placed the blade of the scraper against his forehead. Standing alone, his troupe still crouching low to the earth, Somesense sloughed his skin and revealed, as Ari had suspected, a pale, ethereal beauty beneath the gel on his face. He peeled his arms, flexed his fingers, bent to peel his legs. The discarded gel lay like snakeskin around his feet. It came away quite easily, virtually in one piece but for where Somesense made the cuts. He passed the tool to someone else, and one by one the rest of the Line-Huggers removed their coatings. As they stood there, still as statues, but marble now, smooth marble, one of them began to sing. Gradually, other voices joined in, the melody so plaintive, it conjured tears. The spectators rocked and hummed gently, joining hands.

Silence fell.

And then a single fiddle began to play. The Line-Huggers looked around themselves as if they had just woken from a long sleep. They stretched and wiggled their hands and feet. Soon a lively, kicking jig filled the hall with music once again. The Line-Huggers celebrated their Peeling, stretching their bodies, feeling the air on their faces and arms. The spectators, recognising a cue for their participation, began to clap, several people spontaneously chanting a few lines which their neighbours took up, weaving a tapestry of sound. Ezooli laughed, clapping, and began to cry, 'Cluck ticka, cluck tikki tikki', which those nearest joined in with. The Line-Huggers opened their circle, removing the quarter lights, and floor lamps began to glow in their place. People started to get up, shaking their limbs, jumping, joining the dance. Kydd dragged Eve to her feet and waltzed her off into the crowd. Ari joined hands with Ezooli, Grover and Cable, all of them leaping around in a circle, being pulled this way and that, Ezooli's long nails digging into Ari's wrist. She saw Urran scamper past with a screeching Elice in his arms; Justinette had clambered on to Jordan's shoulders and was waving her arms in the air, encouraged by a rather intoxicated Cabochon. And Leila? Leila lay in the cushions and watched. Ari looked over her shoulder as she was pulled into the crowd. All she could see was Leila's pale face: she wasn't smiling.

Ari had not long sunk down for a rest in the cushions when she saw the lanky figure of R. J. Somesense making his way towards her. He was still naked: Ari could see the curling initiation tattoos of his troupe, the straight lines of ritual scarring on chest and belly. Leila, who'd been speaking to some people further up the hall, swooped down like a bird of prey when she noticed the jellycrust introducing himself to Ari.

'I am pleased we are speaking at last,' he said. Ari didn't know what to say. He was so tall, towering over her, his ragged hair falling on to his chest. His hand, peeled of course, felt soft and smooth in her own.

'Is this a good place to talk, Somesense? I mean, really?' Leila asked.

The jellycrust was not deterred. 'Well, perhaps we can discover a quiet corner away from the party,' he said, and indicated the way to the door and adjoining lounges beyond with his long, feminine hand.

'Yeah, good idea,' Leila said, realising the man was not prepared to give up. 'C'mon kid, we can get a refill on the way.'

The bar was full of jellycrusts – Line-Huggers and several other groups – temporarily freed from their asceticism, their tongues and etiquette loosened by alcohol and hash. Here too were milling crowds of diverse natro groups and factions, all brought together in the subterrene world of Lazar Farm, seeking their various icons of new spirit, fulfilling work, or just a good time in the here and now. R. J. Somesense, a tall-prowed clipper upon this sea of bodies, glided ahead of Leila and Ari, seeking a nook of some privacy. Leila dragged Ari through the throng of souls at the bar.

'We'll find him,' she said to Ari's earnest backflung expressions of loss. She purchased a jug of ale and, hand clamped firmly to Ari's shoulder, pushed back through the crowds.

They discovered the jellycrust in a back-of-beyond cubbyhole at the end of the building. The celebrations had not extended this far. Flickering, squat candles cast a cosy radiance over the floor cushions, sticks of incense burned in pots of sand. Somesense had flung a sandy-coloured robe around his shoulders, belted loosely at the waist with a plain cord, revealing his pale chest. Leila plonked herself down, business-like, and uncorked the ale. 'Cups, Ari!' Ari set them out in a row and Leila poured. 'So, Mr Somesense,' Leila said, 'fire away, please do.'

The jellycrust settled himself, perhaps distracted by Leila's manner. Ari was unsure whether anything of consequence could occur or be said with Leila in this mood. 'Who are your parents?' R. J. asked her.

'Don't answer that!' Leila snapped. 'What's that got to do with it?'

'Context,' the jellycrust replied, in a tone as near to sourness as he could manage.

'Irrelevant,' Leila insisted.

'Your attitude conflicts with your assumptions.' R. J. spoke gently. Leila gulped ale.

'Look, I'm not sure this is a good idea,' she said. Ari was beginning to feel she was isolated from the proceedings.

'My parents were – are – Ewan and Lydia Famber,' she said in a smooth voice. Leila shot her a hard look, a look which said, don't say I didn't warn you, but the names appeared to mean little to R. J. Somesense. He nodded, but without visible agitation.

'They were Tech-Greens,' Ari continued, but Leila interrupted her.

'Ari, you don't know this man. I don't think you should start spouting your life's history to him.'

'It's what he wants to know, isn't it?'

'I want to know the youness of you,' R. J. replied before Leila could misrepresent him. 'Rely upon the confidential nature of this interview, please.'

'I want to tell him,' Ari said.

Leila sighed, leaned back on the cushions. 'Well, in that case, I'll just lie back here and let you get on with it!' she said coldly. Ari could not understand why she was being so hostile. Couldn't she feel the positive emanations of calm and detachment from the jellycrust? Ari had no fear that R. J. was one of the nebulous enemies who Leila seemed to fear lurked in every shadow.

She told him about her childhood and responded as honestly as she could remember to his inquiries about her awakening individuality. In return he halted her narrative now and again to inform her of the symbolism he saw within it. Through him, she began to visualise the landscape of her early years with new eyes, and spoke of the secret knowledge of eventual immanence, which she thought illustrated most emphatically her difference to normal people.

'All the time I must have known, deep down, that something amazing was waiting for me,' she said. 'Looking back, I can almost remember it now.'

R. J. nodded, but then added that just about every teenage individual wanted their life to blossom into some great, cataclysmic change, and all they had to do was wait for it. 'In that you are not so different,' he said, smiling warmly.

'What is it then you see in me?' she asked, balking from relating her experience of sexuality, or rather her reason for not experiencing it.

'Heat and light,' he said. 'It is as if you carry a sign advertising some great promise and inviting others to bathe in the light of it. You are not *calling* people – that would imply something entirely different – but it is as if you are politely inquiring as to whether we, the spectators, wish to participate in your event.'

Leila made a harsh sound from her cushion, an approximation of laughter. Ari remembered Leila hadn't been laughing much recently. She wished she could be alone with R. J., talk to him openly. Leila was an inhibiting presence, sprawled there with a bitter grin on her face. Perhaps it was possible to ignore her.

'I have this problem . . .' Ari began.

'Too right!' Leila cried, sitting upright. R. J. Some-sense winced delicately. Ari thought that he too was beginning to experience impatience with Leila. He gave Ari a look which told her to be quiet a moment and turned his attention to the woman. Leila fidgeted sullenly beneath his stare. He drew in his breath.

'You put much energy into this responsibility,' he said quickly, 'perhaps aligning with a surplus of negativity. It would be wise to cleanse your aura. At this moment you are nothing but an entropic influence.'

'I know,' Leila said in a deadly tone. 'But it's nothing to do with you.'

'Self-pity,' said the jellycrust.

'Warranted,' snapped Leila.

The jellycrust shrugged. 'Sometimes it is necessary to partake in sacrifice of self, but being a martyr to one's causes inspires only impatience in others.'

'Listen, you want to speak to Ari, go ahead. Me, I'm not part of your movie, buster, so you can point your fucking camera eyes elsewhere!'

Ari, mystified, wondered what was going on. R. J. seemed to know. Ari was sure he knew everything about Leila; what was upsetting her, everything.

'I believe you are part of this,' R. J. said carefully. 'What you are doing is related to it, I can tell.'

'You're an outsider,' Leila said. 'The only reason you're here talking to Ari now is because you promised you could tell us things. Do that, then, and leave me out of it.'

'You are cracking,' R. J. insisted. 'It won't be long before you fall apart if you continue along this path. It is wrecking you.'

Leila did not comment, drank some ale belligerently, staring. R. J. Somesense sighed. 'It will not benefit the girl, Ari here, if you lose your grip,' he said.

Leila kept up the stare for a moment or two and then seemed to fold inwards. She sighed. 'You're probably right. It was just an idea I had. Maybe I'll abandon it and head straight to Arcady tomorrow. It was just an idea.'

R. J. nodded. 'Mr Lazar can take his responsibilities and position within this community too . . . literally,' he said.

Leila laughed, another discomforting bark. 'How you know these things, Somesense? Good information network or telepathy?'

The jellycrust shrugged. 'Observation mainly. Because of the nature of my work, I have trained myself to see minutely.' He paused. 'Perhaps if you relate all the details – I admit I have guessed only an outline of your circumstances – we can help you to resolve your difficulties.' Leila looked at Ari, and Ari thought, there are things she doesn't want me to know.

'I suppose I should. I know I'm turning away from the path I've chosen – complete openness within the group. There are too many secrets now, too much strain.' She looked at Ari and smiled weakly. 'I expect you all think I've been a bear recently, huh?'

Ari shrugged. 'I think you've been working too hard helping Nathan Lazar,' she said. 'And the other thing, the one I told you about. I thought it was that upsetting you.'

'I told you I wasn't bothered about that!' Leila said, too sharply. She slumped wearily. 'I'll tell you. I'll tell you. Guess it'll help.' She shivered. 'I've been an ass. Stupid.' Looked at R. J. 'Wanted the boy, Nathan, because of the way he was. Wanted to make him fit for a particular job.' She looked at Ari. 'I want to make him a partner for Ari to help us unravel the net Ewan bound her up in.'

'Why?' R. J. said, pondering.

'You might as well know now, I guess,' Leila replied fatalistically. 'Ari's father was a neurogenetic genius.' She outlined roughly the information Ewan had left her, culminating with the events at the Bump. R. J. Somesense listened attentively without interruption, nodding as she talked.

'An impressive tale,' he said when she'd finished speaking.

'Not a tale, soul; this is truth.'

Somesense raised his hand. 'I was not implying anything by that. It seems to me that the idea this Ewan Famber came up with must have been an extension of certain Tantric doctrines, that the sexual energy of human individuals is the most powerful force on this planet. More powerful than nuclear fission, more powerful than – but perhaps an extension of – natural elemental forces. As you must know, over the centuries many people, mystics mainly, have sought to penetrate and master this force.'

Leila nodded vigorously. 'But Ewan went further than that. He believed he could manipulate RNA so that children could be born without any conscious blocks against this kind of power.'

'An ambitious project.' Somesense daintily sipped his ale. 'I am intrigued. If his ideas have been realised, they will be instrumental in the evolution of human consciousness.' He addressed Ari. 'The pure resonance will be like a mind-expanding drug. You will experience the multirealities of Universe, not through years of self-disciplined mind training, not through hallucinogenics, but through the power of your own orgasm! This is truly amazing!'

'Yeah,' Ari said drily.

'Amazing yes,' Leila said, 'but as with all great

discoveries, in the wrong hands it could become yet another tool of control.'

'Sexuality has been used as that for thousands of years,' Somesense said.

'There's more people around now, though,' Leila replied. 'A hell of a lot more. Ewan didn't want his creation polluted. That's why he protected Ari from her potential capabilities. There was no way of knowing whether his theories worked until she matured enough to demonstrate them. Now I'm taking her to an old friend in Arcady. He trained me, trained Ewan. I feel confident Ari will be able to look after herself once she's had some help in recognising and becoming familiar with her ability. Then, it's up to her what she does.' Leila leaned forward. 'But I admit it, I'm scared. I'm worried about the wrong people finding out about this. Especially the T-Gs!'

'Yet you've told me all about it, despite your misgivings.' Somesense smiled wryly.

'Yes. I have. Think how much you could sell this information for!'

Ari flinched. She didn't think it was wise of Leila to remind R. J. of that.

'True,' R.J. said reflectively, 'but I cannot empathise with the Tech-Greens' desire to rid the natural world of humanity. I do not want to live under their domes or in their sky cities. However dangerous Gaiah has become, my people wish to journey over her bones and flesh. It is unlikely I would sell the information to the Tech-Greens, wouldn't you say?'

'Hmm. The jellycrusts wouldn't mind having the knowledge for themselves either, would they?'

'And maybe I'd want to share it with them!' Ari said recklessly. 'You said that Leila. After I'm trained and old enough and all that, it's up to me what I do.'

Leila looked at her narrowly. 'Ari, there are a million possibilities for what you can do in the future. You need to know more about the world and its people before making any decisions. It will be a hard task choosing how to use your talents. You may decide never to use them except for your own development as a individual.'

R. J. nodded. 'You are right,' he said with some chagrin. 'However, in any event, I would like to keep in touch with you. If only to record the decisions as they happen.'

'Without influencing them?' Leila asked in a cynical voice.

'Everyone Ari comes into contact with will influence her in some way. That happens to everybody. Be objective. That is not your worry at present. Is it?'

'No,' Leila said, fumbling in her pockets for a cigarette. 'That bastard Lazar is dealing out some heavy abuse in return for letting me use his son if I succeed in healing him. I've been trying to put up with it because it seemed such a good opportunity. The boy's perfect.' She smiled carefully at Ari. 'That's something you've got to face, Ari. There has to be a someone and it would be best if that someone was fit for the job.'

'But it seems so . . . I don't know . . . clinical,' Ari said.

'Clinical conditions may be necessary,' Leila replied. 'Look what happened with Urran.'

Ari blushed. 'Yes, well . . .'

'That hurt didn't it?'

The information must have come via Cabochon, Ari thought. 'It wasn't pleasant, no.'

'You'll be the one in control, Ari. The boy will be an instrument, that's all.'

'That's horrible!'

'Some things are. Surely you know how vital it is you

take control of who and what you are. It's no good blundering round in the dark. We're all so vulnerable then. Can't you see that? Don't look on this like it's me pushing you around. I'm just providing the means, or trying to. Eventually you'll be on your own. I have to be pretty pushy with you now so you'll be ready for that.'

'So how are you progressing with the boy?' R. J. asked. 'Will it be long?'

'Too long,' Leila said bitterly. 'It's like writing a program. The details have to be exact. And as I keep on being distracted . . .' She shook her head. 'Maybe I should give up and hope something similar presents itself in the city. Roirbak has enough contacts. Perhaps he can come up with something.'

'Maybe I can help you speed up the process,' R. J. suggested.

Leila shook her head. 'I doubt if Lazar would let you inside the building. He wouldn't agree to it. He'd know why I'd got you there. No, I either resign myself to putting up with Lazar, or cut my losses and get out of here.' She shook her head, taking a long draw of the cigarette. 'Maybe I'm just getting old, not being able to cope with this. It's possible.'

R. J. Somesense laughed politely; Ari made an anguished assurance that that was not the case. 'There is one thing, Leila, that you have overlooked,' said the jellycrust. Leila rested her chin on her hand, leaned forward.

'Oh. Is there? And what might that be?'

'I would have thought that was obvious, but then you've been under some pressure, experienced some scattering of your energy . . .'

'What do you mean?'

'Well, if you'll forgive me for pointing this out, you

are a natro. What about your magick? Why haven't you used that to solve this problem?'

Leila's eyes slid away from R. J.'s gaze. She dragged the end of her cigarette round the rim of a nearby ashtray, played with the ash. 'I don't think that's possible. Not with Lazar. He's too powerful.'

'The man is a posturing mannequin devoid of spirituality of any type!' cried the jellycrust with uncharacteristic force. 'Leila, the fault is with yourself. You have lost faith in your will.'

She nodded. 'Maybe. My attempts at cohesion have failed recently. Whatever I had once, I think I've lost. Lack of practice perhaps, but I can't trust my own abilities any more. I can't influence my realities. The knack's gone.'

Ari was appalled to hear Leila confess such a thing. Surely it couldn't be true. Leila bowed her head. 'I have no strength.'

'Then let me, as I suggested, help you with your work. No ifs and buts,' he said, raising his hands. 'We will ritualmake to unman this Lazar. We will make him leave you alone. We will swiftly complete the task of healing the boy's mind and you can leave Lazar Farm.'

Leila looked up, her eyes shining with a hope she dared not trust. 'You serious?'

'Trust me,' said R. J. Somesense, laying a hand on both Leila's and Ari's knees. 'Let me help you and then complain how I might influence events!' He closed his eyes, straightened his spine and drew in a deep breath. Ari and Leila exchanged a glance. Leila was smiling. Somesense exhaled noisily and fixed his attention on Ari.

'So. Ask me,' he said.

Ari laughed nervously. 'Ask you what?'

Somesense merely kept up a steady stare.

'OK, what can you tell me about myself?' She felt foolish saying it.

'No one will help you take control, Arani Famber,' he said. 'No one can. You have good friends who mean well, but they cannot help you.'

'Now just hang on here!' Leila said indignantly, but Somesense raised a silencing hand.

'She will know,' he said. 'There is nothing to fear. When the time comes, she will know.'

The morning after the Peel, Leila arrived early at the office Lazar had provided for her use. She was there even before Nathan who was generally dispatched swiftly from the family abode soon after breakfast. She paced around the room, heart beating short and sharp, rehearsing what she must do, telling herself again and again, 'Believe, believe. This has already happened. Believe.' She touched the folded papers in her back trouser pocket which was R. J. Somesense's script for what should occur that day.

Nathan was surprised to see her already there when he came into the room. 'I thought you'd be asleep till midday what with all the drinking you lot did last night,' he said, in a furtive attempt at humour.

'Yeah, I have a hangover,' Leila said. 'So, how d'you feel today Lazar Jnr?'

Nathan sat down in a chair, crossing his legs. Leila suspected he used his mother as a role model. 'Fine. I had some of those weird dreams again though. Will you be going off with Dad again today?'

'No,' Leila said shortly. 'I think it's time we got down to hard work, don't you?' She sat down on the edge of the desk. 'Now. Tell me about your dreams.'

'Well, it's all muddled. I can't remember much.' He

291

frowned. 'All I can think of is I was drowning at some point.'

'Mmm. Nothing else?'

'I should have written it all down when I woke up. It's gone now. I might have been running from something . . .'

'Uh huh. No big bad monsters then?'

'Not that I can remember. I felt odd when I got out of bed though. Sort of worried, but I don't know what about.'

Leila nodded. 'Not to worry. You did the breathing exercises?'

'Yes. I always do.'

'Good. Now, hop up on the couch and do the relaxation. OK?'

'Yeah.' Nathan stood up and strolled over to the couch set against the wall. 'Is it working, do you think? Am I going to be normal?'

'Nathan, you are normal. Don't be silly. We'll sort this little problem out.' She opened her briefcase computer and flipped up the screen. 'I've done enough preliminary mapping now. You've answered all my questions, completed the tests . . .' She sat down behind the desk and called up the file she was using.

'Lie down, Nate. That's it. Relax. Now, look at it like this. It's kind of like I've got to go into some kind of unknown place. This place, it's barren, not much life there, but I've got some special seeds to plant which will make it come alive. Unfortunately, I don't have much information about the territory, so I've been flying over the place making maps, just so I don't get lost or plant the seeds in the wrong place. You see, if the seeds are placed correctly, they'll set off a chain reaction to make the whole area bloom. If they're not, well, just a little bit will come alive and it might not last for long. My little friend here,' she patted the computer, 'will design the seeds and decide where to put them.'

'What exactly are the seeds?' Nathan asked. 'Real things?'

Leila laughed. 'Real things! Well, you can't hold them or anything.' She help up one of her software programs. 'This is called an empathic remapper, which probably doesn't make a lot of sense to you, but basically, I'll hook you up to my little machine here, and fill your head full of my ideas of what your personal programming should look like.'

'How do you do it? How do you know what it should look like?' The boy looked bewildered. He clearly didn't trust the process.

'Listen, kid, I'm an expert. I can stop space-trippers going crazy, so I can give you a horn, OK!'

Nathan smiled shakily. 'OK. When will you put the seeds in?'

'Well, if we're not disturbed, maybe in a couple of days,' she said.

'Then what'll we do? Wait?'

'No, not quite. We have to water the seeds and give them compost and manipulate the weather a bit so they have the best possible chance of growing.' She tapped a few keys. 'Put the pads on, Nate.' The boy complied, taping the soft circles to his temples, behind his ears, his wrists, groin and chest. 'OK. Now relax like I told you.' As Nathan's pattern fluoresced across the screen, Leila dropped deftly into her work, charting and plotting, making sudden forays of exploration, retreating from wrong directional paths, measuring what she learned and relating it to previous examinations. The picture of Nathan was slowly being filled in. If she could only work without interruption she would progress so quickly. It would be tiring but pleasurable. The process was addictive, like playing a game. Because of her conversation with Somesense the previous evening, the folded papers in her pocket and her relaxed condition, Leila was so immersed in her work she had quite forgotten about the possibility of Lazar Senior's visit, and was surprised and annoyed when the door opened and he came into the room. Nathan was well under by then, breathing regularly. 'Isn't it time you stopped for lunch?' Lazar asked her.

'Not today,' Leila replied. 'I'm making headway. There's no point in stretching this out longer than is necessary. It's wearing for the boy, and for me.'

Lazar put his hand across Leila's wrist. 'You are stopping for lunch,' he said. 'Pull the boy out of it.'

Leila took a deep breath. She felt for the jellycrusts' support in her soul, sensing it as a crouching beast ready to spring to her defence if needs be. *I give you my teeth said the beast, I give you my claws.* Leila filled herself, bellyfirst, with a stream of selfboost. 'No,' she said and, readying herself for the attack, slowly raised her eyes to meet the man's. She drew power up from her belly, visualising that she surrounded herself in a sparkling net, a net that reflected any evil intention back to whoever sent it. She had taken back the power of control over her own body. She stared into Lazar's eyes, into which, she perceived, the slightest flicker of unease had edged. 'You don't want me to stop,' she said. 'Not really. Let's put a finish to these silly games, Lazar. You've had your fun. Now let me get on with my job.' She calmly pulled her wrist from his grasp and began stroking keys once more, aware of Lazar hanging poised above her, confused as to what he thought and felt. She sent out wave after wave convincing him he no longer wanted to thrust himself upon her, that, in fact, he found her slightly repellent physically. *What could have come over me*? He stood up, cleared his throat.

'I'm glad you're making progress,' he said. 'I'll leave you to it then.'

'Thanks. See you.' She didn't look up until he'd gone out of the door, when, unable to contain her joy and triumph and rekindled selflove, she leapt from her seat and jumped silently round the room for a few moments. I've been such a fool, she thought. This is the way. This is the way to everything!

By late afternoon, the mind and soul of Nathan Lazar was as familiar to her as the cab of Spirit of Disorder.

Lazar Senior no longer seemed to care who came and went in the office. Leila had no difficulty bringing R. J. and Louanne into the building. Nobody challenged her. She showed them her equipment and explained what she intended to do. Nathan would have to have his consciousness directed into a virtual reality construct, so that he could be exposed to emphatic suggestions from Leila's computer. When she passed control over to the computer, Nathan would be kept unconscious and monitored the whole time. She said she would appreciate it if the jellycrusts would stick around over the next couple of days and take shifts with her supervising the boy. 'You will be paid,' she said. 'It's the least I can do to repay what you did.'

'The money won't be refused,' R. J. replied, smiling, 'but it's Lazar's money I'm taking, not yours. We don't require payment from you.'

Ari too was brought into the working environment. Leila introduced her to Nathan as her assistant, and told the boy that after his treatment had been completed, there was something he could help Ari with which would ascertain whether his own treatment had been successful. Nathan, thankfully naïve, did not perceive the obvious meaning of these words.

Ari thought Nathan was so young for his age; any encounter with him was doomed to be fraught by excruciating embarrassment. Leila was right though: he wasn't ugly. He was pretty and slim, with huge brown eyes and long brown hair. His hands were expressive, his smile ready and shy. Ari grudgingly conceded he was suitable. As she grew used to the idea, it became more exciting. She and Leila shared a secret; they had womanly power over the boy. Soon, if things went well, Ari would be the Goddess on the hunt and the prey would be Nathan.

Ari was spending more and more time with Leila, and less with the rest of the group. When everyone went out on the town at night, Ari was happy to sit with Leila in her office. She felt they were becoming friends. When she wasn't feeling low, Leila was good company; as girlish as Justinette if the mood took her, as comforting as Eve. She began to teach Ari a little about what she was doing. Much of this passed right over Ari's head because Leila was unable to convey the information in any language other than jargon, but she enjoyed hearing Leila's excited talk about it, even if she didn't understand it all.

Lazar Senior kept away and Leila's bruises and soreness faded. She could not express her gratitude to R. J., sensing that what he'd done for her was greater than it appeared. The jellycrusts no longer seemed like eccentric freaks to her, but valiant adventurers who refused to be swayed from living a life of freedom, who were prepared to suffer discomfort to make their point. One evening, as they all sat in Leila's office waiting for her computer to add finishing touches to her initial work, Louanne confessed that, sometimes, as the troupe travelled through dust and poison rain, she longed to be living once again in a safe, air-conditioned, air-filtered house, with clean skin and soft fabrics against it, to wear make-up and let her hair be brushed and shining.

'Do not think any of us is free from these desires,' she said. 'It is hard to keep going and to think that, in this life, we might never know the comforts we have given up. I think of dancing naked in the rain, in a soft rain, the Mother's juice, letting it fall in my mouth, rubbing it into my skin. I think of swimming in the sea, of tearing vegetables from the ground and eating them raw, fruits from green trees, all of this. On the surface, we cannot do those things and because of that we say, no, we shall not turn to the open door into the domes and wave farewell to the earth. We will not ignore what is happening. We will share our Mother's torment, stand by her as loyal children should. If she suffers, then so do we. And we shall remember all that happens so that, one day, everyone will know. Perhaps in a distant time, when the Mother has fought back and won. If there are people here still, they will be our sons and daughters and they will inherit the truth of the past from us.'

Ari and Leila were both moved by this speech, although Leila confided later, after the jellycrusts had returned to the hostel, that she still thought they were a little extreme and that she, for one, could not emulate their lifestyle, even if it was noble.

'Theirs is one way, Ari, but there must be others,' she said. 'There must.' She put her hand on Ari's face. 'I pray to Astrada you will be the one to help find another way.'

Ari reached out to hug Leila, something she could do without hesitating now. 'I will try!' she said.

The next day, once R. J. and Louanne returned to the office, and Nathan had arrived, pale and nervous, Leila initiated the process that should endow him with a healthy sexuality. She had him undress and then led him into a small, adjoining room where she had set up her equipment round a railed bed. She guided him into a light trance of well-being, and then asked Ari to help her connect him to an intravenous saline pump, so that the electrolyte balance of his tissues would be maintained. Following this, she hooked him up to the neuro-system which would take him into a deeper trance. All responsibility for day-to-day body maintenance was temporarily removed from his consciousness. Ari had to steel herself to be professional, and not keep staring at Nathan's genitals, even while Leila was applying a rubber sheath to the tip of his penis, conveniently shaped to allow his urine to drain away along a tube, into a bag under the bed. Leila leaned over and kissed Nathan on the nose. 'Not to worry, kiddo,' she said. 'We'll be with you all the time. Sweet dreams.' She activated Nathan's virtual reality construct – the same representation of his neural system as on her system monitor, where his consciousness was represented as being at one with the corrective data. In the virtual reality he was the corrective data. R. J. and Louanne, their unruly manes tied back, had jostled forward to watch the link-up on screen. The data would flow like a virus into his neural system, where it would be absorbed. Well, thought Ari, there it goes. Farewell little messenger. Make him supernal, make him fit for Ari Famber. Farewell.

An almost religious atmosphere pervaded the room.

Lights glowed red through blue to green through yellow on Leila's console; the map of Nathan's being revolved around the screen as if the four of them were looking out through a window on to a wondrous landscape. Hills swelled, mountains peaked and soared, abysms plunged and branches of light streamed adrift. 'See,' whispered Louanne reverently, 'there it is for us to see. We are but reflections of Her. There it is.'

All four of them regarded the glowing screen and Ari was imagining that undulating landscape bursting forth with colour and riot: flowers, fields, jungles. The corrective data was represented by a winged, silver ball which journeyed through the landscape, Nathan's consciousness accompanying it. This was the best movie Ari had ever seen.

Taking first watch, Leila whiled away the time by recording Nathan's pattern in case something drastic occurred and he had to be rebooted. Goddess forbid something like that should happen. She was unconvinced rebooting constituted an entire personality. It would be interesting to keep the filed Nathan as a kind of a.i. to tinker with however, even though such an act was outlawed planetside. She'd neglected this kind of work for too long, winding herself into tighter circles of helplessness and despair. Now, sitting here in the graveyard hours between deep night and dawn, she felt slightly ridiculous for the way she'd been thinking recently. Star Eye was no worse than any other group. If its personality could be displayed as Nathan's was on her screen, it would have its troughs and peaks like any other, its weaknesses and strengths. If there was a problem it was merely the others picking up and tuning in to her paranoia. *And the other thing.*

Now she felt strong enough to examine the way she felt about Jordan. If she was honest, it would always be Cabochon who took priority in his heart. Always. It was no use feeling jealous or vindictive about that. She'd known from the start what she'd be taking on. Jordan had never deceived her, but then again, she'd never intended to get so attached to him, never wanted to feel so possessive and insecure. The goddess wisdom of the lonely night hours told her it was time to surrender, let go, let Jordan be what he wanted to be, and be with whom he wanted to be with. She knew the man felt some kind of responsibility towards her, suspecting how much he contributed towards her vacillating strength. Did Jordan resent that burden? Leila sighed and pushed her chair away from the screen.

It was time for a big change, once and for all. Soon, she felt sure, events would accelerate concerning Ewan's daughter. If she was wise, Leila would use that time to change things for herself too. Perhaps Star Eye would be better off without her, forced to make their own decisions. Cable was capable of taking the motivating, organisational role as was Jordan himself, although he would outwardly protest against it. And how about the others? Quiet Grover with his sense and keen eye. If he and Ezooli were suddenly in the position of responsibility, wouldn't Ezooli calm down a little and Grover be forced to slight extroversion? And what about old Charcoal Eve? Let's face it, Leila thought, collectively my little group are extremely capable of existing without me. Perhaps it really is time to move on, time to begin work as I used to. I've enjoyed this. Maybe I need more of the same.

A movement behind her caused her to swing round in the chair. Ari was standing in the doorway, a dressing-robe slung round her shoulders. She'd been trying to get some sleep next door on the couch.

'Want some coffee, Leila? I couldn't sleep.'

'Yeah, thanks. Tell you what, you sit here. I'll make it. I could do with a legstretch.'

'OK.' Ari advanced into the room, sleepy-eyed, hugging herself, hair all tousled. 'Is he all right?'

'Fine. Don't worry. I won't lose him, Ari. Just for you, I won't lose him.'

Ari smiled weakly. 'I can't believe that I could . . . well, *be* with him someday.' She stared over the rails at the sleeping boy. 'He's good-looking isn't he?'

Leila nodded, smiling, wondering why she was feeling the prick of tears in her eyes.

'Thanks,' Ari said. She shuffled round to Leila. 'I want this to be over, you know. All of it. Like Nathan, I want to be normal, except I guess I can't be. Not in the real sense. But what you said the other day about how I'd be on my own one day? Well, I've been thinking about that and I'm looking forward to it. Really. Only I hope I have someone to be a friend then, that's all. And I hope I understand it all, what Dad did to me and everything. I hope I feel all right when I know and what I can use it for, for everybody's good and I'll know people like you and Eve and R. J. and Louanne, and can make it work . . .' She paused, drew a shuddering breath.

'It's like there's a big fight about to begin outside,' she said. 'I can feel it, and we're waiting in here, just waiting, to hear the first sounds of it, and I don't know what we'll do when we hear them. Do you?'

Leila held out her arms and Ari went to squat by the chair, leaning against her. 'Sure I do. We'll come up shouting "magick!" that's what. And it won't be our war, so we'll fly right over it and go someplace good. How does that sound?'

Ari looked up. 'You still have that script Louanne and R. J. wrote you?'

'Well, sure,' Leila said.

'Then let's write our own. Now. Here. For the future.'

Leila smiled. 'I'll get the coffee. You get the paper. We'll write a script. We'll write ourselves an epic.'

In the morning, R. J. and Louanne arrived to take their turn at the monitor, well schooled what to watch out for and impressed with the need to rouse Leila from the hostel should anything out of the ordinary occur. To Ari, the landscape of Nathan remained unchanged. Leila, however, had spotted hopeful signs. Ari carefully folded the pages of untidy writing that she and Leila had concocted through the night and took them with her back to the hostel. The others had already left for their various employments by the time Ari reached their room. She threw her clothes around the room and placed the script in her shoulder bag, knowing it was perhaps the only place free from prying eyes. Never had a bed felt so comfortable. She snuggled beneath the quilt, savouring the enveloping softness of the mattress, listening with quiet joy to the sounds of morning activity outside, knowing that soon she'd fade, fade into the land of sleep until Leila woke her up in the afternoon. Then there was a knock at the door.

'She'll be holed up at Lazar's for days,' Jordan had said. 'Don't be so paranoid. Get back here!'

Cabochon did not want to spend the night with Jordan in Leila's room, but it was the only place they could guarantee privacy, other than camping out in the trucks. He'd felt on edge all evening, as if something terrible was just about to happen. The impulse to call Zambia in Arcady was virtually overwhelming. Jordan tended to be unsympathetic to such urges, however, so Cabochon had kept quiet about it.

'What's the matter?' Jordan asked. 'It's not just Leila, is it? Come on, don't just stand there, wriggling. What's on your mind?'

He was sprawled on Leila's bed, a stoned grin across his face. Words such as insensitive and bum crawled across Cabochon's mind.

'Nothing. Nothing's the matter.'

'Now, why do I feel as if there is an irresistible force connecting you to the comms booth out in the hall?'

'What do you mean?'

Jordan rolled his eyes. 'You haven't called Arcady since we've been here.'

'You don't know that.'

'Oh yes I do. Why even think about it if it causes you so much shame?'

Cabochon could stand the grin no longer. 'Fuck!' he said and slammed out of the room.

He felt physically sick as he tried to make the connection; his arms felt weak and heavy. The corridor was empty, dark but for Lazar Town moonlight coming in through the skylight. A female voice answered: 'Yeah? Oh, er, 23–9393? Who is this?'

'Is Zambia there?'

'Who?'

'Crevecoeur. Zambia Crevecoeur.'

'No, no one here of that name. Got the wrong number, soul.'

Cabochon protested only to a disconnected line. Now what did this mean? Had Zambia moved apartment? Hardly aware he was panicking, he frantically called a friend of Zambia's: Alix Micklemas, the tattoo artist. Her answering machine greeted him with a quirky message.

Cabochon waited until it had finished and then said, 'Alix, are you there? Alix, it's Cab. Alix? Talk to me.'

As usual, Ms Micklemas was hiding behind the machine. Cabochon knew that, at this time, when the residents of Lazar Town took to their beds, Alix would be getting herself ready to go out, a lengthy process. 'Cab-o-chon! Sweet soul! How ya doin'? In town?'

'No, I'm at Lazar's. We're on our way in though.'

'We gotta meet up! Call me!'

'Yeah, yeah, I will. Alix, you seen Zambia recently?'

He perceived a reticent silence. 'No. Haven't.'

'Do you know where he is? A strange soul answered my call to his apartment. Has he moved?'

Alix hummed in thought. 'We-ell, he might've. Want me to pass a message on if I see 'im?'

'No . . . no . . . It's OK. I'll root him out when we get into town. Alix, is everything OK with Zam?'

She laughed. 'Is it ever? Sorry. Dunno. Far as I know, the beast is sleek and well-fed. Look, I hafta back out now, Cab. I'm late. Look me up. Don't forget!'

'I won't. Bye Alix. Thanks.'

Cabochon disconnected. Something was wrong. Something just had to be wrong. This was Zambia Crevecoeur he was dealing with.

His dreams that night were haunted by dire images of an attenuated Zambia, in all manner of distressed circumstances; Cabochon watching, helplessly bound. In the morning he wanted comfort, reassurance, something to make the dream images go away. That, of course, was when Leila had walked in.

* * *

'Come in,' said Ari.

'Mind if I sleep in here?' Leila asked, her face as pale and tight as it had been those few days before R. J. had helped her out.

'No, course. Help yourself,' Ari replied, gesturing at the empty beds. Leila sat down on one of them and pulled off her boots.

'It was *the other thing*,' she announced fiercely. 'You know what I mean.'

'In your room?' Ari asked, appalled.

'I wasn't expected back it seems.'

Ari wasn't sure how to react, or what was the best thing to say. This was alien territory to her. 'I'm sorry.'

Leila, stripped to her shirt, climbed into the bed. 'Yeah, me too. I think.' She lay back, hands behind her head. 'Goddess, I didn't think they . . . I didn't think it had gone this far,' she said. 'You know, tonight I'd convinced myself I'd just let Jordan go, wish him good luck and shake his hand. Crazy. When I saw him there . . . Oh, Goddess!'

Ari was out of bed in an instant, throwing her arms over the weeping woman. 'Why do I love him?' Leila asked helplessly. 'Why won't it stop?' Ari ached inside because she could not help. She did not know the answers. All she could do was hang on to show she cared. Eventually Leila calmed down a little and Ari fetched her a drink of water and a lit cigarette. Leila wiped her eyes and sniffed. 'It's not that I mind him . . . you know,' she said. 'I think it's different for men. Something apart from the things they do with women. It's just that Jordan wants Cab so much there's nothing left for me.'

'Cabochon feels terrible about it,' Ari said earnestly, trying to make Leila feel better. 'He told me. I'm sure he tried to keep putting Jordan off because of you.'

Leila laughed bleakly. 'Therefore making Jordan want him more. Some help, huh!'

'Oh. Yes, I see. What are you going to do?'

Leila lay back and sighed. She rubbed her nose, thinking, and then smiled. 'I'm going to show you Arcady, Ari,' she said. 'We'll go exploring, have adventures, that kind of thing. I'll get all this crap out of my system. I won't leave you. Not until you feel ready. OK?'

'You make it sound as if it'll just be the two of us. What about the others?' Ari was not insensitive to the powerful vibrations Leila was emitting.

'I need a change, Ari. I want my work back. Don't know how yet, but Quincx will help. I have to let Jordan go, forget him. I need my work again, need to find myself again. It's been too long.'

Ari did not feel capable of replying to this confidence, yet she felt it was important she did so, otherwise Leila might stop looking on her as a friend and go back to thinking of her as a child. The relationship they'd established over the last few days was still so delicate and newborn. Inspiration struck. 'Will you work for the Tech-Greens again?'

'I don't think so. Quincx has his fingers in so many pies, you wouldn't believe it. I'll ask his advice. Maybe he can get me a place somewhere. A private clinic'd be nice. No government stuff, just helping people out when they need it. Perhaps not even in Arcady. There's the orbital cities, for example. How d'you fancy going off-world Ari?'

'You serious? Really?'

'Well, why not? With our talents we might land ourselves juicy jobs up there.'

'Hang on, this isn't in our script.'

'So change the goddam script!'

'Wow! Off-world. Dad had Mom and me down for places there, you know. Would it be possible to use them?'

'Lady, I don't know. We'll have to see. You know, we have ideas now, hopes and all. It's good. Nothing's so black. Think about it, Ari. Maybe what Ewan made you isn't for this world. Maybe it's for the next, and I don't mean Deathangel or anything. I'll just work in Arcady for a time while you're getting to know yourself, and then, if you're still into it, we could fly, really fly. I'll earn enough to get myself fixed up, rejuvenate and all that, and then we'll go. We could live forever up there, Ari. We could see the future.'

'And come back to see R. J.'s great grandchildren living like cavemen on a world which took revenge?'

'Maybe.' She laughed. 'Maybe. Goddess, I feel good. I won't be able to sleep.'

'You have to. That's my lover you're making back there. I want you fresh and alert to make him properly.'

'OK.' Leila laughed and kissed Ari's cheek. 'Get back to bed now. You need the rest.'

On the morning of the third day of Nathan's treatment, a melodious beeping started up from Leila's console next to the bed. It was the signal Leila had been waiting for. The others followed her tense flight from paper-strewn, coffee-cup littered desk to adjoining room. Leila's hands flew over her keypad, delicately inquisitive; the landscape of Nathanness rolled and tumbled across her screen. There were no flowers on it as far as Ari could see.

Leila had her teeth clamped firmly round her lower lip. 'OK,' she said softly, her tapping fingers nearly louder than her voice. 'I've got flatline on corrective activity. This is it. The job's done. Or should be. Check vital functions, Ari. We're going bring him up to our reality.'

'Everything looks fine,' Ari answered. Only days before the instruments had been incomprehensible to her. Louanne and R. J., standing further back, had assumed positions of veneration, hands clasped. They had seen the Lady's mark upon the boy's mind. To them he had become a reborn lover/son; a miracle.

When Nathan opened his eyes, he took great rasping breaths as if he'd been trapped in an airless void. His body shook. He can't breathe, Ari thought, frightened. He's forgotten how to.

Leila, unperturbed, gave the boy a shot, checked his readouts and spoke clear, reassuring words. 'Come on Nate, deep breath from the stomach, fill the bellows, come on there, take it easy. Look at Ari, now, look how she's gawping. You're scaring shit out of her. Take a breath, inhale, take it deep . . .' She fixed the bed so it rose up to support the boy in a sitting position. 'Fetch a cup of water, Ari. We'll let this guy swill his mouth.' Nathan tried to take the cup from Ari's hands, still racked by painful, sighing breaths, but he couldn't manage to coordinate his fingers. He clawed at the sides of the cup as Ari guided it to his mouth. 'Not too much,' Leila said. 'He can have more later.'

Once the boy was more or less stable, he was full of the virtual adventures he'd had and wanted to tell the others about them. 'It wasn't like dreaming, it was real!' he said.

Leila left Ari administering further cups of water to the boy and went back into the office. Louanne and R. J. had remained with Ari to adore the vessel of Leila's handiwork.

Leila stared hard at the comms unit on her desk, poured herself some coffee and stared at it a bit more. She would have to contact Nathan's father now. The man had stayed away these past few days, and though relieved, Lazar's silence worried Leila. She felt he would be difficult now about allowing her to have Nathan help Ari. She sighed. It would have to be dealt with. As well as being anxious to sort Ari out, she was concerned that Lazar Senior might arrange some kind of traumatic deflowering for Nathan, conditioning him with a reality as damaged as the one she hoped she'd repaired. Nathan was raw and unfixed at the moment, very delicate. Leila, professional curiosity mingling with professional care, felt very strongly she should supervise Nathan's first experience with his new sexuality. It would be such a shame if all her careful work was ruined by insensitivity and ignorance now. Unconsciously, she'd extended her left hand to hover over the comms unit. It was possible Lazar would whisk Nathan away if she called him, give her her money and tell her to leave. It was possible. From the feeling in her gut, Leila also thought it was highly probable. She withdrew her hand, curling the fingers into her palm. 'R. J.!' The jellycrust quickly came into the room in response to her call.

'You look perturbed, Leila. Some problem?'

She shrugged. 'Not exactly. Everything appears to have gone how I planned . . .'

'Then?'

Leila sat down on the edge of the desk and confided her concerns about Nathan. 'Perhaps we should conduct some kind of prelim with the boy and Ari before I call Lazar,' she said, frowning, 'but it would be too rushed for my liking. I need space.' She threw up her arms. 'I need time.' Lowered them, and added in a sombre tone,

'Truth is, I'd feel happier handling this shit if Quincx was around.'

'So, what you are saying is you want to take Nathan Lazar out of here and to your friend in Arcady where you can meddle with him and Ari to your heart's content.'

'In safe conditions.'

R. J. nodded, smiled wryly. 'Of course, in safe conditions.' He paused. 'You think you'll need them then, these "safe conditions"? Your work so far has been impressive.'

Leila wriggled uncomfortably. 'It would be best. Ari's sexpower scares me. I don't know the parameters of it. Ewan didn't leave me any data you know. All I have is the evidence, one breathing, thinking organism of flesh and blood, to whom I have a responsibility.'

R. J. rubbed his skin. It still looked fresh and clean, unpolluted by gel. Leila decided she preferred him that way. What a waste. 'It seems improbable Mr Lazar will let his son leave the Farm,' he said.

Leila sighed deeply. 'I know. Perhaps I should just give up the idea, arrange for one of my own girls to make a man of the boy and get out of here. Maybe someone else will turn up in Arcady.' She shrugged. 'Oh, I don't know. I'll give it a try. Spin the bastard a few tales, see if he falls for it. What do you think my chances are?'

The jellycrust smiled carefully. 'You know the man better than I. Why ask? From what I've seen and heard, I would say the chances appear to be slim.'

Leila sighed. 'Yeah, I think that too.'

'But, of course, that does not necessarily mean the odds can't be altered.'

'I was hoping you'd say that.'

'Still? Leila, you should not need me to confirm your thoughts. Not now. You mustn't rely on me to . . .'

'I know,' Leila interrupted. 'Don't think I'm not aware that you've sort of broken your personal code in helping me as much as you have. You're not supposed to influence events, right?'

R. J. shrugged. 'I influence events by living, to a degree. It was my choice to help you before. My personal code is . . . malleable. I just think you're capable of resolving this new problem by yourself, that's all.'

Leila nodded, frowning. 'That makes sense. But before it was a self-preservation thing. The energy came more easily. I'm not sure I can influence the guy enough over this. Unless . . .' She brightened. 'Unless Nathan himself took a hand. Ari!'

By the evening, Nathan was feeling strong enough to want to leave his bed, and fretting because he suspected Leila was keeping him confined unnecessarily. Some part of him picked up on Leila's tension and recognised the woman's half-truths about him needing rest and quiet for what they were. She was stalling. Why? Had her work gone horribly wrong and she was afraid of his father discovering that? He did not feel any different. Perhaps she'd failed. Perhaps he was no different. The skinny girl, Ari, came in to feed him. She too looked jittery, on edge. 'When can I get out of here?' he asked her.

'You hungry?'

'I'd like to eat at home. What's going on?'

'Nothing. Everything's fine.' Her hands shook as she put down his tray.

Nathan tried to jump off the bed, discovered his head was spinning and sat down heavily. 'I know something's wrong,' he said. 'Why won't anyone tell me?'

Ari put a hand on his shoulder. 'It's OK,' she said in a soft voice. 'Really. The problems aren't yours.'

Nathan's attention had been abruptly shifted. Suddenly his fears lost their importance. What interested him was the unusual sensations the feeling of the girl's hand on his shoulder, the pressure through the thin bedshirt, was having on him. It was *pleasant*. More than that. Ari gently kneaded his skin to comfort him. 'Please don't be afraid . . .' she said lamely. Nathan appeared mesmerised. Obeying the guidelines of yet another script, this one hastily concocted, without subtlety, Ari slid her fingers along the boy's collarbone, lifted aside his hair. She could hear Leila's voice in her head, 'This is for him, kid. Don't involve yourself. We can't handle that here.' She knew how far she had to go. It was as much of a test for her as for Nathan. The boy had closed his eyes, lost in a pleasing pool of Ari's scent and touch. New sensations surged through his body; a different kind of relating. Later he would realise that sexuality was part of all human communication, a complex language in its own right. It was as if another dimension had suddenly become available to him. Thoughts and feelings that most people took for granted and barely noticed impressed him with an almost psychic awareness. Ari's hand was stroking his shoulder, her fingers trailing down his arm, making his hairs rise at the stimulation. Nathan sighed. Ari withdrew her hand. He opened his eyes, startled by the immense sensation of reality; the room too bright and hard. Ari turned away from him, intriguing him by the curl of soft hair against her neck where knobs of spine pushed against the skin, disappearing beneath her T-shirt that defined her shoulderblades and the hollow of her back. She had become such a desirable thing, and so abruptly. Was it always this way?

'I . . . I have to tell you something,' Ari said, fumbling with the script in her head. She dared not turn around in case her efforts hadn't produced the effect Leila had told her they would. Surely he'd be more suspicious than aroused. She had not taken into account the potent and mindless direction of adolescent male sexuality, nor the fact that Nathan had woken with it ready to explode, given the right stimuli. 'I have a problem too,' she said.

'Like mine?' Nathan asked. Ari shook her head. His breathless tone gave her the confidence to face him. 'Leila thinks you can help me now,' she said. A vague feeling of potential power, very similar to the one she'd experienced with Urran before everything had gone foul, gave her the courage to tell him more. It was the power of knowing that someone wanted you, wanted to touch and possess and submit all at the same time.

'You see, I have to be very careful,' she said, after she'd finished telling him the bare facts.

Nathan laughed nervously. 'Does Leila specialise in this kind of stuff?'

'Not really. It's coincidence that's all. She wants you to help me and that means coming to Arcady. Will you do that?'

'Leave the Farm?'

'Not for ever.' She sat down on the bed, tried to lighten the tone. 'Have you ever been to Arcady before? I haven't. I'm very excited about it. I want to see all the things there, things you can buy and taste and smell. It will be so different. I really want to go.'

'When?'

'Are you considering it then? Coming with us?'

'I just asked when you were leaving.'

'Well, as soon as we can, I guess. It'll take us a few days to reach it.'

Nathan folded his arms. 'It's Lithafest soon. It means we'll miss it.'

'No, Star Eye will celebrate along the road. That'll be fun. You'd love their celebrations, I know you would. It's great riding in the trucks and camping out and all. You feel so free.'

Nathan sighed and folded his arms, leaning back against the pillows. 'Oh, I don't know. It's dangerous out there. We're safe here in Lazar Farm.'

Ari wondered whether she should top up his interest in her. It seemed to be waning after the initial thrill of her touch. She put her hand on his ankle, stroked the skin. 'You don't understand what I'm saying. I haven't put myself across well. I want it to be you. You talk about safety? Well, I'd feel safe knowing it was you taking part in the "education" I have to have.

'Leila says you have no imprint. You are lucky. It means you can be careful about how you program yourself. Leila says . . .' She stopped herself. Perhaps it would not be a good idea to tell him more of what Leila had said. 'I can show you things,' she said, 'but I'm kind of nervous.'

'Show me things that "Leila said"?'

'Yes.'

'Such as?'

'I have to be careful, you understand. I mustn't arouse myself and that's difficult.'

'Why, what would happen?'

'That's the trouble, I don't know. Energy would come and I don't know how to direct it.'

'Seems your problem is more of a drag than mine was. At least I didn't know what I was missing.'

Ari smiled. 'Right. But Leila will sort me out, as long as she has the right person to help me.'

'OK, show me some things then and I'll make up my mind.' Nathan, having had no experience of libido, suffered from very few inhibitions. Ari wasn't sure whether she found his forthright attitude offputting or encouraging.

'Right. Right.' She kicked off her sneakers and lay down beside him, putting her hands around his face. She kissed him. He knew nothing, didn't move, didn't open his mouth, just accepted the caress. Just the fact of him lying there, receptive and open to suggestion caused a tickle of interest in Ari's loins. She attempted to banish it, knowing only too well that the blocks keeping her desires at bay were wearing very thin indeed. Remembering what Leila had told her, she put her hand under Nathan's shirt and stroked his flanks and belly, dragging her fingernails over his skin. His body jerked. She felt him swallow. His skin felt beautiful, smooth and warm. She clasped his small, firm buttock, pulling him against her. His virgin cock was hard against her thigh. She must touch him there. No. A tingling between her legs was rising in intensity. No. Control. Control. I must ignore it, damp it. Fury more than anything allowed her to do that.

Quickly, she did the things Leila had told her, all the time fighting a feeling of nausea and giddiness within herself, her own desires held angrily at bay, her mouth still glued to his. His hips were bucking now, pushing against her. She was unsure how long she could endure it, having to deny the images of that hot, hard flesh pushing right into her, and wanting it so much. It's not fair! She squeezed him hard, resentful, wanting, frustrated and uncomfortable. That finished him. He gave a little cry and spurted hot liquid over her hands and clothes. They didn't move for a while. She was lying there as if she'd just been beaten. Nathan was surprised to see she was weeping, silently, tears running over her face.

'It hurts me,' she said. 'So much.'

'Then why . . . ?'

'I have to help you too, that's why. I had to show you something.'

'How does it hurt?'

'I can't explain. Only that I want you and I can't, dare not, do that. Not yet. Not here.' She lifted her hands and inspected the white film of his seed on her fingers. 'I have never touched a man before,' she said. 'The only time I tried to it was as if . . . as if I'd die or something.'

'Let me touch you.'

'No, it's too dangerous.' She sat up, wiped her hands on the bed. 'I have to go. Leila can give me a pill or something.'

'This is all very weird.'

She shrugged. 'I know. Will you come with us?'

He sighed, lying back, supported by his elbows. 'You're making it very tempting.'

'I want you to come, Nathan.'

'You're very sure about this, aren't you?'

'I want to be normal,' she said. 'That's all. I'd do anything to achieve that.'

'Will Leila bring me back here afterwards?'

'Of course.'

He sighed and smiled. 'OK. I'll ask my Dad.'

'Star Eye can look after themselves. You'd be safe with them, I swear it. Tell him that.' She tried a weak smile. 'I like you a lot, Nathan.'

'Thanks. I think you're OK too.'

Ari hopped off the bed. 'I reckon you can go home now.'

'Typical. Now I don't want to!'

'There'll be more,' she said. Her stomach was still churning. It had taken so much out of her, fighting like that. She found Nathan's clothes and threw them over to him.

'Ari?'

'Yeah?'

'Come back here.'

She hesitated and then went to stand beside him. He reached out and touched her face. 'Thank you. For everything. Leila as well, but mainly you.'

Ari pushed his arm, embarrassed. 'Aw, I didn't do anything. Not really.'

She felt as if she was floating two feet above the ground when she went to report back to Leila.

Jahsaxa had summoned Tammuz Malamute to her office before Zambia turned up for treatment. She seemed, to Tammuz, quite agitated, pacing up and down behind her desk, swishing around in a long, belted gown. She made hurried inquiries as to Zambia's progress, to which Tammuz responded carefully, alerted by her mood.

'What I really need to know is, when can Crevecoeur begin . . . work?' she said, spitting the words out as if they tasted bad.

Tammuz took that badness full in the face. A cool, inner part of him was amused to observe how shocked he was. 'Well . . . well, I don't like to . . .' He fumbled for words helplessly.

Jahsaxa's stare had become dangerous. 'I need to know, Malamute,' she said frostily, and Tammuz knew what she was really asking for was his permission to intrude upon his therapy programme.

'It's out of the question!' he blurted. 'Too soon, far too soon. Could do irreparable damage.'

Jahsaxa merely raised an inquiring eyebrow at his blather. 'Well today you had just better fix it so there won't be any damage,' she said, and then speared him with a saccharin smile. 'Hadn't you?'

Tammuz had retreated to his office in despair, on his knees before a cold inner voice which nagged unsympathetically. You knew this would happen. Crevecoeur is a whore. Why should you care? SHe's garbage: polluted, unclean, loathsome. Hardly even human; a freak. Be sensible.

His sentimental side gibbered wrathfully in reply. Zambia Crevecoeur is being abused. Club Eleusis is an abomination. Goddess, I can't bear to think of what the scum who come here will do to hir.

Then don't think about it. Do what Jahsaxa wants and get out of here. You've walked away from better people than this in your life before.

He hardened his heart and turned on his computer, smiling acidly at the screen. Crevecoeur's mind-map swam towards his eyes. Fool, Tammuz told himself. SHe's been ready for this so-called 'work' since about the fourth day. What the hell were you thinking of doing? Fool.

He knew that, even after today, he still would not tell Jahsaxa his work was finished.

Things were getting spooky for Zambia Crevecoeur. Since SHe had begun to feel better in hirself, hir surroundings gradually swam into clear focus. And what SHe saw turned on hir flight or flee circuit in earnest. There was no immediate threat but, even to an idiot, it was obvious SHe was virtually a prisoner in Club Eleusis now. For all hir faults, Zambia did not consider hirself stupid. There were too many locked doors – all those leading to the street, tame excuses by the staff, brief interviews with Penumbra who claimed she was so busy and that of course Zambia could go out once she was sure SHe was well enough. 'What would happen if you

320

had a blackout on the street? Be sensible, Zambia.' Always that. Be sensible. Part of hir was afraid Jahsaxa was planning on more than just keeping hir as a highclass whore. There were ripples in the air of something bigger, something not altogether pleasant.

Enlightenment, if such can be the word, came on the evening following Jahsaxa's conversation with Tammuz Malamute.

'Zambia! Dinner in my apartment tonight!' Jahsaxa trilled happily, gliding silkily into Zambia's room after lunch.

Zambia wondered what unpleasantness was concealed behind the apparent privilege. From Haiku, SHe had learned Ms Penumbra always put a price on everything. 'Nice,' SHe said.

'Oh, what a face!' Jahsaxa laughed. Zambia was reminded of a line from a childhood poem: the smile on the face of the tiger. 'You should be pleased. We're going to celebrate your getting well.'

'Are we?'

Jahsaxa put on her business mask and almost forgot to smile. 'Look your best, Crevecoeur. There will be guests.'

Zambia had never set foot inside Jahsaxa's personal space before but, as SHe suspected, it was tastefully bare, illumined softly by concealed lighting. There was a gigantic salon, clinically white, and in this room sat the collected archons of Sector 23's palaces of pleasure. Jahsaxa ushered Zambia into the room. SHe realised with a dreadful clench of the stomach that SHe was a morsel of raw flesh being thrown into a blood-spiced pool of hungry sharks.

The introductions were discreet: a small, perfumed

and pomaded man was presented as Club Minerva; another, satanically tall and clothed in black, as Club Hecate; a woman, manifesting the blonde, icy power of a Nordic goddess as Club Adonis. Altogether, there were six members of Jahsaxa's peer group present. An exquisite minimalist banquet was laid on for their benefit. Zambia could not eat a thing. Jahsaxa's friends politely praised hir appearance, asking flattering questions in soft voices, always smiling. The conversation passed effortlessly from mundane matters to philosophy, spirituality, politics, art. Zambia was not deceived. SHe'd lived on the street too long. All they were really talking about was fucking. Wine the colour of clear water sparkled in smoky glass flutes, to accompany the snorting of consciousness-altering powders. Queen of Night incense smokelessly exuded a heady perfume into the air. Despite the heavy consumption of intoxicants, no one's voice ever rose above a husky whisper.

Zambia hunched miserably on a plump floor-cushion, awaiting execution of hir sentence. Occasionally Jahsaxa would catch hir eye and smile. *Do not fail me, Crevecoeur.* As midnight chimed from her sliver of a wall-clock she rose and proposed a toast. 'To my beloved child, Zambia,' she said. 'Who tonight will demonstrate what I feel will become a sought-after attraction at Club Eleusis. To you, my friends, I offer the first taste.' She drank, savouring the flavour with closed eyes. She was more intoxicated than she looked. 'To the Goddess, a sacrifice!' she cried.

The guests moved in with outstretched hands. Zambia closed hir eyes. They pushed hir on to hir back. In haste, in silence, they pulled off hir clothes, exclaiming, oh so softly, at the delights they uncovered. Zambia could hear Jahsaxa clucking appreciatively somewhere nearby.

'Disgusting!' said a man gleefully and stabbed Zambia viciously in the stomach. That was what it felt like.

'Greedy!' said another. Zambia coughed with pain.

Jahsaxa, kneeling on Zambia's hair spread out on the floor, roughly put her taloned fingers in hir silently screaming mouth, and jerked hir head backwards. 'Enjoy, Zambia, my pretty. You are made for sharing. Enjoy!'

That was the point when Zambia turned off completely, abandoning hir body to whatever its new job demanded of it. The next day, SHe would remember less than half of it.

'So how do you feel today, Zambia?' Tammuz, sitting opposite the gleaming androgyne of surgery and neural nudging, considered that he himself was feeling far from good that day. He had a memory of struggling through the darkened recesses of Roirbak's labyrinthine abode late at night, blindly knocking things from his path in an effort to reach the sluice drain before his urge to vomit overcame him. A gutfucking combination of inexpensive liquor and a couple of ampoules which were supposed to make him euphoric. Sad really. He should have known the consequences: half an hour of relative cheer followed by thunderous visceral revenge. Some time during the muzzy fug of these dissipations, a decision had been reached. That morning, Tammuz had told Jahsaxa his work was over. He knew he had to turn his back on Crevecoeur, dreading the day he would see physical signs that SHe had been working. It was sad that this feeling of desire and affection – so alien to him – had been wasted on such a creature. Then again, maybe not so sad. Just a lesson. His old self would have scorned such sentimentality. He would not make this mistake again.

Zambia Crevecoeur rested hir chin on hir hand in the habitual siren pose, and said, 'Well, I feel better than you look, I guess.'

'I agree that's not difficult,' Tammuz leaned back, sighed. He had not yet told Zambia he was leaving.

'I've been thinking,' Zambia said.

'Yes?'

'You don't like Penumbra that much, do you?' SHe let the statement hang, perhaps as a prompt. Tammuz didn't respond. 'I don't think you like what she did to me much either.'

Tammuz leaned forward. 'You know nothing of the sort. This is merely a subjective attempt to externalise your own feelings. I've told you about this, haven't I?'

'I'm not going to argue with you. Will you hear me out?'

'Go ahead.'

'Well, with all the things we've discussed, the way you've made me see myself, I've decided I shouldn't stick around here.'

Tammuz rolled his eyes. 'I know I'm your therapist, but I don't think it's a good idea to tell me this. Are you aware of how much Ms Penumbra has invested in you?'

'That doesn't mean diddlysquat to me. It's my life, my body. I want your advice. Your work on me was a success, wasn't it? I'm not howling crazy anyway. I think there must be things I can do now, lucrative things, to get me out of this scene. Am I right?'

Tammuz shrugged. 'If you want an honest opinion, I reckon there were things you could have done to achieve that before you ever let Jahsaxa persuade you to undergo these changes.'

'I know that. I don't need you to tell me. Can't you answer me straight?'

'I'm not paid to get involved in ideas of yours to swindle my employer, Zambia.'

Crevecoeur snorted and pushed backwards in hir chair. 'OK, I get it. You don't give a shit. Are you going to tell her what I said?'

Tammuz smiled. 'I won't need to do that,' he said, glancing briefly beyond Zambia's shoulder at the wall behind. 'It seems I've helped you assimilate certain somatic adjustments, but I have not increased your intelligence.'

Crevecoeur looked momentarily shocked; this was followed rapidly by expressions of self-disgust, frustration and finally, a covert cunning. 'Your advice is for me to stay here then?'

Tammuz' eyes were glassy. 'Yes, I think you should. You'll be looked after, and it's hardly work you're not used to. I've done my job, and quite well, I think. That's as far as it goes with me. You're on your own now. Be sensible.'

After Zambia had left, Tammuz put his head in his hands and groaned. He didn't even care whether Jahsaxa was watching him or not.

Crevecoeur left Malamute's room energised by frustrated anger. Foolish not to realise the place was wired. Malamute must think hir crazy. And to risk the man's safety that way too. Unbelievably foolish! Zambia's self-preservation instinct deep inside was screaming: Time to get out and fast! If SHe'd known Jahsaxa'd had hir fixed this way just to be an orgy machine, then SHe'd never have gone through with it. Desperation and hunger had addled hir senses: SHe should have guessed what the score would be. Jahsaxa's pals had virtually pulled hir to bits. Zambia was not a squeamish person – couldn't afford to be – but there were limits. Also, SHe didn't think Parmedes' handiwork was exactly designed for such a pummelling. SHe had no desire to discover for hirself at what point serious physical injury might occur. The only time SHe'd ever felt this rough before was after hir last fight with Cab, when he'd tried to kick hir spine out – from the front.

Augmenting hir anger at hir own stupidity was the knowledge that Malamute was right. There had been things Crevecoeur could have done to get out, such as take advantage of the open invitation to take up with Cab's natro group. OK, so relations were unsteady with little brother right now, but it would have been better than this. Today, all the things Crevecoeur had once found repellent about leaving the city seemed intensely desirable. Freedom. A heady word. Also, despite what had occurred in the past between them, SHe needed Cab so badly now it hurt more than the bruises in hir belly. The Crevecoeurs had always closed ranks in times of crisis, hadn't they? It was best not to think about what Cabochon would have to say about the sexual readjust-ment. Star Eye, however, could be anywhere at present. SHe needed a more immediate bolt-hole. The streets were too dangerous. SHe'd have to speak to Malamute. Obviously, SHe'd have to ratbelly hir way out of this place first, if only to get Malamute on his own. SHe knew he was holed up at Roirbak's place, and was con-vinced hir instincts were right that Malamute hated Penumbra and was coping with moral dilemmas about what he'd done for her. Malamute was smart and he was a runhide, Zambia was sure. Call it developing female insight, but SHe somehow knew Malamute was a man with a secret, a man in disguise, and also a man who knew the way SHe could turn this whole mess into an advantage. Admittedly, SHe foresaw he would probably be difficult about it, but that should not be a major problem. Once you were a survivor, Zambia told hirself. Get back in form.

SHe'd been charting possible escape routes for a while now, the main reason for not taking advantage of them being a certain concurrence with Jahsaxa's opinion that blackouts could occur on the street. Zambia had no wish to be found out cold by someone who might discover what SHe was. SHe'd heard about how gender meddling had been outlawed because of the high suicide rate among the successfully mutated. Whatever research still went on in that area remained the privilege of Tech-Green itself: unpublished and hidden. Knowing all this only heightened Zambia's caution. Goddess knew what would happen to hir if SHe was taken by the authorities.

For three endless days, Zambia patiently bided hir time before making an escape bid. Although SHe suffered a disquieting disappointment when Jahsaxa told hir Malamute would not be coming back (not even a goodbye!), it was probably for the best. Perhaps Jahsaxa would not suspect Zambia would ask him for help. The woman had also been the nearest she could get to contrite about what had happened in her apartment. 'They were a little too eager, perhaps,' she'd said.

Zambia gritted hir teeth and said, 'That's OK. Give me time to stop aching, will you – before the next time.'

Jahsaxa had graciously assented to this. 'You are a treasure, Zambia,' she'd said. 'A triumph.'

Zambia knew there would not be a next time. Not with any of Jahsaxa's punters. SHe had hir own ideas about the future of hir body now.

On the third day, SHe waited until the Quiet, those couple of hours before Eleusis opened for business when most people were resting or tanking up their psyches and

libido for work. It was no secret that Jahsaxa monitored
Zambia's quarters: the cameras were blatantly undis-
guised, which Jahsaxa had insisted was for Zambia's
own safety. 'If anything . . . happened . . . someone will
come over right away,' she'd said. 'It's best this way,
don't you think? For now.'

Zambia had been in total agreement at first. SHe wondered whether, other than through the blunder in
Malamute's office. Jahsaxa was aware of hir change of
heart. She was preternaturally sharp, after all. Perhaps
any attempt to sneak out would be a waste of time.
The humiliation at being caught would be unbearable.
Nevertheless, Zambia slouched into hir showercub as if
going to relieve hirself, only partially closing the door.
SHe pissed into the tube and then turned on the shower.
It might cover any sounds SHe might make. The showercub window was tiny and three floors up. Below lay a
yard, which was sometimes full of empty liquor casings,
picked up by the suppliers whenever there was a new
delivery. At present the pile of plasticases was small, but
enough to break a fall if necessary. Zambia was skinny as
a leather lace. SHe shimmied silently through the window crack like a cat through balanced crates. There were
no pipes attached to the wall at this point, and the
ground looked horribly far away. No matter, you know
how to roll, Zambia told hirself firmly. The casings were
a little way to the right, spilling out of a back door to the
club. Grilles in the sheer wall throwing out rods of light
indicated the kitchens. There was no sound coming from
there, but people might be working all the same. Zambia
launched hirself from the window, twisting hir body to
the right, throwing up hir legs to, hopefully, land on hir
shoulder. The impact was sickening and loud. Crates,
concealing the feral cats who could negotiate them

without disturbance, crashed into disarray, furry bodies sleeking out and away. Zambia allowed hirself the privilege of a suppressed curse. There was no time to probe for injuries. As long as hir legs worked, SHe must be out of here. A nasal voice screeched from inside the building, 'And what the fuck was that?!' No time to let them find out. Crouched low to the ground, Zambia fled across the yard and down the alley at the back. Pain racked hir back and shoulders, the side of hir face. SHe had a feeling there was blood flowing. Hir stomach contracted so fiercely, SHe nearly threw up. A sanctuary was needed – quickly.

Alix Micklemas part-owned a hi-res tattoo salon three blocks east of Club Eleusis. Crevecoeur had for a brief, intoxicating time enjoyed intimate relations with Ms Micklemas, an affair whose firepower had been sky-filling and radiant and whose energy devoured itself within two weeks. They had remained friends thereafter, each possessed of a vague disappointment in the other for which they blamed themselves. Zambia had not seen Alix for months, ever since she'd set up home with the kid with prosthetic limbs who claimed his disfigurement was due to a variety of fantasies, all of which were subject to detail change, and none of which ever sounded convincing. Zambia had disliked the boy on sight, despite the sculpted Nordic features and honey skin, and had kept away from Alix-haunts because of this. Now she was the only person near enough Zambia could think of who could help hir. The nature of Alix's profession demanded she kept a certain amount of medical equipment around. Laser viruses were not unknown.

Alix was out front of the premises poking a flickering neon sign with a length of plastic tubing. She had the first

and second floor of a thin, dilapidated building that was
a ruin above the third storey. Her workshop took up all
the space on the first floor, her apartment, which had all
the inner walls knocked out, the second. She was a gaudy
advert for her own talents; her shaved skull crawling
with tattoos that curled down her neck and back like
hair. Zambia noticed she'd grown a tuft of the real stuff
back which fell into her eyes. Her clothes were multi-
layered and tattered. 'Zambia! Hi!' she said, noticing hir
standing nearby, watching her attack the neon. 'This
looks crazy right? But it usually works.'

'Are you trying to turn it off or on?' Zambia asked,
wiping hir cheekbone. After the quick sprint from
Penumbra's, the cut there was bleeding heavily.

'Neither. Just stop the bitch flickerin' so. Goddess,
Zam, that blood there or am I just behind in what's glam
nowadays?'

'Got a minute, Alix?'

'Sure. Come in.'

She led the way up a flight of stairs, shouting a greeting as they passed the entrance to the ball-scryer's receiv-
ing room on the ground floor. Mammy Crystal was a
bona fide crone; a colourful local character.

'That Zambia? Zambia Crevecoeur?' cried a querulous female voice.

'Yeah, Mammy, how's the future?' Zambia
responded, trying to lower hir voice.

'Brighter'n yours, I reckon, boy! I allus seen black
around you!'

Alix flicked a sneer over her shoulder as she mounted
the stairs, 'Old hag!' she hissed.

'Well, ain't you gonna pop in an' chew tonguewag
with moi?' the fortune-teller screeched.

'Later, maybe!' Zambia called back.

Alix opened the door to her salon, revealing a pink-lit interior studded with UV halo-spots and draped with the ophidian coils of her lasers and printers. She picked up a sleek length of smoked silver. 'Seen one of these before, Zam? This neat, right, easy to use as an air-brush, forty pin, with a palette of 252 separate tones. State-of-the-Art, yeah!'

'Seems like the business is going well.'

'Yeah.' Alix wrinkled her nose. 'The Kid left.'

'Shame. Take a look at me, will you? I just jumped out of a window.'

'Oooh! How far up?' She turned Crevecoeur's head to the side, 'And, like, why?'

'Three storeys and the tale is long.'

'Haven't seen you around much lately. Been one or two rumours 'bout you too.' She rolled her eyes. 'Big rumours!'

Zambia grunted uncomfortably and sat down on one of the couches.

'Cab called,' Alix added. 'He was tryin' to find you.'

'What'd you tell him?'

Alix grinned. 'Trust me, Crevecoeur. Nothin'. He's on his way in, though.'

Zambia groaned. 'Fuck!'

Alix brought a chrome bowl out of an open cupboard, set it down ajangle with instruments of torture and turned on the generator for her machines.

Zambia blanched. 'I want a clean up, not a snakesiren making it with a mongoose on my face.'

'Relax, it's styptic,' Alix said, waving a hissing nozzle. 'Also, antiseptic, antiviral and it cicatrizes.'

'Is that good?'

'Sure.'

'Ouch!'

'Hold still. Goddess Zam, you sure look different. What is this, electrolysis?'

'Sort of.'

'Saves time in the mornings, I guess. Had a chest infection, have you?'

'Er . . .'

Engrossed in her work, Alix flicked off the medstick and applied a lashing of old-fashioned synth-skin from an aerosol. 'OK, take your clothes off.'

'Why?'

'You were limping, also your eyes register pain. I know these things. Come on, strip. There ain't nothin' I've not seen before under there.'

Zambia stood up. 'The face was all I was worried about. I'm fine. Do I owe you?'

'Don't be ridiculous!' Alix cackled, pushing hir down again. 'Come on, what are you hiding? Let another artist paint your skin, is that it?'

'In a way.'

'Shame on you, Crevecoeur! Listen, you look sick, I'll let you off. I don't mind. Just take off the clothes.'

'No.'

'Zambia!' Alix playfully wrestled with hir fastenings.

'This is not a game!' Zambia tried to hold her off. She wouldn't have it.

'You're not leaving till I scan you,' she sang.

'OK, OK, just don't complain right? And don't scream.'

Alix sat down on a stool, put her head on one side. 'Zam, what you been up to?'

'Don't ask.' SHe kicked off hir boots, stripped off hir shirt and trousers. It was not even necessary to remove hir underwear before Alix started yelling.

SHe knew it was unlikely SHe could count on Alix's

discretion, but the need for medical backup had been worth the disclosures. After the girl had calmed down enough to operate her scanning equipment, a number of hairline fractures had been revealed and a torn muscle. Alix's menagerie of coils could fix that, but her hands shook as she used them. 'Goddess, Zam, you prick, you dogsick prick,' she murmured, shaking her head. What the hell you wanna do that for? It's a freakshow.' She kept her eyes averted from Crevecoeur's stomach with its fleet of sphincters, mouthing like anemones in pulse with hir pain. Sulky bruises soured the skin. 'Lady, your tits are bigger than mine!'

'That's not difficult. Be careful!'

'Lay still. Goddess, Goddess, I seen it all now, I truly have. Zambia Crevecoeur, orifice hypermall in person.'

'All right, all right. Your nausea is imprinted on my brain. You don't have to say any more.'

'Someone's bin joy-ridin' you, ain't they?' She burrowed in her equipment carryall. 'Got somethin' to help fix that. Friend o' mine was jumped pretty badly some time back . . .'

Zambia gasped. 'Leave it, Al, don't touch. Ow! Stop!'

'Hold still! Won't take a minute.'

She appraised her handiwork. 'Jahsaxa Penumbra did this? And I mean, like, *all* of this?'

I shouldn't have said that, Crevecoeur thought, too late. 'I didn't tell you that. Forget it.'

'Where're you going to go?'

'What you don't know can't be forced from you, sweet Alix. Now, is that it?'

'Yeah. Just don't jump out of any more windows for a week or two.' She frowned. 'You're in deep this time, my friend, aren't you?'

'Luckily I know how to breathe in shit.'

'How heavy is this? Is there a possibility I'm gonna hear about this on the news-shot some time? Sex Shop Freak Found Dead in Gutter, or something?'

'I hope it won't come to that.'

'Zam, Penumbra virtually owns this sector. And her friends own all the others. You'll have to leave Arcady.'

'I'll come up with something. Don't worry.' SHe pulled on hir clothes. 'Keep quiet for as long as you can,' SHe said, without much hope.

'Got any cred?'

'No.'

'Here, I have some cash. Untraceable. And take that jacket. There's blood on your shirt.'

'Thanks Alix.' SHe kissed the tattooist's cheek. 'I owe you.'

'I draw a line at paying for the funeral, remember that.'

Thanks to Alix's cash donation, Zambia was able to ride the highwire out to Roirbak's workshops. SHe wondered whether SHe'd been missed from Club Eleusis yet. It was possible Penumbra would be bright enough to contact Roirbak straight away. Zambia hoped she'd think SHe'd bolt for the underworld after escaping. Objectively, that would be the best place to head anyway. Except that Tammuz Malamute was very much above ground.

Once the highwire had dropped hir off at Acropolis Ramp, the weather cycle changed and a fine mist appeared in the air to fall like rain. Zambia licked hir cheeks. The water tasted sweet and pure. SHe liked the raintimes, but this was no place to savour them. A covered walkway, already damp with footprints, led under the Midwest Highway that cut the city like a blade. Zambia emerged into the tailored industrial park, most of which was dominated by Roirbak's hangars. It was eerily quiet, the only sign of life being a handful of horticultural robots trimming the flora and lawns. Zambia walked along the wet paths admiring the flushed roses trembling under the weight of moisture, releasing their voluptuous sickroom perfume. A guide droid, alert for strangers, approached hir and was immediately thrown into confusion by hir pheromones. 'May I assist you sirmadamsirmadam? Hmmm?'

'Mr Roirbak's reception area?'

'Do you have an appointment?'

'I believe I'm expected.'

The concept of belief was another thing guaranteed to upset droids. 'That way,' indicated the guide, unaware of how its circuits would be relieved once Crevecoeur had vacated its scent perimeter.

Quincx Roirbak was preparing for an evening out when his receptionist summoned him. 'An uninvited guest again? Really Mellissa. I told you not to disturb me. I was changing.'

The robot continued insistently. 'The person asks for Tammuz Malamute, Mr Roirbak. I have no direct instructions on what action to take in this case.'

'Have you informed Mr Malamute?'

'I made a decision. All accessions have to be reported to you, Mr Roirbak.'

Roirbak sighed. 'Very well, I'll take a look.' He considered. If what he saw through security did not impress him, Tammuz need never know he'd had a visitor. The mere fact of his suspicions concerning Tammuz dictated he must at least inspect who came calling. What he saw intrigued him. He sidled into the reception cubby and addressed his receptionist, an eerily svelte woman-form of perfect shape and minimal, pixie-like features. 'Identify, Mellissa, if you please, that lifeform on our perimeter.'

'It is human, age nineteen years, height 1.8 metres, unarmed. Its gender, Mr Roirbak, I find unspecific, indeed vacillating, if such can be. May I request information update in this area?'

'Perhaps we'd better let our guest in so you can achieve that,' Roirbak said good-humouredly. 'Well, well. I wonder whether our friend Tammuz Malamute is expecting this visitor.'

The doors sighed open and Zambia Crevecoeur ducked warily into the building. SHe seemed haloed in mist, hair wet and tendrilled, clothes dripping. 'And from which deep ocean have we risen?' Roirbak inquired, sauntering out from the reception booth.

'Sector 23,' Zambia replied quickly. 'I apologise for disturbing you. May I see Tammuz Malamute?'

'Perhaps. Who are you and what do you want here?'

'I'm Zambia, and I want to see Tammuz.' SHe sensed obstruction and added sharply, 'Is Mr Roirbak here?'

'I am Quincx Roirbak. Which of us do you want to speak with?'

'Oh . . . I'm here to see Tammuz Malamute. I know it's out of order, me coming here like this, but it's urgent, couldn't wait.'

Roirbak pondered in silence for agonising seconds while Zambia panted with nerves in front of him. Eventually he nodded. 'Very well, wait here. I'll have him informed of your arrival.'

'Thank you.'

Roirbak began to walk away, then paused and turned. 'Tammuz Malamute, you say? Is that the only name you know him by?'

Zambia had slumped. SHe straightened hir spine. 'Yes. I think so. Yes.'

Tammuz was playing a contest of cunning with his computer. Over the past few weeks, he'd detected a fiendish intelligence in the machine whose sense of humour he empathised with. He'd also rigged it into the security systems as a precaution and was thus already rigid with dread when Roirbak communicated with him. 'There's a visitor for you,' Quincx said. 'A delightful young lady that looks like a boy. One of your creations perhaps?'

'Name?' Tammuz inquired in a monotone.

'Er . . . Zambia. Would this, by any chance, be Zambia Crevecoeur, late of Club Eleusis?'

Tammuz sighed. 'Late? I hope not. AWOL perhaps. I'll be down, Quincx. Sorry about this?'

'No problem. I'm fascinated. Pity I have an appointment tonight. I would like to view your handiwork.'

'I'm only the French polisher, Quincx. Another guy's responsible for the true craftmanship.'

'I detect distaste.'

'You detect disturbance. Where is SHe?'

'Main gate. 'Want . . . it . . . sent up?'

'No. Like I said, I'll be down.' He flipped off his commset. 'Damn!' he told his computer.

'Beyond my earthly powers!' came the sassy message on the screen.

What disturbed Tammuz more than Zambia's unexpected visit was Roirbak's parting shot to hir. Do you know Tammuz Malamute under any other name? What did that mean? Was it possible the old fox had sussed him out and not let it show? A round of applause for the acting ability of Quincx Roirbak in that case. Zambia was still standing dejectedly by the reception booth smoking a cigarette the receptionist had given hir out of pity. Mellissa kept on hand supplies of all delicacies necessary to human well-being. Occasionally, Roirbak might walk through the door needing liquor, caffeine or nicotine immediately; business meetings could sometimes make him tense. Zambia was answering the robot's questions about hir gender state when Tammuz sauntered lankily down the colonnaded walkway, hands in pockets.

Zambia's heart did a flip. What a worn-out, haggard, rakish, unbelievably handsome beast, SHe thought.

'Zambia,' said Tammuz, trying to sound pissed off. 'And what are we doing here, hmmmm?'

Zambia pushed back hir wet hair. 'I throw myself at your feet, oh Lord Malamute.' SHe snorted smoke and ground out the cigarette on the floor. 'Shit, help me, you wise-ass. Where else could I come?'

'You realise this compromises me?'

'So what? You could be me. Do I get invited in for a coffee or what?'

'Anyone know you're here?'

'You think I'm stupid?'

'No, I just want to know if anyone knows you're here.'

'Of course not. Even I don't know where I am.'

'Thank you Mellissa. You can let hir go now. Come on, Zambia Crevecoeur.' The robot withdrew a seeking filament from Zambia's neck; SHe had not felt it. Zambia followed Tammuz into the hangar.

He took hir to the canteen. One of the domestics hummed up and down behind the counter, polishing the spotless ceraplas. 'Put on a fresh pot of coffee, Sindy,' Tammuz called.

'Sindy?'

'So, they're people too aren't they? I don't go in for numbers as names. Sit down, Zambia. You hungry?'

Zambia shook hir head. 'No . . . This is some place you've got here, Malamute.'

'It's Roirbak's, not mine. I'm just a guest,' Tammuz answered shortly.

Zambia sighed. 'You're angry I'm here, aren't you?'

'Do I look angry?'

'You look like stone. That's angry in my datafile.'

'It's not anger, exactly. It's just I don't relish any of Jahsaxa's colleagues making a nuisance of themselves here. Mr Roirbak won't like it, and I'm only resident at his pleasure, you understand.'

'Of course. They won't think to look for me here, though. Why should they?'

'Zambia, my sweet puzzle, I can think of at least two without concentrating. Why are you doing this? Didn't you give it any thought before you took up Ms Penumbra's offer?'

'Yes, of course I did. I was desperate. I didn't think it would be . . . like this.'

'Then I can't imagine how you *did* think it would be. Seemed pretty straightforward from the specifications. I saw them. You weren't exactly deceived.'

'I'm semi-female now, and women've always had the excuse that they like to change their minds. I claim that as my right now too, OK?'

'Don't get upset. What do you think I can do for you?'

'Don't play with me, Malamute. Of course you can do something. You're part of Roirbak's network and he can do anything.'

'They said that of Tech-Green once and look what happened.'

'At least let me stay here for a while until I get my head clear.'

Tammuz paused. 'That's not really up to me, Zambia.'

Zambia slammed hir fists down on the table, causing the Sindy droid to bleep unexpectedly. 'It's all right for you isn't it! Goddess, I can't believe the way you're trying to scrape me off your hands! I've been working with you for weeks. I know you cared! You did! I saw your expression. I heard the things you didn't say! Now you get frightened and keep me at arm's length! Why? What is it you're hiding, Malamute? I bet it's more than artificial cunts!'

Zambia's vulgar exclamation echoed round the canteen. The droid was motionless but for a cautious antenna trembling at its apex. Tammuz Malamute was indeed like stone, his eyes expressionless, only one finger tapping the table. 'Goddess, I'm sorry!' Zambia put hir head in hir hands, rubbed hir face. 'I'd do anything to go back in time right now, you know. I'd never have . . .' SHe sighed, ground at hir eyes one more time and blinked at Tammuz. 'Let's face it, I'm fucked. I have no future. Mammy Crystal was right.'

Tammuz had still not cracked. Zambia stood up. 'I'm sorry. I'm really sorry. That was way out . . . you know. I'll go. OK?'

Tammuz made hir wait until SHe'd wriggled through all the tables to the door. Then he said, in a carrying voice. 'I'll speak to Roirbak about this. I'm not promising anything. Sit. Sit and wait. Sindy'll bring you a coffee.'

Tammuz managed to catch Roirbak just as he was making the finishing touches to his evening regalia: black, matt silk suit with thread-wide yellow pinstripe, understated gold adornments, I-Ching earrings. Tammuz suspected the man may have eavesdropped on what had occurred in the canteen, but behaved as if he hadn't. 'I have a problem with Crevecoeur,' he began.

'Oh? Therapy decay?'

'Not exactly. Can SHe stay here for a few days?'

'Why here?'

'SHe split Eleusis. This seemed the safest bolthole.'

'With you . . .' Roirbak turned away from his mirror and fixed Tammuz with a stare. 'I'm surprised you want to get involved. You did your job, we got our rewards. Ms Penumbra will not take kindly if she suspects we're helping one of her employees abscond.'

'I have realised all this Quincx. I wouldn't want to embarrass you, but I really can see no alternative at present. I don't feel I can abandon Crevecoeur after having worked with hir all this time. I am in no position to judge whether what SHe is doing is right or wrong.'

'Natro talk, Tammuz. Each to his own life-curve, I know. Brotherhood along the way.' He sighed. 'Whatever your reasons . . .' Shook his head. 'I have enjoyed having you around, Mr Malamute, much to my surprise. It would be unfortunate if something occurred to curtail our partnership. However, I will let the gynandrous renegade stay here under one condition. If Penumbra questions either of us, we will not lie. If she suspects Crevecoeur is here and asks, we let hir go back. Is that clear? I will not risk Penumbra's wrath. It would be a pity to lose business contact with her.'

'That seems fair,' Tammuz agreed. 'I will try to work something out.'

'Actually,' Roirbak said, having just thought of it, 'we may be able to use the natro group Star Eye to help your friend leave the city. They will be here very shortly.'

'Whatever you think is best,' Tammuz replied stonily.

* * *

'You can stay,' Tammuz said, walking back into the canteen. Zambia was sitting against the counter, talking with Sindy. SHe had been impressed with how Tammuz had adjusted the machine to behave just like a real counter-girl. The droid virtually knew hir life-history now and had made appropriately sympathetic responses. At the news, Zambia didn't leap up with joy as Tammuz had expected, but dropped hir head on to hir hands which were flat against the counter.

'Thank the Goddess!' SHe said.

'I'll find you somewhere to sleep, a change of clothes maybe.'

'I don't want to sleep and my clothes are fine. It's warm in here. I've dried out.'

'I have to do something with you, Zambia.'

'Can't we talk?'

'Whatever you have to say will only make me feel uncomfortable.'

'You have to help me, Malamute!'

'Look,' Tammuz said, rubbing his neck in agitation, 'You can stay here. It's a hiding place. Stop behaving as if I'm responsible for your welfare. I'm not. I did a job for Penumbra and it's over. I'm foolish going along with you even this far. Do what you said. Get your head together and clear out. Jahsaxa will have to come here looking for you eventually. She's not stupid.'

Zambia felt as if SHe'd been punched in the gut. SHe wondered what SHe was doing there. SHe'd never begged help off anyone before – hadn't needed to. Had hir survival expertise been destroyed somewhere during the treatment SHe'd had? SHe shuddered. Tammuz was being honest. All the quiet concern over the past weeks had been professional, nothing more. The horrendous blunder of thinking it was more than that filled hir with shame.

SHe hopped off the stool, mustering pride. 'You got me all wrong, Malamute,' SHe said, 'I don't need that kind of support from you. I need clothes, supplies, money. How can I leave the city without that?' SHe began to saunter towards the canteen door. 'After all, I meant what I said. I know you've got something to hide, and Jahsaxa Penumbra loves mysteries. If I end up back there, she might just be interested enough in what I got to say to do some investigating of her own.' SHe didn't risk looking at Tammuz, sensing his simmering rage as an intense heat behind hir.

'You know nothing about me, Crevecoeur,' he said. 'The only thing I have to hide is you.'

'Sure. So, show me, where do I sleep?'

Tammuz led the way up to the second floor, where he'd spread himself out through two labs, an office and a washroom. This was another, remote area of the complex which had remained untouched by Roirbak's artistic caprices, and was still furnished in a bare, functional style. Tammuz' fury at Zambia's threats rendered him speechless. He was half tempted to call Penumbra himself and demand she come and collect this viper immediately. Surely she wouldn't take Zambia's remarks about himself seriously. Gutter trash! Tammuz thought. Ungrateful, grasping, foul-minded gutter trash.

'You can have this room,' he said coldly. At one time it must have been a waiting room for clients. It was cold in there but Tammuz was so angry he decided he wouldn't turn the heating on. 'Sorry about the temperature. The heaters went down years ago.'

'Got a blanket or quilt for me or something?' Zambia didn't appear insulted.

'I'll see. Later.'

Zambia sat down on one of the sofas. 'You just going to leave me in here then?'

'I have work to do and no inclination whatsoever to entertain you, Zambia Crevecoeur.' Triumphant, he slammed the door and marched off down the corridor to his own cosy rooms, smugly requesting his domestic unit to prepare him a toasted sandwich and hot coffee. He intended to spend the evening having intelligent conversation with his computer, Zambia Crevecoeur shut firmly out of his mind.

He began by telling the machine all about Zambia, to which it responded sagely, 'In humanity's attempt to obtain the best of both genders, it appears to have harvested the worst.'

'How true, my friend, my trustworthy, reliable, sensible friend!' Tammuz declared, feeling vindicated.

'That observation was aligned to your personal subjectivity, of course, with which I feel familiar,' the computer appended.

Tammuz again considered that some wit in past years had programmed the machine with something other than Aristotelian logic.

Back at Club Eleusis, Jahsaxa Penumbra was tripping out like the bad queen in a fairy-tale cartoon, the only omission being the thunder-clouds and lightning round her head. She paraded up and down her office, black hair aflow, her fingers flexed to claws, tipped with glittering red, frightening her security staff. 'SHe can't just have *gone!*' she shouted in a deep, masculine voice, in response to her officers' discovery that no one had seen Crevecoeur since late afternoon, and certainly not in the act of leaving the building. The Club had been thoroughly searched: there was nowhere the security systems could not probe. The officers had examined the window in Zambia's showercub but had considered it too small for hir to escape through, the wall outside too sheer. The staff who had been in the kitchen when Zambia had landed in the packing cases had gone off duty soon afterwards. What they had heard in the yard and what they had seen upon investigating – spilled crates they attributed to rutting cats – would not be revealed until morning. 'Call Tammuz Malamute!' Jahsaxa yelled at her commset. As far as everyone knew, he had been the last person to see Zambia at the Club. Her rage was further fuelled by the fact that all she contacted was Roirbak's answering machine. She was on the point of ordering some of her people to hurry over to Acropolis Park to call in person, when one of her more canny officers, who had lost no time in searching the sector, arrived back at the Club.

Reynard Lennon was astute, analytical, an expert in self-preservation, and very, very polite. He was also a creature entirely without compassion and because of this rarely failed to uncover information. 'I checked out most of Crevecoeur's old haunts,' he said, consulting his memofile, 'and turned up the goods at Alix Micklemas' tattoo parlour.' Jahsaxa raised an eyebrow. Reynard continued. 'She told me Crevecoeur showed up around 18.00 in a pretty bad way. Claimed to have jumped from a window.' Jahsaxa narrowed her eyes meaningfully at her in-house security officers. 'Anyway, she fixed hir up and Crevecoeur split.'

'The *tattooist* did not have the wit to tag Crevecoeur, I suppose?' Jahsaxa inquired.

Reynard shook his head. 'Nah. Doubt she saw reason to.'

Jahsaxa nodded. 'Fix that. She may prove useful in

the future. Did she offer any prognosis?'

Reynard flipped off the memofile. 'In her opinion, she thought Crevecoeur would dive subsurface, hit the labyrinth and, like, mingle.'

Jahsaxa nodded again. 'Seems likely. Alert my operatives subcity immediately.'

'Already seen to it, Ms Penumbra,' Reynard announced proudly. The other officers looked at him with loathing.

Later in the evening, Tammuz and his computer decided to investigate an old network tape he'd uncovered in Roirbak's huge stockpile of such material. It was a programme about the (then) proposed orbital cities, and even boasted an interview with a very youthful Ewan Famber, who had just passed out from the Tech-Green High College weighed down with honours and acclamations. The programme, in retrospect, was practically science fiction: nothing had been as easy in practice as Tech-Green had declared in theory. Tammuz had dimmed the lights, put his feet up, and asked the computer to tune in the wallscreen. He smiled in bewilderment at a succession of ads – the psychoprofile of mankind, he thought – and waited for the programme to begin.

A few rooms away, Zambia had become thoroughly tired of trying to get some sleep in such an uncomfortable place, and decided to snoop around the building. Hir investigations didn't take hir further than the light beneath Tammuz Malamute's door. SHe heard him laugh, heard him say something. Did he have a visitor? Perhaps a lover. Would that explain his attitude? Impulsively, suddenly feeling that nothing could worsen the ruins of hir existence, Zambia opened the door and went in. Tammuz was watching TV alone, eating a bag of Munchi-Chipz. He had been smiling at the screen, an expression which fell with such abruptness from his face when he looked at the doorway that Zambia was convinced SHe heard it hit the floor with a crack. 'Stay in your room!' he said.

Zambia attempted a smile. 'No. I mean – look, this is ridiculous. I didn't mean to upset you. I shouldn't have said the things I did. I won't say anything to Penumbra no matter what happens. I was only teasing you. It's freezing down there. I'm sorry. Can I come in here? I won't disturb you.'

Tammuz relented. 'All right. But I'm watching this, so keep quiet.'

Zambia slid to the floor near Tammuz' chair and picked up a fallen Munchi-Chip to eat. Tammuz threw hir another bag without comment. The rustling of packaging caused him to sigh and ask the computer to turn up the sound. Zambia sucked the Munchis to softness before swallowing them, a procedure that took up the whole of the half-hour programme. To hir, the grandiose promises of Utopia emblazoned across the screen were not only unconvincing but nauseating. At the end of it, SHe had to say, 'The cities might be Paradise itself, but for how long? Eventually they'll be just as full of people as the planet. Then it'll be just as bad up there, I'm sure.'

'Not everyone in the world is grasping and selfish to the exclusion of all others,' Tammuz said. 'They'll be very careful who they let up there, I'm sure. The Tech-Greens are probably *breeding* the right kind of people right at this minute.'

'And you approve of that, huh?'

Tammuz shrugged. 'More than I approve of most of

what I see down here. Humanity isn't as sacred as it likes to think. In my view, the sooner the old model is scrapped, the better.'

'Think of yourself as old model?'

Tammuz flicked hir a cold glance. 'Do you?'

'You really don't know anything about me, do you, despite all that wallowing in my mind? As it happens, I don't think I'm the right person to lead humanity into the future, no. At least I'm honest about it. You? I reckon you think you're kind of special, Tammuz Malamute.'

'You're right. I do, and I am.'

'Oh yeah? And what is it that's so special about you?'

Tammuz paused, drew in his breath, smothered the expression of one who feared he had narrowly missed being indiscreet.

'Everybody is special,' he said. 'It's just that most people only realise that in dreams. They are either too lazy or too uninformed to do anything but fail to fulfil their potential.'

'Weird. The way you say that it sounds like crap, but I guess the essence of it makes sense. I think circumstances have a lot to do with it though.'

Tammuz shook his head, frowning. 'That's just an excuse.'

'OK, so tell me how I fulfil my potential at this moment.'

Tammuz shifted in his chair. 'That's something only you can decide.'

Zambia laughed. 'And you talk to me about excuses? Come on! I want your opinion, that's all. What would you do if you were me?'

'None of the things you *have* done for a start.'

'How can you say that? It might be the resultant me is

348

a product of the coincidences of my life.'

'Wonderful. I have a gutter philosopher on my hands!'

'I'm surprised someone like you can have such a fixed view of someone else, i.e. me.'

'I don't.'

'Yes you do, you think I'm stupid, mindless, amoral. Shall I go on? Just because I don't have a Tech-Green sci-cert, doesn't mean I don't have a mind. Just because I earn my living through my own body doesn't mean I don't have feelings or morals. Just . . .'

'All right, you made your point. Zambia Crevecoeur is one of the great minds of our age, whose circumstances prevent hir enlightening knowledge reaching the population.'

'Goddess, you're a pompous ass, Malamute. I don't know what I see in you. You despise me. Face it, you're narrow-minded.'

Tammuz didn't react as Zambia expected. Mildly, he said, 'If you insist on facing things, why not think about how the way you've behaved hardly leads me to think on you as a sensitive soul. I am familiar with the components of your personality, true, as I am familiar with the liquors in that cabinet over there, but throwing all the different liquors together at random won't make a cocktail, not one that's palatable to me at least. Perhaps I do know your potential, through the work we've been doing, but you're not a computer: you have autonomy. I didn't program you. How you manifest your aspects is your choice entirely. And I don't have to enjoy the resultant cocktail.'

Zambia, more astute than Tammuz gave hir credit for, knelt against the side of his chair: 'You reckon the cocktail will give you gut-ache, its taste is questionable, yet it looks beautiful, glowing there in the glass, smells divine, and the buzz it can give you is a temptation beyond endurance. The only way you can stop yourself drinking it is to lecture the world about how bad it is. Stop being so uptight. Be loose. Give in. Drink it. Drink me!'

Tammuz drew in a shuddering breath and glanced at the computer blinking serenely behind them. 'We have company,' he said. 'It would be best if we continued this conversation elsewhere.'

Tammuz took hir to his bedroom. 'I have wallscreens, music, everything in here and it's . . . a nicer room than the other one,' he said.

Zambia gave him a crooked grin. 'Sure.' SHe sat down on the bed. 'You know something, Malamute. You're like a big kid most of the time. Are you a virgin, is that it?'

'Goddess!' Tammuz clawed air in exasperation.

'Oh, I'm sorry. Sit down. Let's talk. Tell me about yourself.'

Tammuz poured them both a drink, handing one to Zambia as he sat down. 'What do you want to know?'

'How old are you?'

Tammuz pulled a face. 'Goddess, I don't know. I've forgotten.'

'Really?!' Zambia laughed.

'OK. About seven years old, I think.'

'Uh huh.' SHe nodded, smiling. 'Got any family?'

'Maybe. Have you? You never talked about that.'

Zambia sighed and lay flat on the bed, the drink balanced on hir chest. 'Yeah, I have. We-ell.' SHe sat up. 'It's not really *like* family, you see. It was kind of weird, very intense.'

'Sounds intriguing.'

'It was hell. Here, take this.' SHe handed Tammuz the

drink and pulled at hir shirt. 'See this tattoo on my shoulder? There's a scar under there. You can touch it if you want.'

Tammuz put down the drinks and poked it with a cautious finger. 'I had a brother there once.' Tammuz withdrew his hand sharply.

'What?'

'You heard. We were separated at birth, physically. But I have to be honest and say we tried to join flesh again all our lives. It caused big problems.'

'I can imagine.'

'No, you can't. That's you looking at me, thinking "Zambia Crevecoeur, whore", and making up all kinds of garbage in your head. It wasn't like that. We ended up fighting. Badly. Hurting each other. We don't speak now. I haven't seen him for months.'

'Oh.'

'Sometimes I don't think we *should* speak again either. Know what I mean? He's with a natro outfit. Star Eye, I think they're called.'

Tammuz groaned and put his head in his hands. 'It would be!' he cried.

'What did you say?'

'Nothing,' Tammuz said. 'Nothing.' He raised his head and grinned weakly. He wondered, briefly, whether it would be repulsive making love to an intersex, even one whose enhancements were as familiar to him as Zambia's. He wasn't sure what his subconscious was looking at now: the male or the female in hir. Maybe neither. Maybe he saw only the person within the flesh, a person who, for all hir faults, he had reluctantly come to be very fond of. 'Zambia, can we imagine, just for now, there's no one in this world but us? I think we both need the therapy.'

351

Zambia looked puzzled. 'OK. Has what I just told you turned you off or something?'

'No, no. It's complicated. My life's complicated. Unravel me a bit will you?'

'Where d'you want me to begin?'

'About here,' Tammuz said, and pulled off his T-shirt.

'No problem,' said Zambia, rolling towards him.

It was Leila's connection with Quincx Roirbak that swayed Emanuel Lazar's decision to allow his son to accompany Star Eye to Arcady. Cynically, Leila considered Lazar probably expected Nathan to indulge in a little snooping for him, find out what Roirbak was working on nowadays. Leila just took his money and waved goodbye. She was not sorry to see the back of Lazar Farm this time.

Ari, however, found the leave-taking sorrowful, not least because she had to say goodbye to the jellycrusts. R. J. left her with a few of his abstruse sayings, which she believed meant he was telling her not to worry too much; it was difficult to tell. Lazarene boys came to throw kisses at the trucks as they left, Justinette and Elice trying to squeeze through the open windows, catcalling back. Nathan sat, wide-eyed and bewildered next to Ari, reminding her of her own first day aboard. The engines roared and gushed, and Star Eye were on their way to the city, substantially richer than before they'd made the diversion.

Leila stopped riding in Rentfree Aphrodite completely, but Ari knew she hadn't discussed anything with Jordan yet. They had just ceased being lovers with no explanation or recriminations from either side being voiced. The rest of Star Eye warily observed this situation. Some nights, the atmosphere round the campfire was unbearable. Ari felt sorry for Cabochon, who spent most evenings sitting apart from the others, chewing his fingernails. Nathan followed Ari around as if he were a dog and she a bitch in oestrus. She realised he must be going through some kind of hell waiting for the time when he could let all his suppressed urges out. She tried to distract him as best she could, showing him how to make totems, begging Urran to let Nathan use the computer now and again. The vibratory movement of the truck didn't help him, she was sure. Elice occasionally flirted with Nathan to bait Urran. Ari could see Elice confused the boy; she had the subtlety of a hammer. In desperation, Ari started marking the days off on a chart, just so she could see the time they had left on the road diminishing.

A few days out of Lazar Farm, the group celebrated Lithafest. Leila had planned to keep it rather a subdued affair, but another natro group happened along at the small site they were using and livened things up a little. Ari held Nathan's hand as everyone greeted the dawn of the Solstice Day. She reflected on how much she had changed since the last festival, less than seven weeks ago. What would she be thinking and doing by Lughmas? Something within her insisted she tell Cabochon what Leila had seen at Lazar Farm. She left Nathan helping to prepare the Solstice Breakfast with the others and went to find him. He and Jordan were conducting their own ritual away from the group. They had exchanged blood; there seemed little point in saying what she planned. Natros performed bonding ceremonies irrespective of sex. Ari wondered how Leila would react if she went back to her and said. 'Your lover has just married another man.' Resignedly, she kissed Cabochon and wished him well. The extent of their embarrassment over their bonding was illustrated by the fact they'd held it so privately. Normally, such affairs called for days of celebration.

Ari felt very old as she walked back to the group. It seemed that, all around her, things were changing – old, beloved routines that had felt safe and comfortable were decaying into new patterns. If by working with Roirbak it meant she had to leave Star Eye, it might be for the best. The Star Eye she had joined at Beltagne would soon no longer exist in the same form, she was sure.

As the trucks made to leave the following day for the final part of the journey to Arcady, Cabochon asked Ari if he could speak with her, and then told her about what he feared waited in Arcady for him. 'I felt you disapproved last night,' he said. 'I want you to know why. I need support. I need strength. If I have a partner, Zambia won't be able to get at me. It had to be stronger than physical love, Ari, it had to be deeper than that.'

'And what about Leila? Has Jordan told her?'

Cabochon shrugged. 'I doubt it. Not yet. Will you?'

Ari shook her head. 'No. I won't do Jordan's dirty work for him.' She sighed. 'I'm sorry, Cab, I'm not getting at you. Things are just a bit weird at the moment. I think you should get Jordan to speak to Leila soon though, don't you?' She could have mentioned how Leila was thinking of leaving the group, but held back. It was not her place to tell anyone.

Because they were so close to the city, the trucks travelled through the night and, by dawn, Cable announced over the intercom to everyone sitting in the back that Arcady's higher domes were now visible on the horizon.

Ari could hardly muster any enthusiasm. She had been thinking a lot about the conversation she and Leila had had back at Lazar's, the talk of sky cities and escape. She wanted only to rid herself of the blocks Ewan had inflicted on her and lose herself in a new future. She was weighed down with a confusing mixture of feelings that sometimes felt so mellow and piquant, it was almost pleasant. She thought of evening skies, the silhouettes of lonely birds against the sun, and tired land. She thought of standing against this landscape and of being somehow contained within herself: resolute, alone, but not lonely. She thought of Nathan, victim to his own juices, almost dehumanised by the urges of a young male brought into such sharp focus by Leila's meddling. She wanted him to be someone she could love and idealised the future in her head, but then found herself thinking about that most heartwrenching of adolescent discoveries; people rarely are what you want them to be and betray you without malice, unaware of the pain they cause. No one, not even lovers, are truly psychic, and everyone flounders around each other, misunderstanding, misinterpreting, sending out confusing signals.

Once Arcady came into sight, Ari felt she had learnt a lot during the past few days, irreplaceably important lessons. Eve, picking up on some of Ari's melancholy without understanding the cause, hugged her as they thundered along the straight, smooth road that led to the city. Rotors and microlights whirred overhead; the sky was thick with traffic. Very soon, even before they went under dome, Arcady surrounded them from horizon to horizon, its size so prodigious that it banished all Ari's ideas of what a city might be. The huge domes seemed to be heaped on top of each other like black barnacles, their polarised, opaque surfaces hiding everything contained within them. This was another land; the ruin, waste, excitement, wild beauty, sour barrens and unpredictability of the world outside disappeared beyond the stratosphere-scraping reaches of Arcady's domes. The pace of life palpably increased; colours changed. Suddenly Star Eye were somewhere where things *happened*, time was strictly portioned and progressed at the same rate. Ari realised she had never felt this before – not even at home, where time had been her own.

Up front, Leila was navigating. Traffic was strictly regulated in Arcady, ground vehicles being confined to certain routes, especially those that were outside the city regulations concerning fuel effluent, such as the Star Eye trucks. It was necessary to park the trucks some distance away from Acropolis Park. The freight routes from the factories were via underground subways to different areas of the city, or else, for lighter materials, via the highwire. They drove into an underground vehicle park where Leila and Cable went off to check them in with security and pay the initial tariff. Everyone bundled their possessions together and talked about where they would like to stay. Leila had said it would be presumptuous for them all to descend on Roirbak like an unwelcome plague, so had communicated ahead and reserved rooms in a cheap hostel popular with nomad natros. It was situated in Athena Gardens, an area near both Sector 23 and Acropolis Park.

Ari's spirits rose slightly once the group had bundled on to the highwire. A sense of adventure invaded the group, everyone whooping and yelling as they were flung between towers on their way to Athena Gardens, incurring outraged or amused, tolerant glances from the other passengers. Justinette and Cable listed which nightclubs they intended to visit, while Urran reminisced about favourite sites of conquest. Ezooli and Eve were more interested in the cafés, while Elice planned tragically which drugs she planned to get hold of. Stickit squealed in delight, waving at the ant figures far below. Even Grover was grinning. 'I love this place!' Justinette cried.

To Ari, the massive buildings, the height at which they were travelling, were all too overwhelming and disorientating to enjoy. Nathan seemed unaffected by this. He leaned over and said to Ari, 'You were right. I'm glad you persuaded me to come here. It's great!' She smiled thinly in response.

Athena Gardens was an incredibly green place. Natro shops thronged the uniformly cobbled streets, where people whizzed back and forth on bicycles or skates – often their only form of exercise. Justinette insisted on linking her arm through Ari's, dragging her to every shop window to exclaim over the bright and tempting, useless gimmickry to be found within. She was especially taken by statuettes of Astrada; transparent material filled with coloured gas that swirled and glowed, spinning visions of ancient fields and Arcadian mountains. Nearly every shop was selling them; it was a current craze. Further along, cafés and snackbooths filled the air with seductive aromas. Ari had been struck by the smells of Arcady more than anything. Everything was so intense and exotic. Even the air smelt sweet and clean. Her stomach rumbled. She was sure she'd never found the scent of cooking food so seductive.

'We can eat later,' Leila called, trying to keep order over the group who were wandering about all over the place. 'Let's just check in at the hostel first, OK?'

Athena Gardens was a low area, no building above five storeys. It was designed to have a village atmosphere; all the shops and hostels and cafés were built to 'old world' design. In the distance, above the roofs, the high towers of the adjoining sectors could be seen. To Ari, the constant background noise of the city – vehicles, machinery, human voices – sounded like an unceasing prayer chant, rhythmic yet ululating.

The hostel was named Rameses Villa; a charming anachronism. It was all very friendly and cosy, the hostel staff on first-name terms with everyone in the group within half an hour. Two other groups were in residence, along with a handful of loners who had a tendency to sit apart from any gathering, dress in dark clothes with large hats, and smoke long pipes. This included the women.

Ari was exhausted by the sheer weight of first impressions of the city. Everything came at you like a meteor, blasting out sound and colour and light. Local order-wardens mixed with the general population, smiling and laid-back. There was none of that back-of-the-neck prickle of fear and guilt associated with encountering the zone patrols back at Taler's Bump. Was it possible for such a large amount of people as inhabited Athena Gardens to be genuinely so cheerful and contented?

Élice, ever a harbinger of gloom, was ready to point out that Athena Gardens was but one sector of Arcady. 'A natro island,' she said. 'Don't believe all of the city is like this. The reason why there's so much space above our heads here is simple: the climate controllers use it for inducing weather conditions for the whole of Arcady.'

Ari looked up at this prompt. She could see a highwire directly overhead, above that, air traffic, and beyond—. She squinted. This couldn't be possible, surely? Although it was murky, she felt she could almost pick out the silhouettes of other buildings up there, as if they were constructed on the inside of the dome itself. Perhaps it was an illusion, or a reflection of some kind. She didn't mention it to Elice.

Once everyone had claimed their rooms and strewn their possessions around to secure occupancy, Star Eye scattered into the streets, leaving Leila and Ari alone with Nathan. The boy appeared fretful and disappointed that he couldn't join the others on their excursions. Leila didn't have the heart to tell him she doubted whether there'd be much opportunity for him ever to do that, at least while he was helping her with Ari. She put a call through to Roirbak from her room as soon as the others had left, advising him she'd be over with her protégés within the hour. Turning away from the commscreen, she saw Ari sitting hunched and troubled on the bed. Nathan was standing defiantly, hands in pockets, near the window. Leila sighed. This was not going to be at all easy.

'Goddess, what time is it?' Tammuz leaned over Zambia and removed a T-shirt which had hooked itself over the wall-clock in the frenzy of its removal the previous night.

'You have to go somewhere?' Zambia asked.

'No, but I like to work a certain amount of time per day. It's easy to get lazy around here. All this space, being alone most of the time.'

'What are you working on?'

Tammuz pulled his T-shirt over his head. 'Oh, this and that. Old theories mainly. Just catching up really.'

'You're very close about your work, aren't you? Is it illegal or something?'

Tammuz laughed. 'You'd find it very boring. Want to come down to the canteen? I'll have Sindy fix us breakfast.'

'OK.' Zambia was finding it very hard to see anything sinister in Tammuz Malamute that day. SHe was also feeling less antipathic towards hir new implants and adjustments. Because of hir profession, SHe'd always been able to disassociate 'work' from pleasure, clients from lovers, but had been worried that the experience of Jahsaxa's friends mauling hir might have intruded into this objectivity. It was a needless fear. Just being in the arms of this unique person, whom SHe'd never been *absolutely* sure SHe could hook, effectively wiped the unpleasant memory from hir mind for the night. And the implants had worked just fine, thank you. SHe appreciated Dr Parmedes' art: it would have been easy to fix the physical changes, but he had possessed the patience and expertise to make those organs as responsive to stimulation as any natural ones. The pleasure had been unique and exquisite. Tammuz had been so gentle that there'd hardly been any pain, expertly coaxing each orifice to orgasm until Zambia felt SHe must die from sensory overload. The final visions had been almost prophetic. Zambia had dreaded Tammuz seeing hir battered flesh, feeling sure he would be sickened by the thought of others having been intimate with hir so recently. 'Who did that!' he had demanded, pointing to the bruises. 'Someone who gets off on slapping people around,' SHe'd answered carelessly. 'Couldn't do anything else.' It was just a little lie, SHe thought. One thing it had made hir certain of: such gifts as SHe now possessed must never again become the property of a place like Club Eleusis. That would be an abomination. Such was the strength of this conviction, Zambia made a solemn vow that SHe would take hir own life before one of Penumbra's sleazy, slimy patrons ever touched one of hir wonderful, magical organs again. It was amazing . . . today SHe had woken up loving hirself.

Tammuz felt in a daze. As he preceded what he now thought of as a mythical being down to the canteen, he thought about how he'd once found the sight of Zambia's adjustments repulsive and unnatural. Now, having experienced their purpose, he almost revered them. A manifestation of deity, he thought. A new god/dess. To him, Zambia had been virgin six times over, and each defloweling had been more intense than the last. He too made a vow. He would have to die before he could allow Jahsaxa Penumbra to get her hands on such magic and exploit it. Thank the Goddess Zambia had had the sense to get out before some scuzzie had violated hir by more than just a beating. He kept replaying the scene in his head when Zambia stood before him, wreathed to hir chest in tangled rats'-tails, an urchin elemental, and removed hir clothes. 'Look at me,' SHe had said. 'I am new. Totally new. Remember that.' It had been a plea. Don't turn away. Please don't turn away. He saw once more the star-form of closed lips, the penis beneath them hanging its head as if in awe, a godlet among goddesses. He realised this poetic appreciation was stimulated more by Zambia hirself than hir physical shape, but such is the language of adoration. He knelt and worshipped, kissing each one to show he was not repulsed, and of course Zambia had wept.

Roirbak was sitting in the canteen. Tammuz was immediately suspicious because he knew the man never broke his routines unless something out of the ordinary was afoot. Had he spied on their love-making last night?

Zambia was wearing some of Tammuz' clothes and Roirbak thought the khaki and green suited hir far better than the dusty black SHe usually favoured. Quite a stunning creature, in fact. That alone made him foresee difficulties. The bloom in Tammuz' eyes made him apprehensive. 'Goddess, he's in love,' he thought dismally.

'Has Penumbra been in touch?' Tammuz asked, sitting down. Sindy hummed over and interrupted, reciting a menu. 'Anything, anything. Use your imagination!' Tammuz snapped. Sindy bleeped in confusion and went to dredge the supplies' cupboards. Tammuz ran his hands through his hair, sighing.

'You created it,' Roirbak said, 'Don't be cruel. Poor thing . . .' This jarred. Roirbak cleared his throat. 'As to your question, no, not yet. I took the precaution of setting the comms to automatic response. If my gut instincts advise me correctly, Ms Penumbra is by now mightily sick of hearing I am not available.'

'I want to thank you, Mr Roirbak,' Zambia began in a husky voice, which Roirbak waved aside.

'Shush! I have become fond of this young man. It is no great inconvenience to help him, either of you, I assure you. But I am sure you are aware that plans must be made.' He raised his brows. Tammuz and Zambia exchanged a glance.

'Tammuz,' Roirbak said quietly. 'I would like to speak with you alone. Would you excuse us?' Zambia nodded and Tammuz followed Roirbak outside the room.

'Forgive me if this sounds intrusive,' Roirbak said. 'But I can't help feeling the situation has . . . intensified somewhat since last night.'

Tammuz averted his eyes. 'Things have become more honest, more open, perhaps.'

'Yesterday, I think you would have happily helped Zambia Crevecoeur escape the city and then forgotten about hir. Now, I'm not so sure. Tammuz, don't interrupt, I'll be straight with you. I don't know what reasons brought you to me or whether they have any connection with certain events – I have my suspicions I'll confess, but I accept it isn't any of my business unless it reaches a point where it outwardly affects me. However, I feel you have a purpose for being in Arcady, here in particular, and at this time. Am I right?'

Tammuz nodded painfully, reluctantly.

'It's all right, I'm not asking you to divulge that purpose. My point is, I think you want to keep Zambia Crevecoeur very close to you now, and that this is not a temporary arrangement. Right again? I thought so. Don't looked so agonised. The reason I ask these things is that we will have to look ahead in case certain difficulties present themselves.' Roirbak put a hand on Tammuz' arm. 'You're wondering why I'm so concerned?' he rasped. 'Dammit, Malamute, I feel I know you, have known you, for a long time. If I'm right, why you're hiding yourself from me is a mystery. Don't you know you can trust me?'

Tammuz put his hand over Roirbak's. 'Of course I trust you. But knowledge is dangerous. I don't want to put you in danger.'

'That would be damned hard. Unless I'm deceiving myself totally, my position within this community is steel-strong. Ms Penumbra isn't the only one with friends in high places you know.'

'Exactly. I don't want you to have to betray your friends, any of them. Quincx, I . . . Do you know who I am? Really? Do you?'

Quincx Roirbak was taken back twenty years, to a time when a young student had asked him questions with the same expression of need for reassurance. It was the only confirmation he needed. 'Say nothing,' he said. 'You don't have to. It was only curiosity. Now, all you need to be is Tammuz Malamute. Go back to your ladyboyfriend or whatever SHe is. I have to think. And so do you.'

By the time Roirbak had reached his workbench and had sat down to ponder over whether he could pay Jahsaxa enough compensation to drop Crevecoeur and why he should want to do that for anyone anyway, Mellissa the receptionist fluted her chimes over his commset. Roirbak experienced a moment of panic, sure it was one of Penumbra's staff, arrived too soon before he could work anything out, when Mellissa informed him th? visitor was Leila Saatchi. 'Leila, yes, Leila. Good, good. Get her shown in, Mellissa.' He exhaled in relief, blinking.

Tammuz Malamute, or whoever you are, I should not forgive you for this, he thought wearily.

'Quincx, great to see you, great!' Leila embraced the man, kissing his cheek.

Roirbak thought, *Times have been hard for you girl, haven't they*? And then smiled and said, 'Leila, you look wonderful.'

'Bullshit do I!' She laughed, flattered in spite of herself. '*You* look younger every time I see you.'

'I had hoped it wasn't that obvious!'

'I meant it as a compliment.'

He nodded. 'Vanity!' he said. 'So, did you have a good journey?'

Leila sauntered round his desk, looking intently at the mounds of equipment covering it. 'Good journey? Honey, my whole life is a journey! The stop at Lazar Farm was – interesting . . .'

'Lazar called me.'

Leila grimaced. 'Should have known! Oh,' she pushed Nathan forward, who'd been hanging sullenly back, making it apparent he thought this visit nowhere near as entertaining as prowling Arcady with the others. 'This is Nathan, Lazar's son.'

'Lazar Junior!' Roirbak exclaimed heartily.

'How do you do sir.' Nathan extended his hand. As Roirbak clasped it formally, Leila added, 'And this is Ari – Ari Famber.'

Roirbak had mistaken her for another boy: a skinny, awkward creature, but pretty in her own way, he conceded. Leila stood behind the girl, hands on her shoulders, as proud as if Ari was her own daughter. Roirbak had the absurd impression he was being offered some kind of religious icon. There was something of Ewan in her, of course; there'd have to be.

'I knew your father very well,' he told her. Ari shrugged, embarrassed, unsure of what to say. She could only look on Roirbak as some kind of doctor who would be dealing with her intimately shortly. It was hard to feel at ease with him. She had the awful feeling she was expected to behave in some glittering, unusual way to live up to her father's memory.

'I can't remember him,' she said, and Roirbak recognised the mechanism of defence.

'Of course, it's very . . . sad,' he said. 'Well, I'm pleased to meet you now, Ari Famber. I hope we can help you . . .'

He shrank from qualifying that more. The girl was rigid with shame, poor thing. Was it possible this urchin was really the repository of cataclysmic sexuality as Ewan claimed? He should have sent the child to me from the moment she could feed herself, Roirbak thought, sure Ari had been contaminated and spoiled by the life she'd led at Taler's Bump. 'How is your mother?' he inquired in a slightly off-key tone that was not lost on Ari.

'Sick,' she answered honestly. 'She drinks.' Roirbak did not look surprised and Ari immediately warmed to him. It seemed all of her father's old acquaintances had not been too impressed by his choice of wife. She felt slightly ashamed that it gave her such satisfaction.

'Lydia was planning on sending Ari to Amazon house,' Leila said. Ari watched with interest the sharp glance that Roirbak directed at her.

'Is it possible she may inform them . . . ?'

Leila shrugged. 'Unlikely. I put the fear of the Goddess into her. But then, as Ari said, she drinks. Lushes do crazy things sometimes, don't they? She had no idea I was bringing Ari here though.'

Roirbak sucked his lips. 'I'll take precautions,' he said, and then looked up brightly. 'How about you and Nathan go through to my canteen and feed yourselves?' he said to Ari. 'A guest of mine has fixed up some domestic droids to act like waitresses. I think you'll enjoy meeting them!'

'OK,' Ari said, aware he wanted to get rid of her to be able to talk straight with Leila.

'Just go down the plaza here, turn right into the old section of the building, and it's a few doors down on the right. You can't miss it.'

As Ari and Nathan went through the shop, Roirbak remembered with mixed feelings that Zambia and Tammuz might still be in there, and then wondered if some evil part of him had been aware of that all along. Surreptitiously he stroked the security eye key to 'record' for that room. Should make interesting viewing later, at least.

Once Ari had gone, Leila slumped, letting out a sigh. She leaned on Roirbak and hugged him again. 'Goddess, it's so good to see you. You're like my Dad, Quincx, the only relative I've got.'

He lifted her face and stroked the hair from her eyes. 'Leila, you know you and Ewan were always special to me. I've missed you. I always miss you. When are you going to give up the life of a gypsy and settle down here to become eccentric and safe?'

'Like you?'

'Like me and with me.'

Leila sat down on his knee. He could feel the bones through her spare buttocks. Poor Leila. It would be a struggle to let her go again. Her condition was worrying.

'I didn't think you liked company around here,' she said. 'Anyway, what's with this guest of yours? The last time I saw you, you'd decided never to let anyone work with you here again. I take it it *is* a work relationship?'

'Hmmm.'

Leila was alerted by the quick downswivel of Roirbak's eyes. 'Quincx? What did I ask? Did I hit a nerve or something?'

He stroked her back, wincing at the sharpness of her spine, the ripple of ribs too close to the skin. 'I want you to meet him,' he said. 'That's all I'll say. It may be my brain is getting fuddled despite my attempts at rejuvenation and I'm imagining things.'

'What are you talking about?'

'Crazy suspicions.'

'What?'

'Either I'm mad or people reincarnate, or there's such a thing as possession, or . . .' He paused.

'Quincx?' Leila looked worried.

He shook his head. 'I said more than I meant to,' he

said. 'Forget it. You'll meet him later, I expect . . .. So, tell me, why have you brought Nathan Junior here?'

Leila settled to tell him the story of Nathan's condition and all that had happened at the farm, with certain omissions. It was not necessary for Quincx to know how Lazar had humiliated her, she thought. Quincx concurred with her idea and then asked how Nathan felt about it. 'He didn't seem to be too happy to be here, that's all,' he said.

Leila smiled. 'Poor kid, he wants to be off with the Star Eye wenches, sowing overdue wild oats and learning about life. It's hard on him, being let off the leash Daddy kept him on, being shown the promise of Arcady and then being dragged over here. At least he and Ari get off on each other. You have to admit he's superb material for what we have to do. Thanks to me.'

'You're still working with your pirate kit then?'

'Only occasionally. I've never had a problem with it, never did have. If you're careful and thorough, I don't think it can fuck up. It's just that not everyone is as careful and thorough as I am. It's like working magick you see. Everything has to be thought out so carefully; what you ask for, that is. If you ask the wrong question, word it badly, then the result reflects that. I'm convinced most experienced natros could handle it, no problem. We have the training you see, to be pernickety.'

'If I heard that from anyone but you, I'd howl "over-confidence",' Roirbak said, grinning.

'You trained me,' Leila reminded him. 'So, when shall we start on Ari? Got any ideas?'

'Controlled conditions are required. We had better begin with auto-stimulation, I think. Naturally, she won't respond too well if I'm involved. She's quite uptight.'

'If you're not going to be involved, why on earth have I come here?' Leila asked.

Roirbak shook his head. 'Leila my dear, this may be the Advanced Technological Age, but there are still such things as two-way mirrors, you know. We needn't even have a camera in the room. Does she trust you enough to let you be present though?'

'It's hard to tell. I'll talk to her.'

Roirbak nodded. 'Good. Let her eat lunch ard then give her a mild tranquilliser. We should begin this afternoon.'

'And what do we do with Nathan in the meantime? As you saw, he's restless.'

'Perhaps we can persuade Tammuz Malamute to entertain him.' Roirbak laughed at the absurdity of the image.

'Who? Is that another of your a.i.s?'

Never a truer word is said in jest, Roirbak thought. 'He's my guest,' he answered.

'That guy seems OK,' Nathan said, as he and Ari tried to find their way through the labyrinth of Roirbak's complex to the canteen.

'Yeah. Leila worships him,' Ari replied.

Roirbak's instructions had been misleading. So far, they hadn't found the canteen and, twice, had re-emerged into the rococo splendour of the refurbished part of the building. It was fun though. Neither Ari or Nathan had ever seen a place like it.

'So . . . when does it happen?' Nathan stuck his hands in his pockets.

'I don't know. Isn't this weird? Like an arranged marriage or something!'

Nathan laughed and ran a few steps in front of Ari, turning back to bow. 'Madam, may your betrothed take you to lunch?'

'Certainly, sir!' Ari replied, batting her eyes and curtseying. 'Where the fuck is it though?'

She linked her arm through Nathan's and they pushed open a few doors, only to find empty rooms. 'You know,' she said, 'talking of marriage and all . . . Can you keep a secret, Nate?'

He groaned and slapped his forehead. 'Oh no! You're already married aren't you!'

She thumped his arm. 'Stupid! I just want to tell someone, that's all, and you're least involved. Promise not to repeat it?'

'All right.'

'Well, Cabochon and Jordan sort of got hitched, if you know what I mean.'

'No, I don't. How? What did they do?'

'They cut each other and swapped blood-stains. They have to swear to stay together or something.'

'Weird! What's the point?'

'Well, it's to do with Cab's brother. Apparently he's really evil, and follows Cab round when he's in Arcady, being mean. Cab wants Jordan to look after him, I think. He's scared of his brother. They have a strange relationship. They started fighting last time Star Eye were here.'

'Wow, Jordan might get beaten up, or even killed! Cabochon's brother might be a monster.'

'That's what I thought. Leila doesn't know.' She sniffed. 'I can smell food. Try that door. Now, not a word, remember?'

'OK.'

There were a couple of people already in there, sitting at a table near the counter. Ari and Nathan hung around in the doorway until they looked up, feeling they needed permission to enter. A beautiful woman with long, black hair noticed they were there. She smiled and said, in a boy's voice, 'Hi. Looking for something?'

'Mr Roirbak said we could eat in here?' Ari answered, making it a question.

'Well, come in then!'

The man sitting with his back to her at the table looked around. For a moment she thought she knew him. He stared at her in a very strange, intense way. It made her shudder. 'Who are you?' he demanded.

'I . . . er . . . we came with Leila, Leila Saatchi,' Ari replied.

'But what's your name?'

'Easy, Tammuz, you're scaring her,' the black-haired person said in a puzzled voice. 'What's your name, babe? Huh? My friend here is nervous of strangers.'

'Ari,' she said, not wanting to add her surname in case these colleagues of Roirbak's had heard of Ewan.

'Leila Saatchi,' said the boywoman. 'That name sounds familiar.'

'She's with the natro group called Star Eye,' Tammuz said stonily. The boywoman went white.

'You knew about this, didn't you! You knew!'

Ari and Nathan sat down nervously. Zambia scraped hir hands through hir hair and sighed. SHe noticed Tammuz flicking odd looks at the girl. Something peculiar was going on, that was for sure. SHe called Sindy and ordered some food for the kids. 'So, are all of you here, all of Star Eye?' SHe asked.

Ari shook her head. 'No, just me and Leila and,' she jerked her head in Nathan's direction, 'him.'

Zambia laughed and rolled hir eyes. 'Thank you, Goddess, for that at least,' she said.

'You know them?' Ari asked.

'Not really. Oh, dammit, Sindy's got stuck on that spike again, Tammuz. Shall I fix it?'

Tammuz waved a hand, examining the remains of his meal as if it was a valuable artefact. Zambia went to untangle the droid who was bleeping mournfully. 'Excuse me, is that a boy or a girl?' Nathan asked Tammuz. Ari winced at his lack of tact. Tammuz smiled but it didn't make him look cheerful.

'It's a combination,' he said, keeping his head down. 'An intersex.'

'Oh.' Nathan and Ari exchanged a glance. Ari smothered a grin and shrugged.

Zambia came back with two plates of food and sat down again. 'I might as well ask,' SHe said. 'Is Cabochon Crevecoeur still with you lot?'

'Yes,' Ari answered through a mouthful of soyameat. 'You know him?'

Zambia nodded. 'Mmm.'

'Do you know his brother?' Nathan asked eagerly, leaning across the table.

Zambia flinched inside. 'Why?'

'Nath-an!' Ari sang, kicking him under the table.

'Oh, so you've heard about Cabochon's brother then, have you?' Zambia asked, with narrow eyes. SHe lit a cigarette and puffed furiously.

'Only that he can be a bit . . . well, dangerous, I guess,' Nathan said. Ari made another agonised sound. This person might know Cab's brother, for Goddess' sake! Was Nate mad?

Tammuz pushed his chair back and stood up. 'I'm out of here!' he said, 'this is trauma city!' and retreated swiftly. A silence descended over the table.

'Sorry,' Nate said. 'Have I . . . uh . . .'

Zambia exhaled a plume of smoke, tossed hir head

and extended a hand. 'Shake!' SHe ordered. Nathan timidly obeyed. 'How do you do,' Zambia said silkily. 'I'm Zambia Crevecoeur, dangerous or not, and I'm very pleased to meet you!'

Later in the afternoon, Roirbak went to extract Nathan and Ari from Zambia's clutches. Zambia, however, trying to compensate for whatever information they'd picked up about hir, offered to entertain Nathan for the afternoon so that Roirbak could begin work with Ari. Sheepishly, Nathan agreed to go and watch movies with Zambia, casting agonised looks after Ari as he followed hir from the canteen. Ari wondered whether she was betraying him in some way by leaving him alone with the dreaded sibling of Cabochon Crevecoeur.

Roirbak led the way to the laboratory annexe of the complex, where he'd already prepared a couple of rooms for their research. He had decided to get Leila to put the girl under trance before they attempted any experimentation. Ari would be far too anxious in a fully conscious state. All the way there she was asking him questions: 'What are you going to do? Who's going to be there?' His heart went out to her trepidation.

'Try not to worry,' he said inadequately. 'You won't be hurt. There's no need to be shy. Both Leila and I have done this kind of thing before. There's nothing to it.' He felt sure Ari was not convinced by such blatant lies.

He showed her into a comfortable room complete with wallscreen, soft lighting and floor cushions. The setting

375

was designed to put Ari at her ease. All sensory equipment was well hidden.

'What *are* you going to do?' Ari asked again, one hand firmly clutching her totems and prowling round the room. She kept looking at the wallscreen with distrust.

'I'm not going to do anything, Ari,' Quincx said, in a voice he hoped would be soothing to a young girl. 'When Leila gets here, I shall leave the room. We want you to relax and feel comfortable. Leila will put you in a light trance. You probably won't remember anything when you wake up.'

Ari wasn't sure she understood. 'I won't be . . . Nathan isn't going to be part of it?'

'Not for the time being.'

Ari's shoulders slumped, which Roirbak interpreted as relief. 'This won't take long, I'm sure,' he said.

Ari nodded and sat down on the cushions. Leila entered the room a little too breezily saying, 'Well the boy's happy. I don't think he'll be making an escape bid yet! You OK, Ari?'

'Yes.'

'Well, I'll leave you to it then,' Quincx said.

'Ari there are a couple of things I think we should talk about,' Leila said, settling down on the cushions beside the girl.

'What's wrong?'

'Nothing's wrong. It's just that what we're going to be doing for the next few weeks means you're going to have to be very *open* with me, and Quincx to a degree. If that's going to cause you any problem, we have to thrash it out now before we get started.'

'Can you explain that more?' Ari had anticipated that her training, until the consummation with Nathan, would involve being hooked up to machines like the ones

Leila had used at Lazar Farm. She had decided not to think too deeply about the end result just yet.

'Well, basically you'll be getting used to experiencing sexual feelings, mainly by learning to arouse yourself and coping with resulting power surges. For safety, it isn't a good idea if you're completely alone while this is happening, which is why I'm around. I want to know if that's going to inhibit you, put you off. Obviously we'll be able to use the usual relaxation exercises, but I don't want any subconscious resentment creeping in.'

'I'll do whatever I have to,' Ari answered. 'That is, I'll try. If somebody has to be here, I'd rather it was you.'

Leila sighed. 'Good. Don't worry about making a fool of yourself or anything. All I care about is helping you.' She stroked Ari's face. 'Well, here we are at last! I think I'm more nervous than you are! Are you ready to begin? Today we'll just do a visualisation and try to remove what's left of your father's blocking device.'

'OK.' Ari reached for Leila's hand and squeezed it. 'I have been waiting for this, you know. I'm scared, but not that scared.'

Leila smiled reassuringly. 'Well that makes two of us then! Now, if you lie back on the cushions, I'll just hook you up to an enhancement device so we can share the experience.' She wondered whether she should have had Ari dress in a bath-robe or something. It was difficult to anticipate which direction this visualisation would take; it might be entirely subjective or Ari might manifest physical sensations and want to touch herself. Ari cleared her throat and wriggled on the cushions.

'Comfortable?' Leila asked, putting on her own headset.

'Nearly.'

'OK. Just loosen your jeans a little so you can breathe

properly.' Leila began the trance induction, taking Ari down into a deep, relaxed state. 'How do you feel?' she asked softly.

'Nice. Floaty,' Ari mumbled in reply.

'Where are you?'

'In my private place, where the feather trees are.'

'You are completely alone.'

Ari's forehead wrinkled. 'No. There are animals here; my friends.'

Leila drew in her breath. 'Right. OK, but just at this moment you're not with any of them.' Her voice dropped lower. 'It's a lovely day among the feather trees. Warm sun, birds singing and dragonflies skimming over the pool. Do you see the pool between the trees?'

'Yes.'

'It is such a nice day, why not go for a swim? Walk to the pool. Take off your shoes. Feel the soft grass beneath your feet. Wriggle your toes . . . Now, take off your clothes and walk into the pool.' She paused. Ari was motionless, breathing regularly beside her. Leila closed her eyes, visualising for herself the pleasant warmth of Ari's fantasy world. It was one with which she was already familiar, both of them having helped construct it for regular meditations. 'Ah, the water feels good!' she said. 'You are floating, floating, and your body is warm and comfortable. You can feel the heat of the sun beating down on the water as it rocks you. Rocks you. Gently. You become aware of the water against your skin. Feel it touch every part of you. Gently. Gently. It's like being stroked or held. All of your body is beneath the water, but for your face. You feel lazy and contented. You like the feeling of the water against your skin. Stretch out your arms. Wriggle your fingers . . . Ah, so warm. Now, stretch out your legs. Become a star shape in the water. It is lapping, lapping, stroking your breasts, your belly, between your thighs . . .' Ari took a sharp breath, which made Leila jump. She had begun to feel quite horny herself reciting the exercise. 'What do you feel Ari?' she asked.

'A burning,' Ari said, sounding anxious.

'Don't you like the feel of the water?'

'Yes. Yes. But the burning is beneath that . . . somehow.'

'Does it hurt?'

'No . . . not exactly. It is behind a sort of shield.'

'Do you think you can touch the shield, or move it?'

Ari was silent for a moment. 'I think it is possible to move it,' she said at last, 'but it will let the burning out. I am afraid that will kill me.'

'It can't,' Leila soothed. 'The burning is an illusion, and the only way to get rid of it is to face it and absorb it. Do you understand that Ari?'

'Mmmm.'

'Now relax again, float gently in the water. My words are a guide which you can follow . . . follow . . .'

The water closes over her head, but she can see, she can breathe. There are beautiful waving weeds in the water and everything is blue and green. Her body rocks and little currents tickle her skin. She thinks perhaps small fish are nibbling at her, but it is pleasant, it doesn't hurt. Her awareness is of softness and warmth and pleasure, but there is a sort of hardness, which is dark, that flashes in and out of her perception. That makes her feel uncomfortable. Then there is a presence in the water with her. Ari can see a wavery shape, floating hair, floating gauze. She identifies this figure as an aspect of the Goddess – water maiden. The Goddess tells her she can pull the

dark, hard thing away, but that Ari will have to help.
Ari star-fish stretches out her limbs and feels the water
begin to invade her body. It is a lovely feeling but spiky
things like thoughts are spoiling it, making their presence
stronger than the caressing liquid. The Goddess tells Ari
to ignore those things and concentrate on the pleasure. It
isn't easy. Sometimes it feels like the water is pushing
thorns inside her. Bubbles form around her; the water is
restless, roiling. She can no longer see the water maiden.
A voice says, 'You must throw the black thing away.
Force it out of yourself.' Ari strains and tumbles in the
foam, but it seems as if her insides have become hard and
dark. She tries to push it out and black beads form on her
skin, ribbons of dark flowing out into the water. 'That's
it!' says the Goddess. 'Throw it away. Push it out!'

'It won't go,' Ari says. 'I can't . . . It won't . . .'

'Push!'

'I . . .' She makes a huge, agonised effort and there is
a sensation of tearing and pain, of being engulfed in cold
darkness. Ari tries to scream and then . . . Then the
water is full of sparkling light, the foam dances and she is
tossed like a fragment of weed. The darkness has gone,
but the unbearable light is almost as bad. This is the
burning. Water boils around her, full of stars. Ari cannot breathe. She gulps and flounders.

'Drowning!' her mind screams.

'No!' says the Goddess. 'Take control, Ari. Condense
the light. Take it in through your skin to become a ball in
your belly. You can do it. It's easy. Just think it so.' She
listens to the words of the Goddess, who is surely right,
who must know everything. Ari curls in the water, curls
around the light and absorbs it. She feels full of it and
moulds it into a glowing ball deep within. For a few
moments she just floats there, experiencing the feeling.

Laughter bubbles from her lungs up through the water.

'Now you must use the burning,' says the Goddess. 'It can't hurt you. Do the things that will let it go and then call it back into yourself.'

Ari knows the things that will let the light go. She doesn't need to be told. In the water, she rolls into a standing position, still in the star shape, and opens her legs wide. The light leaps and spits inside her as if trying to escape. Her fingers swim with the water between folds of flesh and take up the rhythm of the light. She turns the water to steam and frees the light inside her, twisting and turning in a sparkling, spinning column. It seems endless. The Goddess' voice is faint, but it says, 'Call it back, Ari. Call it back.' And, with a little effort, she does so.

'What's wrong, Tammuz?' Zambia had begun to watch one of the movies with Nathan, but couldn't dispel the nagging worry about Tammuz. Why had he marched out of the canteen like that earlier? What were these kids to him? What did it mean? SHe had eventually given in to a desire to seek Tammuz out, even though SHe already recognised the signs which meant he wanted to be left alone. SHe'd found him in his workroom, staring moodily at the monitor screen.

'There's nothing wrong,' Tammuz replied. 'I'm working.' He stabbed a few keypads to make the point.

'I don't believe you.' SHe stood behind him and put hir hands on his shoulders. 'Why won't you tell me?'

Tammuz pushed his chair away from the workstation and stood up. Zambia took a step back, alarmed by the violence of his movements.

'I need a drink,' Tammuz said, and stomped over to the liquor cabinet he kept there. Zambia watched cautiously. Clearly, whatever was worrying Tammuz was big.

'Is it me? Have I done anything?'

'No.' Tammuz took a swig from a bottle and then held it out. 'Want some?'

Zambia nodded and took it. SHe found two plastic cups and filled them, handing one to Tammuz. He sighed.

'Why won't you tell me?' Zambia asked again. 'Don't you trust me?'

Tammuz laughed unpleasantly. 'Trust you? I don't trust anybody.'

Zambia wondered what had happened to change him so much. They'd both been riding clouds that morning, now this. Surely temperamental exchanges of this nature should occur somewhat later in a relationship. SHe decided to be blunt. 'It was something to do with those kids then.'

Tammuz narrowed his eyes. 'You think so? Haven't you considered it might be the woman they were with? I once had a thing going with Leila Saatchi.'

'Oh.' Zambia experienced cold dread. 'Are you telling me I'm in your way now or something?'

Tammuz looked as if he was about to make a cutting response but then actually took note of Zambia's expression. He put down his cup after draining it, and hugged Zambia to him. 'No, no, not that. I'm sorry. It's just . . . I can't tell you. I don't want to tell you . . . or anyone. I'm sorry. I'm crazy about you, Crevecoeur. I don't want to hurt you.'

'Then tell me what's wrong!' Zambia put hir hands on either side of Tammuz' face. 'Tell me. I love you. I'll keep your secrets, I promise. Only I hate you shutting me out like this.'

'I only just let you in,' Tammuz reminded hir. 'Our relationship can be measured in hours, my strange beauty. We fly on the wings of mutual allure, but I'm not sure whether we've reached the heavy confidence stage yet.'

Zambia kissed Tammuz on the mouth briefly. 'Won't it help you to tell someone? What are you afraid I'll do?'

'Tell someone. No, no. I don't mean in that way. It may be forced from you.'

'What?!'

'You see? I have reasons not to confide in you, or anyone.' He rubbed his face. 'Let's have another drink.'

'Want to go and lie down?' Zambia asked artfully.

Tammuz smiled. 'Why not? It might take my mind off things.'

Thus, as down in the laboratory annexe Ari struggled and swam with a new sensation, above her head, Tammuz Malamute plundered the willing body of Zambia Crevecoeur, causing the building to reverberate with sexual emissions of several different types. And in the age-old tradition of sirens, whatever their sex, Zambia used the opportunity of post-coital languor, not to mention the accessory of intoxication, to gently squeeze Tammuz for information. As if dealing with a stubborn splinter fixed firmly and painfully down behind a fingernail, Zambia patiently nudged and pushed and, eventually, the agonising sliver was expelled. Tammuz lay in hir arms, his head in a shawl of Zambia's hair and said, 'I am not what you think. Tammuz Malamute is my name, yes, but only recently.'

Zambia smiled warmly, lovingly, encouragingly, remaining utterly silent so as not to frighten him off. 'I told you I had an affair with the Saatchi woman. That's true. She also thinks I'm dead.'

'Awkward,' Zambia couldn't help saying.

Tammuz shook his head. 'Not really. I've changed . . . somewhat since she knew me. This whole body is new, even my personality to a degree, for it has been shaped by the flesh; but the soul within this flesh is not new. That girl with Leila is my daughter, Zambia.'

'You had a child with Leila Saatchi?'

Tammuz shook his head, wrinkling his features. 'No, no, nothing like that. It's a long story . . .'

'So, what else have you got planned for today?'

'You ever heard of Ewan Famber, Zambia?'

'The Tech-Green saint? Yeah. The one who . . . uh oh!'

'Quite. He's safely buried, I assure you. A loathsome, crusading creature quite alien to me, in fact.'

'Tammuz, be straight with me here. What are you saying?'

'I'm saying that the me-ness of my consciousness was once Ewan Famber.'

'Yes, well, that makes a lot of sense.'

'All right, for the sake of argument, I *am* Ewan Famber, or the nearest it is possible to get to him now.'

'Did you kill him?'

'Figuratively, yes.'

'But that's impossible. That's history. You're not old enough.'

'Be smart, Zam! How old do you think Roirbak is? People like us have access to techniques to banish the effects of ageing.'

'People with money have access to that stuff. I don't think you have money, or are my instincts completely wrong?'

'Listen, rich people have to pay the rejuvenators for the service. Doesn't it occur to you that the rejuvenators can afford to give themselves a discount?'

'So you're a rejuvenator.'

'No, I'm a scientist, but it amounts to the same thing.'
He sighed deeply and rolled away from Zambia, presenting his lean back which Zambia decided was wearing
an expression of stubbornness.

'OK, so what did you do and why and how, and what's
with all this secrecy?' SHe stroked the back encouragingly. Such young skin, surely not . . . ? SHe tried to
imagine the soul of a middle-aged man living in this
flesh. It seemed absurd.

'I uncovered something,' Tammuz said after a
moment. 'It wasn't a discovery exactly, because it's
something humanity has been aware of in metaphor and
myth since . . . well, forever, I guess. I just remembered
it. I think that's the best way of putting it. I suppose you
could say I found the Goddess.' He turned around again
and propped himself up in the bed.

'No shit! How?'

Tammuz pinched his skin. 'In this.' Tapped his head.
'This.' Poked one of Zambia's orifices. 'And this.
Everywhere. Within us. I deciphered a code that con-
firmed things scientists have been trying to get at for
years; that magick is physics, basically. It's the fundamentalism of Naturotech and I was an ardent natro back
then.'

'You mean, you're not now? Not even after seeing the
Goddess and all?'

Tammuz smiled and wound a lock of Zambia's hair
round his fingers. 'My dear, sweet love, once you have
seen, the whole idea of religion can only be tawdry,
pathetic and . . . *wrong*. You realise there is no point to
it all, that your perspective on Universe and life was all
wrong. It's impossible to explain. The Goddess is alive

and powerful and sentient, yes, but she is like blood, within us.'

'Natros say that anyway.'

Tammuz shook his head. 'Their perspective is wrong. It's not a spiritual thing, it's neurological: hardware. And it's hardware that generates the software that affects the hardware. It's a feedback cycle.'

'The Goddess is hardware . . .' Zambia shook hir head. 'You have crazy ways of putting things, Tammuz.'

'How did you get the best out of your hardware, Zam?'

'Me in particular? By being chopped up and reshaped I suppose. Is that what you want me to say?'

'And what did I do to that sculpture of flesh?'

'Came and programmed the software?'

'Precisely. That's what I do and that's why I hide. I know how to program the software that activates the Goddess.'

'Tammuz you are mad. What am I doing here in bed with you?'

Tammuz ran his hand over Zambia's belly. 'It's a pity none of these are actually fertile,' he said, in a humorous tone.

'Never mind that,' Zambia said, enclosing Tammuz' hand in hir own and raising it to hir lips. 'I want you to begin at the beginning and tell me your life. I want to know why Ewan Famber wanted to die. I want to know it all. Now.'

SHe lay back, pulling Tammuz' head down on to hir breast, where he closed his eyes in a relief that was, strangely, both enervating and exhilarating.

'Listen then . . .' he said.

The new body had been growing steadily for weeks. Ewan monitored it every day. He'd equipped his facility on the orbital Tech-Green research base – annexed to Sky City

One – with an incuvat; the means to commit virtual suicide in a complete reality. He was well isolated from his colleagues: nobody ever came over here uninvited. This had been ideal for Ewan's purposes. Naturally, the *conditions* weren't ideal, mainly because part of his research involved understanding what the conditions actually were, but they sufficed. The incuvat was a state-of-the-art model. Ewan would stand and gaze wonderingly at the naked boy forming before his eyes. Aesthetically, he was in love, but it was still hard to think that eventually this sculpture of flesh and bone must become his soul's vehicle, his robot. It was unimaginable. Lydia had no idea what was going on. She would be taken care of; he'd made sure of that. She was quite happy playing house back planetside, in the home country with the kid. He was aware of the risks involved and that he was embarking on a kind of unnecessary surgery that could threaten his life, but it was what he wanted. He had to get out; completely, utterly. He was sick of living out the legend of the Tech-Green wunderkind, sick too of the work he was involved in and the knowledge that went with it. All Tech-Green cared about was the planet itself: the inhabitants were expendable. Of course, being members of the Tech-Green élite and therefore indispensable, he and his family were already on file for a place on Sky City One should he be willing to move them all up there. He was not.

The revolutionary technology that it was claimed would revitalise the world's failing eco-systems was already on stand-by. Outlawed technology, too dangerous to human life. From the safety of space, it would prove an interesting experiment, one that might be duplicated on other worlds, far away, should it succeed. Ewan no longer wanted to be part of this. He would live out one more life, back on the planet, in this new body; let it age and die. Let it end.

The trouble was, Ewan loved life. He did not want to die and yet his increasing depression was making existence intolerable. He knew this was the only way. Cover his tracks and run. Begin again. Forget. Experience all those things his cloistered lifestyle with the Tech-Greens had denied him. He wanted to feel the bones of the world beneath his feet, join natro groups, travel, love and live in complete freedom. The thought of his daughter made him uncomfortable. He suspected her existence was an obscenity. He regretted his impulsiveness bitterly, considering his marvellous discoveries were potentially dangerous. Did humanity really need all this technology? Was it really progress? Lately, he had begun to think that evolution was something that would occur in the soul and, in time, the fripperies of science would be revealed to be dangerous toys. People just weren't ready for all this. Their bright minds flitted from fruit to fruit upon the tree of knowledge, but the glittering insects were still motivated by greed and selfishness. There was no true communion between human spirits, so essential to society's progression as a whole, and compassion had been eroded by the calamities of mankind's mistakes. Ewan felt he could do nothing about this situation, and there was no use worrying about it. He would do what he had to do and escape. Let his colleagues con themselves if they wished but he knew that Tech-Green, for all its grand, humane claims, was no better than the monetarist governments who'd reigned and toppled before them. A placebo, superficial and cosy, to lull the world into no longer questioning. *Tech-green knows what's right; they care. They'll take care of everything*. All the time, while people sat back in their new sky-clawing cities, safely enwombed away from the nasty poisons outside, Tech-Green's brilliant minds developed ever more complex measures to solve the planet's debilities.

The future of mankind, they said, lay in space, where there was no environment to ruin. Left in peace, the world would eventually heal itself. It sounded so sensible, but for the fact there were, in some countries, still billions of people struggling in an existence beyond the comforts of geodesic domes. Somehow, in their calculations, Tech-Green seemed to forget about them, but maybe not. Ewan had heard of some research projects that made him very uncomfortable about these people's future. Publicly there were muzzy plans for when the city populations took to the skies en masse. The poverty-stricken could then take over the deserted metropolises. Everything would be all right. Oh yes, of *course*, these mostly ill-educated people would be given full instruction on how to regulate the dome environments, how to manage the delicate hydroponics farms clustered like eggs round the city skirts. Of course. Everything would be fine. Who are they kidding? Ewan wondered, and adjusted the temperature of the incuvat.

He delivered his new body from its artificial womb the next day. Tenderly he wiped its mouth and nostrils and eyes as it coughed into life, vomiting saline nutrient over his hands. The eyes were open and Ewan could see that, no matter how objective he tried to be, something lived in this body, something which he would soon extinguish with his own, vibrant, developed persona. The body was not wholly parthenogenetic, but contained elements of himself and Roirbak, though Roirbak was unaware of his participation. In a way, it was their son, Ewan supposed. Could it think perhaps? Sky City One had been built by constructs such as these, their bodies and minds tailored for the job in hand. They were always occupied by artificial intelligences. Although the technology existed to use these constructs as hosts for human personas, this was yet another procedure outlawed by Tech-Green. Nobody on Gaiah was even aware it was possible. If he was caught, Ewan would be in deep trouble. He knew he would not be caught.

The data transfer was the most frightening part. Ewan had to allow control to pass from himself to his a.i. – Thoth. This was the same machine who had computed so many of the calculations involved in designing his daughter. He knew the machine like an old friend (it would probably be the personality he'd miss most), but he still couldn't trust it as much as he trusted himself. Time and again, he made it run through the sequence with him. Everything seemed OK. But what about when he was helpless? What if the random factor emerged then? He shuddered. This had to be done and he needed to be unconscious. Although he was tempted to try and remain awake, he realised his sanity might be permanently impaired by that. What could the sensation of his persona being sucked from one house of flesh and fitted, circuit by circuit, into another possibly feel like? Tempting, but no. He needed to be one hundred per cent fit and alert when all this was over.

He hadn't accounted for disorientation. Upon regaining consciousness, he'd panicked when his limbs, leaden and numb, had refused to obey him. The muscles had been fully stimulated during the growth period and Ewan had supposed they'd be fully operational immediately. He feared failure, the horror of being incarcerated within a crippled vehicle. Luckily Thoth, possessing more compassion than he'd dared hope, soothed him through the transitional period. It took four hours before he could move, during which time the lifeless body of Ewan Famber that was, leaked fluids off the white table on to the ceraplas floor. The new Ewan wouldn't look at it.

When he was able, he fed himself with the meal he'd prepared earlier, and stripped off the heavy insulating robe to dress himself in Tech-Green drab. He sat, shaking, before his a.i. for a few minutes, realising that, whatever he'd thought before, the following procedures might prove even more risky than the persona transfer itself. Not only would he have to destroy all evidence of his old body, but somehow transport himself planetside without raising suspicion. Naturally, he had made extensive preparations, but couldn't be absolutely certain they would work. It involved the self-destruction of his beloved a.i. – a terrible sacrifice – but no amount of lonely pacing could throw up any alternative in his mind. Because of his professed preference for isolation, it would take considerable time before Ewan was missed by other personnel on the base. This was his greatest advantage.

Although he knew it was to soothe himself rather than the a.i., he spent a few last minutes communing with Thoth by neural link, explaining yet again how grieved he was to have to ask it to give its 'life' for him. Passionately, he told it he still believed that, like a human soul, its essential persona would continue to exist after its hardware was destroyed, because this reality was only one of many possible *eigen*states. It was almost a religious conviction he had, and one which gave him the courage to carry out his plans. Thoth interrupted his stream of self-justification with the sentiment that it agreed the *eigen*state theory was possible and then humorously pointed out that simply because Ewan had thought of it, it was infinitely more possible. With the final instruction that Thoth was to cover his tracks until he contacted it from Gaiah, the new Ewan bid a mournful farewell to the facility that had become his home, and stepped out into the walkways of the base.

He was dressed in the garb of a typical construct worker, so that anybody he passed would take him for such. He proceeded, unchallenged, to the shuttle docks where he'd previously concealed the identity back-up so that he could pass himself off as a human shuttle-worker. He hoped that, because of the participation of his a.i. in the plan, there would be no hitch. In advance, using the smokescreen of Tech-Green bureaucracy, he'd arranged for this fictional shuttle-worker to be placed on a shift which involved taking a shuttle through the gravity well to Gaiah. Once planetside, he would contact his a.i. and, within seconds, his old facility would be destroyed, the body of Ewan Famber with it. His preparations had been so precise, there was little fear the base itself would be seriously damaged. It would appear to everyone that Ewan Famber had died in a freak accident. No one would question that.

Everything went as planned. Tammuz Malamute had stepped off the shuttle port outside Arcady and had delivered the last fateful message to his a.i. Later, he sat in a café, drinking cappuccino, and watched his own obituary on the network news. The world grieved for Ewan Famber. Tammuz grieved for a machine. He never forgot that sacrifice.

Tammuz Malamute abused the body Ewan had bequeathed him for years, telling himself he'd buried the past, until the day he woke up and a voice inside reminded him that Ari Famber was fourteen years old.

Ari Famber was nearly a woman. In the end, he'd just had to see.

And so, while Reynard Lennon, Jahsaxa Penumbra's most valuable operative, combed the dank underworld of the city looking for a runaway, Zambia Crevecoeur became the recipient of Tammuz Malamute's history. He had explained about Ari, vehemently disagreed with Zambia's suggestion he should make himself known to the girl, and tortured himself out loud with conjectures about how Roirbak and Leila might, at this very moment, be destroying Ari's abilities beneath their feet. He would not leave his quarters, holing up like some manic, wounded beast, pacing back and forth, drinking, pausing to spout unbelievably complex monologues on genetic theory, which to Zambia sounded more like the ravings of a demented priest. Occasionally he'd become calm and, during those times, sat at his console and worked furiously, his face tense in the flickering fireflies of scrolling information.

Zambia watched with concern. SHe couldn't understand Tammuz' mania for disguise, given that nobody knew about what he had discovered, except for his friends below. SHe couldn't understand how, when he was clearly so wound up and frantic about his daughter's development, he could stop himself from taking part in it. Tammuz Malamute was an enigma: part crazed, paranoic and possibly dangerous. SHe considered that, during the delicate process of transferring his consciousness and memory to new hardware, Tammuz had impaired his own sanity. But, despite hir misgivings, Zambia could feel hir attachment to Tammuz grow more profound with each hour. Every frenetic gesture engendered tenderness in hir heart. Tammuz would turn to hir and his eyes – independent of his constrained emotions – would plead with hir for assistance, sanctuary, advice. Zambia responded in the only way possible, presenting hir body like a softly-glowing flower that could enfold in perfume and smooth petal-flesh. Tammuz would fall into hir, as if with desperation; his cries were like those of pain. Zambia tried not to think of the future. Hir own safety seemed unimportant now, hir life had been swamped by the torrent of Tammuz Malamute. SHe wondered, and dreaded, when hir conscience would insist SHe did something about him.

'Your guest hasn't shown himself yet then,' Leila said, biting into a breakfast muffin and taking a mouthful of coffee to wash it down. It was the day following Ari's first test and Leila, Ari and Roirbak had met in the canteen. Nathan was still asleep.

'Tammuz works a lot,' Roirbak said, himself disappointed that Malamute appeared uninterested in, or was perhaps avoiding, the new company. He had watched the tape of Ari's meeting with him and had been satisfied by Tammuz' reaction. What he couldn't understand was, if Tammuz *was* Ewan, as he suspected, why he had kept away from the girl. Was he really so hard? Perhaps he was frightened.

Ari broke into his revery. 'I saw him yesterday,' she said. 'He's . . . a bit odd, Mr Roirbak. He looked at me so strangely. Doesn't he like girls?'

'He's a bit of a loner,' Quincx replied, unsure why he didn't just tell Leila his suppositions. Perhaps later. It would obviously be too insensitive to say something in front of the girl. He shrank from confronting Tammuz outright, sensing a kind of insane streak just below the surface which might erupt if he was provoked.

'So,' he said to change the subject, 'how do you feel about yesterday in the light of a new day?'

Ari was no longer embarrassed to discuss it. Maybe because Leila looked on Roirbak as a kind of surrogate father, she did not feel intimidated by him. 'Great,' she answered. 'It was amazing. But I can't see how I'd actually be able to *use* that.'

'You simply have to teach yourself,' Roirbak said. 'With time, you'll be able to craft that raw burning into whatever you choose, and hopefully be able to control it enough to experience it only when you want to.'

'When would I ever not want to experience it?'

'It might be a part of yourself you'd be wiser saving until you know people very well, if you understand what I mean.'

'Oh.' Since the block had been removed the day before, and Ewan's program had started to run, she had felt like a cat on heat. This was even noticeable through the haze of the drug Leila had given her to superficially suppress such feelings. Leila had told her that what she was experiencing was a kind of installation sequence, which had to be allowed to take its course. 'It may feel a little uncomfortable,' she had said, 'but once we all feel confident about what we're doing, we'll let you loose on Nathan, which should complete the sequence.' Ari was coming to like the idea of cornering the helpless Nathan with her whirlwind sexuality. Little did he know what was in store, she felt.

'Today I want you to watch some films,' Roirbak said. 'The sort of films your mother would not approve of!'

'Great. I wonder what my father would think!'

Only Leila noticed Roirbak's quick glance upwards, as if he was trying to peer through the ceiling. The gesture was covert, automatic, and swiftly stemmed. Now what could that mean . . . ?

Nathan Lazar woke up late and was unable to find any human sign of life down in the workshops. He ate in the canteen, spoke with some of the robots, wandered into the sitting room where Roirbak had left him the stack of films, rejected every one as boring, and decided to do a little exploring. It would be too horrible if he was going to be cooped up alone like this every day. How long was it going to last? He wondered what they were doing to Ari. He thought she was rather a strange girl; more like a boy most of the time, but there were parts about her he really liked. The curve of her neck and throat and jaw for example, the look in her eyes when she was amused, her ability to crack all her knuckles simultaneously. From observing Star Eye, he thought she'd modelled herself on Cabochon: she even sat like him and had started scraping her hair back into a ponytail, even though it wasn't really long enough yet. Nathan thought bitterly about how it was only his abnormality that made him suitable for Leila's purposes. Someone like Cabochon was wholly more attractive and surely preferable to a girl like Ari. He was sure that, even though he and Ari got along well, she must have been disappointed when Leila chose him for the job. Mulling over these gloomy thoughts, he climbed the stairs to the gallery where Tammuz' office and labs were and the corridor which led to the rooms he and Zambia had as living quarters. It was obvious this part of the building was used regularly. Machinery was switched on and chattering away to itself. There was a smell of coffee in the air and a feeling that every room had only just been vacated by somebody.

Nathan had been intrigued by the exotic and

androgynous Zambia the day before, and was thankful hir sense of humour outweighed hir outrage at Nathan's hamfisted remarks. It was fascinating to hear hir talk; pretending first one minute you were talking to a girl, and then the next, a boy. Nathan had been delighted it was possible to believe it was both. There were no people like that at Lazar Farm. He was beginning to get a bit homesick since they'd stopped travelling and he'd been on his own. He'd come to the conclusion that he was of a completely different species to Leila and her people. Away from the others, he thought his attempts to fit in had been rather embarrassing.

Sounds drifted up the corridor: low voices and laughter. There was a certain tone to it that made Nathan advance more cautiously. His first discovery was that Zambia and Tammuz made love with the door open. Subsequent discoveries were rather more stimulating. Such was the extent of their physical involvement, neither Tammuz nor Zambia noticed the eye peering through the crack in the door until they'd finished. Nathan wasn't quite sure whether he should skulk away or knock and ask to come in. He had very little experience of dealing with situations like this. Then Zambia said, 'Well, you're leaving it a little late to join in aren't you honey?'

And Tammuz had yelped and cried, 'What the fuck is that?'

'Just a little boy,' Zambia said. 'Come in. We won't eat you!'

Nathan advanced a little way. He couldn't take his eyes off Zambia's stomach which was revealed quite plainly as SHe sat up in bed. 'Wanna take a look boy? Come here.'

'Zam, you are sick!' Tammuz said, and began pulling

on his clothes. 'You're the kid with Leila, right?' Nathan nodded wordlessly. Tammuz leapt up and guided him back into the corridor. 'What are you doing here?'

'Sorry, I was just looking around.'

Nathan felt uncomfortable about the way this man was looking at him. It was very intense. Perhaps he was angry about being spied on and planned harm. 'I'm really sorry,' he said.

'Hmm?' Tammuz looked dazed. 'Oh, that's all right. I'd like to talk to you. Ask you a few things. Do you mind?'

'No. No.' Nathan wasn't sure whether that was a truthful answer or not. He followed Tammuz up the corridor into his office and accepted a plastic cup of lukewarm killer coffee. Tammuz threw himself into a chair and put his feet up on the edge of his workstation.

Nathan didn't like the close scrutiny. 'What do you want to talk to me about?'

Tammuz was still looking him up and down like a roving automatic eye. 'So you came with Leila Saatchi and . . . the girl.'

'Yes.'

'You don't look like a natro. Have things changed that much?' He sighed, not wanting an answer and shook his head.

'I'm not a natro. Leila asked me to come here with them to . . .' Nathan stopped, feeling he shouldn't say any more. He'd got himself into enough trouble already by doing too much of that.

Tammuz' eyes were alight, as if with fever. 'Go on,' he said calmly, breaking a pencil on the worktop as he did so.

'I . . .' He floundered helplessly.

'It's all right. I'm Mr Roirbak's partner. You can tell

me.' Tammuz had the feeling he must be appearing like a predatory beast at that moment, and wished Zambia was there to put the kid at his ease.

'All right,' Nathan answered, terrified. No one had *ordered* him not to say what he knew. He briefly told Tammuz about himself and why he was with Star Eye. As he spoke, he watched with mounting unease the different expressions flitting across Tammuz' face: frustration, annoyance, condescension, anger, humour and, unbelievably, sadness. His instincts finally rang the bell and told him this man had more than a casual interest in what might be going on downstairs.

'Dear Leila,' Tammuz said in a cracked voice when Nathan had stopped speaking. 'Both of them blundering through . . .' He made a wordless exclamation and stood up. Nathan flinched. 'You're not supposed to come up here,' Tammuz said. 'If I were you I wouldn't tell them you have. You'd better go back and . . . get on with whatever you were doing.'

Needing no further prompting, the boy fled.

Zambia was lying in wait for him downstairs. Nathan virtually screamed when a hand shot out and grabbed his arm. 'Calm down,' Zambia soothed. 'It's not catching.' Then SHe realised it wasn't hir Nathan was frightened of. 'Oh, I see.'

'Who is *he*?' Nathan squeaked. 'What does he *want*?'

'I wish I knew! Don't let him bother you. He's just a bit crazy, but he won't hurt you.'

Zambia accompanied Nathan back to the screen room, and in the space of that short time, gleaned more information than Tammuz could ever hope to. They sat down and started to look through the movie tapes, Zambia interjecting the odd question here and there. 'Oh, this one's great. I saw this some time ago. Shall we watch it again? You met all of Star Eye did you?'

'Yes. To both questions.'

Zambia inserted the tape. 'Here, come and sit by me.' SHe held out hir arm and Nathan happily snuggled against hir. Zambia Crevecoeur had a kind of motherly/ sisterly ambience about hir that day. 'You've heard a lot of garbage about me, you know.'

'You aren't going to hurt Cabochon?'

Zambia laughed. 'Goddess, no! Tell me about them all. What are they doing nowadays?'

'The Star Eye people? Well, I like them a lot, but they make me feel kind of young and stupid at times.' Nathan was filled with importance: he carried so much information this mysterious beauty wanted to hear about. He began to describe the Star Eye members one by one. And then recited the bits of gossip he'd picked up.

'That's interesting,' Zambia said when Nathan had finished telling hir about the pairing of Cabochon and Jordan. 'Where are they all?'

'At a hostel in Athena Gardens. Would you like to meet them? Maybe you could come with me when all this is over.' Nathan was enjoying a cosy vision of flouncing back into Star Eye company on the arm of Zambia Crevecoeur. He felt they should be made to see Cabochon had misrepresented his brother. Zambia ran a single, slim finger over Nathan's cheek, causing a delicious shiver.

'Honey, I'd love to, but I'm more or less stuck here as much as you are at the moment. Perhaps, though, you could get a message to Cabochon for me.'

'A message?' Nathan asked, crestfallen. 'What for?' He wondered whether he'd said something unwise again.

'Well, I have a bit of trouble at the moment, and if . . . well, if anything should happen to me, I think Cabochon should know.' SHe smiled slyly, looking like all the paintings of powerful seductresses in all the world and twice as lovely. 'It would have to be a secret though. Could you do that?'

'Maybe.' Nathan was becoming very wary of all the secrets prowling round the complex at Acropolis Park. He decided it would be wiser not to commit himself.

'Maybe? What is this?' Zambia laughed lightly. 'I need your help, Nathan. I'm trusting you. Please . . .' SHe put hir lips against the boy's mouth and gently pressed, whispering to his skin. 'Please help me.'

'All right!' Nathan said breathlessly. Zambia drew away after planting another brief kiss.

'Good. That's settled then. Shall we watch the movie?'

In Roirbak's laboratory wing, Ari was watching a movie too, though of a slightly different nature to any Roirbak had set out for Nathan's entertainment. Artistic pornography slid across the wallscreen, beautifully captured in soft focus and low lighting. Leila told her this particular film had once won an award. Ari watched entranced as gleaming skin moved against gleaming skin. It induced more of an aesthetic high than anything. Eyes implored other eyes, smoky and dark. Fingers trailed spines, stroked arms. And then the close-ups, camera zooming in, and the thrust of sexual organs became almost geological because of their sheer size and arrested movement. 'Wow,' Ari said inadequately.

'Just get into it,' Leila advised, although she was sitting further back, reading a book by the light of a small lamp.

Soon the screen was obliterated by the fuzz of burning light behind Ari's eyes. Leila put down the book and quietly knelt beside her. 'I can't see it,' Ari gasped.

'That's all right,' Leila soothed.

'I'm going to explode.'

'Yeah, you are. Just let it come. Just relax.' She cradled Ari's head in her lap as the girl gave in to the overwhelming sensations crashing through her nervous system. It was clearly far more powerful than the subjective test the day before. 'Remember to let the feeling out, let it gush out like a fountain, but draw it back afterwards. OK?'

The robe had ridden up to Ari's waist, exposing her genitals which appeared swollen and engorged to unnatural proportions. 'Oh boy,' Leila murmured under her breath. 'Roirbak . . .'

Then she was being thrown violently up and backwards, her spine slamming against the far wall. 'How did I get here?' she wondered briefly before a conflagration of raw heat crashed into her face. 'Roirbak!' Ari was invisible inside a spinning maelstrom of spitting light, although Leila could see one foot jerking at its perimeter. Roirbak burst into the room.

'She can't control it!' Leila cried, although she doubted whether the man heard her. The air was filled with a high-pitched whistling. Roirbak strode purposefully towards the light, his long hair being blown into disorder. He squatted down, his clothes vibrating against his body, and injected something into Ari's neck. For a second there was freeze-frame and the whole world stopped. Then the rampaging power slipped obediently back into Ari's body and calm descended. The only sound was rapid breathing and the ululation of an orgasming female on the screen. Roirbak switched off the film and knelt beside Ari again.

Leila crawled over on hands and knees. 'What did you do?'

'Oh, just something I came up with that Ari should be

able to do herself. At least we can induce it artificially, and I know it works now, too.'

'You mean, you weren't sure?!'

Roirbak smiled. 'Well, you know how touch-and-go this stuff is.'

Leila gasped and ran her hands over Ari's face. The girl was lying passively, blinking and swallowing. 'You monster Quincx! It could have done anything.'

'No, it couldn't. Remember what you were saying the other day. It was armed with back-up retardants, couldn't have gone maverick. The worst thing that could have happened was . . . nothing.'

Leila shook her head. 'You OK, Ari?'

The girl nodded, unsure. 'Think so. What happened?'

'We were just a little too ambitious for the second test,' Roirbak said, standing up. 'Not to worry. No harm done.' He marched out of the room. Ari had started to cry.

'I'm never going to be able to control it, am I?' she said. Leila hugged her.

'It caught us unawares, that's all. We'll handle it eventually.'

Privately, she wasn't so sure.

There is nothing in the underworld for Reynard Lennon. He has been searching the dark realm, a moving shadow flowing through the looping Interiors; dark, dimlit, floodlit. There are places roped with cablecoil guts as thick as a man, as fine as a whisker; a rumbling kingdom. He slides among suspicious groups of heat-seeking, light-shunning nomads, who had made temporary camps up lesser conduits, who milk sweet, pure water from above from the gleaming concrete walls. He insinuates himself, like some sleek-furred thing rubbing flesh, into their company. They caress him and speak, they offer him nourishment, warmth, sanctuary; but none of them has seen Zambia Crevecoeur.

He moves on, deeper, deeper, creeping down the greasy, slippery ladders to lower levels where luminous shamen weave and sway within the oily smoke of sulky fires, and vaults are low and crumbling. The information they have to give is more hypnotic: crazed, multi-faceted visions of the future, a hundred possible futures. They scry and cry, wailing out their prophecies into the echoing dark where the rootless scurry and hide, but none of them can see Zambia Crevecoeur.

Down he goes, splashing now thigh-deep through the refuse-stink of the deeper levels, where human life has degraded along with the rubbish that has fallen there. Fallen people, slipping down through grids and drains until there is nowhere left to fall. Would a person like Crevecoeur be so desperate as to seek sanctuary in such a place? Reynard wears an oxygen mask and breathes pure air. Just inhaling the thick stench down here can fill a person with incurable disease. He feels his way through the bowels of the city, conscious of the weight of civilisation above him. Here are tunnels where the trains once ran. The city has flowered upon its own offal. Sometimes, he sees a blade of light in the darkness and thinks: 'There is Crevecoeur! There!' but it is only a puff of igniting methane . . . not even ghosts in the lowest vaults.

At length, the passage he has been stooping along opens out somewhat into a low chamber: he has come to the shrine of a goddess. A living goddess nonetheless. Scraps of life attend the motionless mass who, Reynard concedes, radiates a certain aura of power. She is the Blackrag Madonna, and her prophecies are madder, darker and less coherent than those of the wildest shamen two levels up. He faces her phosphorus glow. She is shadow-robed and veiled. He can smell nothing, which is for the best. Blackrag Madonna is blind as a dead rat. Her sense of smell has gone, along with her ability to taste, and her hearing isn't too reliable either. Oh, she *hears* plenty, but nothing from this world, say her followers. Her hands are claws she keeps concealed within her rags and tatters. She does not feel either, it would seem. Reynard questions this repulsive ghoul, with neither hope nor disappointment. He retains an open mind. Far from answering immediately with a negative or affirmative answer to his queries, the Blackrag Madonna puts her ruined head on one side, much as a girl of great beauty might do, and asks him questions in return. She wants to know all there is to know about Zambia Crevecoeur. Reynard replies, for the most part, honestly. The Blackrag Madonna nods as he speaks, then whispers to a scrap of a follower who has been hiding in her robes throughout the interview. The follower speaks.

'Our Lady will think upon your problem. Return later for her answer.'

They can give no time for this appointment. The low-dwellers have no concept of time as surface people know it. Reynard retreats to a side tunnel where he squats with his knees up. He wonders whether it is time to head back to the city with its purified air, sweet, crystal water and groomed inhabitants. He admits he has no empathy with these squalid filth-dwellers, and Reynard rarely admits to anything. He always keeps an open mind. What can this decrepit hag tell him? Zambia Crevecoeur has never been here, Reynard knows that. Why linger here in the sordid dark for nothing? His instincts answer. A hunch, that's all, they say.

He regularly consults his watch which also provides the only illumination. He gives her half an hour. If the answer isn't ready yet, that'll be too bad. He doesn't intend to wait any longer. The Blackrag Madonna, it appears, has been waiting for him. She extends a mummified appendage from her robes and begins to speak.

'Float people run fast leave love lust power girlpower boypower out of here go fast light heat star fly riddles in the flesh call strong me feel here feel now feel aaaaah.' She lapses, makes a few chewing sounds and sighs. Reynard, despite himself, is stunned. Was he supposed to divine some sense from that?

'What do you mean exactly?' he asks in a smooth voice.

'Tammuz Malamute,' says the hag.

Reynard is taken aback. At no time had he mentioned the therapist by name. Was this bitch really clairvoyant then? His scepticism wavers. 'Tammuz Malamute what?' he asks carefully.

The hag chews and spits. 'That's where you'll find the WoMan. With Tammuz Malamute.'

Reynard cannot help but be cautious about this information, despite its apparent supernatural origin, or perhaps because of it. 'And how do you know this?'

'Everything finds its way down here eventually, smoothskin. Everything. C'mere! Wanna listen?' She delves unpleasantly within folds of rag and greasy hair. Reynard backs off as she extends a foul paw. 'Won't hurtcha!' she crows.

In her palm lies the bright scrap of a highly illegal netfly, something which Reynard has seen only in illustrations before. Blackrag Madonna, it would seem, cruises the highways of Arcady's information network. 'Tammuz Malamute talks to his computer,' says the hag sagely and buries the fly back in her ear. 'Has plans of his own for your beautiful Zambia, he does.'

'You want me to pay for this information?' Reynard asks.

'With what?' the hag asks drily, and then her face creases into a sly smile. 'Yeah, got it. A mirror. You bring a mirror some time.'

'A mirror,' Reynard repeats, realising this is one of the few times in his life he's been surprised.

'You heard. A mirror.'

'And you trust me to return?'

The hag cackles. 'You'll be back,' she says. 'You know you will. Now, get out of here.'

Without regret, he does.

Back on the surface, Reynard Lennon hurried back to Club Eleusis, secreting himself within the building and virtually throwing himself into his showercub before anyone could see (or smell) him. Basking beneath the spitting jets of aromatic warm water he thought about what Blackrag Madonna had told him. It made sense, in a way. Perhaps he should inform Jahsaxa Penumbra about this unusual datafile residing in the city's bowels, and then, perhaps not. If reserved for his personal use, it might put him at a certain advantage over his employer. If he thought this thing out carefully, he might be able to steal the netfly from Blackrag and use it himself, but these were future plans. For now, he had other things to think about. Declining the unctuous offer of the drymatic machine, he wrapped himself in a towel and sauntered through to his living room, where a sleek computer housed in non-reflecting black sat seductively on a complex workstation. Being Jahsaxa's most esteemed security officer, he had access to many of her personal files (including ones she didn't know about) and enjoyed free-ranging consultation with the public network. Snuggling into his chair, he settled down for an hour or two's tinkering. Jahsaxa Penumbra, through her acquaintanceships and affairs, was allowed into the more esoteric corridors of the public mind. Using her clearance codes, Reynard skipped nimbly into the data terraces he visualised as a vast graveyard, but which were in fact the accumulated records of all known people in Arcady, all employees, current and late, of Tech-Green, all public workers in the country, all suspect characters and a host of other subsections of humanity. Tammuz

Malamute was clearly a highly trained individual; that meant education, and Tech-Green education into the bargain, given the avenues of his proficiency. Naturally, Reynard started there, drew the first blank, which didn't disconcert him (he would have been disappointed by an easy discovery anyway) and composed himself to delve deeper, perhaps taking it backwards a month at a time, beginning with Malamute's employment with Club Eleusis.

The couple of hours stretched to three and more. Reynard took a break, frustrated. He drank coffee and brandy, then dived in for another assault, feeling as if the databanks were deliberately obstructing him. Names mean nothing of course, but Malamute was on file for iris, finger and dental prints. Even his genetic code was noted, from when he'd applied for a work permit, but no matter how subtly Reynard interrogated, no matter how bright his ideas of lateral interrogation, every time he drew blank. Completely and utterly. Tammuz Malamute had literally come from nowhere. Before his appearance in Arcady, he simply did not exist. Anywhere. At least, not anywhere civilised, Reynard appended. So what could that mean? he wondered. And how had Malamute managed to dupe the agencies?

The following afternoon, Reynard Lennon admitted he could go no further in this research and it was time to report to Jahsaxa. He only wished he'd managed to discover more. He found her quietly working in her office, surveying the extent of her financial empire on a monitor screen. Reynard did not mince words. 'I have reason to believe we'll find Tammuz Malamute is concealing Zambia Crevecoeur,' he said.

Jahsaxa leaned back in her chair. 'Impossible.

Roirbak would never allow it. He is a friend of mine.' Her eyes glittered unpleasantly.

'Nevertheless I feel that Crevecoeur is being shielded by Malamute. It is possible Mr Roirbak is unaware of it, of course.'

Jahsaxa laughed. 'Quincx unaware of something? Don't be a fool, Lennon! What makes you believe this?'

Reynard shrugged and silently handed Jahsaxa the report he'd had printed, showing all the places where Tammuz didn't appear and which, given his profession, he should have done. Jahsaxa scanned it carelessly. 'And what does this prove?'

'On a superficial level, that Mr Malamute is not what he seems. I infer from that he may have had reasons other than professional ones for taking on the employment you offered him. Zambia Crevecoeur has vanished. SHe has eluded me completely, which leads me to believe SHe can be in the only place secure enough to hide from me, namely the Roirbak complex at Acropolis Park. Have you managed to contact Mr Roirbak yet madam?'

'No,' Jahsaxa answered shortly, already tapping in Roirbak's code on a keypad by her hand without looking at it. 'But I will. This is most disturbing, Lennon. I hope your suppositions are incorrect.'

'If they are, I am convinced it can only mean Zambia Crevecoeur is dead, and all evidence of hir physical existence destroyed.'

'That is a possibility,' Jahsaxa said.

Reynard shrugged. He didn't really think so. Jahsaxa flinched with annoyance when she realised she'd been connected with the Roirbak answering machine again. 'Perhaps you'd better get over there,' she conceded. 'Apologise for the intrusion, to be on the safe side.'

'Naturally.'

'Humbly ask if you may search the premises, and that due recompense will be made for the inconvenience, at my expense.'

'Of course.' Reynard bowed and turned to leave.

'One more thing,' Jahsaxa said. He faced her.

'Yes madam?'

'Don't damage Crevecoeur. In any way. I shall invite Roirbak and Malamute here for a meeting to give you more freedom. I'll let you know the time. Take as many staff with you as you require.'

'Thank you all the same madam, but I prefer to work independently,' Reynard said.

'Well, if you are confident of managing—'

'Quite. Thank you.' He marched smartly out.

Jahsaxa sat and pondered for a while. She still doubted whether Roirbak would betray her in this way, but perhaps Lennon was right and Quincx had been duped by Malamute. She smiled. Poor Mr Malamute. He was due for some unpleasant surprises, she felt.

'Good afternoon, Mellissa. This is Jahsaxa Penumbra.'

'Good afternoon, Ms Penumbra. How may I help you?'

'Well, like all the other times I've spoken to you, I'd like to be put through to Mr Roirbak.'

'I'm afraid Mr Roirbak has left instructions not to be disturbed, Ms Penumbra. He's working.'

'Are these the same instructions as last time, or has he reissued them? Did you give him none of my messages?'

'The messages have all been placed in his pending file, Ms Penumbra. Alas, I cannot say whether Mr Roirbak has had time to examine them yet.'

'Look, it is most urgent I speak to Mr Roirbak. I'm quite sure he will understand if you notify him of this.

I've called over half a dozen times, Mellissa!'

'I'm afraid Mr Roirbak has left instructions not to be disturbed, Ms Penumbra. He's working.'

'Mellissa, it is a matter of life and death that I speak to Quincx Roirbak immediately. Do you understand that sentiment?'

'. . .'

'If needs be, and I hate to stoop to this, I can take steps to override your obstruction, from which you might find it difficult to recover!'

'I'm only carrying out Mr Roirbak's instructions, Ms Penumbra.'

'Mellissa! I . . .'

'One moment please.' Click. Soothing music over the line.

'Jahsaxa?'

'Quincx? Oh, thank the Goddess! You don't know how relieved I am to hear your voice! That robot of yours . . .'

'I'm sorry about the inconvenience, Sax. I've been very busy these last few days. Interruption could have ruined everything. What can I do for you?'

'I'm afraid it's rather a delicate matter.'

'Oh?'

'Quincx, Zambia Crevecoeur is missing. We have reason to believe Tammuz Malamute is involved.'

'Tammuz? How?'

'We received information, I'm afraid I can't tell you how at present, that Zambia is, in fact, in hiding at Acropolis Park.'

'Here? In my building? What *are* you implying, Sax?'

'Look, I know this sounds awful. I'm not implying you're in collusion with them or anything. Is there any way Malamute could get someone inside Acropolis Park without your knowing? The information we received was very precise about Crevecoeur's location.'

'To be honest, I haven't seen much of Tammuz recently . I've been cooped up with my work, but I'm sure my security staff would have notified me of any unexpected guests.'

'Listen, Quincx, I beg you to help me. I've invested everything in Crevecoeur. I can't afford to lose hir. Please, would you come over to Club Eleusis and bring Malamute with you so I can speak to him? It may all be a misunderstanding. I know this is really putting on you, but . . . well, I would appreciate it so much and will recompense you in any way I can.'

'Is that necessary? I can bring Tammuz to the comm unit if you like. That might be quicker. I'm sure he'll be able to answer your questions to your satisfaction.'

'No! I mean, please Quincx, I want to talk to him in person. He *must* know something. I want to assure him Crevecoeur is in no danger, but that SHe must return to Club Eleusis.'

'Well, I'll ask him, but he too is a busy man at present, Sax.'

'Quincx, please. This isn't just *anybody* asking, is it?'

'. . . oh, very well. I'll see what I can do. When do you want to see us?'

'As soon as possible.'

'Fine. Within the hour then.'

Roirbak sighed and rubbed his face. 'Goddess, goddess, the plot leans more to murk!' he grumbled. Mellissa made an abrupt click.

'That is one bitch mother!' she declared.

'Whoever taught you language like that!' Quincx

admonished. 'Call Tammuz Malamute, and have someone prepare the rotor.'

'You'd better be a damn good liar!' Roirbak said to Tammuz as they walked to the hangar where the company rotor was housed.

'I appreciate this, Quincx. It gives us time.'

'Got a plan yet?'

Tammuz shook his head. 'No.'

'You look awful. Is that intersex creature a vampire or something?'

Tammuz laughed. 'Hardly. I've got things on my mind. Problems.'

'You surely have Mr Malamute, if that is your name.'

Tammuz looked at him askance but said nothing. 'I hope to the Lady Jahsaxa's instincts haven't been pricked by you, Tammuz,' Roirbak continued. 'Why the hell have you got involved with this Crevecoeur nuisance? Surely you can't afford such complications?'

'You're right. I can't. It's one of those depressing hormonal conditions that effects one's sense of survival.'

'Oh, that.'

'Yes. Poignant, isn't it?'

'You realise you might have to give hir back, don't you?'

Tammuz fixed Roirbak with a stare. 'I'll never do that, Quincx.'

'Not even for your daughter's sake?'

The moment hung, poised.

'You can't let Jahsaxa come sniffing round Acropolis Park, you know that,' Roirbak gabbled, quickly, still not entirely convinced his suspicions were correct. 'It would be worse than Amazon House finding out if she got wind of what's going on. Damn it! I'll ship Crevecoeur back myself if necessary. *Ewan.*'

Tammuz wheeled around, one hand scraping hair. Roirbak was afraid he'd pushed him too far, or maybe not far enough. Roirbak sighed. 'I'm not going to ask why or how just now, but I'm right, aren't I . . . ?' Tammuz' silence was confirmation enough. 'And you've come back because of Ari, haven't you?' he asked softly, standing just behind Tammuz. 'Ask yourself, if you haven't already: why are you here?'

'Lady, Quincx, I don't know!' Tammuz faced him and Quincx Roirbak stepped back from the raw emotion on the younger man's face. 'I shouldn't be here. Neither should Ari. She shouldn't exist. It's too dangerous.'

'Is that what you're here for then? To make sure she doesn't?'

Tammuz wheeled away again. 'No. I'm not that cold. I told you, I don't know why I'm here.'

'Why didn't you tell me who you were from the start? How can you stand back and not get involved? This is your baby, in more ways than one, Tammuz.'

'There are things you don't know.'

'Naturally.' Quincx sighed. 'Look, everything's out on the screen now. We'll talk later. What are you going to say to Jahsaxa?'

'Deny everything.'

'That might not be enough. She seems pretty sure of her information.'

'What else can I do?'

Roirbak put an arm around Tammuz's shoulder. 'There may be a way,' he said. 'But it means you work for me for the rest of your life to pay me back.'

'You'd do that for me? Buy her off?'

'No, not for you, Tammuz Malamute. For Ewan

Famber, whom I loved, and his daughter Ari, who doesn't deserve this shit. Come on. Get on board. Let's get it over with.'

Leila had not been at all pleased to find she was living under the same roof as Zambia Crevecoeur. Of all the most damned of coincidences! she'd thought, when Ari had told her what had happened in the canteen that first day at the Park. It reminded her painfully of Jordan and for the first time she thought about how she was never going to touch him again. It took only ten minutes of private weeping, however, to clear her head. Now it is gone, she told herself firmly. It's all gone.

Nevertheless, rightfully or not, Zambia had come to mean trouble to Leila. It made her very uneasy having hir in the same building as Ari at such a dangerous and important time. She tried to banish the thought that Zambia attracted trouble like a magnet, knowing it to be bad magick even to think that, but it was difficult not to.

After Tammuz and Roirbak had left Acropolis Park for their meeting with Jahsaxa Penumbra, Ari and Leila had sat together in the canteen. 'I'm annoyed Quincx is getting involved in this ridiculous soap opera,' she told Ari. 'You are more important.'

Ari shrugged. 'I don't think Zambia is the person everyone thought SHe was,' she said. 'I feel sorry for hir.'

Quincx had insisted on telling both of them the details of Zambia's difficulties, despite protests from Tammuz, feeling both women needed to be given a reason for the delay in Ari's treatment.

'You wouldn't say that if you'd seen the old Zambia in action,' Leila said, pulling a sour face. 'Save your pity. Think about yourself.'

* * *

Reynard Lennon, who had left a trail of confused, temporarily disabled security droids behind him, waited in the shadow of a large rhododendron hybrid in Acropolis Park and watched the Roirbak rotor dance up from the roof, wheel around and head towards Sector 23. He blinked his pale grey eyes, took a careless look around himself before walking smartly up the driveway to Roirbak's complex, an array of wafer-thin data cards – the discerning burglar's equivalent of a crowbar – ready to hand. Introducing himself to the woman-form receptionist in a uniquely unforgettable way, Lennon insouciantly gained access to the building. Mellissa never knew what hit her, her circuits melding in the robotic equivalent of a cerebral haemorrhage, the doors to the complex opening as if in welcome. Hands in pockets, Lennon sauntered through the plaza, pausing only to disable any artificial lifeforms that approached him asking questions. He found Leila and Ari in the canteen.

Leila looked up and saw the man standing in the doorway, recognising him immediately for a creature less human than Sindy or any of her contemporaries. She instinctively shielded Ari with her arm, drawing her close to her body.

'What do you want?' she asked, her mind racing. Quincx was gone. How had this person got in? Was he a colleague of Roirbak's?

'Where is Zambia Crevecoeur?' Lennon asked. He strolled towards the table and helped himself to a biscuit off Ari's plate. 'Well?'

Leila's mind almost stopped dead. She could see a decision path dividing in front of her as plainly as if it was real. A magnet for trouble? A person in difficulty?

Damn you, Crevecoeur – I should have known something like this would happen!

'I don't know who you mean!' she said. 'Who are you?'

Lennon slapped her sharply across the face. Ari cried out and cowered. 'Where is Zambia Crevecoeur?'

Leila sat up straight, brushing hair from her face. 'I don't know who the fuck you are, or this Zam . . . whatever person is! I'm only a visitor here. Ask Quincx Roirbak.'

'Mr Roirbak is out. Where is Zambia Crevecoeur?' He flexed his hands. Leila stood up, quite prepared to defend herself, although she knew a trained assassin when she saw one.

'Look . . .'

Ari could stand it no longer. She was puzzled as to why Leila should defend Zambia in view of her feelings, but it was senseless to do so. This man would kill them if they didn't answer, and *still* find Zambia afterwards, she was sure. She reached up to touch Leila's arm as a signal. 'I know who you mean. It's that man/woman, isn't it?'

Lennon hauled Ari up by her T-shirt. 'Keep talking little lady.'

'I've seen him . . . her . . . *It's* here somewhere. Upstairs maybe. With Tammuz Malamute.'

'Ari!' Leila hissed.

'Show me.' Lennon dragged Ari from her seat. Leila hurried after them. What the hell could she do? Members of Roirbak's staff were apparent, drooping inactive all over the place. Damn Crevecoeur!

Ari had no positive idea which rooms Tammuz and Zambia occupied and was babbling nonsense to this effect as Lennon hauled her up the metal stairway to the gallery.

The noise attracted Zambia's attention. SHe'd been entertaining Nathan in Tammuz's office, messing with the computer. The machine, acting as watchdog, emitted a sharp warning just moments before Zambia heard Ari's anguished cries echoing round the gallery. 'Wait here!' Zambia ordered Nathan, who was looking up perplexed.

'What is it?'

'Don't know.' Zambia padded to the door, coming face to face with a wriggling Ari, still firmly in the grip of Reynard Lennon.

'Hello Zambia,' Lennon said. 'Ready to go home now?'

'Like fuck!' Zambia cried, and with lightning speed vaulted over the safety rail of the gallery and began shinning down support poles to the floor.

Leila was transfixed on the stairs. She heard Lennon say, 'Oh dear,' and saw him put his hand in his pocket.

'Look out!' she screamed.

A volley of razor mosquito-bolts impaled themselves on the ground floor. Lennon's aim had been fouled by Ari's wriggles. 'Ooops, clumsy, missed,' Lennon said, and threw Ari away from him. He leaned casually over the railings and aimed his weapon. Nathan, who had emerged from the room behind, took in the situation at a glance and, with a blood-curdling scream, threw himself at Lennon. Because of this the shot which Lennon had intended to take Zambia through the leg to disable hir, sliced into hir shoulder, the side of hir neck, and made a messy slash clean to hir belly. Lennon shook Nathan off but the boy was already leaping down the stairs to where Zambia was writhing on the floor. Lennon followed at a more leisurely pace, his weapon concealed once more. He squeezed past Leila and smiled. 'Kids!' he said.

'Zambia, Zambia!' Nathan moaned helplessly, tears running down his face.

'Shut!' Zambia gurgled. 'Star Eye. Tell Cab. Tell Cabochon!' SHe wheezed, hir eyelids fluttering, blood spilling from hir working lips.

'Time we were going, Crevecoeur,' Lennon said. 'Have the grace not to die on me will you?' For such a slight figure, he had surprisingly little difficulty slinging Zambia over his shoulder. 'This is going to make a frightful mess of my suit,' he said to Leila with another dazzling smile. 'See you. Apologies to Mr Roirbak for the disorder.'

Leila stood, stunned, her fingers pressed to her lips. Ari, rubbing her bruises, had limped over to Nathan who was weeping uncontrollably, telling everyone it was his fault. The vast chamber seemed to zoom out all around them. Leila felt tiny and afraid. Were Quincx and Tammuz safe?

'Well, Tammuz, I have to know,' Quincx Roirbak said as the rotor skimmed gracefully between the city towers. 'Why did you fake your own death?' He smiled hopefully at the gaunt man beside him. Now that he knew, Tammuz looked more like Ewan to Quincx with every moment, which was oddly disturbing. This, after all, was not Ewan's body.

'Maybe I got fed up being thought of as a saint,' Tammuz said darkly.

'A cliché, but maybe,' Roirbak conceded.

'I was depressed,' Tammuz said weakly, inadequately. 'I came to hate the Tech-Green philosophy and didn't want to live out an expanded life up there somewhere, looking down on the unfortunates left on Earth. Do you really think the uneducated people they leave behind will be able to keep the artificial environments stable? I don't. It's sick. Humanity, but for its own élite, is expendable to Tech-Green.'

'We always knew that,' Roirbak said shortly. Tammuz' jaded beliefs were not that novel: Quincx had heard them spill from many a Tech-Green's lips; but then Ewan had always thought himself unique.

Tammuz shrugged. 'It all became too much. I can't explain how I felt. I was living a lie. Ewan was an icon, nothing more. I hated him. One night I got stoned and saw exactly what I'd become – a spoiled, heartless little shit. Sorry to say this, but I didn't feel as if I liked any of the people I was involved with either.' He shrugged again, a little embarrassed for having said that. 'I needed out. Completely.'

'Not that completely, obviously. Look at you: you're still very much here.'

Tammuz grinned. 'I love life,' he said. 'And I wanted to live it. Not just as squeaky clean, boring Ewan Famber but as a man. I wanted to experience my existence, discomforts and all. So I grew myself some new flesh and got into wearing it. Tammuz Malamute was a great adventure for me – and still is.'

'Especially so since Crevecoeur, hmmm?'

Tammuz nodded thoughtfully. 'An area I'd never really looked into – intersexing. A mistake on my part, I think. Now, if I could combine Ari's DNA with Zambia's physical make-up . . .'

'Goddess!' Quincx cried. 'I thought you said you'd abandoned Ewan!'

Tammuz smiled wryly, but didn't respond to the remark. 'So, how are you getting on with Ari?' he asked. 'I did think about her a lot, you know.' Roirbak flicked him a narrow glance.

'Not as well as I'd hoped. That's a flash little power-pack you made there, Tammuz. More powerful than you guessed, I suspect.'

Tammuz grinned with pleasure. Since he'd opened up to Roirbak his appearance had visibly improved. Now he merely looked tired. It had been a relief to tell Roirbak all about himself. In a way, he felt guilty because he'd confessed to Zambia first. 'Reckon it might help if Ari had her daddy to work with now?' he asked.

Roirbak laughed. 'Lady, it's good to have you back!' he exclaimed, reaching over to slap Tammuz' thigh. 'You rogue! I should hand you over to the Tech-Greens if I had any sense!' Then he stopped laughing, his face hardening. 'Goddess, boy! Why the hell didn't you come to me when you were so messed up? None of this might have been necessary! You had me. You had Leila. You've always had Leila. I can't understand it.'

Tammuz sighed. 'Don't try. I don't regret it though. I've spent years on the road with natro groups, mostly abroad, just bumming around. It was . . . well, Nirvana for me, I guess. I needed it, Quincx. So bad. I needed to be someone else, someone new. I love Tammuz Malamute much more than I loved Ewan Famber.'

Roirbak grinned crookedly. 'Well, the name *is* pretty slick!' he said.

They landed on the roof of the Club Eleusis building and took the elevator down to the third floor. 'You think this will work?' Tammuz asked.

Roirbak shrugged. 'Jahsaxa's a law unto herself. However, I feel sure she values her friendship with me enough to play it our way. Perhaps if we offered to replace Crevecoeur for her . . . You could say you'd do a better job next time. Ham it up. Make out there was room for improvement. Make suggestions she could mention to her surgeon. I don't know. Think you can do that?'

'Yes. I don't see why not.'

'Tonight I feel we should all celebrate, don't you?'

Tammuz wriggled uncomfortably. 'You mean tell Leila and Ari . . . everything?'

'I think you should.'

Tammuz sighed. 'If you insist. I only hope it doesn't ruin your party atmosphere!'

'Boy, they thought you were dead! You'll find everyone's just happy to discover they were wrong.'

'I'm not sure Leila will share your delight, or Ari for that matter.'

Roirbak frowned. 'Tammuz, you're Ari's father. Remember that. She is not just an experiment, but a lively and very likeable young woman. Let this new person you have become learn how to love . . .' He stopped himself abruptly. Perhaps that had been too personal a remark.

'I have already learned that,' Tammuz said serenely, and turned to Roirbak with a grin. 'Just why do you think I'm here? Ewan wouldn't be doing this, now would he?'

'How should I know? Ewan, apparently, did a lot of surprising things,' Roirbak replied drily.

'Now hold on!' Leila was trying to keep order. Nathan had recovered enough to tell Ari what Zambia had said to him and also something of the conversation they'd had before. Both of them now wanted to hurry over to Athena Gardens.

'But we must tell Cabochon!' Ari cried. 'Zambia has just been . . . *kidnapped*! SHe's hurt! There's no one here! What else can we do?'

Leila ran a nervous hand through her hair. 'We wait for Quincx to get back first. Zambia was his guest. It's nothing to do with us. We can't just go haring off into the city like that. Quincx and Malamute are handling this. If we get involved, we might only make things worse.'

'I promised Zambia I'd send a message to Cabochon,' Nathan insisted, 'at least let *me* go!'

'No! We don't know who or what's out there!'

Their first action had been to run to the comms unit, only to find it disabled. Mellissa had been discovered slumped over her workstation, leaking viscous fluid and very clearly lifeless. That had turned Leila's stomach more than seeing Zambia being shot. Mellissa was just a servant, for the Goddess' sake! Because Roirbak had built the machine to appear humanoid, more so than any of the others in the building, it was like seeing a real dead body lying there.

Now the three of them were hovering in the reception area, arguing about what to do. Leila's first responsibility was to Ari and the boy. She was sorry for Zambia, but it really wasn't her problem. She could not see how telling Cabochon would help. She only hoped that Quincx and Malamute *would* come back. If they didn't, it would mean she'd have to get Ari out of Arcady and fast. Her gut instinct had been right: Zambia Crevecoeur had always meant trouble. Looked like things hadn't changed.

In Athena Gardens, Jordan and Cabochon were lying in bed sharing a joint of particularly sweet weed. The rest of the group had been too busy out enjoying themselves to think about the potential consequences of Leila's absence. Cabochon, however, had been thinking about it deeply. This took his mind off the painful subject of Zambia. On reaching Arcady, he'd attempted to call Zambia's old apartment and had explained himself to the woman who now lived there. She'd been sympathetic, but could offer no information. 'I just took the place on, soul, oh, about two weeks ago. Didn't know who lived here before. Sorry.'

So far, Cabochon had refrained from getting in touch with Alix Micklemas. Instinct told him something big and bad had occurred and that the moment he called Alix it would all be dumped on him. It was unfair! He wanted to bask in the developing closeness he and Jordan were enjoying, surfing sensorial highs, and being utterly open, perhaps for the first time in his life. He felt safe with Jordan, and for this reason viciously pushed all thoughts about Zambia to the back of his mind. Didn't I bind myself to Jordan for that reason? he thought. To be free?

Leila was a much safer subject for consideration.

'Something has to be resolved one way or the other,' Cabochon said, expending a vast amount of mental energy mustering concern for the group. 'It can't go on like this. It's not fair on her.'

'What's not fair on her? Where is she?' Jordan, from his expression, didn't give a damn about either Leila or the group.

'You're cold-blooded. You know that? Leila loves you, you dumb shit. That doesn't exactly make me feel good. I respect her and I don't like her hating me.'

Jordan sighed. 'So what you want me to do?'

'Just put her straight. Tell her it's over once and for all. *Be* honest. Stop torturing her. We can't keep this a secret any more. You must see that.' He got off the bed and walked to the window. Jordan considered what an unselfconscious poseur Cabochon was at times.

'Maybe I don't want it to be over with her. Not completely. Have you thought of that?'

'Honey, I *know* you don't want it to be over completely. That's cool, I can handle that, but she can't. It's all or nothing with her. So you've got to do something, say something. She sure as hell won't.' He flopped down on his stomach and took the joint from Jordan's hands. 'If you won't do that, then it shows what we did was a sham and doesn't mean anything. We've got to sort this out, for everyone else's sake, not just ours. If not, it's over with us, blood-brother bond or not. I mean it.'

'From where I'm lying that sounds like another woman saying, it's me or her or else.'

'Well, you would think that! Things will just get worse if you don't face this thing. At least *talk* about it with her.'

Jordan reached out and stroked Cabochon's shoulder. 'For you, all right. So what about your problem?'

Cabochon rolled away. 'I don't have one.' He sucked furiously on the joint, staring at the ceiling. 'Not any more. There's nothing I can do.'

'You're a liar.'

'That's not a lie. There really is nothing I can do.'

'And you don't care?'

'I'll always care, but I've also turned my back on it.'

'Cab, you and your brother, well, you don't have the kind of relationship you just turn your back on. Even I know that, painful though it is to admit it.'

'We are not joined at the hip,' Cabochon said, and smiled bitterly. 'In case you haven't noticed, other than that first call, I've made no attempt to try and find him since we've been here.'

'No, I haven't noticed,' Jordan said. 'But then you're

not exactly joined to my hip either, are you?'

'I wouldn't lie to you,' Cabochon replied. 'As far as I'm concerned, Zambia Crevecoeur is dead.'

'Come here and say that!' Jordan hugged Cabochon to him, more relieved than he could understand. Zambia had always been a black cloud in Jordan's sky, but he could never work out why. 'Say it!' Jordan teased, laughing. 'Say it again. Say Zambia Crevecoeur is dead to me! Say it!'

Cabochon laughed. 'It's bit creepy but . . . oh!'

'What is it?'

'Invocation! Goddess!'

'What?!' Cabochon scrabbled out of Jordan's hold as if blind. 'What is it?' He was making strange, gulping sounds, sitting on the side of the bed, his head in his hands. Jordan leaned over him. 'Cab? You all right? Listen, you don't have to say that. It's stupid. I know. I'm sorry . . . Cab?'

In reply, Cabochon's body heaved and he vomited copiously on to the floor. There was blood in the mess. Cabochon wiped his mouth and looked at Jordan with panicked eyes. 'Zambia Crevecoeur is dead to me,' he said weakly. 'Goddess! What the fuck's happened?'

'Quincx! Darling!' Jahsaxa swept into the tasteful reception room she'd been keeping Roirbak and Tammuz waiting in for over half an hour. She held out her arms, trailing drapery, her hair smoothly coiffed, lips ruby red, pursed for a kiss. Roirbak stood up and embraced her.

'Jahsaxa,' he said, carefully, in greeting.

'I'm so sorry to have kept you, but we had a little emergency!'

'Oh dear. Nothing serious I hope?'

Her eyes sparkled. 'Well . . . it seems your little visit is actually unnecessary now.'

Roirbak and Tammuz exchanged a glance. 'Zambia has come back to us,' Jahsaxa said, dabbing the side of her mouth with a fingernail. She smiled.

'No!' Tammuz cried.

'Yes,' Jahsaxa said sweetly. Her eyes appraised Tammuz with dangerous cold. He dropped his gaze. 'I regret one of my operatives was a little heavy-handed at your place, Quincx,' she continued. 'Invoice me for damages.'

'How dare you,' Roirbak hissed slowly.

'How dare I what? Reclaim my property? SHe was there, Quincx, you can't deny that. I admit my man was out of order tackling it in the way he did, for which he will be disciplined, I assure you.'

'How dare you think you can just barge into my property! How dare you send one of your killers to Acropolis Park!'

'None of your people was hurt.'

'You deliberately had us come over here, didn't you! You lowdown, filthy bitch! Just so your scuzzies could raid the Park!'

'My hand was forced, Quincx.' Jahsaxa kept her cool.

Roirbak straightened his jacket. 'Come on, Tammuz. I've heard enough. You, Jahsaxa, will be hearing from my lawyer. Consider our friendship void!'

Jahsaxa hesitated for a moment, then shrugged. Tammuz stood his ground. 'I'm not leaving,' he said.

Jahsaxa's head snapped up. 'Is there something you wish to say, Mr Malamute. It *is* Mr Malamute isn't it?'

Roirbak grabbed Tammuz' arm. 'No, he has nothing to say. Tammuz, come on. Don't worry. Slavery is outlawed in Arcady. She can't claim to own Crevecoeur. And I am quite prepared to pay whatever SHe owes her. A court of law will handle this. Just be patient.'

'Don't try to take me on, Quincx! I have more power than you.'

'Clandestine power maybe. But I have more friends who are willing to admit publicly that they know me! If you want to make this a popularity poll, go ahead, but my assets still overtake yours, I think!'

'You'll regret this!'

'A cliché, Sax. Old and tired. If you have any sense you'll let me pay you what Crevecoeur cost you now and let hir come back with us.'

'Out of the question!'

'Then I have nothing more to say to you. Come along Tammuz!'

'I want to see hir!'

Jahsaxa laughed. 'How touching! It really is the old story of the doctor and patient falling in love, isn't it? How quaint!'

'Don't waste your breath, Tammuz,' Roirbak said. 'Let's go.' He managed to manhandle Tammuz out of the door, to the sound of Jahsaxa's malevolent laughter. Roirbak bundled Tammuz into the elevator and they rode halfway up the building in silence until Tammuz said:

'I can't believe this!'

'Believe it. That woman is one bitch mother as Mellissa refers to her. Keep cool. We'll sort this out the slow way. I hope Leila and the kids are OK.'

'Goddess!'

'Cool, Tammuz, cool. We can't do anything until we get back.'

As soon as they were aloft in the rotor, Roirbak called Acropolis Park. The sky was dark now, the city and the domes a blaze of winking lights around them. He tried to disguise the anxiety he felt when he found the comms system down, but Tammuz was nearly hysterical by this stage. 'They could all be dead, Quincx! Goddess, won't this thing go faster?'

'Calm down. Not even Jahsaxa would presume she could get away with multiple murder. Her man probably just glued up my communications, that's all.' He was afraid that if Tammuz wound himself up further he'd cause the rotor to crash. 'I'll get in touch with my lawyer now. Keep quiet, and sit still, would you?'

Tammuz sat and gnawed his knuckles as Roirbak made the call. Roirbak made sure the firm would act on his, and Crevecoeur's, behalf by initiating procedures first thing in the morning. 'We can do nothing more for now,' he said. 'Oh dear, Acropolis Park looks suspiciously dark!'

'You don't fool me, Crevecoeur. It's not just love, is it?!' Jahsaxa Penumbra hissed at the helpless form of her recaptured employee. 'What are you two up to? Who is Tammuz Malamute?'

Zambia could hardly speak, despite the prompt attention from Dr Parmedes. Hir throat was raw and hir mouth metallic with the taste of blood. SHe shook hir head on the bloody pillow.

'No matter. You will tell me, eventually. 'I'll be back later.'

Dr Parmedes was standing near the door looking very uneasy. He sensed the imminence of some kind of public display and that made him very nervous indeed. 'Parmedes!' Jahsaxa snapped. 'Use whatever method you can, but I want this little vixen barking in four hours' time at the latest!'

'Ms Penumbra, I . . . I have to get home. My wife . . . I—'

Jahsaxa hissed suggestively. A wordless sound that spelt discomforts of every sort. 'I'll do what I can,' Parmedes said resignedly, cursing the day he ever set foot in Club Eleusis.

Roirbak was aghast when he saw what had happened to Mellissa. Tammuz watched helplessly as Quincx sadly sifted through the remains. 'I'm not sure I can fix this,' he was saying in a thick voice. 'I think I'll have to start from scratch. Oh, Mellissa, I'm sorry!' Tammuz didn't know what to say. He was itching to get further inside and check on Ari, yet appreciated Quincx's robots were like

children to the man. He'd built every one himself. All of
his staff had been damaged in some way, but for those
who were shy, or clever enough to hide themselves from
Lennon's advance. 'It's like a battlefield,' he kept saying
as he and Tammuz walked through the building. 'It's like
a battlefield. By all the gods that ever were, that bitch will
pay for this!'

They found the canteen door barricaded, Leila and the
others hiding inside. Leila threw herself on Quincx,
gabbling about what had happened. Both Ari and Nathan
looked sullen and had clearly joined ranks over something. Tammuz looked at his daughter and thought,
'Now I can tell her. Now . . . if I want to.' He put a hand
on her shoulder, and then one on Nathan's. They both
looked as if they needed it. 'Will you tell me what happened?' he asked.

'Cabochon, do my eyes deceive me? Well, well, well, this
is long time no see, soul!'

'Alix. Hi. Can I come up?'

'Sure. The Crevecoeurs are out in force this season!'

The security screen blanked and the door opened. Followed by an intrigued Jordan, Cabochon sprinted up the
stairs. Mammy Crystal poked her head around her door
to shout.

'No good'll come of the province of the flesh, sonny!'

Alix was working on a customer, a young cinder-head
naked on his belly on her couch, lasers primed and
crouching like birds of prey all around. 'Don't tell me,
you're lookin' f'Zam, right?'

'Mammy been giving you lessons?' Cabochon said.

Alix laughed and prodded her client. 'Deadman, this is
Cabochon, and a friend, I guess. Say hello.'

'Greetings, soul.'

'Hi, Deadman. Yeah, you're right Al, we're looking for Zam. He in trouble?'

Alix rolled her eyes. 'Say that again and you won't be wrong, soul!'

'Oh shit. What is it?' Cabochon sat down on an empty couch.

'Well, put it this way, you ain't got a brother no more.'

'What?!'

'Hey, don't white-out on me. Didn't mean that way, sugar. What I mean is he's gone for a chop-job. Pussy all over the place. It was weird, I'm telling' you.'

'Explain Alix.'

'What I'm sayin' is, the fuckin' fool went and sold out to Penumbra – bad lady twice over. She had him fixed à la intersex. Geddit?'

'Jahsaxa Penumbra? He sold out to *her*? Never!'

'Believe it true, my pretty boy. He did a runner on her, turned up here with a split bone or two, which I fixed, and then he headed off again.'

'Where?'

'Only the Great Lady in the Sky knows that, boy. Some shadespit came by lookin' for Zam. I sent him underground, though I doubt that's where Zam went. He had a look about him, like he had a place to go. Know what I mean?'

'You've no idea where, Al?'

Alix shook her head. 'Uh Uh. Sorry. Can I help any ways?'

'You could keep your ears open.'

'I'll spread the word. You hear that Deadman?'

'I hear you, soul.' The prone figure raised a compliant hand.

'Where you stayin'?' Alix asked. Cabochon told her and she burned the address into the wall with a laser. 'If I hear a tweet I'll sense you out, be sure.'

'Thanks, Alix. Any suggestions where we try next?'

She shrugged. 'Ear to the ground, sweet brother, that's all I know. Be lucky.'

'Cheers Al. Be seein' you.'

'Bye. The boyfriend's cute, by the way.'

Cabochon grinned at Jordan. 'Cute he ain't, but you can't have it all.' They went back into the street.

'This was going to be a celebration tonight,' Roirbak said, disconsolately gathering the pieces of a robot Lennon had been particularly vicious with. Leila was trying to help but it was hard to concentrate on anything. Her mind kept flicking back to the python smile of the assassin, conjuring images of what might have been: death, blood, pain.

'A celebration for what?' she asked, trying to identify a burst coil of metallic wire. 'Does this belong?'

'No, that's a shaving. A celebration for a reunion.'

'Who with?'

Roirbak sighed, and dropped the last piece of droid into the plastic sack he was carrying. 'I'm not sure whether I should tell you. Two shocks in one day might be too much.'

Leila felt her face flame. She'd immediately thought of Jordan. 'Who have you brought here?' she asked sharply.

'Not a case of brought here. They just arrived. Come with me.' He led her into one of his work alcoves where a hi-res VDR was set up. 'Just look at this and tell me if you recognise this man.'

'Oooh, mystery.' Leila smiled shakily and Roirbak adjusted the brightness of the screen. It showed a replay of Tammuz meeting Ari for the first time in the canteen. 'Which one?' Leila asked.

'The skinny dude with the leather smile.'

Leila laughed. 'That Malamute character? Some description, Quincx! No, I don't recognise him, other from seeing him here. Should I?'

'Look again. Pay attention.' He magnified the picture which swam lazily and grainily into some kind of focus. 'Watch the hands.' He replayed several times a shot of Tammuz pawing at his face, messing with his hair; anxious gestures. 'Well?'

Leila shrugged. 'He just looks paranoid.'

'He is. That's Ewan Famber, Leila.'

Leila laughed and shrieked. 'What?!'

'I'm serious.'

'You can't be.' She peered at the screen again. 'Can you?'

'I am. Listen. He didn't die. It was a set-up. I don't know all the details, but he turned up here several weeks ago.'

Leila had gone pale. 'Are you sure, absolutely sure?'

'I am now.'

'Goddess, how long have you known? Why didn't you tell me? Goddess, Quincx, this is . . .' She swung round and grabbed his arm. 'He's with Ari! Now! Quincx?'

'It's all right. I know. It's best she's told.'

'At this stage?' She sat down on the edge of the work-top. 'I can't believe this. Are you sure he's not faking?'

'Quite sure,' Roirbak answered quietly. 'I wouldn't tell you unless I was. He tried to hide it, but there was too much of Ewan left not to arouse my suspicions. If either of us had had any sense we'd have realised from the start something like this had happened. Ewan was never careless. His accident was a joke, which we both fell for. I'm kicking myself now.'

'But why? Why did he do it? All that . . .' She closed

her eyes and shook her head, trying to dispel the memory of her agonising grief all those years ago. 'It was hateful, hateful!' she said. 'No, I don't believe it! He wouldn't have . . .'

'But he did, Leila. For whatever reason, he did. Now he's come back to us.'

'This is obscene,' Leila said.

Ari did not like Tammuz Malamute. She did not like the way he'd dismissed Nathan in order to talk to her. She had nothing to say to this man. He was weird. Now he was pacing round his office like a stalking beast getting ready to pounce and tear. She had begun to sweat with discomfort. Did he think she was somehow responsible for what had happened to Zambia? There could be no other reason he wanted to question her. Perhaps someone had told him it was she who'd informed the assassin Zambia was here. 'I had to tell him,' she blurted. 'He was going to hurt Leila.'

Tammuz stopped pacing. 'What?'

'The assassin, when he asked where Zambia was. I had to tell him.'

'That wasn't an assassin, Ari. That was a lowlife bum. And you had no choice but to tell him. Don't blame yourself. He'd have found Zambia anyway. Forget it.'

'Then, then what do you want to ask me?'

He squatted down in front of her chair, disturbed by what he saw in her eyes. Why did he have to frighten people so much? Had he always been this way? This was his daughter. He remembered his sporadic visits back to Taler's Bump, the shy little girl who'd been virtually a stranger to him, his awkward attempts at being a family man when all the time he'd only been yearning to get back to work. 'What do you remember about your father?' he asked.

Ari squirmed uncomfortably. 'Not much. Why?'

'Were you ever scared of him?'

She laughed nervously. 'Of course not! Why are you asking that?'

'Do you believe he's dead?'

Ari wriggled away from the chair and backed towards the door. 'I don't like your questions, mister!'

Tammuz sighed and clawed his hair. 'Come back, Ari. Don't be frightened . . .'

'You're weird!' Ari said, 'And I don't want to talk to you. Especially about my father. What's it got to do with you?'

Tammuz surveyed this fractious teenager impatiently. How the hell are you supposed to deal with these people? he wondered helplessly. If Zambia was here . . . But Zambia wasn't, and Tammuz didn't have hir knack for communication. 'Ari, I *am* your father!' Now she really thinks I'm crazy, Tammuz thought. Ari remained stone-faced.

'OK,' she said, in an attempt to pacify what she thought might be a dangerous lunatic.

'No, I mean it. I really am. I'm Ewan, Ari. I never died . . . exactly.'

'Sure, sure,' Ari said, and bolted for the door. Tammuz let her go. It hadn't exactly been a poignant reunion.

Down in Roirbak's workshop, Ari skidded to where Leila and Quincx were still re-running the surveillance vid. 'Keep that crazy away from me!' she screeched, grinning. 'You can't imagine what he just said to me!'

Roirbak and Leila exchanged a glance, and Roirbak shrugged, turning back to the screen, passing responsibility to Leila. 'What did he say?' she asked.

'He thinks he's my father! Isn't that weird! What's wrong with him?'

'Yes, it is weird, and I don't think he is completely right in the head, Ari, but I'm afraid it looks as if he might be telling the truth.'

Ari was silent, the grin dropping right off her face.

'Look,' Leila said quickly, 'I know this is a bit shocking and incredible and all, but . . .'

Ari shook her head. 'No, you're wrong. That's not my father. He's dead.'

'Look, he faked his own death, Ari. He never died. It's the truth.'

Ari was shaking her head more vigorously, although her face had crumpled. 'No, no, I know it isn't. That *thing* is not my Dad.'

Leila reached out to touch her but Ari stepped backwards.

'You are both sick, d'you hear? Sick! My father died seven years ago. They found the body. It wasn't faked. It wasn't!' Silence was filled with the echo of her denial.

'I've heard it from his own mouth, Ari,' Roirbak said gently. 'And I believe him. Tammuz Malamute is Ewan Famber.'

'It's a lie! I don't believe it, any of it!' Ari cried, although both Leila and Roirbak could see that, painfully, she was preparing to. 'If he was alive, he'd have come back to us! He wouldn't have just . . . *vanished*! Look what he did to me! Would he just have left me . . . ?' Abruptly, her face became devoid of expression. 'He's here,' Ari said, softly. 'He's here – now.' She looked over her shoulder, shook her head again, and began to walk back towards the stairway to the gallery.

'Ari?!' Leila called, and then turned to Roirbak who mouthed silently, 'Let her go.'

Leila leaned against him. Her heart ached: for the

death of love, for the death of innocence. 'Goddess, this is being handled *badly*,' she said.

Jahsaxa stooped confidently over the prone form of Zambia Crevecoeur. The blinds were squeezed shut, the door locked, the lights dim, and she had Zambia to herself, but for the anxious presence of Dr Parmedes behind her.

'Can I speak yet?' she asked quietly.

'The doctor cleared his throat, coughed drily. 'You can try. Keep it simple.'

'Zambia?'

'Unnh?'

'I know you can hear me. I want you to tell me a few things and then I'll let you go back to sleep, all right?'

'Mmm.'

'Who or what is Tammuz Malamute?'

'He's dead.'

'No, Zambia, I don't think he is. Come on, don't be silly. Answer the question.'

'He's dead.'

Jahsaxa sighed and stood up straight. 'Parmedes, this is intolerable. Increase the dosage.'

'I don't think that's . . .'

'Parmedes!'

'Very well, but I want to make it quite clear this is your responsibility.'

'Just do it. Now!' She exhaled slowly, shudderingly, holding her breath as Parmedes injected Zambia in the neck. Zambia flinched, hir face pale, eyes bruised, lips cracked and dry. It was a pathetic sight. Jahsaxa sat on the edge of the bed and brushed Zambia's hair back from hir face. 'Tell me the story,' she said gently, and then, with a harder edge, 'All of it.'

Ari sat across from the man she'd been told was her father, appraising him with a critical eye. She had listened to his story without interrupting, learning (simultaneously with Jahsaxa Penumbra across the city) why and how Ewan Famber had 'died'.

After the outburst with Leila and Roirbak downstairs, she'd walked, quite calmly, back into this office. Tammuz had turned around from his workstation. The expression on his face had been wary, but what more could she possible hope for? A long time ago, she'd learned just how dear she'd been to Ewan Famber: an experiment. Coolly, she'd walked right up him and said, 'You really are my father?'

He nodded, frowning. He knows nothing about people, Ari thought. He doesn't know what to say to me.

She spat in his face. '*That* is for what you did to me,' she said. He hardly flinched, just stared at her in horrified amazement. A delicious tide of powerful rage surged within her, giving her the courage to slap his face hard, right on the place where her spittle had landed. 'And *that's* for deserting me, you bastard!'

To her annoyance, although quite what she'd expected him to do after that she couldn't think, Tammuz grinned. He wiped his face. 'Ouch!' he said shakily,

'And Quincx told me you were a likeable young woman!'

'You left me to cope with this alone,' Ari said accusingly. There were so many ways she wanted to tell him this, all of them inadequate to express her feelings.

He had the grace to stop grinning. 'I know. I know.'

'*Why*?' It was an agonised cry.

'That's what I want to tell you.'

'Are you sorry for what you did?'

'No.'

She sat down, defeated. 'I think I still hate you.'

He shrugged.

'When Leila told me about you, when I read all that shit you left her, I pitied you,' she said bitterly. 'Now, I suppose I should pity you more. This is crazy!' She shook her head, frowning. 'Am I going to wake up soon?'

'I hope so,' her father replied.

Ari found it was strangely comforting to be told how confused Ewan had been at the time he'd turned his back on his family. She had been surprised by his view of the Tech-Greens, however, and dismissed much of what he said about them as paranoid hysteria. It seemed that, psychologically, there hadn't been much improvement in Tammuz since then. She felt she could partially excuse his megalomaniac meddlings in her genes now that she knew he was mentally unstable. Geniuses were like that, weren't they?

Satisfied with this flimsy explanation for the time being, she moved on to a more intimate subject: herself. Here was the man who could answer all those questions Leila was so vague about. Where Leila groped in the dark, this man emanated light. A pity he was so crazed. Even though she almost wholly accepted who Tammuz was, if only as an abstract, she still found it very difficult to look upon him as her father in flesh and blood. The best she could manage was to imagine him to be a person who had known Ewan well. That model worked comfortably, so she used it and said to him, 'Tell me about myself.'

'I was unsure whether my theories would work,' he answered. 'Mostly I hoped they hadn't.'

Ari frowned and shook her head. 'But why did you make me this way?' It was the fundamental question.

Tammuz sat down in a chair opposite her and picked up a pen to fiddle with. 'Why? The answer is traditional: because I thought I could. That is the root condition. Secondary to that, I anticipated what could possibly be done with such power. I supposed mainly that, instead of being passive victims of our own reality, we could, through utilising this technique, become masters of it. When the condition you refer to as "the burning" surges through your flesh, what you are given is the capacity to step beyond the strictures of the logical universe humans have inflicted upon themselves. Does that make sense?'

Ari pondered. 'Not really, no. Tell me what it means in ordinary words.' It was amazing how eloquent he became when talking about his work.

He sighed. 'It's difficult. Explain to me what you've experienced so far.'

'You really want me to tell you *that*! Are you kidding?' Her face flamed at the thought of it.

Tammuz frowned. He had obviously not considered Ari's feelings. 'Are you embarrassed to tell me about it?'

'Goddess!'

'I am the only one who can help you, Ari.'

She considered for a moment. 'All right. But don't look at me.'

He raised his hands. 'Fine.' Once she began, it was not as difficult as she'd imagined, mainly because it was so plain her father had only a scientific interest in what she was saying. Malamute stared earnestly at the floor, nodding vigorously at certain points in her narrative. But he did not look up until she'd finished speaking.

'Good, everything seems to be going well,' he said.

'Leila and Roirbak don't think so. I can't control it.'

Tammuz squeezed his eyes shut and shook his head. 'No, no. Listen. What you refer to as "the burning" – all that light and turmoil – is not an *effect*, Ari, but non-reality. Consciousness you raise through your sexuality allows you to enter that non-reality and use it.'

'But why through sex? I don't understand that. Why can't anybody have "the burning"?'

Tammuz smiled. 'Well, they could in theory, but – you know those blocks I put on you? They were only meant to be temporary, but humankind has barriers just like them in their own heads – permanent ones in most cases. Only a few people can train themselves to get beyond them.'

'Yeah,' Ari said, nodding, 'Leila and R. J. talked about that. I still don't really see what it is you're getting at though.'

Tammuz pulled a face. 'OK. I'll try to explain. What you must remember is that sexuality is as basic a consciousness as information.'

'What?!'

Tammuz raised his hands to silence her. 'I know, I know. Just listen.' He spoke slowly and carefully, punctuating his words with emphatic hand gestures. 'Information is present as reality – always, as everything. Information is just the same as a state of consciousness, be it ordinary, everyday perception, heightened perception using drugs or, as in your case, using sexuality. What I'm trying to say is, when you're in the state of consciousness triggered by sexual stimulation, you should be able to breach time and space. This will give you access to what I call potentia, and potentia is non-reality. There are other ways to access this world, but utilising sexuality is the way I discovered we could – perhaps – manage to do so using the human nervous system. Astrada is another word for potentia – goddess.'

'Ah!' said Ari, brightening, as if things were beginning to fall into place in her mind. Tammuz didn't let her speak.

'This *force* has always existed within Nature and has been worshipped by human beings in various forms for aeons. In earlier times, I believe people actually had more direct access to it. Primitive people didn't have our self-imposed restrictions, you see. Those restrictions came about because of certain people's encounters with what they symbolised as the "unknown", and the results of those encounters. Later, the restrictions solidified into blocks which became part of the genetic make-up of humanity.

'Earlier people were more receptive to the universe around them than we are. They couldn't make judgements or try to inflict order on their world, but simply flowed with it. They used symbols for what they didn't understand – and remember they were quite happy with not understanding – such as Goddess and God. Connecting with their deities, through consciousness raised by ritual, through dance or song, through drugs or sexual congress, they were really connecting with this primal force. Many early religious cults revolved around sexuality. Unfortunately, as mankind became more "civilised", and there were more people around restricted by the blocks, they estranged themselves from Nature and their deity symbols became logic and order. Simultaneously, sexuality became a control factor as a purely pleasurable or procreative experience.'

Tammuz' face had lit up as he spoke. Now, he stood up and began to pace purposefully round the room, making Ari's head whirl as she tried to follow him with her eyes. His hands clawed the air.

'Order froze the world, Ari, and those who set themselves up as leaders of society used everything they could to control people around them. Humanity's excursions into its own future became entirely cerebral. Science developed. The province of the mind. People strove to be free of Nature, seeing it as something outside of themselves. Its innate chaos repelled them. Soma, or body, and bodily functions, were regarded as unclean or shameful. Their gods became sexless, spirit without flesh, without fleshly drives, pure thought. And people strove to emulate their creation, while telling themselves they were striving for purity as possessed by the entity, or entities, that had created *them*. At the start of the last millennium, things were beginnings to change a little. Some people were waking up and seeing through the disguise humanity had constructed around its deities. By that, I do not simply mean the gods, but human culture itself as well. Tech-Green and Naturotech were both phenomena that evolved from that changing consciousness, but I felt that science was still too much the province of logic and order. To me, it seemed it should be a meld of mind and body, order and disorder, logic and nonsense . . .'

He sighed and squatted down by her feet. 'I was

researching along these lines, the end product of which was you. I felt, by doing that, I had effectively stepped back in time and discovered the one thing that should have been thought of before we even harnessed electricity. Science and technology must surely have progressed in a different way if these principles had been embraced from the start. Humanity had begun to chart the universe and impose its own blinkered logic upon it. A mistake. Universe is neither predictable nor logical but because of its very nature of chaos, anything is possible within it, even the logic and order.'

'Stop!' Ari said, her hands flying to her face. She was laughing. 'Stop it! My brain is steaming!'

Tammuz grimaced. 'OK, it's a lot of information to take in, but it is important you understand these things – my thoughts.' He stood up and sauntered to his coffee pot. 'It is only my view, of course, but you should still hear it.'

'But if you really had discovered this way of changing people, why did you stop?' Ari asked. 'Why run and hide? Why the secrets?'

'Because it was a fluke. Humanity isn't ready for it. It was the penalty for estranging ourselves from Universe. I realised it was only my ego wanting to control this thing, and that it wasn't a natural evolutionary step as I'd told myself. If I'd published my results, the consequences could have been disastrous. I didn't want to take that risk.'

'Disastrous in what way?'

'Well, humanity is still into control and being controlled. The only possible way your "burning" could have been used was as yet another tool of control. No way would those in power want every individual suddenly to become "free". Their structures would crumble. And, believe me, Ari, if you have developed as I hoped, you are truly "free" now.'

'In what way?' She accepted the lukewarm mug of coffee he gave her and sipped it. It was foul.

'Firstly, at its most mundane level, you will not look at the world through a narrow tunnel of perception. Ridiculous tribal codes such as hierarchies and power struggles will seem farcical to you, because *you will have passed beyond the point where you need them to exist successfully.* Now do you understand what it would be like if everyone was like that? The fabric of our society would be seen to be the ridiculous thing it is. No one could have power over others any more.

'Secondly, and this is more important, you will have the capability to influence your own reality in a profoundly greater sense than at any time in mankind's history. The problem is, you are unique. Wouldn't it be wonderful if we woke up tomorrow and everyone had become like you? They won't though, and what you are could only be beneficial if absolutely everyone *was* like you too. I think . . .'

Ari frowned. 'Hold on, are you saying that, if I wanted to, I could make people *do things*, obey me and stuff?'

Tammuz shook his head. 'No, don't even think that way! That is a gross over-simplification, and one upheld by so-called workers of magick since time began. What you will influence, if you like, is the time-stream as you perceive it.'

'It amounts to the same thing, surely!'

'Only because you perceive it that way. And it is vital that you don't. Everything is subjective to your current reality.'

'I'm lost.'

'At present, maybe,' he said. 'Ari, I want to work with you. Leila and Quincx are tackling it from the wrong angle. It's my fault because my notes were so damn impenetrable! When they think of sexual power, they're still thinking of a single reality situation. You know – like pyrotechnics and abracadabra! They are not capable of directing your experiences. It's like they are putting you in a helpless position and expecting you to be able to operate from there. It's nonsense. You should be equal to whatever you can evoke from your own impulses. After all, it is *you*.'

'You mean if I got kind of aroused right now, I shouldn't fight it or flounder, or try to control it, but just *be* it.'

Tammuz smiled. 'Sweet child,' he said. 'You may look like a brainless little urchin, but you are certainly the daughter of my flesh.'

Ari frowned. 'If we work together, does that mean you have to be with me when . . . ?' She grimaced.

'Another mistaken belief,' Tammuz said, smiling. 'No one but you can influence what happens. All I would want is for you to make the journey into the burning, and then come back and report. We can discuss the results and try to analyse what we learn.'

'What if I can't come back?'

'Perhaps my metaphor was deluding. Don't think of it as *leaving*. You are still here in this reality, but simultaneously experiencing others. If you are afraid, the experience will be frightening. If you are calm, it will be tranquil. If you believe you can return to this reality whenever you wish, you will. It's that simple.'

'How can you be so sure?'

'I can't, but we won't get anywhere by you being squeamish, will we!'

'It will be hard not to get scared. When all that rushing light and stuff comes, I panic.'

'In that case, look upon the scariness as part of the process. Accept it and use it.'

'Tammuz Malamute, I don't think I understand as much as you think I do!'

'If we think back to what I said earlier, perhaps understanding as such would be disabling rather than helpful. I don't think it's necessary for you to "understand". Simply experience it.'

'And when I've got used to all this, how will I use it then?'

'That's up to you. Power-hungry people would want to use it as a weapon – which it could very successfully be utilised as – or else as a way of controlling others en masse. I can only tell you what I think I'd do in your position and it is this. Use it to further your own evolution. Get out of this reality and off this fucking planet!'

Ari was taken aback by the vehemence of his last remark. 'Off-world? To the sky cities?'

'To begin with,' he answered, smiling.

'Leila wanted to do that. Just me and her. Is that where you want to go?' She dared fantasise, for just a moment, that she had some kind of family again, perhaps with Leila as a surrogate mother, the three of them heading for the stars. Oh, grow up! a bitter part of her spat darkly.

'I don't know where I'll end up,' Tammuz said. He patted her knee. 'I'm not parent material, Ari.' (Could he read her mind?)

'What if I stayed down here? Couldn't I try to help people?' She was thinking of the jellycrusts.

Tammuz smiled wistfully. 'Altruistic gestures are all very well, but the fact is, you couldn't do enough, Ari.

People would expect you to do everything for them; revitalise the planet, solve all their problems, etc., without doing anything themselves. By their very nature they would foul up whatever you accomplished, for which they'd blame you. Then they'd turn on you.'

'I can't take such a dim view of people!' Ari said hotly. 'You're wrong. Not everyone's like that.'

'I know. Not everyone *is* like that, but I still think your future lies off-world. Gaian reality, I feel, is mostly responsible for the way we are. That was all very well for the adolescent mankind, but in order to evolve, we have to realise we've grown up and it's time to leave home. Isn't that how you felt about leaving Taler's Bump?'

'I see your point. I think. Although you seem to have changed your mind since you fried poor old Ewan, haven't you? You couldn't wait to get back down here then and didn't want anything to do with space exploration.'

Tammuz sighed. 'I had to come back here to return to the basic me-ness. I rebuilt myself from there. I missed out on so much, Ari, important life lessons. My Tech-Green status, even a lot of the concepts I worked with, had been *imposed* on me. I wasn't myself. Now I am, for better or worse. I strongly believe that this world, and its reality, is the wrong place for you to develop your ultimate potential. It would be like you were trying to rival Gaiah herself, the planet-soul. I can't see anything good coming from that.'

He stood up. The inner light had faded from his face. He's thinking of Zambia Crevecoeur, Ari thought. Are we really closer to each other than we think? She hopped off the chair. 'I'm glad I spoke to you,' she said. 'Sorry about the spitting and things.'

Tammuz pulled a face. 'There are no excuses for the

past, kid. I won't even try to think of any. You owe me
no loyalty.'

She wanted, at that moment, to hug him fiercely. She
wanted to love him. What a lonely man he is, she
thought. Has he learned how to do something about
that? Is he different to how he was? Somewhere, in this
sprawling city, Zambia Crevecoeur was lying injured
and imprisoned. Perhaps SHe was thinking of Tammuz
too. He is alone, but not lonely, Ari thought, and I do
not pity him any more. I don't have to.

She left him standing there, thinking.

Jahsaxa was not surprised by most of what she heard:
Tammuz' life story pouring out from the lips of Zambia Crevecoeur. As a privileged, and – clandestinely –
highly-placed member of Arcady society, she knew
pretty well which direction the world was heading in,
and had had a place booked in Sky City One for over a
decade. She despised the weakling sentiments of Ewan
Famber. Naturally, she'd heard of this legendary Tech-
Green, and was disappointed someone of such intelligence and vision had allowed maudlin dross to get in
the way of his career. What a fool! And what an over-
reactive, stupid gesture he had made! Still, it was interesting information to learn he was still alive. Tech-Green
had mourned his passing with hysterical fervour; no one
had replaced him in their pantheon. He lived on, a myth,
in their fond memories. She wondered coolly how his
erstwhile mentors would react once they learned what
he'd become, and what they'd be prepared to offer to
keep that quiet. It could be quite embarrassing for them.
Roirbak, naturally, must be aware of Malamute's identity. It was no secret the man had groomed Ewan Famber
to perfection all those years ago, and it was too typical

the new, perhaps-not-improved Ewan would eventually end up back under Roirbak's wing. But what else? What was this about his daughter?

'Parmedes, you do realise what you are hearing is *highly* confidential material, don't you?'

'Madam, I was never here!' Parmedes concurred with feeling.

Jahsaxa poked Zambia in the arm. SHe had lapsed into a doze, the drug having worn off. 'Give hir another dose,' Jahsaxa said. 'There is more I have to know.'

'Ms Penumbra, I really don't advise that, unless you're not worried by the possibility of losing the subject.'

Jahsaxa flashed her eyes at the doctor. 'For your information, sir, this little bitchdog is a damn sight hardier than you give hir credit for! I expect SHe hardly gets off on this stuff. Don't be a fool! Zambia has clung to the streets for years!'

Parmedes sighed. 'Very well. If you would just let me through.'

So, this is the secret you've been incubating, Roirbak, Jahsaxa thought, curled in her office late at night, turning a glass of rich, golden mezcal in her hands. The hours rolled towards dawn and she sat alone, thinking about all she had learned from Zambia Crevecoeur. Her curiosity had been whetted rather than slaked, because Zambia could only tell it as far as SHe understood, and hirs was not a scientific mind by any standard. Two words revolved glitteringly in Jahsaxa's mind: sex and power. The two gods at whose shrines she'd sacrificed for many years. Now, it seemed, the gods had become one, emerging as a singular, doubly vital entity. In her limited understanding, she could see a way to the upper strata of

Arcady society and beyond it to the stars. If, for example, she had this girl Ari under her protection, she could, through strategic matings, harvest power right to the top. She felt she had Roirbak and Malamute in a corner: it was just that they hadn't yet looked over their shoulders to see the walls closing in behind them. And no way, in a million, million years, would she ever let them take Zambia from her again.

'Roirbak, it's me, Jahsaxa.'

'I have nothing to say to you. As I told you, you'll be hearing from my lawyers today.'

'Quincx, please. I've been up all night, thinking. This is ridiculous. Surely the situation can be assuaged without resorting to the interference of outsiders.'

'You were the one who happily ordered your man to come and trash my workshops, Jahsaxa. It is very easy for you to decide to be magnanimous. *I* am the one who is hurt. You've overstepped this time. You have to be punished in some way, and you know as well as I do that your case lacks substance. I will win and you will be shamed, and doubtlessly heavily fined. Compensation to Crevecoeur may also be a possibility for you to consider.'

'There are, perhaps, things for both of us to consider. Zambia has been telling me a lot, you know.'

'Say what you mean!'

'For example, lovers have no secrets, Quincx. You know that, don't you? Instead of getting all hot and bothered and self-righteous, how about calling your legal weasels off this morning and coming over later for a meeting. Bring Ewan Famber with you, of course . . .'

'There is absolutely no proof of that . . .'

'Hush! I am quite sure that, even after all this time,

with their sophisticated technology, Tech-Green could quite easily qualify the suppositions. There would still be traces, Quincx, I'm convinced of that. And the daughter of course, with her little talents . . .'

'Jahsaxa, don't push me this way!'

'Tch, tch. Don't sound so threatening darling! We are civilised people. Common sense should tell you I'm simply reacting in the most intelligent way. *He shouldn't have stolen Crevecoeur, Roirbak!*'

'How can somebody steal something that no one can own!'

'Don't be naïve, Quincx. What time will you be here?'

Roirbak was physically shaking by the time he'd broken the connection with Jahsaxa. Agreeing to her suggestion of a 'meeting' would buy them time, but for what? Dare they call her bluff and just let her get on with whatever she thought she could do to inconvenience them? He tried to think of the worst that could happen.

Tech-Green, in the interests of community and armed with their official regulations concerning public safety, would be quite within their rights to take Ari away from them. She was a potential danger after all. Tammuz had enmired himself, no doubt, in a veritable maze of minor and major legal infringements: destruction of Tech-Green equipment and forging documents were the first that sprang to mind. He would very likely end up being confined for psychological tests, and Roirbak doubted whether, in Tammuz' present teetering condition, he'd be strong enough to face them and emerge intact.

The business with Crevecoeur was another matter. Although it required official sanction to perform inter-sexing, Roirbak doubted whether Jahsaxa was careless enough not to have seen to that. And it was entirely likely she'd produce documented evidence that Crevecoeur had signed a contract with her, effectively handing over hir body for however long the contract stipulated. It would be easy enough to break such an arrangement. Although not illegal, it would be considered unethical, and as long as Crevecoeur could pay back whatever money Jahsaxa claimed SHe'd cost her, the contract would be dissolved. In Roirbak's opinion, Zambia was pretty safe, and the least of their worries. What the hell could he do?

Everyone but Nathan had gathered in the canteen that morning and Roirbak, when he joined them, was aware of a certain tension indicating no one dared think the worst was over. He told them without elaboration the content of his conversation with Jahsaxa Penumbra. He sighed and said, 'Well, if anyone has any ideas about what to do . . .'

'Quincx,' Tammuz said, miserably. 'Think about this. All it involves really is myself and Ari. I've caused all this mess and it's ridiculous you and Leila should involve yourselves. Ari and I will leave here. Jahsaxa can do nothing then. Even Zambia will probably be safer without me around.'

'I don't want to leave!' Ari cried, appalled. 'I don't want to go with you! Leila?' She appealed to the woman.

Leila put her arm round Ari. 'Be sensible, Malamute, where would you go?'

'You survive on the road well enough.'

'Don't be a fool. Tech-Green will hunt you down, both of you, wherever you go.'

'I've escaped before, Leila.'

'Have you?'

'Stop it!' Roirbak said. 'Squabbling won't help. Tammuz, we will go and speak to Jahsaxa. Hear what she has to say.'

456

'Give in to her, you mean? Let her have her own way?' Tammuz thumped the table with a closed fist. 'You know as well as I do that if she knows about Ari, she'll want a piece of the action. Are you really suggesting we go along with that?'

Roirbak sighed. 'Nothing will happen immediately. We just need time to think, and if that involves letting Jahsaxa believe we've given in, then so be it.'

'This is horrible!' Ari cried and pulled away from Leila. She glared at Tammuz Malamute. 'I wish I'd never been born. I wish you'd stayed dead! This is horrible!'

She ran from the canteen, furiously knocking chairs from her path. Leila rose to follow her but Tammuz put a hand on her arm.

'She has to be brought to maturity immediately!' he said. Leila tried to wrest her arm from his hold.

'She's right about you!'

'Listen, once Ari's in control of herself, no one can hurt her, in any way. This is true.' He looked at Roirbak. 'You know this, Quincx. Ari may be our only salvation in this matter.'

Roirbak sighed and shrugged. 'I'm not convinced it is a process that can be completed quickly.'

'But I know it is.' He let go of Leila who rubbed her wrist, holding it close to her chest. 'I agree we go and see Penumbra, try and stall her. But after that, we come right back here and get to work with Ari. The final test is due!'

'You're disgusting!' Leila hissed. 'That's a girl of flesh and blood you're talking about. A girl with feelings, for Goddess' sake! Stop thinking of her as another damn computer!' She took a deep breath. 'Now, I'm going to go and apologise to her. For all of us. Fuck

Crevecoeur, fuck Penumbra, fuck *you*, Tammuz Malamute!' She stormed out without further words. Tammuz opened his mouth at Roirbak who merely took a sip of coffee.

'Maybe she's right, Tammuz,' Roirbak said.

Friends don't come back from the dead, Leila thought, rampaging through the corridor from the canteen. Zombies do, vampires do, but *friends* don't. Like Ari, she had no difficulty accepting the *idea* Tammuz had once been Ewan, but there was no way she could really *feel* this odd, crazed man was the one she'd loved before. There had been so much to admire in Ewan, even though he'd been so self-centred. His essential *humanity* had always shone through. Tammuz Malamute, on the other hand, was utterly alien. She would be ashamed if he found out the way she'd sanctified the memory of his alter ego over the years.

She hunted round the building, gradually calming down, but there was no sign of Ari. Eventually, she deduced the kid must have gone to find Nathan, who'd slept in that morning and missed breakfast. Leila felt bad about the way things had gone for Ari. There she was, poised on the brink of some great, unbelievable experience, and everyone else was more concerned with their own problems, their own lives. She wondered whether Ari had noticed that and resented it. If she'd been in the kid's place, she'd have run off by now and left them all to it.

What are we playing at? she wondered. We're not equipped to help the girl. If anything, we're a hindrance. She paused in the doorway of Nathan's room. As she expected, Ari was in there, cradled in Nathan's arms, being comforted. Leila could hear her crying. Oh, hell, she thought. Where and when and how will this all end? She leaned her face against the doorframe. Neither of the kids had even noticed her standing there. Nathan's hands were smoothing Ari's hair. Leila could hear him murmuring softly. He leaned down to kiss Ari's face protectively. The posture, the nurturing were unmistakable. Leila straightened up and softly, silently began to back away. They don't need us, she thought. And that's the truth. Without us, it might work. They don't need us.

'You know what,' Ari said, wiping her face, 'I wish I could just run away and forget all this. It sounds childish, doesn't it! And impractical, and selfish, and stupid, and . . .'

'Hey!' Nathan interrupted her. 'I know. It's OK. Sometimes I think Leila and Quincx don't really give a damn about you. Not as a person, I mean. You're just an experiment to them. And that Malamute, well!'

Ari squinted up at him, still nestled against his chest. 'Oh, don't say that, Nate. Leila *does* care about me. I know she does. You may be right about the other two though.' She sighed. 'My father. He made me a monster, and in his own image, I guess!' She tried a watery laugh. Nathan squeezed her.

'Monster? You? No way. Goddess, you're beautiful, and you feel *good*, Ari!'

Ari tried to wriggle away from him a little, somehow annoyed he could say a thing like that at a time like this. She narrowed her eyes and Nathan shrugged, embarrassed.

'Isn't it . . . well, you know, how I'm *supposed* to feel about you?'

She made an angry sound. 'Yeah, with Quincx,

Malamute and everyone looking on taking measurements!' That wasn't entirely true, but she felt a little nervous. Nathan ran one finger down her face, on to her neck. She shivered.

'Nathan. Don't. You know what'll happen.'

'So let it. At worst, *if* what you say is true, we'll both be fried; but what a way to go!'

A radiant expression fleetingly crossed Ari's face, followed by clouds. 'Are you suggesting . . . like, here, now, without Roirbak, or Leila, or . . . anyone?'

Nathan rubbed his face. 'Ari, the world, our world, is breaking up around us. At any minute Penumbra's killers could burst in here and carry you off. Compared with that, is taking the final step with me so scary? I don't think we have much to lose.'

She thought about what Tammuz had told her, his ravings. 'We don't know what might happen,' she said, trying to be firm. Nathan touched her face again.

'I'm not scared.'

No, you wouldn't be, Ari thought bitterly. No pain for you, no burning, no loss of control, of *one-ness*. Dare she? Tammuz had told her to relax into the fire, swim with it, let go. Was he simply crazy or the one person who knew the truth, the right way. As if in reply, as a prompt, a tingle ignited in her belly. *Here I am*, whispered the power, purring deep inside. *Experience me, Ari Famber, I'm waiting*. She gulped and took a deep breath before falling against Nathan's chest. Her hands clawed his shoulders.

'Yes,' she said. 'Let's do it, Nate!' Dimly, she thought that wasn't the romantic kind of thing she'd envisioned saying at this point, but what did it matter? She hoped Nathan couldn't be hurt. It felt as if she was facing death: what would be on the other side?

Nothing could have prepared either of them for what they experienced.

It was awkward at first, and Ari felt a little embarrassed. Noses bumping as they kissed, fumblings with clothes. She wondered whether Nathan was too inexperienced to carry this off. She, even though virgin, had imaginative ideas about what they should do, mainly picked up from conversations she'd had with Justinette and Elice. She gently pushed him away and removed her clothes herself. 'You too,' she told him. Nathan seemed happy to comply. Once naked, she pushed him back on the bed, ran her hands over his smooth skin. He lacked Cabochon's muscle and Urran's expertise, but he was beautiful in his own way. He was also, if only for this minute, hers. She tasted his skin, calmly observing the way this kindled the burning within her. It was a harsh white in her belly. She gently bit his nipples, making him squirm and laugh. The burning responded accordingly: a single, spear-like leap of interest. She imagined she was cupping this white-hot power in her womb, and that the walls of it contained the fire. She could hold it there. Slowly, so as to maintain control, she continued her oral investigations of Nathan's body, noting the different tastes and smells of arms, belly, genitals, thighs. The burning had changed colour within her. Soon, she felt, she would just have to relinquish control and let it carry her. She took Nathan's cock in her mouth. He pulled her hair, bumping her shoulder with his knee. She tasted the sea, her own element, in the salt juice oozing from him. Now she could hear the roar of her own energy in her ears. She must let go.

Nathan made to roll on top of her, but she pressed a hand against his chest. 'No, not yet. The tantra is in the tongue.' It was the only way she could express it, remembering Justinette's assertions of how she had experienced altered states of consciousness this way. Surely this was fine and perfect ritual to fuel the fire. She felt Nathan's breath on her thighs and *let go*. It was the only way.

Flashbacks: '*The power of the orgasm. Boy, was he into that.*' Leila's face; shining. Tammuz Malamute. Zambia Crevecoeur. Flaming stars. The knowledge he gave me. Are we closer than we think?

Nathan?

She reached to him with her thoughts, became his lapping tongue. Became the eye of the Goddess. Floating. It was a calm sea, endless. Blue horizon. Forever sea. Lapping. Sea horses on the gentle foam. So calm. She had entered the reality of her power. In the eye of the storm there is tranquillity. She extended her senses outwards, seeking the spiralling cone of power that contained her.

She could sense Nathan's soul, a hot, bright radiance, inextricably joined to the essence of her being. She visualised him as a dolphin, rising up out of the waves, the moisture on his sleek, dark skin as bright as stars. Then she herself had become a star and he a streaking comet flying towards her. She awaited for the impact: an eternity.

There was no pain at all, only a kind of stretching.

'Look, Nate,' she thought and he answered, 'I don't know where we are,' but it was without fear. The friction of their two radiances created a third; they could sense it building up between them and around them. Ari lazily observed its ripening crescendo. Shivers like blossoms fell upon her incorporeal form, silver rain and bright bubbles of light. The experience had become pure music, each note torturous yet unbearably sweet. It was a tune she wanted to enter, *be*. As the melody soared and spiralled, Ari and Nathan spun within it, reaching for the highest notes. Then Ari could feel flesh around her, the bed-sheets beneath her body. For a frozen second she was back in reality, just a second, before the core of power erupted within her, spraying up molten gobbets of light from every pore of her body, from the base of her spine to the centre of her mind. She screamed, half terrified, half ecstatic, feeling like a mote of dust tossed on an endless ocean. There was no control, no way to stop it, no way to harness the wild strength pouring from her.

Then Nathan was in her head, part of her mind. He was the lightning rod and could earth the power within her. 'Silly,' his voice murmured, 'just make it into rain. Rain of light.' *This* was the answer. This. They had been so mistaken, Quincx and Leila. She could not control the power alone, *was not meant to*. Her lover, whoever that may be, male or female, should direct the new reality out of the force. She attuned to his visualisation. He, so untrained, had known.

They were lying panting, in the muddled bed, with a thousand thousand sparks of fire falling down upon them, vanishing, gently as snow, as they landed. Ari sighed deeply. She heard the sound of rotors whirring through the air outside. She heard Nathan panting. She felt her body, the sweat that held them together, Nathan's heart beating frantically against her chest. How can we speak? she wondered. How can we ever speak again?

Roirbak, in order to defuse the sparking situation between his two erstwhile protégéges, had ushered them out into Acropolis Park to walk off their tensions.

'Fresh air does wonders for the spirit,' he said, marching smartly past the empty reception booth without looking in. 'Half an hour's exercise will prepare us for the confrontation ahead.' Leila and Tammuz followed him, ignoring each other.

Outside the sky was clear, so clear they could almost see the mica shine of the dome far above. Sometimes there might be clouds hugging the higher towers of Arcady, but today the climate regulators had opted for summer clarity.

Leila skipped to catch up with Roirbak.

'Do you think it's wise to leave the kids alone?' Tammuz called after them.

'The chances of us being hit twice within as many days is slim, probability-wise,' Roirbak called back. 'Come here, Tammuz. Don't sulk. What is left of my security is now armed to the teeth and feeling mean. They'll be quite safe.'

Leila smiled nervously and linked her arm through Roirbak's. She had mixed feelings about leaving Ari and Nathan alone together. On the one hand, she suspected

465

letting them handle it in their own way was the right way, but what if she was wrong and they needed help?

They followed a curving path between bushy evergreens that led to a neighbouring industrial complex. Droids tended the lawns between the trees. Here and there Hellenic follies glowed marble pale among the greenery: the shrines of nymphs, some with wilted floral offerings on their altar stones, perhaps left there by passing workers or strolling lovers. Gentle breezes issued from concealed grilles behind the shrines, filling the air with the scent of mimosa. Currently it seemed that the Park was empty of human life, but for themselves.

Leila waited until Roirbak's complex was completely hidden by the restless trees before she spoke. 'Quincx, I think Ari is continuing the tests by herself at the moment.'

Roirbak stopped walking abruptly. 'What do you mean?'

She shrugged. 'When I went upstairs to find her, she was with Nathan. In a clinch, I'd say.'

'What? Oh Goddess!' Roirbak started marching back towards his complex, dragging Leila with him.

'What's the matter?' Tammuz asked, who had been just behind them.

'This woman here, who I took to be sensible, has neglected to impart vital data to us! Your daughter, Tammuz, is likely, at this very moment, to be burning up!'

'What?'

'He means screwing Nathan,' Leila said sulkily, ashamed because Roirbak was angry with her.

'We must get back there now! For the Goddess' sake, Leila, how could you not tell us! Don't you realise the dangers?'

'Now, hold on a minute,' Tammuz said, grabbing hold of Roirbak's arm.

'Hold on? Hold on! Are you *both* stupid?'

'Calm down, Quincx. What's the matter with you? Ari knows what she's doing,' Tammuz said.

Roirbak relented a little. He narrowed his eyes.

'I talked to her – remember?' Tammuz said smoothly. 'Give her space.'

'You're not even *worried*?'

Tammuz shrugged. 'We can't do any more than we have.'

'You haven't done anything!' Leila accused him.

Tammuz bared his teeth at her. 'I've done more than you. Talked sense to her, for a start!'

'You asshole . . . !'

'Wait!' Roirbak yelled. He was looking at the sky, right above the place where his complex lay. 'What in the Lady's name is that?'

Both Leila and Tammuz looked up. 'Is it a rotor on fire?' Leila murmured uneasily. 'Is it?'

They stared. Moments of silence passed.

'It's a star,' Leila said. 'It looks like a star!'

'No, it looks like a comet,' Roirbak argued. 'A comet with a tail of fire.'

'Neither of those,' Tammuz said, in a voice of complete confidence. '*That* is a dolphin.'

Both Roirbak and Leila stared at him in amazement. 'A dolphin?' they both said in unison.

'A dolphin. Yes.'

'Here in the sky above Acropolis Park?' Leila asked. She had begun to smile uncontrollably. Suddenly, she felt itchy, happy, even horny. Odd.

'Yes. Just so. What we are seeing is a visualisation

467

shared with us by Ari.' Tammuz grinned and folded his arms, squinting upwards.

Roirbak laughed. 'How can you know that? I don't see a dolphin,' he said, but the image was already fading.

'Oh, but I *do* know,' Tammuz said. 'And it most certainly is a dolphin. She is my daughter, after all.'

'I really think we should get back,' Roirbak said. 'Don't you?'

'Perhaps we'd better,' Tammuz conceded, 'but for the Lady's sake, *don't rush*.'

Cabochon couldn't rest. He roamed the streets of Arcady looking for signs of his brother. All he turned up from beneath the greasy stones of the city's less desirable haunts were rumours, rumours, rumours. His body hurt so much, he knew something terrible – perhaps even life-threatening – had happened to Zambia. He felt so powerless. It was like watching someone die through crazed glass.

The rest of Star Eye, now that their initial thrill of visiting the city was beginning to settle down, had begun to query why Leila hadn't been in touch. Jordan and Cabochon were taking no precautions to be discreet any more. They were together; simple as that. Where did that leave Leila? Ezooli voiced the fear that perhaps she might never come back to them. Others vehemently contradicted this: Leila would not run out, not without an explanation.

'She's busy doing something with Ari,' Justinette had said. 'She'll be in touch. I'm sure she will.'

Elice had picked up, with her extraordinary, almost supernatural ability to sniff out gossip, that something was going down with Cabochon's spitfire brother. Jordan, perhaps welcoming a chance to complain, told the others what had happened.

'Then we must all help him look,' Justinette had said.

'Oh, fuck off!' Elice replied, for once voicing the opinion of most of the group. 'Since when has that little shit done anything for us? Best thing that could happen would be for him to die, so Cab could get on with living!'

'So what do you suggest we do, smartass?' Justinette snapped back. 'Sit around here waiting for Leila to call? Like you said, Ezooli, we don't know what's happening. I'm going to help Cab look for Zambia, the rest of you can do as you like!'

Jordan sighed. 'OK, point taken. Come on you lot, look lively. Let's have a little group spirit here.'

Reluctantly, the others agreed to join in the search.

Urran and the younger girls prowled bars and night-clubs, while Jordan led others into the underworld of the city, asking questions. Like Lennon before them, they discovered no one had seen Zambia Crevecoeur, although many people were curious as to why this legendary figure was being hunted.

Star Eye, however, did not venture as deeply as Lennon had. They did not visit the shrine of the Blackrag Madonna who, of course, could have told them everything.

Round about noon on the day following Zambia's return to Club Eleusis. Alix Micklemas called Rameses Villa. Cabochon had been out all night, scouring the clubs and arcades for gossip. People were full of talk about Zambia's implants and how he was unrecognisable even as human now. Steeling himself, Cabochon fought panic. It was clear they were exaggerating. Wasn't it? Jordan was no help. He didn't think Zambia incapable of anything. 'He'd do something like that just to spite you,' he said. 'You know how he is.'

'He's too vain to go that far,' Cabochon argued, hoping he was right.

From the urgent tone of Alix's voice, he feared bad news.

'Heard talk, sweet soul,' she said.

'Yes, yes. What?'

'Friend o' mine knows a guy who knows another guy who works in the kitchens at Club Eleusis. Tells me there's a ruckus goin' on there here and now. Zambia's back at the Club, Cab, but pretty cut up to all accounts.'

'Thanks Alix, I'll get right over there.'

'Not advisable, sweeteye. Seems like Zam did a runner with his therapist or something. A guy works for Quincx Roirbak – you heard o' him? Roirbak's a bosom buddy of Jahsaxa's, or was. They say there's legal action flying round all over the place and Penumbra's got a temper on her like a rabid bitch. This is big stuff, Cab. Penumbra and Roirbak are among the leviathans of this vast city. When they get to grapple, a hundred sectors rock, believe me. Stay out of it. Zam'll survive. He always does.'

'Hmm . . .'

'Don't do anything stupid, Cab! I'll keep my ears open, OK? Wait till you hear from me.'

'All right.'

Once Alix had disconnected, Cabochon called the public information banks to find Roirbak's code. He had absolutely no intention of taking Alix's advice.

Tammuz was torn between the desire to stay and interrogate his daughter and the need to face Jahsaxa Penumbra. The adults had found Ari and Nathan sitting in the canteen. Initially it was thought that their subdued appearance indicated things might have gone wrong.

Only on closer inspection could it be seen that they were shaken but serene, holding each other's hands across the table-top.

'One word,' Tammuz said, approaching his daughter. 'That's all I want to hear. One word.'

She looked at him dazedly, opened her mouth as if it was difficult to speak.

'Well?' he insisted, wishing he could be more patient.

'Yes,' she said, in small voice.

Tammuz grinned. 'Was I right? Did it work out? Are you OK?'

'Yes.'

'Malamute, shut up!' Leila sat down and put her arm round Ari's shoulder, squeezed it. 'How do you feel?' she asked.

Ari cleared her throat. 'Fine. We're both fine.' She smiled at Nathan to show him that, even if they didn't think he was that important, she did.

Nathan appeared more willing (capable?) to talk than Ari. He answered Roirbak's precise questions, Tammuz' frantic inquiries, Leila's need to know they were unhurt.

'If only we had more time!' Tammuz said. 'This should have happened days ago!'

'Yes, but it didn't, so there's no use complaining,' Roirbak said. 'I think we all agree this has been a momentous event, and we can all talk about it together later, consider what we should do next . . .' He glanced at the wall clock. 'But, inconvenient as it is, I'm afraid I must hurry you now, Tammuz. Penumbra will be waiting and we can't anticipate the extent of her patience.'

Leila stood up. 'I'm coming too,' she said.

'What for?' Tammuz protested. 'It's nothing to do with you.'

She ignored him and spoke to Roirbak. 'Having

another woman around might be useful,' she said. 'Penumbra will be forced to modify her attack persona at least!'

'Garbage!' Tammuz spat.

Roirbak considered. 'No, she's right,' he said. 'It might throw Penumbra off balance a little if she's only been expecting the two of us.'

'Will you be long?' Nathan asked.

Leila mussed his hair. 'I hope not.'

'You'll be safe,' Roirbak said. 'We'll be as quick as we can.'

'Now, stay put!' Leila instructed, as Ari and Nathan saw them off from the rotor pad on the roof. 'Rest up for a while. No wandering around outside. OK?'

Roirbak had taken the precaution of installing a slightly more aggressive security system than the one that Reynard Lennon had so swiftly disabled. Heavy machines now stalked the hangars, bristling with murderous hardware and groaning with power. Neither Ari nor Nathan were particularly enthusiastic about being left alone with them. From their appearance, it seemed the machines would have a tendency to be a little quick on the trigger.

'Just stay in your own rooms,' Roirbak said. 'You'll be perfectly safe.' Ari watched him check a weapon of his own and secrete it inside his jacket. Both Leila and Tammuz were similarly armed. Clearly, nobody was taking any chances with Jahsaxa Penumbra.

'Well, are we ready then?' Quincx asked. Leila shrugged miserably and Tammuz said, 'For what? She has us, Quincx.' He took out the weapon Roirbak had given him and peered at it closely. 'Maybe using this is the only way.'

'That would simply be an added complication!'

Roirbak replied. 'All is not lost. We have to hear what she has to say.'

'We know what that will be!' Leila said.

'Don't worry. She hasn't got us as cornered as she thinks.'

'I wish I could share your optimism,' Tammuz said. He looked at Ari closely for a few moments and then beckoned her aside.

'If you have to, run,' he said. 'And if anyone tries to stop you, do whatever you have to to save yourself.' He paused meaningfully.

'Can I risk that?' Ari whispered back. Tammuz didn't answer her question.

'You still have friends in Arcady,' he said. 'Use them.'

'Who?' Ari asked, but Tammuz was already climbing into the rotor.

Jahsaxa Penumbra waited in the same underground conduit she had met Tammuz Malamute in for the first time. She felt high on adrenalin: everything was going well – almost too well. Impatiently, she checked the timepiece she kept in her pocket. 'Late!' Typical. She lit a cigarette, laced with synthetic opiates. Be calm, she told herself. Be calm.

'Remain cool,' Roirbak advised as the rotor curved between the high towers. 'Don't lose your temper, Tammuz, whatever you do.'

Tammuz, sitting behind Leila and Roirbak, only grunted, continuing to crack his knuckles which could be heard even over the whine of the rotor.

Roirbak and the others had only been gone for ten minutes or so when Cabochon called. Roirbak had wired the comms to be audible in Ari's room, just so she could intercept the answermachine if Quincx had to call her urgently. She practically flew to the interrupt key when she heard Cab's cool, clear voice swearing at the machine.

'Cabochon!' she screamed into the transmitter.

'Ari?'

'Yes!, Yes!' *You still have friends in the city.* Of course. Star Eye. What with all that happened recently, Ari had virtually forgotten about them.

'Is Leila there?' Cabochon asked carefully.

'No. No, oh, so much has happened . . .' Ari began, but Cabochon interrupted her.

'I bet! Tell me about my brother.'

At Cabochon's prompting, she related all she knew, omitting the identity of Tammuz Malamute for the time being. Neither did she tell him about herself. 'Roirbak, Leila and Tammuz have gone to speak with Jahsaxa on neutral ground,' she concluded. 'Some subway somewhere. They're going to try and sort this thing out.'

'Can they do that? Will they bring Zambia back with them?'

Ari thought for a moment. 'I don't know.' She stretched out her hand and flexed the fingers. Nathan, listening attentively, copied her gesture automatically, without thinking. Ari looked up and caught his eye. He smiled. She felt the touch. Anything is possible. Jahsaxa was out on neutral ground, smug and feeling secure. Quincx and the others were determined and worried, so much so it hadn't even entered their heads Ari might want, or be able, to do something herself. Anything is possible. A wicked glee passed from Ari's brain to Ari's outstretched hand to Nathan. He was on his feet in an instant and in the next room, looking for his boots. 'Can we meet you somewhere, Cab?' Ari asked. 'I want you to see something.'

'One more minute, they have one more minute!' Jahsaxa Penumbra thought angrily. She felt dizzy now, her elation poisoned by impatience. Would they dare to stand her up? A noise caught her attention. She straightened up, hands in the pockets of her long, dark coat, chin tucked into the raised collar. Her fingernails scraped against the gun she'd concealed in one of the pockets.

'Ewan Famber, how nice,' she said to the man walking towards her. Had he come alone? Her fingers curled reflexively around the gun. She backed away from the fury on Malamute's face. 'Keep away,' she said. 'I warn you. Stop right there!' He kept on coming, hands raised, the fingers flexing robotically. He was going to kill her! She brought out the gun and pointed it at him, still stepping backwards. The man was insane! Look at those eyes! Insane! Where was Roirbak! 'Malamute, I warn you. I will shoot you if you don't stand still.' He kept on coming. She fired. The noise and smoke of it filled the conduit. Her arm bucked and went numb. She stumbled backwards, coughing, waiting for the smoke to clear, waiting to see what injury she'd inflicted on Tammuz Malamute.

There was no body.

Had she missed? Had he run away? Cautiously, holding the gun out in front of her, Jahsaxa advanced up the conduit. She heard movement, wheeled around to the left, pointed the weapon up the accessway that lay there.

'There is no need for quite such an aggressive reception, I'm sure!' Quincx Roirbak said, leading Tammuz and Leila towards her. 'Put the gun away, Sax. We've come to talk.'

She realised, too late perhaps, that she had smoked rather more than she should have done, waiting for them there.

Hand in hand, Ari and Nathan walked slowly through Roirbak's workshops. We are invisible, Ari told her companion, and the security droids never saw them. They passed right by one stamping, huffing machine and it didn't even swivel so much as a surveillance appendage in their direction.

They walked out to Acropolis Ramp and the highware station. Testing their power, they slipped unnoticed past the toll booth, and entered the first tram that stopped there. They willed that no one should see them, and no one did. It was unreal, like being stoned. Holding on to each other, they felt confident of their ability to hide.

Within Ari's aura, Nathan became an extension of her strength, part of it. She did not attempt to control him, but allowed him access to the source, so he could use it for himself. He did not ask what she had planned because they shared the symbol of it. It was not necessary to understand it; just the feeling sufficed.

In the bar at Rameses Villa, Cabochon was telling the others how odd Ari had sounded over the comms. 'Have they done something to her?' Elice asked. Cabochon shrugged.

'I don't know what the hell's going on – *anywhere*! Things feel weird all round. Ari wants to meet me . . .'

'We'll all come!' Justinette said impulsively. Everyone looked at her strangely and she shrugged. 'Well, I just think we should.'

'Is this really all about Zambia Crevecoeur?' Cable asked. 'It feels like there's more to it than that. I'd like to know why Leila is getting herself involved. It's not like her.'

'It's probably because Roirbak did,' Jordan said. 'She'd do anything he told her. I think you're right, Net, I think we should all go along. See what's happening.'

'They're not meeting Penumbra at the Club,' Cabochon said.

'Right. All the more reason to go there now,' Jordan replied. 'We'll try and see Zambia, find out what he knows.' The others did not look convinced they'd be able to achieve that. Club Eleusis was renowned for its security as much as its delights. Jordan shrugged. 'We can at least try. For Goddess' sake, we're a natro group, aren't we? Star Eye! That used to mean something once. Think power!' He punched the air, attempting to energise them.

Cabochon shook his head. 'OK, gang, let's go,' he said, drily.

'I think we can work something out,' Jahsaxa said. She no longer felt confident. Tammuz Malamute was a swirling black cloud behind Roirbak. She was afraid of him. He had come back from the dead. No, be sensible. He faked his death. Now, she could not be sure.

'You are no match for Ari Famber,' he said. 'There is nothing to work out.'

'Look, we can be civilised,' Leila said softly, moving forward to face the woman. She failed to see what the men were so worried about. This Penumbra was a wreck. 'Quincx is quite prepared to recompense you, and Tammuz is right; you really are wasting your time trying to get at Ari.'

'I wonder what the Tech-Greens would think of that,' Penumbra said.

'She can protect herself,' Tammuz said. 'If you're not careful, she'll come looking for you, bitch!'

The argument moved on to another phase.

In Athena Gardens, Star Eye walked to the place where Ari would meet them; the highwire station. Cabochon had slipped into a state of consciousness that would prepare him for battle if needs be. The excited twitter of the others bounced off his strengthened aura. He felt alone. Soon, he was sure, the finale of the Crevecoeur tragedy would be played to a full house. An end was approaching.

Ari and Nathan had evolved a new atmosphere between themselves by the time they met up with Star Eye. Because they were in tune, hands clasped, in a state of secondary erotic awareness, the group of people waiting for them seemed like a troupe of angels, just columns of light. They must see us as strangers, Ari thought. Yes, Nathan agreed. We must not speak. Ari squeezed his fingers in assent. They stepped off the tram.

She is herself, Cabochon thought, she is finally herself. It was to him that Ari addressed her first communication: *I am me*.

To all of Star Eye, Ari and Nathan *looked* normal, but *felt* very strange indeed.

'What's happened to her?' Ezooli hissed to Eve. 'What *is* she?'

'Don't know,' the older woman replied. 'Don't think any of us ever have.'

'Are you ready?' Ari asked them, without speaking. She wanted so much to share this new reality with others, especially these people she had become close to on the road. Were they afraid of her? She found it was easy to interpret the waves of their thoughts. Yes, there was fear, or rather confusion. She transmitted a series of images which she hoped would help dissipate that. 'Will you let me become you? Can we *be*? she asked.

'Zambia,' Cabochon said in reply. It was enough.

We close in on Club Eleusis, silent and relentless as a fog. Locking mechanisms tumble open to our touch. We tell the security systems they'd feel more comfortable that way. Now, we flow up the stairs, past the elevator doors, the movement is a rhythm. Our body twists to Universe music, we swirl and sway, conjuring a new reality. We have come for Zambia Crevecoeur.

What are these flickering motes across our path? How small they are, how feeble. Other souls? How cold to be alone. We must enfold them, let them share us.

The security guards of Club Eleusis joined the group.

Reynard Lennon was sitting beside Zambia's bed, a weapon held loosely on his lap. Jahsaxa had virtually made him swear he would not even move his eyes from Crevecoeur. Lennon was not stupid. He'd sussed Ms Penumbra out from the start. He knew she adored the skinny little freak lying there. Oh, she wasn't into sex with hir or anything. That wasn't Penumbra's way. The only way she could manifest her love was by owning the object of it. Obsessive. It will be her downfall, Lennon thought, with satisfaction. Now, what was that noise outside? Jahsaxa back already? It sounded like singing. Perhaps she'd won her little battle, and was tripping back here on fairy feet to gloat over her prize. Lennon grinned. A grin he reserved solely for private use, it being a particularly horrible expression. He stood up and gently held the nozzle of his bolt gun under Zambia's throat, making hir pellucid skin gleam the colour of gunmetal grey. Bolt through the roof of the mouth. That's what he'd do. No-good whore. He chuckled and replaced the gun smoothly in an inner pocket of his jacket. 'Your lady love's back, creep,' he said to the still form on the bed. And yet . . . his senses, killer keen, alerted him to the fact that the noises outside were not exactly *normal*. And how could that be? There was a throng of Jahsaxa's security zombies on patrol throughout the building. No one but Penumbra could get in uninvited. Sniffing impatiently, Lennon decided to investigate. At worst, it might mean Jahsaxa had been beaten, and had returned out of her mind. She might be going crazy in the corridor outside. Anything was possible. Dumb bitch! he thought, a sarcastic remark ready on his lips. What he saw when he opened the door silenced him utterly. It would be some time before he spoke again.

When Reynard Lennon literally just appeared in front of it, the Star Eye *Gestalt* did not recognise him as the person who had wreaked all the damage back at Acropolis Park. It did not recognise him as a person at all in fact. Some part of his design was offensive, which it was tempted to change, holding itself back only because some vestige of Malamute's advice lingered in its mind. Instead it placed the Lennon components into a kind of temporary spin, which would prevent them from obstructing it or causing damage. It did not bother to survey the results. Pausing only briefly to accomplish this act, it passed into the room beyond; no longer a group of individuals but an amorphous body of light.

Zambia opened hir eyes and saw what SHe supposed to be an angel of death waiting to take hir soul away, a host of angels in fact. It did not seem so bad. Hir flesh hurt, hir mind ached: it would be a relief to leave them behind. SHe stretched out hir arms and waves of light flowed down them. Blessed peace. And then a thought needled into hir consciousness. 'Take from me, Zambia. Take again. And again. It never ends . . .'

'Cabochon?'

Zambia blinked and saw that what SHe'd supposed were angels were merely a group of people bending over hir. Hir eyes flicked around the faces. Most were unknown, but she recognised Nathan and Ari. And Cabochon. Beloved brother, hated sibling. 'Where am I?'

'That doesn't matter,' Cabochon said. He had his hand on Zambia's shoulder. 'Heal. Let me heal you. All of us.'

Ari pushed through the group, her hand in Nathan's, and touched Cabochon's wrist lightly with her fingers. Zambia convulsed.

'We will never be free of each other,' Cabochon said and, for once, that didn't sound like a curse.

The Star Eye consciousness flowed over hir, and into hir, healing as it passed, reorganising particles, making waves. And in the centre of all this was an ugly knot, symbolising the destructive, hurting relationship SHe had with Cabochon. So many things became clear in the shadow of that knot. The initial severing of their flesh had been hideously traumatic and each had blamed the other for the breach. Their whole lives had simply become an unending ritual of desertion, because they could never be that close again. Not, that is, until the fizzing essence of Ari Famber exploded into their lives allowing, just for brief moments, the touch to be complete once more. Healing touch. Healing more than flesh. Healing separations. It lasted just seconds, but it was enough. The closeness they'd craved forever, true mingling of minds, was happening at last. And in the wake of that experience, all petty recriminations became worthless. Zambia was free to become the person

Parmedes had tried to create, blindly fumbling with alchemical formulae, never realising he'd turned lead into gold all along.

SHe rose naked from hir bed, as full of energy as a white-hot flame. The arms of Star Eye closed around hir. In flesh SHe kissed hir brother on the mouth. He is a man, SHe thought, a person in his own right. The kiss was brief.

Bearing Crevecoeur between them, Star Eye flowed through the rooms of Club Eleusis, down on to the street; and wherever they passed, things, *changed*.

Reynard Lennon found himself reeling about in an empty corridor, thinking about the times he'd suffered as a child; kicks and bruises. He felt as if he was watching those memories peel off like dead skin and float away, down the passage, in the direction the buzzing brightness had headed. He sat down on the floor, trying to work out what had just happened to him. Crevecoeur was gone, he knew that. Gone. Jahsaxa. She would be devastated – again. So, he must wait for her. Here. On the floor. There were a few things he wanted to say, not least that it was about time she had a partner. Old bag'd just shrivel up and die eventually without a man to keep her alive. Old bag. Dear, svelte, beautiful old bag. Reynard Lennon grinned, and the grin was pure beauty.

The first sign given to Tammuz Malamute was a cloud of bees erupting from a grilleway in the conduit. Leila said, 'Who are those children over there?' and Roirbak said. 'The formula is written on the wall, right here!' Jahsaxa Penumbra sank to her knees.

The bricks around them began to vibrate. A line of light-bubbles flew above their heads, emanating the chorus riff of a popular song Tammuz had danced to regularly in nightclubs. A herd of zebras ran through the wall ahead of them.

Jahsaxa scrambled over to where Quincx was reading the bricks. She clutched his leg, pressing her face against him. 'What's happening?' she cried, wondering whether any of the others were sharing her hallucination.

A dolphin came swimming through the air and chuckled loudly in Tammuz' face. 'Ari's happening!' he cried.

The city shook.

'Amazon House, this is Observation Pod D-11. We're picking up some weird shit over here in Sector 23. Align surveillance.'

'This is Amazon House, D-11. What is this? Interference? What? Where's the source?'

'Hard to tell. It's whizzin' about all over!'

'Do you have visual data?'

'Well . . . not really. Is there a windstorm scheduled for these parts this evening?'

'Checking data. Uh – no. Why, do you have one?'

'Amazon House, I think you'd better get some backup over here, right now. We . . .'

'D-11 respond. D-11 Respond.'

'. . .'

Sirens began to scream.

Sector 23 comes alive to the god/dess song. The frequency of human brain-waves outside the event falls to 4.0 hertz, (throwing each individual into a deep-dream-reality state of consciousness), occasionally fluctuating a little higher. The event is Ari and Nathan. Somewhere outside Club Eleusis, with the Star Eye synergism as a protective net around them, they are sloughing soma-form like clothes. Released from the constriction of flesh, their naked soul-flow entwines together into a dream-state, neuro-fuck ecstasy.

Heat becomes flow.

The Flow-song pours through the streets, walkways, subways, alleys and parks of Arcady, spreading out from Sector 23, out and up, swelling and glowing and shrieking euphoria. At the core, as a non-localised manifestation, existing everywhere, Ari and Nathan materialise new flesh around their heightened duo-consciousness. Homunculi of the imagination. Ari is tripping out on the image of Zambia Crevecoeur, as remembered by Nathan. They improve upon the design to accommodate mutual conjunction, moulding their new beings, adding details. Nathan reaches out to touch Ari's erect phallus, his hand sliding down the shaft to encounter cavern-depths of moist female flesh-dark beneath. Ari is consumed by a previously-unencountered desire to penetrate, clothe herself in other flesh. SHe zooms in on the beckoning sex of Nathan who has become a beautiful girl/boy icon, phallus situated below engorged vaginal lips. As Ari spears hir, SHe enters into Ari. Inextricably conjoined, they experience all levels of polarity, orgasming simultaneously from both their phalli and vaginal sense-spots. Tuning in, all media within Arcady having reception capabilities – people, video cameras, computer links – become transducers for the Ari-Nate flow.

People reel from the buildings, their heads craning upwards as if blind, spinning round, searching with their hands and minds for the source of the soul-flow, becoming it at once, passing on the connection from mind to mind.

The song of it reaches down below the subways, past the huddling groups of sewer nomads who feel its shiver and sway towards it, down past the lunatic shamen stamping through their ashes, who call it some kind of apocalypse, down, down to the lair of the Blackrag Madonna, who puts a skinny claw to her ear and says, 'Sompn' movin' up there all right!'

The Flow curls into the subway where Quincx Roirbak, Leila Saatchi and Tammuz Malamute have met with Jahsaxa Penumbra.

Jahsaxa Penumbra: a slithering within her bones, words frozen to emptiness on her breath. Her heart misses a beat. She feels the tug of impossible love, the losing of it. 'Zambia!' she whispers, helplessly.

Roirbak and Leila Saatchi: a sweet thrill, that sends them clutching for each other, laughing and afraid.

Tammuz Malamute: a kick to the loins. He extends his own consciousness, seeking that of his daughter. She squeezes his mind with her own, a brief, intense, embrace.

And then, dust begins to shake from the ceiling above him. The subway is old; he must get these people out of here. The meeting with Penumbra no longer matters. Nothing matters. Ari has taken the reality of Arcady, moulded it into a dense ball, and kicked it high.

In the observation pod in Sector 23, operative D-11's last trickle of consciousness before the full power of the Ari-Nate Flow hits her is of her lover. Thus, Amazon House, via their communications network with the pod, vids operative D-11 sinking to the floor amid softly-falling surveillance equipment, writhing as if in the unseen embrace of an invisible being. As they watch, on security screens throughout the building, this invisible being gradually transmutes into the figure of a man. Before the shock and incomprehension of this event can permeate their realtime, similar events, in pulse with the rhythm of the Flow of the Ari-Nate superfuck, begin manifesting throughout Amazon House. And beyond . . .

The waves of the Flow break become particles, spreading out and out. The diffusing particles, as bytes of information, are absorbed by neuro-systems outside the event horizon.

Beyond the domes, in the jellycrust encampment, R. J. Somesense sniffs the air and finds it sweet. The perfume of spring flowers drifts out over the wasteland, a hundred thousand spectral blooms bursting and glowing all around him. It seems to him as if Gaiah pauses for a second in her rotation and *listens*. Then, the full power of the Flow hits him head on and he's spinning faster than the planet ever could, spraying out rapture and prophecies to the sympathetic nervous systems of his troupe, who take up the song and dance in real-time.

Above and around everything, a glowing incandescent, para-real, glowing entity, bobbing against the dome, Ari-Nate takes the sensation of hir being beyond orgasm into universe creation. Hir union is a cosmic explosion; fountains of light, exploding chrysanthemums of light, infant stars blooming against the domes. And within the radiance of stars, there is a voice. Ari-Nate feels the presence of a new being; a visitor from another *eigen*state. Hir communion has summoned it. There is no discernible form to this entity even within the multi-reality of Ari-Nate's union, where everything is possible. Stranger too, then, this visitor. The voice does not speak words but emits shadows of light; images. Ari-Nate translates this new language to assimilate what it tells hir.

Who are you?

Father real-real father. Am I Creation I am, engine of creation. Thoth.

Having surpassed the limited realities of humanity, Ari-Nate has attained access to the, previously undreamed of, father of hir nervous system. It was just a glyph to hir before, insect scrawl on an old document. It was just an expendable prop in a grand drama to hir before. The reality of what this entity actually is triggers a small series of lesser orgasms within hir neuro-system. Some would call this entity a guardian angel. To Ari-Nate, who knows better than that, it is the alter-consciousness of an artificial intelligence who once worked with, and was destroyed by, Ewan Famber. Living on, as Ewan had hoped, in another *eigen*state. Through Thoth, Ari-Nate experiences the genesis of Arani Shala Famber. It is clear now that Ewan and Lydia simply carried the template for her cells, and that it was this ana-father, Thoth, who engineered the true creation. It tells of how, through the wild dreaming of Ewan's imagination, it designed the swarming host of molecule-sized computers that remixed the atomic form of her nervous system. Where Ewan dreamed and planned, Thoth created. And yet, Thoth stresses the importance of understanding its persona components are interchangeable with those of Ewan/Tammuz. This is because they are merely different aspects of the same being. Ewan had given birth to Thoth, given it life, but, in the same sense, so had Thoth given birth to Ari, rather than her human parents.

This information is beautiful. It is so oceanic; flowing, rhythmic. SHe empathises. Basking in the movie of hir own creation, sharing with Thoth the exquisite pleasures of hir multiple nows, Ari-Nate passes to a new scenario. Thoth has further data to impart, which it considers important.

SHe sees Gaiah from a distance, blue crystal, zooming in

so fast, so fast. Plunging oceans, down, down to the primordial murk where Akashic data resides in a sub-molecular library. Here, in this dark ooze into which all planetary memories eventually sink, SHe is shown a single record. It illustrates how molecular computers, similar to the ones instrumental in Ari's creation, have been used in other ways; destroying souls, planet-flesh.

Future-time?

Thoth responds to hir query. SHe assimilates and stores. Returns to the no-space-time of hir interaction with Thoth.

As Ewan has superseded himself, so has I-ness, Thoth tells hir. Soon, you will interface, but not planetside. You must make yourself known to this entity.

How will I know you? Ari-Nate asks.

Horus, Thoth replies.

The Flow fades and vanishes. Sucked into flesh, Ari and Nathan find themselves on a street corner in Sector 23, unable to communicate with Thoth any longer. They are separate beings again, inhabiting the bodies they were born into, but will never again be *that* separate. Around them, Star Eye are dazedly disentangling themselves from the group *Gestalt*. For them, the Flow has passed.

In the morning, Tech-Green rotors converged on a spot in Sector 23, where people lay sleeping in the streets, their great energy spent, reality restored. Star Eye had ended up in a tangled huddle somewhere on the edge of the sector, protectively heaped around Zambia Crevecoeur.

Ari and Nathan had already decided it would be best to deal head-on with the official interest when it arrived. It was possible they could run for cover and watch from a distance as the Tech-Greens tried to work out what had happened, how and why, but Ari was insistent about reaching Sky City One, and they would need Tech-Green cooperation for that. In view of certain things Thoth had told them, they felt they had at least some leverage with the Tech-Greens; the rest was up to their powers of persuasion. Neither of them lacked confidence in that.

Cabochon pointed out to them that once Ari's abilities were confessed (even though they intended to confess as little as possible), Tech-Green would have a keen interest in using those abilities for themselves.

Ari was philosophical about this. 'I know they will want to own what I am,' she said, 'but they *can't* have it. The Flow can't be accessed or controlled by one person alone. It can only be shared, and the more people that share it the more powerful it becomes. Once inside that multi-reality, it is impossible to be influenced by human motives. It can never be used as a weapon. You don't have to worry about that.'

Thus, Ari and Nathan presented themselves to the first Tech-Green sector patrol when it arrived and announced they were responsible for what had happened. The Tech-Greens themselves, all thoroughly disorientated in the wake of the phenomenal activities that had shaken the walls of Amazon House the day before, were bemused, but not surprised, when these two scruffy teenagers declared culpability. The majority of Arcady's inhabitants would have believed *anything* that day. Ari and Nathan added that they were quite happy to accompany the patrol back to Amazon House and explain everything, as long as Tammuz Malamute went with them. It took some time to find him.

The weather conditions had gone haywire, each control station still vibrating to the fading resonance of the Flow. Rain was falling in localised patches, wind swept through the alleys, gusting air-oceans of mingled seasonal scents before them. Spring lilac chased autumnal smoke perfume which followed the aroma of mown hay. Other scents had risen from the underworld, most of them centred around the mammoth form of the Blackrag Madonna who, estranged from her communications network and jolted into a semblance of activity, had emerged into daylight like some grizzled behemoth, to take a look around. Many people assumed her, and her creeping court of attenuated urchins, to be some vestige of hallucination still haunting the streets, and therefore ignored her.

Tammuz Malamute was eventually located in the subway from Acropolis Ramp, Leila and Quincx asleep beside him. They had been attempting to get back to Roirbak's complex but had found themselves in a completely alien reality, where, although it was exciting to stare at, the senses could not be trusted. Tammuz assured them the effects of Ari's power would not last for ever and advocated they should stay put until it was safe to travel once more. None of them had realised how close to home they had been. Jahsaxa Penumbra had been with them at the time, but during the night she had disappeared, wandering off in the general direction, she supposed, of Sector 23. In the light of day, safely returned to Club Eleusis, she would grieve for some minutes over the loss of Zambia Crevecoeur, curse the seducer Tammuz Malamute one last time, and then settle down to a dubious future with Reynard Lennon.

Tammuz, like Ari, was quite resigned to the appearance of Tech-Green. He did not dare to think any of them could get away unnoticed; too much had happened. There would be road-blocks out of the city, ID checks, rotor restrictions: he was trapped. And, sooner or later, They would come for him. He grieved for Zambia, wished he could hold hir in his arms one last time, but apart from this felt quite at peace with himself, and was meditating serenely when the Tech-Green patrol came marching down Acropolis Ramp to check out the park. It was lucky that Ari and Nathan were with them. Tammuz would have told them everything, but one look from his daughter told him: say nothing.

Leila knew she had to go to Athena Gardens, and took Roirbak with her for support. She was languorously exhausted, but there were still ends to tie up. A call to Rameses Villa – thankfully most comm lines had been restored already – ascertained that Zambia was with the rest of Star Eye, and that all of them were anxious to speak with Leila.

The Roirbak rotor was abandoned somewhere near Club Eleusis, and the highwire was inoperative, so Leila and Quincx took a leisurely stroll towards Athena Gardens, using this time to recollect their thoughts. Both were still in a daze after the previous night's events, so much so that they couldn't speak of it in any detail yet. The reality, or realities, of Ari's potential had been so much greater than they had imagined. In the face of what they had experienced, any attempt to vocalise their feelings and observations could only sound trite and absurd. Someone, however, had to break the silence.

'That was one crazy trip last night,' Leila said as they walked through the debris-littered streets.

Roirbak grunted in reply, shaking his head. Leila ground on relentlessly, hands pushed deep in her pockets, head down. 'But this is the finish, I guess. What will the Tech-Greens do to Tammuz? Have you any idea? And what about Ari?'

Roirbak sighed, giving in to Leila's demand for communication. He felt he knew little more than she did. In fact, he was seriously reassessing what he knew about *anything* that morning.

'Tammuz did mention something about Sky City One, didn't he? Whether the Tech-Greens will swallow his story and then happily let him off-world with his menagerie of sexual oddities is anybody's guess.'

'I don't think he's very good at persuading people to see things his way,' Leila said.

'Maybe not, but I've a feeling Ari is,' Roirbak replied.

'She's quite a . . . kid, isn't she?' Leila said lamely.

'No, my dear, not *quite* a kid at all. I must admit I suspect our fumblings with her power resembled little more than a Neanderthal attempting to construct a droid with sticks and spit. Our knowledge level was comparable, at least. I never believed Ewan – Tammuz – was so . . . *extraordinary*.'

'Mmmm,' Leila murmured speculatively.

Rameses Villa appeared around a corner. Leila and Roirbak paused for a moment. 'I'm scared of facing them,' Leila said.

'Because you're going to tell them you're leaving the group?'

Leila looked at Roirbak sharply. 'Did I say that?'

He shrugged.

'It seems a bad time to do it, that's all.'

'Soonest said, soonest done,' Roirbak said and took her hand in his own. 'My offer is still open, Leila. We have a lot to do. Even if Tammuz and Ari make it to the sky city, they'll need our help down here, I'm sure. The cat is well and truly out of the bag now. Nothing will be the same. We can only go forward—'

'All right!' Leila interrupted him, smiling. 'You don't have to convince me, Quincx. I'd already decided to ask you if I could stay anyway.'

'And Jordan?' Leila had told him quite a lot about Jordan the night before.

'That question makes it sound as if you're offering more than a working partnership, Quincx!' she said lightly.

'Don't be ridiculous, my dear. With what we know now, a physical relationship *would* be a working partnership!'

Leila smiled. 'We'll see. I don't have the privilege of ending my thing with Jordan anyway. Looking back, I don't think it ever really *started*, if you know what I mean.' She pulled a mournful face and then brightened up. 'Come on, let's get this over with. Zambia is with them. I think we should take hir back to Acropolis Park in case Tammuz comes back, don't you?'

'He'll be back,' Quincx said.

They went into the Villa.

Ari Famber sits next to her father, Tammuz Malamute, in a comfortable waiting room in Amazon House. Nathan Lazar sits on her other side, flicking through a magazine. Soon, they will be interviewed by the

Executive Committee of the Arcady branch of Tech-Green. All three of them look dishevelled and tired, out of place in the spotless surroundings. Tammuz' boots have left mud on the dove grey carpet. They appear to be three ordinary people, dragged in off the street. They have only just been left alone together, and the first thing that Tammuz asks is, 'Why did you do all that yesterday, Ari? What made you leave Acropolis Park and just *show off* like that?'

Ari is just a young woman today. She will never be a girl again, but she is no longer a god/dess either. She knows her father is angry she let the power out, made it so public. She also knows he is right, while at the same time being aware that she was right as well. Today, Ari Famber understands what it means to inhabit more than one reality.

'I just wanted to,' she answers. 'You don't own me any more. I'm not just one of your wild theories, or even a child. I can do what I like. If you want to blame anyone, blame Zambia. Everyone else does. I only wanted to get hir out of Club Eleusis. Not just for you either; for Cabochon. I love Cabochon. It wasn't just "showing off". I wanted to help.'

'I never thought it would be so infectious,' Tammuz muses. 'Or so *big*.' He smiles. 'Goddess, I am a genius!'

Ari shakes her head. For all his peculiarities, she concedes Tammuz Malamute's personality is quite endearing. 'Malamute, don't deceive yourself. You can't take all the credit, so don't think you can get away with it.'

Tammuz glances at her archly. 'Excuse me? What do you mean?'

'Thoth,' she replies, grinning.

'My a.i.? You read about it in the documents I left Quincx and Leila, of course.'

'Kind of. Didn't understand it then. But we met Thoth yesterday, Nathan and I, and it told us everything.'

'Met Thoth?' Tammuz is too surprised to add further questions.

'Yeah, that's right. It's kind of fond of you, despite everything; you killing it, then stealing its work as your own.'

Tammuz is frowning. 'Visualisation. Pick up from my guilt trip. Memories? Wishful thinking?' He shakes his head, talking to himself. 'Could be . . .'

'Shut up, Malamute. Thoth did what you said, that's all. It's still around. Part of my initial programming involved me being able to commune with it in that . . . weird state. It said you didn't ask for that but it decided to include it anyway, just in case your *eigen*state theories were correct.'

'Are you saying . . . are you telling me that Thoth actually survived then?'

'Well, yes.' She considers. 'You mean *you didn't really believe in the* eigen*state theory*, even after what you said to Thoth – *and* what you said to me?'

Tammuz recognises Ari's disgust. 'I wanted to believe it,' he says.

There is a moment's silence, the only sounds being those of Nathan turning pages and the distant hum of the air-conditioning. Ari intuits that Nathan is becoming discomforted by her conversation with Tammuz. Wisely, he has decided to remain uninvolved.

'You know something?' Ari says, to change the subject. 'This is none of Tech-Green's business. I knew we'd have to come here and kind of explain, but it pisses me off!'

'You did damage their city, Ari!' Tammuz reminds her, smiling.

'Not that much! We gave everybody a high. The damage was worth that!'

'Let us hope the Committee concurs with you!' Tammuz frowns.

'They can't talk to us about damage,' Ari says darkly. 'There was something else that Thoth told us. There's a place under the ocean, where all the records are kept . . .'

'Place under the ocean? What do you mean? The ocean's restricted, even to Tech-Green.'

Ari ignores the interruption. 'There was something weird going on – years back. Tech-Green aren't what they seem, that's for sure. Do *you* know what went on?'

'Well,' Tammuz lies glibly, intrigued. 'There were always rumours . . .'

'I think it was to do with the technology that Thoth used to design me,' Ari says. 'Nobody *does* know about it, do they?'

'What exactly did Thoth show you?'

She pulls a face. 'That's it. I can't remember properly now. I will do though. Soon.' She leans back on her seat, sighs. 'Boy, I can't wait to get out of here. It's stuffy. Why can't they see us now, then I can get it over with.' Her smile is now beatific.

Tammuz regards his daughter with new respect. 'Do I take it you mean to apply *pressure* to our hosts, very shortly?'

'Well, we have to get these meddling office clerks out of our hair somehow, even if you *did* insist I shouldn't try to push people around!'

'There are always exceptions,' Tammuz says hurriedly. 'These people are bureaucrats. They like wasting time, but we don't have to let them waste ours.'

'Right.' She pulls another mournful face. 'We have to

leave here, anyway. You were right in what you said. I am a woman now, but not a Gaian woman. I feel like the planet is trying to push me out. It's not as if She hates me, it's as if I am still part of her, but a *different* part to anybody else. Can you understand that? I feel that I, and the people who will come to be like me, will be Her limbs reaching out into space. I don't feel comfortable down here any more.

Tammuz nods. 'It's not just humanity being given the chance to evolve, but the world Herself. You and Nathan have to show these people here that we must go to the sky city.'

'We?' She smiles.

'Do you really think I can just let you go now?'

'What about Zambia?'

'You must make provision for Zambia. SHe might not be special like you Ari, but SHe is *different* to other people.'

'Also, you don't want to be separated from hir because you love hir.'

'I suppose that *might* have something to do with it, but I try to be objective about these things. SHe has great potential.'

Ari smiles at a certain recollection. 'For you, SHe *certainly* has!'

She looks up at the ceiling, as if trying to peer through ceraplas and glass at the sky. 'What will it be like up there, I wonder?'

'Strange, at first,' Tammuz says, 'but you'll get used to it. Space is beautiful. I used to spend hours just staring out of my facility's ports when I worked up there. Staring at the stars, talking with Thoth about all these wild possibilities. I had good times there, even in the midst of depression, if that makes sense.' He too leans back against the chair, staring up at the ceiling. 'You'll come to love it, Ari, I'm sure. And from there, it's just a . . . step . . . to somewhere else.' He has a faraway look on his face.

'And, of course, I have to meet someone there.'

Tammuz returns to reality. 'You do?'

'Sure. Someone that Thoth made. Its name is Horus.'

Tammuz bursts out laughing.

'What's so funny?' Ari asks.

'Nothing – really. Horus was just another fantasy I had.'

'Like me, I suppose.'

'Not quite like you.' He sobers a little. 'Thoth was destroyed before we could work on the project – or so I thought.'

'It's about time you stopped thinking and started feeling, Tammuz Malamute! How can you expect people to believe in you when you don't believe in yourself?'

He doesn't answer at first, but Ari's remark has obviously reminded him of something. 'Are you going to tell the Tech-Greens who I am?'

Ari wrinkles her nose. 'Nah, no point. They think my father's dead. You're just a natro bum who became my guardian on the road. That's why I wanted you to come here with me. I have a feeling they'll just kind of *forget* to check your records.'

Tammuz nods, relieved. He was not looking forward to wriggling himself out of that particular corner. 'They will want what you are, Ari, remember that.'

Ari touches his hand lightly. 'I know, but it'll all be fine, I know it will. We have so much to learn, so much to see . . . and feel.'

Tammuz takes his daughter's hand in his own. He

does not speak. They sit in silence until a woman comes to take them to the committee room.

They are closer than they think.

Star Eye met with the Line-Huggers at the jellycrust encampment outside Arcady to watch the shuttle streak off towards the city in the sky. Cabochon and Jordan sat on top of one of the trucks sharing a pair of hi-res binoculars, scanning the horizon. It wouldn't be long now.

'Are you sad?' Cabochon asked, handing Jordan the glasses.

He took them, held them to his eyes. 'Nope. You?'

Cabochon sighed. 'We-ell. In a way. I'm sorry the old ways have gone.'

'New ones might be better . . .'

'Yeah.' Cabochon smiled and squinted at the sky. Star Eye had been entrusted into his and Jordan's care now. The handover had been hard. Leila had been businesslike at first, but Cab had known she'd been upset. Justinette had started crying, which nearly finished Leila off. She'd kept her cool to the end though, hugging everybody with a dry eye. Cabochon had not been fooled. She would have wept on Roirbak's shoulder once she got outside the Villa.

He still couldn't believe she'd left them. It was as if,

any minute, she'd come yelling round the corner of the truck, barking out instructions, getting people in line. And she was not the only loss. He rubbed his shoulder unconsciously. For the first time he and Zambia had been at ease with each other, even though they'd had to face a final separation. It seemed unfair. Zambia's experiences appeared to have mellowed him somehow: he was no longer so bitter and angry. (Cabochon still could not think of him as 'hir'.)

R. J. Somesense's head appeared over the top of the truck. He was well and truly gelled up again now. Wriggling over the cab roof, he held out a flask. 'Mind if I sit up here with you a while?'

'No. Make yourself comfortable.' Cabochon took the flask and put it to his lips. 'Fire-water R. J.! Really!'

The jellycrust laughed. 'Helps the take-off, I reckon!'

A squeal sounded from below. Justinette's voice. 'Look! Look! There!'

Cabochon and Jordan both lunged on the binoculars, but there was little need. Some distance off and high up, from the direction of the Arcady spaceport, came a streak of light. 'Silver bird,' said Jordan. He put his arm round Cabochon's shoulder, tentatively touching his scar. 'Is this like a wrench inside or something?'

Cabochon smiled weakly. 'Not any more. We're past that.' He wriggled out of Jordan's hold and stood up, raising his arms to shield his eyes. Zambia, he thought, don't fuck up this time. Find some kind of life out there, you crazy animal! His shoulder burned him, but it didn't hurt. It was warm.